ENDANGERED MEMORIES

an Expired Reality novel

David N. Alderman

Visit **DavidNAlderman.com**

This book is dedicated to the memory of my late grandmother, Priscilla Bailey, a woman who never stopped remembering my stories.

THE DAWN OF EVIL

For years, the planet of Anaisha (An-ā-sha), especially the continent of Enera, suffered violence. The criminal mastermind, Mr. Big, had the world in his grip, squeezing as hard as he could to bring brutality and chaos to the planet...

...until a group of junior high school students banded together and put a stop to him. Known as the Lazerblades, the four heroes—David Corbin, Carrie Green, Veronica Amorou and her brother, Sean—fought for years against Big and the other villains who plagued the land, conquering them and bringing peace in what almost became a time of war.

With Anaisha's most dreaded criminals defeated, the teens were left to live their lives as they pleased. To embark in once forbidden relationships, to pursue careers, to achieve higher education, to take a well-deserved rest.

But what was to be a time of respite quickly became an era of confusion and instability as certain events pushed the heroes to their separate ways to walk the roads of their lives alone.

Now evil has returned in a form never seen on Anaisha, fulfilling prophecies given ages before, forcing the young champions back together again to either fight against the evil or fall into the growing darkness with the rest of the world.

FROM THE DIARY OF CARRIE GREEN...

Friday, May 22, 1998
Dear Diary,

Today was it. David told me that he loves me, and it's something I can't handle. So, I'm leaving to South Ryshard, far away from his love and the potential disaster it could bring upon the both of us. I'll find a job out there and hide away until someday we can see each other again.

I'm not going to tell my mother where I'm going. She doesn't accept anything I do anyway. She crossed the line tonight, drilling me about David and my future again, and on the evening of this horrible day. Besides, Sean is leaving for Mecca soon. Veronica is going to start college for fashion design. And David...he'll probably wonder where I went...but I can't let him know, at least not right now. I love him so much, but I can't do this anymore. I can't hide my feelings from him or risk him dying because of them.

The LZR Project is shut down now, the major criminals of the world have been caught—even Mr. Big—and now there is nothing left but to start over. I hate this feeling inside me, the feeling of having to leave my best friend, Veronica, and my one and only true love, David. But this is something that has to be done.

Maybe, when things settle down and everyone has finally gone their separate ways, I can contact David and let him know where I am. Maybe then things can work, when the world doesn't need saving. Then we can be together without looking over our shoulders to see if there is a gun pointed at our heads.

I'm not bringing you with me, Diary. I will leave you here, so when I come back someday, I will remember the things I went through, the things that made me stronger and wiser, the things that made me leave here in the first place.

Goodbye, Diary.

1

Chaos

Tuesday, November 10, 1998

The icy wind rushed against Kimberly Sebastien's face, sweeping through her long blonde hair as she bounded through the vacant dirt field. The blue crescent moon lit up the ground just enough for her to see her way across the damp surface. The chilly air induced a burning sensation in the mark on her right cheek, causing it to sting more than when she received it only an hour ago.

The cell phone jostled in her hand, the blue screen illuminating her beaten face. The time on it read 6:34 p.m. She hit the redial button on the keypad, her heart wishing that this time someone would pick up on the other end. Holding the phone to her ear, she heard a steady busy signal, just as she had the last three attempts. *This can't be happening.* She closed the phone and shoved it into the pocket of her jeans, glancing behind her briefly to make sure the monster wasn't closing in on her. *No one.* Well, no one she could see anyway. That didn't mean he—it—wasn't there.

She scanned the tops of the giant trees in front of her,

1

making out a small orange spire glowing on top of the roof of the stalus beyond. The stalus—a building designated by the government for weddings and funerals—was the only building she could hide in for miles, and she hoped it would, by some miracle, be open. Her body relentlessly quarreled with her, scolding her for pushing so hard, pleading with her to stop and rest. But she couldn't rest, not yet, not when her life was at stake.

Plowing through the trees, thick leaves that hung from crooked branches slapped Kimberly, each one a stranger's hand reaching out to snatch her and carry her off somewhere dark and dangerous, somewhere she would never be able to escape. She fought through them and stumbled into a parking lot, her knees meeting the asphalt with a flash of pain.

Kimberly stood to her feet, ignoring the pain swelling through her kneecaps, and pressed on across the lot, finally slamming herself into the glass doors of the building. Inhaling a deep breath, she grabbed the door handle. *Locked.* Panic seized her as she tried the next door and the next, all of them locked as well. She pounded madly on the glass. "Help! Somebody, help me! Open up!" Her voice came out hoarse, and she suddenly realized that wasting her breath would do no good if nobody was in there to hear her pleas.

She turned and leaned her back up against the door, clutching the burning cramp in her side. Gazing into the distance, she saw nothing but the trees reaching into the wind. Her heart throbbed, threatening to leap out of her chest while she fearfully waited for something to lunge at her. *Don't be scared*, she thought. *Keep moving! Get away from him!* A gust of frosty air slipped through her white sweater, chilling the sweaty mess that spread itself under her tattered clothes. The chills warned her to run.

She peered through the glass at the dark lobby inside. She could see the desk where the receptionist who handled the wedding and funeral parties sat during operating hours. Stacks of flyers covered the counter, accompanied by mysterious shadows that seemed to dance around as if a party was going on in the desk owner's absence.

Kimberly had nowhere else to go. Only orchards and farms stood between her and the city. The closest house was too far to run to, unless she wanted to backtrack, which was impossible without risking running into him.

Turning back toward the lot, she pulled out her cell phone and hit redial. Her heart skipped a beat with the brief silence that ensued, but then the busy signal droned in her ear and she sighed loudly, despair covering her like a dark blanket.

She shoved the phone back in her pocket and watched with fright as the tree branches shook vigorously in the distance. Her eyes narrowed, trying to make out the figure stumbling through the barrage of giant leaves. A face peered out, red eyes glowing in the night.

Kimberly's voice caught in her throat.

Swinging around, she tugged at the handle again. This time the door swung open, almost knocking her off balance. A bit confused, she passed into the stalus, not stopping to ask herself questions. She pulled the door shut and turned the latch, locking it. She swung back around toward the desk to try and make out what little she could from the light that shone in from the parking lot lamps.

The large round government seal hung on the wall in the

foyer. The symbol of the Enera Government—three triangles overlapping each other at different points—was etched into the stone slab surrounded by the words "SECURITY, EFFICIENCY and CONFIDENCE." The first time she had seen the seal was when her parents died and she had been forced to come to a stalus for the funeral.

She shook the thought away and peered to the left and right of the desk, where double doors stood tall and erect—doorways to other dark places. Farther to the left and right, hallways swarmed in shadows. *I should be able to hide in the main sanctuary until daylight.* She approached the left set of double doors and made her way through them.

She couldn't see anything in the sanctuary except for the red glowing EXIT signs and the doors they perched above on each side of the room. Kimberly stepped forward and bumped her leg on something hard. Reaching down, she felt the glossed wood of a bench. She knelt down and crawled underneath, creeping through the sanctuary until she figured she was in the center of the room. Lying still, her back to the floor, she closed her eyes.

The quiet stillness invited her mind to wander. Thoughts flew at her at lightning speed: *Where is he? Why did this have to happen to me? I can't believe he's dead! It's all a dream, just a nightmare.* Tears broke from her eyes and streamed down her cheeks as her gut convulsed with torment. She wanted her family back. She wanted this man—this creature—to stop chasing her. Events rushed through her mind: the man with the dark eyes at her doorstep; the chunk of cold crystal her uncle gave her from the freezer; her uncle being broken like a toothpick in the jaws of a giant.

The vision of her uncle's face blurred into view each time she remembered him begging her to "take this and keep it safe." He handed her that piece of crystal, wanting her to flee with it. But the man with the dark eyes had just as quickly slapped her to the floor, knocking the crystal from her hands, taking it for himself.

Kimberly remembered getting to her feet and running from the house, the man yelling for her to come back. His face couldn't be placed exactly, just dark and round, with an evil, hollow gaze peering out from under his bald head. He had an uncanny familiarity about him, something that seemed to have escaped from the nightmares Kimberly had when she was younger.

Only a miracle can save me now.

Her thoughts diminished and fatigue kicked in. She slipped in and out of consciousness. It was hours to daybreak, and there was no way for him to get into the stalus without her hearing him first. At least that's what she told herself. She needed to drown everything out long enough to regain her strength for her journey to the city in the morning.

A clicking sound echoed through the sanctuary, waking her senses. Her eyes shot open as a door creaked slowly and then thudded shut. She knew it was him by the dark presence she suddenly felt seeping into the room. Kimberly held her breath. His squeaky footsteps passed the aisle she hid in. She followed that sound to the other side of the room and then back near the door he entered the sanctuary through.

She quietly bent her arms and legs, rolling onto her stomach, and shuffled out from under the bench. Moving to her knees, she glanced up at the red EXIT sign over the hallway door. That was her only escape, and there had to be only a few rows of benches in the space between.

The footsteps stopped and silence thickened. Her heart thrashed in her chest like a caged animal. She took a few quick breaths and sprung up, rushing for the door. She maneuvered and stumbled around the benches, relying on all of her instincts to get her through the maze of wood and darkness. Her body plowed into the door, and she grabbed the cold metal handle to open it.

"Kimberly."

She turned around slowly and found herself staring at two glowing red wedges that seemed to float in the air. Her voice caught in her throat again, like she was trying to vomit up an apple. Her nails clawed frantically at the surface behind her, scraping against the hard wood, peeling away part of her fingertips.

"Kimberly Sebastien." The man's raspy voice released a foul smell into her nostrils as he came under the red light, the crimson eyes matching the EXIT sign's glow. The repugnant scent turned her stomach in knots.

"Wh…wh…wh…," her lips quivered. She turned her face to the side, attempting to avoid the stench that permeated the air between them.

"Your sssoul, Kimberly. That issss what I want."

She closed her eyes as he moved in closer. She could feel the sensation of his breath floating across her skin. His hand touched her cheek, turning her wound cold and sending vibrations through her whole face. The wound stung and then burned like fire. She let out a yelp, and the hand retracted for a moment. She started shuffling across the wall toward the front of the sanctuary.

"Go where you want. You can't essscape me. I am everywhere and in everything." He moved in front of her, like an ethereal arrow, so quick. The red eyes dangled in front of her like demonic puppets suspended by shadowed strings.

She felt tears crawling into her eyes. "What do you want with me? Why can't you leave me alone?" The tears broke out and she cupped her hands over her mouth, terror engulfing her. "Why can't you leave me alone? You killed my uncle. You killed my uncle! What more do you want with me?"

"I need you. I need your sssoul, your ssspirit. Then I will leave. Then you can rest in peace, without the nightmares, within the darkness."

She shook her head and fell to her knees, her face covered in a moist film. She had a boding feeling that she wasn't going to make it out of the building alive. The doors to escape seemed so far away. *This is where I'm going to die.*

He reached his hand out to her again, the silence in the stalus falling on her like a ton of bricks, allowing her to experience the dreadful sound of her sobbing. The thought of her life ending here, in this place, was violent and yet comforting to her. She could be with her uncle soon...

"Stop!"

The man retracted his reach and spun around. Kimberly looked up through her blurry vision at two silhouettes in the open doorway at the back of the room. One was tall with the chiseled build of a man. The other had the thin, hourglass shape of a woman.

"You?" the evil stranger squealed.

They stepped into the stalus and allowed the doors to shut

behind them, darkness swallowing everyone in the room.

"Let her go," a female voice demanded.

Kimberly wiped the tears from her eyes and slowly started to her feet, her mind racing to figure out who these people were. *Probably Anaishan Sentries. If that's the case, they're no match for whatever he is.*

The man grabbed Kimberly from behind, wrapping his arm around her neck. His fingers moved across her throat, and she felt the cold tip of his long, sharp fingernails begin to etch their way through the tender surface of her skin.

"Show yoursssselves!"

Kimberly's neck burned, and her body drooped in his arms like a sack of manure.

The two strangers said nothing, yet their shuffling movements could be heard throughout the room.

Kimberly, a female voice whispered in her mind. *We are here to help you. When he releases you, leave this stalus and go to the city of Lysallis. Wait for us there. We will catch up with you.* Her eyes struggled to stay open as she tried to put together the words floating through her thoughts.

The dark man's fingernails pressed harder into her neck, carving through the skin. She felt a small amount of blood trickle down.

"I told you two to show yoursssselves. I will ssspill her blood all over thisss place!"

"Not tonight!" the female shouted. A strong force slammed into Kimberly and the dark stranger, knocking them back to the floor. Kimberly rolled to her side, her strength rapidly coming back to her, allowing her to scramble to her feet. The creature reached out and tried to grab her, but only managed to rip the bottom edge of her sweater as she escaped from his clutch and reached the exit. She grabbed the handle and swung the door open to the dark hallway.

"Go, Kimberly. We will meet again." The confidence in the male's voice filled her with ease. She darted out into the hallway.

Kimberly made her way to the front doors of the stalus and retreated outside. She stood in the lot for a moment, taking deep breaths and staring at the line of trees, picturing the field that stretched behind them. Across that field stood the housing community she had escaped from. *I can't go back. There's nothing left for me there.* The only place to go now was Lysallis and hope these strangers were true to their word. *Doesn't really matter. As long as they're keeping him occupied, I have a chance to escape.*

She cautiously made her way around the stalus and headed into the orchards that stood between her and the city.

***

You are cordially invited… the front of the card began. *Hmm*, David Corbin thought, *wonder who this could be from. No return address.*

A faint ringing sound droned from his black leather jacket. He pulled out his cell phone and glanced down at the caller ID, rolling his eyes when he realized it was his sister. "Hello?"

"You actually answered your phone?"

"What do you want?"

"Why haven't you returned my messages?"

He stared at a young couple sitting under a nearby tree. They appeared to be in an argument, but from his distance, David

9

couldn't tell what about. The girl was crying, and the man was throwing his arms up in the air in surrender. "I've been busy."

"I've left at least a dozen messages on your phone! You're too busy to call your own sister back?"

"What do you need, Cybil?"

A long pause. *"To borrow some credits. Nicolas and I are broke and need groceries."*

He let out a slow, deliberate sigh. "Groceries?"

"Yeah, groceries."

"Hmm."

"What's that supposed to mean?"

He closed his eyes and rubbed the bridge of his nose.

"You think I'm still doing drugs, don't you?"

"That's not what I said."

"No, but that's what you meant."

David glanced up at the young couple again, just in time to witness the girl smack the guy across the face. The young man sprung to his feet and stormed off, leaving the girl there to pour out her tears. David wanted nothing more than to go over there and comfort her, but she wasn't the reason he was at the mall tonight.

"Look Cybil, I didn't say—"

"You don't have to. Who do you think you are, huh? Mr. Perfect? Who are you to criticize me and my boyfriend? Do you think just because you saved the world that you can treat your family like garbage? Is that what you think? I'm your sister, for crying out loud! Flesh and blood!"

David couldn't help but sigh again. Exhausted, his sister was only wearing him thinner. This wasn't the first conversation like this with her. "Look, I don't have any credits to lend you. Simple as that."

"You don't have any credits, or you don't want to give me any credits?"

"Why do you ask questions like that?" He knew his sister was setting a trap for him, a trap to satisfy her thirst for a battle that he could never hope to win. "You're not getting any credits out of me, it doesn't matter why."

"I see. Someday when you need help, see if I'm there for you. If only everyone out there knew the real you, they wouldn't call you a hero. At least Mom and Dad still care about me."

"Why don't you call them?"

"I already did. They can't help me because…whatever." She sniffled. *Fake,* David thought. *"I don't want to talk to you anymore."*

The call disconnected. David slid the phone into his pocket, shaking his head. The young girl that had been crying left. He could still see her faintly in the distance, crossing the parking lot. He felt sorry for her.

He looked toward the Jewelplex Mall and spotted Amber standing in front of the entrance. She wore a pink sweatshirt and let her blonde hair flow freely down her back. Her gaze peered out toward the parking lot, no doubt searching for him.

David shoved the invitation back into the red envelope and placed it in the inside pocket of his jacket. Glancing quickly at his watch, he saw that it was already 7:50 p.m. Amber was twenty minutes late. He ran his hands through his short brown hair, dismissing her tardiness as a small nuisance. Then he blew into his hand and checked his breath: *Hmm, could use a mint…or some gum.*

He made his way toward the entrance, hoping his time with Amber tonight would be less strenuous than the rest of his day had been. He glanced around the courtyard, first at the giant stone fountain in the center and then at the tall feathery trees adorned with strands of small white lights. The sound of rushing water from the fountain calmed his nerves.

Amber checked her watch and formed an irritated expression on her face. She was the late one, but David had a feeling she would try to pin the blame on him.

"Amber!"

She smiled briefly as he went in for a hug, the intoxicating vanilla scent of her perfume filling his head. She pulled away first, and when she did, her expression morphed from irritated to nervous.

"How are you?" she asked.

"I'm better now." He went in for a kiss, and the world seemed to stop when he did. Her tender lips and the warmth of her body close to his made the last few days worth waiting through.

She pulled away again, and as if to make up for the abrupt halt to their public display of affection, she quickly grabbed his hand in hers and led him toward the front of the mall.

"It's been a long three days." He smiled as they reached the glass doors. He opened one, motioning for her to go first. She entered the building and he followed behind her. "And today's been an especially long day."

"Boy, don't I know what you mean."

They approached the giant stairwell that led to the second story of the mall and started up toward the food court. "This break has really helped me see things a little more clearly. You know…"

She stopped and turned to him. "Could we hit customer service real quick? I have to get a gift card for my parents. They're out of town for their anniversary and I couldn't think of anything else to get them."

He shrugged. "Sure." They started back down the stairs.

"Do you think I could borrow twenty credits, just until tomorrow? I forgot to grab some before I left the house."

He pulled his wallet out as they turned around the bottom of the stairs and walked toward the customer service counter. "I don't think I have many credits on me."

"You know," she started, hesitancy in her voice, "these past three days have helped me see things more clearly too, only I don't think in the same way."

He lost his calm stride at her change of tone. "What do you mean?"

"What I mean is…well…" She looked down at the tan tiles in the floor, stepping so as not to have her tennis shoes hit the cracks in between.

David's instinct warned him where this conversation was headed, but he didn't want to believe it. He had hoped over the last few days that if she really wanted to break up with him, she would have done it before or during the break, not after.

They approached the counter, where a young girl in a white-collared shirt greeted them. David swore he caught a brief look of recognition in the girl's brown eyes when she looked at Amber, but dismissed it as a sliver of paranoia from his tired mind.

The girl smiled at David. "Can I help you?"

He placed his wallet on the counter, motioning to the girl that he needed a minute. He glanced at her collar, eyeing the silver name badge: Bubbles. He turned back toward Amber. "What are you trying to say?" His tone had become impatient. He attempted to calm himself by taking a deep breath as Amber looked up at him and frowned, her blue eyes revealing icicle shards hidden behind the pupils.

"What I mean to say is…well…I need some more…space. You and I've been seeing a little too much of each other and I…"

He took a step back. Amber took a step toward him, reaching her hand out to keep him steady. Her eyes glanced quickly at David's wallet on the counter and then returned their gaze to him. Bubbles turned around and went back to checking log sheets for the mall baby strollers, pretending not to listen in on the conversation.

"I don't think we should see each other anymore." Amber wrapped her hand around his wrist and tried to tug him toward her. "I mean, we have been dating now for almost two months and I…well…you're a little too much for me." She winced a little, letting her last sentence hang in the stale air.

He quickly ripped his arm out of her grip. "Too much? Where did you come up with that?"

"Well, for example, you're always calling me. You call me every morning and every night. How am I supposed to have any time to think with your voice in my ears all the time?"

"You're breaking up with me because I call too much? Are you serious? You're the one who wants me to call you all the time. You actually tell me when to call you!"

She grimaced, her eyes searching the random people walking the mall. "Lower your voice. It's not just that. You want to spend all your free time with me too. We're always going out to fast-food places, the park, the library, anywhere you can possibly think of for no real reason than for us to just spend time with each other. Frankly, I'm feeling…I'm feeling very smothered."

"Smothered?" David gawked at her. *I can't believe she's really serious about this.*

"Smothered. Yes, smothered. Maybe even suffocated. These three days we had away from each other really helped me think clearly, David. I don't want to be in a relationship with you right now. You're too…dependent on me."

His eyes widened.

Bubbles scribbled nonsense in her logbooks while peering over her shoulder at the arguing couple. When she caught David's annoyed glare, she brushed her brown hair behind her ears and averted her attention back to the logbooks.

David turned his attention back on Amber. He tried to calm himself, but found it too difficult, especially after the day he already had. The things Amber was saying seemed to come out of nowhere, sideswiping him with a terrible force he wasn't prepared to deal with. "I've treated you like a princess since the day we met. A princess. I've given you all my time, all my attention. I've poured more than two hundred percent of myself into this relationship to make it work, and you're going to stand here and tell me that all of this is why you're turning away from me?"

"Well," Amber hesitated for a moment and shrugged, "yeah. Sure."

"This is ridiculous!" he shouted, causing a few passersby to stop and stare, and Bubbles to drop her logbook on the floor.

"Please don't make a scene."

He heard Amber's words but chose to ignore them. He felt the blood rushing to his head and his temperature rising like the screech in a tea kettle. *She's actually going to stand here and tell me that she's dumping me because I gave all of myself to this relationship?*

"I love the poems, the flowers, the gifts, everything you've given me in the last two months, but it's not what I want. You're not what I want."

"But you like to be spoiled."

She stepped back at the comment. "Excuse me?"

"You heard me. You like to be spoiled."

"I know you didn't just say that."

"I did. You know, I don't get it. What is it you're looking for? Is it muscles? Wealth? Fame? What the heck is it that you want, because the last time I checked, every other woman on this planet liked flowers, poems, gifts, time and you know, the simple things."

"I'm not like other girls, David. You should have figured that out in the time I gave you."

He ran his hands through his hair and took another deep breath. *Stay calm. Keep control of your emotions and you'll get through this. It's just been a long day. Amber's just another girl. If she doesn't want to be with you, then that's her loss. Just stay calm.*

He stared into her frosty blue gaze and rehashed the whole day in his head. His car had broken down on him twice, he had received a call from the bank stating his account had been overdrawn because of the groceries he purchased the other day, and then he had the call from his sister—one of many in the past few days—all of them to ask for credits for things he knew she was lying about. All he wanted to do was get to the mall and see Amber. *Stay calm, buddy. Stay calm.* He could feel his heart bracing to jump out of his chest, ready to escape the hurt she was inflicting on him, but at the same time he wanted to rip his heart out himself and beat it up against a wall, punish it for developing such strong feelings for her in such a short amount of time.

Amber took a deep breath and refigured her posture, standing tall and making direct eye contact with him. "I'll make it real simple for you because I know it takes you a while to look at things realistically when it comes to being in a relationship. You and I are finished. I am breaking up with you. We are no longer together. Understand?"

Sharp pains stabbed at his chest. Three days ago, he could have sworn that this break would only benefit both of them, but now he realized how wrong he had been. As he gawked at her like a deer in the headlights, he realized that she wasn't the girl he had fallen for. The sweet-smelling hair he had put his hands through, the lips he had kissed, the body he had held so tightly during the cold nights, everything seemed suddenly foreign to him, as if none of it had been real. This wasn't the Amber he had come to know.

A muffled ringing resounded from Amber's purse. The anger in her face turned to surprise, and after pulling the cell phone out and checking the caller ID, the surprise changed back to the nervous glance she held when they first entered the mall.

"Hello?" she answered, stepping a few feet from David. "No, not yet...Yes...Look, I have to finish something up here. I'll talk to you soon." She glanced up at David and then turned around to talk privately. "All right. I'll talk to you soon. Bye...What? I can't...No, I can't." There was a moment of silence. "Fine...I love you too." She quickly slid the phone back into her purse. "Goodbye, David," she said as she casually started away.

"Whoa!" he shouted as he grabbed Amber's shoulder and swung her around toward him.

A wild glare and a violent shake of her head caused him to release his grip. "Don't you ever touch me again," she growled. "I thought I made it clear just a minute ago that we are no longer together. Can you handle that, David? You're a big boy. After all the adventures you've had in your life, I would think you could take a breakup maturely."

"Is that it, Amber?" He held his hands out toward her, as if begging for his life. "That's the end of us? You call for this break and then you dump me at the mall?" A moment of silence fell between them as he suddenly felt suspicion sneak in. "You were cheating on me, weren't you?"

Bubbles gasped lightly, but not loud enough to draw their attention away from each other.

"You can think whatever you want, David. You can think whatever you want." She frowned and then headed toward the mall exit. He could feel the anger and other twisted emotions building up inside of him, crisscrossing through his chest, racing through his veins. He didn't want to handle this the way he knew he should. He should just take it like a man and go on his way, less one very stuck-up, snobby girl. But curiosity beckoned like a siren, luring him to find out what was really going on. He had to know who she had been cheating with. He had to know what mystery guy had singlehandedly toppled their relationship and caused him this grief.

David dashed across the tiles and reached toward her. He grabbed the shoulder strap of her purse and yanked it toward himself.

"Let go, you idiot!" Her screeching voice echoed through the mall as she tried to pull the purse out of his grip.

He dug his hand in it, fished around and pulled out her cell phone. *Got it!*

She swung around, pulling the purse back as his hand retreated with the desired object. His fingers fumbled with the phone's buttons, trying to scan for the number that had just called. *I know it's here somewhere!*

"Give that back to me now!" she demanded as she thrust herself at him.

He stepped backward. She lost her footing and fell, knocking the phone from his hands. She smacked into the floor as the cell crashed into the tile and shattered to pieces. People stopped and gaped as the debris scattered across the floor.

Bubbles cupped her mouth in awe while David looked down at Amber.

"You IDIOT!" Amber screamed. "You stupid idiot!"

A crowd began to gather around the two of them. Amber propped herself on her knees and pushed blonde strands of hair out of her face.

A security guard came running from the center court of the mall and grabbed David by the arm. The dark hand held tighter than a vice and made some of the reality of David's situation sink in. He glanced up at the guard's emotionless face and knew it would be pointless to struggle, to try to explain himself. The deed had been done, and he had done it. Simple really.

The guard turned toward Amber and his deep voice rolled like thunder. "Are you all right, young lady?"

"Yes, thank you," she answered as she buried her face in her hands, too embarrassed to look at the crowd gathered around.

"I hope you realize that no one will ever treat you as well as I did," David whispered with a weak voice as he watched Amber scramble for the phone pieces, shaking her head in disbelief.

"He already does," she responded loudly without turning toward him. "Next time, why don't you try to act your age for once and keep your emotions in check and maybe you wouldn't do stupid things like this. This would have been a little easier if you had."

The security guard escorted David to the glass doors of the mall exit and opened one, motioning for him to leave. "Don't show your face here again tonight, is that understood? I don't care who you are or what problems you guys are having, you had no right to do what you did."

"Yeah," he replied in agreement as he took one last look at Amber. She was getting to her feet, disgusted and perturbed. He didn't have the strength to argue with the guard or try to explain the why of what he had done. He simply shook his head and stepped out of the mall. *A nice ending to my already wonderful day.* Cold air hit him as he zipped up his jacket and headed back toward his car.

2 Backflash

Kimberly stumbled along the bumpy canals, making her way through the orchards as the moon's light guided her path. She turned around every so often to make sure nothing—and no one—was following her. She didn't know what those strangers did to her attacker, but she decided not to question any help they had to offer. Rubbing the front of her throat, she felt the scratches she accrued and considered herself fortunate that they hadn't gone any deeper.

The orchards looked all alike at night. Kimberly's feet staggered across the dirt rows, the long mounds jabbing at her heels and toes, causing her to trip and stumble occasionally. Minutes earlier, she tripped and fell face-first into a pile of rotten jewel fruit. The stench caused her to dry heave, but she managed to pick herself up and continue on.

Kimberly emerged from the group of jewel trees and entered a field with a small house in the distance. Next to the house stood a barn, a place of rest for the night as long as she didn't get caught. She knew farm people were notorious for killing anyone who crossed their property. It was legal of course, since the government enforced the "No Trespassing Treaty" a couple of years ago. Horror stories spread of the ways some farm people decided to kill their "crossers."

She didn't care to entertain those thoughts at the moment. She already had enough of a scare for one evening and was plenty worn out. Her stomach rumbled for food and her muscles ached. She knew if she had the chance, she would sleep for days, mainly to avoid thinking about what happened.

She approached the barn and couldn't help but notice the giant tree that overshadowed it, elephantine branches clutching the building, mammoth leaves sweeping the roof. She could hear nothing but a small gust of wind blowing through the tree as she approached the barn's huge doors. She quietly pushed against the edge of one of them as it creaked open. Pitch blackness engulfed her inside, except for a small spot of moonlight that pierced through a hole in the roof, spotlighting a section of the flat ground in a sapphire hue.

Too tired and worn out to worry about what else might be in the barn with her, Kimberly made her way to the spot of light and collapsed on the ground, resting her head on her hands. *It's safer in here than out there*, she thought. Her eyes closed to the world around her, only to open to the nightmares within…

"Wake up, little girl. Wake up."

Kimberly opened her eyes. A police officer stood over her bed, staring down at her.

"Sorry, little one. We need to get you out of here."

"What? What's going on?" she asked, her voice cracking.

The officer reached down and picked Kimberly up into his arms, carrying her out of the room and into the hallway. "It'll be all right, sweetie. We're going to get you out of here." He walked down the stairs to the first floor of the giant house with her slumped over his shoulder. As he reached the bottom, a familiar man wearing a brown overcoat took her, putting her over his shoulder.

She rubbed her eyes and yawned. "Where's Mommy and Daddy?"

No answer.

"Where's Mommy and Daddy, Uncle?" she asked again, inhaling a large whiff of his musky cologne.

His bifocals slumped down the bridge of his nose, his eyes glancing at the officer. A dispirited look grew on his face.

"Um..." Uncle Grey started as he patted her on the back and set her on her feet.

She stood in her red pajamas, looking up at him and the officer, rubbing her eyes again.

"Mommy and Daddy had to leave suddenly."

"Where did they go?"

Uncle Grey shook his head and closed his eyes, taking a deep breath. She was too young to understand it all. Too young to understand the violence that had just taken place, the slaying of her parents.

Kimberly suddenly realized she was dreaming. Her young eyes glanced up the stairs she had just been carried down. The banister railing began to creak and twist as red liquid oozed out of the wooden surface.

She backed up and turned around to find nobody there. "Uncle? Uncle, where are you?"

The house's foundation creaked loudly as the lights started to fade behind a thick black smoke filling the house. Her back slammed against the front door as her gaze moved toward the warped stairs. Her body tensed, paralyzed with fear, while her nerves waited for the scream

23

to escape her throat.

The black smoke and the red stain spilled down the stairs and swirled together to create a black mirror or void, the central core of her darkest dreams. She peered into the void closer...closer...closer...and then the crimson eyes appeared.

"Ahhhh!" Kimberly screamed, as her eyes shot open.

She found herself lying in the darkness of the barn, the moonlight on the other side of her now. She sat up, rubbing her eyes. Her cheek stung from pressing it into the dirt. She pushed her sweaty hair back away from her face and brushed the dirt from her cheek, glancing around, quickly remembering her whereabouts. The barn door remained open partway in front of her, the orchards in the distance. She couldn't help but wonder if anyone from the house heard her scream.

Her nightmare started her heart racing as the images passed briskly through her mind, despite her efforts to push them out. She looked around at the darkness surrounding her. Goose bumps rippled down her arms and across her back as she shook the dream from her mind. She hoped to wake up to daylight but hadn't been so fortunate.

Suddenly, she heard a door slam in the direction of the house. *Oh, no!*

"Who's out thar?" a deep voice bellowed. Kimberly scrambled to her feet. Her reflexes felt sluggish as she stumbled into a dark corner of the barn behind the wooden door. Her breath came in pulses. She felt something hard near her foot and reached down to pick it up. The rough texture felt like a chunk of wood.

"Who's thar? I've a gun! I'll shoot ya!" The voice drew

closer as the sound of footsteps approached the barn.

Kimberly leapt out from the shadows, swinging the piece of wood as hard as she could, striking the man in the head. She heard a grunt as the gun fell from his hands and his body collapsed to the ground. She dropped the wood and rushed out of the barn. *Did I kill him? No. I hope not. Don't really have time to check. It was self-defense, right?*

She trudged through the dirt, trying to stay alert and focused on escaping the fields. *He might not be the only one with a gun.*

The lights inside the house flicked on as she turned her head and saw the white lace curtain open. A young girl peered at her through the window, her hands pressed against the glass, a frown on her face.

"Kimberly..." a soft voice drifted through the air.

She couldn't tell where it was coming from. *Is it the girl?*

"Kimberly. They will find you and that's when it will begin. Do not be afraid. This is all meant to be."

Kimberly sprinted into the groves, hoping to make it to the city of Lysallis alive.

***

David sat in his car, peering through the frost-covered windshield at the mall. *How could this have happened? How did things turn so suddenly?*

He closed his eyes and felt the cold air around him. He remembered the incident that took place the same day he and Amber decided to take a three-day break from each other. In hindsight, it had been the turning point of their relationship, but he hadn't seen it that way at the time. They had come to the Jewelplex Mall on a Friday night, and her behavior should have been cause for alarm…

"Okay, so do you think that pink is better on me, or red?" Amber held up two T-shirts with the word "Flirt" printed on the front.

David gave her an awkward glare. "Is there really that much of a difference between pink and dark pink?"

She looked down at the shirt she was holding up against her chest. "It's not dark pink, it's light red."

"Okay. Sure it is."

She smiled at him. "Just answer the question, silly."

He glanced around the Girly *brand clothing store. About a dozen or so other females were wandering around, some of them casting flirtatious smiles and giggles toward David. He didn't know if it was because they recognized him or because of the fact that he was the only male there. It could have been both. "Did you notice that I'm the only guy in here?"*

"Oh, that's not true." Amber waved her hand at him, dismissing his remark as if it was an annoying fly buzzing about her ear. She held the shirts up against her chest and glanced down at them. "Which one of these do you think matches the pink skirt I'm wearing? Do they match my pink shoes?"

He wished he was somewhere else. He should have brought Veronica with him so he would at least have someone to talk to. He knew Veronica wouldn't let him hang in a store like this without keeping his mind off the fact that it was the most feminine store in the mall. Well, besides that lingerie store at the other end on the first floor.

"David? You haven't answered any of my questions. Are you awake?"

"Unfortunately." He couldn't figure out why she was acting so…obnoxious. Then again, this was the first time they had been through a long day of shopping together.

She pouted her lips and hung the shirts back on the rack. "Fine." She walked over and took his hand, tugging him out of the store and back into the mall. "Where do you want to go?"

Finally. "Arcade. Or the toy store. I hear they have new *Super Spy 2* toys in stock."

"How old are you, David?"

He watched two kids throwing pennies down to the first floor of the mall. One of them hit a security guard in the head. David held his laughter back.

"I don't know. If I say I'm nineteen, you'll ask me why I would want to go to a toy store. On the other hand, if you say I'm two, then I'll have to ask you what you're doing going out with me. So, how about we ignore your stupid question and go to the arcade since I've had to go to six of your stores in a row?"

"Fair enough." She tilted her head and rolled her eyes, holding her hand out for him to lead the way. On her other arm hung five bags of clothes.

David took her hand, wondering why she had even asked him to go to the mall with her today. He didn't have anything to shop for. Then again, it wasn't like he had better things to do other than sit at home and sulk.

He led them through the eating area, shifting through the maze of tables and chairs. He turned to her at the entrance of the arcade with a big, genuine smile on his face. "I love this place. It's kind of like my home away from home."

"No surprise there," she replied under her breath.

David's smile flat-lined. "What?"

She shrugged. "I didn't say anything."

"Hmm." David turned and entered the arcade. The bleeps and bloops of video games, mixed with laughter and cheers, rang through his ears. He looked over at the *Chronic Fighter* game and remembered when he and Carrie had played against each other the last time she was here with him.

"Hey, David."

David turned to see his friend, Jake. He wore spiked hair and all black clothing, his usual attire. He held out his hand, shaking David's as they both smiled. David cringed at the blue ring protruding from his friend's bottom lip.

"I haven't seen you in a while. When did you get the…" David pointed to his own lip as Jake nodded.

"Yeah, man. I got it the other day. Isn't it cool? Yeah, I've been helping my dad build the extra room on our house for the past few months. We finally finished it the other day. How's it going with you?"

"Okay."

"Still haven't heard from that Carrie girl yet?"

He shook his head and frowned. "No."

They stood in silence for a brief moment.

"I'd like to introduce you to my girlfriend, Amber." They turned to her, but she grimaced.

Jake held his hand out to shake hers, but she shook her head instead. "I'm Amber. That's all you really need to know."

"Oh. Okay." He pulled his hand back and raised his eyebrows at David.

"Could you excuse us for a minute, Jake?"

"Yeah, man. I'll see you around." He glanced over his shoulder. "I've got some people at the prize counter anyway."

"See ya." David grabbed Amber's arm and walked her back into the mall. "What is your problem?"

She shrugged. "I don't know what you mean."

"Enough of your sarcasm, okay? All of a sudden, you've decided to become extremely annoying and now you won't even acknowledge my friends. What is the deal with you tonight?"

"Oh, if by friends you mean a walking oil spill with 'STUPID' written all over him, then, yeah, I chose not to shake his greasy monkey hand."

David's eyebrows tipped inward at the insult. "Excuse me? Jake has been a friend of mine for almost a year now. Just because you don't like the way he looks doesn't mean he's not human."

Amber set her shopping bags on the floor and crossed her arms over her chest. "You know, I don't get you, David."

"Enlighten me."

"Okay. You are one of Anaisha's greatest heroes. Well, you were. Or you are. I don't know. Anyway, you've fought against dozens of criminals, put Mr. Big away for life, saved countless lives and you have a ton of reward credits put away in a bank account that will be released to you in a few years. Is all this correct?"

"What is your point?"

"You're Mr. Popular! Why the heck aren't you hanging out with popular people? Why aren't you on TV or doing autograph signings or having dinner parties? Why the heck are you hanging around and associating with people like Jake? Why do you insist on hanging around stupid places like the arcade? You have so much going for you, and you just choose to waste it."

David closed his eyes and pinched the bridge of his nose. "Sorry, Amber, if I can't be little Miss Pretty-in-pink-drama-queen like you, but I choose who I hang out with, what I do and what I don't do. And I don't choose to use my popularity for publicity. I just want to live a normal life, okay? I just wanted to come here with you tonight and have a nice, relaxing night." His eyes opened to her hands on her hips and a look of astonishment on her face.

"Did you just call me a drama queen?"

He sneered. "If the shoe fits."

"Whoa!" She pointed her finger accusingly at him. "You went too far with that one."

"And your comments didn't go too far? Are you kidding me?"
She huffed. "I think we need to call it a night."
"Agreed."
"I think we should take a break from each other for a few days. Maybe give us time to try and understand each other."
"Whatever. Let's just cool off and I'll see you on Tuesday."
"Fine."
"Fine."

Maybe it was to his advantage that things ended. But questions still plagued his mind, questions about Amber and what had taken place at the mall tonight. He hadn't felt that much chaos in a long time. One day, they'd agreed to work out their relationship problems, give each other a little space, and three days later she was with someone else. He had taken a chance, trusted again. But he was wrong this time. Wrong like he had been with Carrie.

It was over now. He didn't want Amber back and he didn't want to be held down by the emotions he still felt tugging at his heart, making it difficult to make sense of anything. He knew he had treated her right, and he knew it had all been a waste of time. He wondered if he would ever meet the right girl. He didn't want to waste any more time or energy on these inferior relationships he found himself falling into. He wanted his soul mate. At one point, he thought Carrie was his soul mate, but that all changed long ago when she left to go who-knows-where.

His attempts each day to put Carrie at the back of his mind continuously failed. He couldn't forget her beautiful eyes, her warm smile. She taunted him each day, like a carrot dangling in front of a starving rabbit. It had been six months since she left, and he found himself wondering where his life was headed. He didn't have the same close friendships anymore, except for Veronica.

He missed the days when he and his team fought crime in the city of Lysallis and the rest of the continent of Enera. He missed the LZR Project and, in a spurt of irrational thinking, regretted finally locking away Mr. Big and his thugs, putting himself and his friends out of a job and shattering their circle of friendship.

David's hand lay steady on the car key, ready to turn the ignition, but for some reason, he couldn't pull himself away from the mall. Amber was probably still in there, filing a report against him or something. His eyes opened and he breathed out a long trail of white mist. He had to leave. He knew it was time to go.

He began to turn the key when he realized that he forgot something. He sat back and thought for a moment, then remembered that he left his wallet on the counter at the customer service station. He cursed himself for being so negligent, stepped out of the car and headed back toward the building.

3

Mirrored Wallet

S outh Ryshard. A city of beauty. A city of credits and coin. A city of greed. South Ryshard rests in the middle of the ocean about a hundred miles off the coast of the continent of Enera. A contrast in itself, South Ryshard houses the wealthy aristocrats and the underground club hoppers. With the largest collection of banks on Anaisha, almost all of Enera's transactions move through South Ryshard.

Each day, Carrie Green found herself wondering why she was here. She wasn't rich nor did she consider herself a clubber. She felt out of her element to be in such an elegant place, in the richest city in Anaisha.

She stared at herself in the oval-shaped dresser mirror. Her straight brown hair trickled past her bare shoulders and ended in the middle of her back. Her green gaze sparkled in the light of the many candles scattered about the dresser's marble surface. Her eyes shone with bluish-green eye shadow, her lips glistened with red lipstick, and her cheeks were as rosy as the cinnamon-scented candle to her right. It was all to impress her future husband's business partners.

She noticed, as she stood before the large mirror, that her body was thinner. *Almost too thin in this dress.* She ran her hands behind her ears, pulling her hair away from her face as she moved in closer to the mirror, staring awkwardly at herself. *Smooth complexion*, she thought, *almost flawless.* Yet, she felt so old and tainted.

Her room was one of many in the large house owned by her fiancé, Jerad Montlier. He retained a mansion somewhere in Anaisha at a location she knew not of, and he owned a number of houses—like the one Carrie currently resided in—which he moved in and out of on a yearly basis.

She slept alone, which was the way she wanted it until they were married. She made the firm decision in the beginning not to sleep with him until they wed. He agreed, but it seemed to her a reluctant decision on his part. Besides the two of them, the only other occupants of the house were the maid and the live-in cook, making the place somewhat lonely when her husband-to-be wasn't around.

Staring in the mirror, Carrie saw a girl with no memory of who she was. She couldn't remember much of her past, and Jerad never seemed to ask her about it. She didn't have any childhood memories whatsoever, including high school or the years in between. She was told that her parents died in a house fire shortly after her high school graduation, and she would have died too, had it not been for Jerad rescuing her from the fire. He had been visiting a house across the street when he noticed the cloud of smoke rising from the blazing building and saved her just in time. Unfortunately, the large amount of fumes the fire emitted wiped her memory.

She tried on several occasions to convince Jerad to research her past, but he advised her that the past didn't matter, only the present and the future. He said she should be grateful to be alive. She hesitantly agreed. Even though he was thirteen years older, Carrie loved Jerad. Loved him for the security he offered, loved him for his romantic personality. He saved her life, and she was indebted to him for doing so. He was her personal knight in shining armor.

She gazed deeper into the mirror and saw hints of a nineteen-year-old in her features. She definitely felt more mature than a teenager, but some of that maturity felt like an illusion that stemmed from the mysteries entangled within her.

Carrie turned from the mirror and glanced behind her at the small digital clock radio on the nightstand by her bed. The red numbers told her it was 8:10 p.m., time to impress some more of her fiancé's associates. Her brain was already overloaded with thoughts of the upcoming wedding this weekend. Lately, her wedding had become her highest priority, and she had to convince herself numerous times that she couldn't be wasting effort with thoughts of anything else.

Exhaling a deep sigh, Carrie blew out the candles, watching the smoke curl up along the mirror.

***

Kimberly careened through the farmlands, stopping frequently to drop to the ground and take a three-minute nap before the chilling wind woke her again.

She had enormous trouble keeping her eyes open, let alone

finding the strength to keep the rest of her body moving toward Lysallis. The city wasn't far now. She could make out a large complex ahead and wondered if it was a mall. She didn't really care what it was as long as she could get to a bathroom and a phone. She tried again earlier to call the number her uncle had given her but realized in despair that her cell phone battery had completely drained. *I don't even know who I'm trying to call.*

She staggered through the fields, reaching the outer parking lot. A large sign with dark blue letters read: Jewelplex Mall. It seemed to be the only establishment in the area, besides a gas station in the far distance.

Trudging across the lot, she found her strength returning in waves of adrenaline. She had finally reached her long-awaited destination.

***

Approaching the large glass doors of the mall, David hoped the security guard who escorted him out wasn't anywhere nearby. David placed his palm on the handle just as the cell phone buzzed in his pocket.

"Hello?"

"David, where are you? I've been trying to get a hold of you all night."

"Veronica? What are you talking about?"

"I keep getting a busy signal every time I try to call you."

He shrugged, as if she were in front of him instead of on the phone. "My phone's been on all night. I don't know what's going on with this stupid thing. It's been giving me all sorts of problems lately."

"I have a fashion exam tomorrow, and I was wondering if maybe

you'd want to get together tonight and help me study."

He glanced down at his watch. It was already creeping up on 8:30. "Yeah. I could use your company tonight anyway."

"What do you mean? Are you all right?"

"I'll explain later. Meet me at my apartment at 9:30."

"You sure you're okay? You sound a bit down."

He nodded to the fountain ahead of him and turned back toward the mall. "I'll be fine. I'll see you soon."

"Okay. I'll be there at 9:30."

He stuck the phone back in his pocket and entered the mall. It had been a little over a half hour now since he met up with Amber. A small part of him wished he could go back to that moment in time and somehow change the way things had turned out, but he knew he couldn't. Amber already had her mind made up to leave David behind in the dust, and he was trying his hardest to make it sink in so he could move on.

He made his way underneath the stairwell and approached the customer service counter. Bubbles still stood behind the counter. She looked up as David threw a half-hearted smile at her.

"Hi. Remember me?"

She nodded. "Yup. I sure do."

"I was the one—"

"You and your…um…now ex-girlfriend were here earlier. Yeah, you were the one who threw her phone in a temper tantrum."

"I don't want any trouble. I just left my wallet here," he set his hands on the tan countertop, "and I was wondering if I could get it from you."

She turned her eyes upward, trying to think, and then returned her gaze to him. "Don't have it."

He stood up straight. "What do you mean you don't have it?"

"Exactly what I said, I don't have your wallet. Why would *I* have your wallet?"

"Because I left it here, right in front of you, on the counter. You saw me put it here. Did she take it? Did Amber take it?"

"Well, I don't remember seeing you leave it here. I do remember you telling me to hold on a second because you and your girlfriend needed a moment to be stupid."

"Okay, first off, none of that is any of your business."

She snapped her head back a bit, her eyebrows shifting downward. "Excuse me? You were the one who made it everyone's business. Remember that? Remember the whole scene that played out here?"

"Listen, I'm not here to talk about my relationship. I just need my wallet."

"I don't have it. Do I need to record my voice on CD so you can listen to me tell you I don't have it until it sinks in?"

He ran his hand through his hair while the other hand rested on his hip. *She was nicer a while ago,* he thought. *She was so quiet.* "I really need my wallet."

"I don't have it." She shrugged. "Sorry."

He felt the heat rising in his neck, but he tried to keep calm. If she wanted to, she could call security and have him hauled out of the mall again. Then he'd never get his wallet.

"Look," David leaned in closer to the counter, his voice a whisper as his lip curved into an annoyed sneer, "I really need my wallet, okay? Now, the only place it could possibly be is here, around this counter somewhere, unless you saw the girl take it."

37

Bubbles leaned in closer to David as they stared eye to eye. "Let me explain something to you. I've been working all day. I'm tired and don't have time to put up with your stupid antics right now. I'm going to call security if you don't get away from my counter and leave the mall this instant."

He closed his eyes and felt the remainder of his patience flee. "Excuse me?"

He opened his eyes to see a young girl in a tattered white sweater and dusty blue jeans stumble to the counter. Her dirty blonde hair stuck in tangles here and there. Her face advertised a huge red mark on one side and streaks of mud on the other. Eyes that looked as if they had been sewn shut and were being used for the first time peered out at him.

"Are you all right?" David asked.

She slowly turned toward him and nodded, motioning for him not to touch her.

He stepped back, acknowledging her request. *She looks as if she's been run over by a train. And what is that smell?*

Kimberly turned to Bubbles. "I need...to use your ...phone."

"A phone? You look like you could use a body bag."

Kimberly mumbled her words in a hoarse tone as she tried to get them all out, "I need...a phone." Her body swayed as she fought to keep her balance.

"I'm sorry, but all the phones in the mall are out of service right now. They've been installing a new phone system today, and the phones won't be back up until tomorrow."

Kimberly dropped her head in her arms on the counter.

"I have a phone you can use," David started to reach his hand into his jacket pocket when Bubbles let out a long sigh and rolled her eyes.

"Okay, look, I might know where your wallet is, but you have to promise to leave the mall once you have it, all right?"

He halted his reach and placed his hands on the counter. "Where is it?"

Kimberly started to tip sideways as David instinctively reached over and grabbed her in his arms. She tilted her head up, blinking her eyes repeatedly at him. "I need…" she started, but quickly buried her head in his chest.

He turned to Bubbles. "Please just tell me where my wallet is." He turned back to the bedraggled girl in his arms. "I'm just going to get my wallet and then I'll get you to the hospital."

"I'll take you to our lost-and-found room where your wallet might be." Bubbles walked out from behind the counter and motioned for them to follow her through the mall.

Kimberly hoisted herself up and gracelessly walked beside David. She tried to keep her eyes open, stumbling left and right while they passed dozens of people in the mall who were pointing and staring at her.

"Don't worry," David whispered into her ear. "It looks like you had a night worse than mine. I'll help you get yourself together as soon as I deal with this stupid girl, all right?"

She nodded slowly.

"What's your name?"

Her lips trembled a few times before uttering, "Kimberly."

Bubbles took them up the escalator, through the food court, and led them down a hallway of rooms to the back doors of food stands and other shops in the mall.

Suspicion creeped into David as to why this girl had a sudden change of heart about helping him find his wallet. He hoped she wasn't planning any trouble for him or this Kimberly. If he could just get his wallet, he could get out of here and help this poor girl.

They approached a door with the numbers 334 in brown plastic numerals on the top frame.

"This is the room where all of our found items are kept. I'll give you clearance to check it out to see if your wallet is in there. If it is, take it and leave the mall. I know that if security catches you in here after tonight's incident, they won't be as nice as they were earlier." With that, she pulled a ring of keys from her khaki pocket, shuffled to a silver one and unlocked the door. "Good luck." She held the door open as David and Kimberly stepped into the room.

He reached over to the closest wall and flipped on the light switch, revealing a white square room with a small rectangular table in the middle and half a dozen chairs spread out across the tiled floor.

"Hey, wait a second." David turned back toward the door in time to catch the girl's malicious smirk.

"Security will be here soon to arrest you for trespassing, Mr. Corbin." She shut the door, and the lock made a loud click, sealing them in.

"No!" He tugged on the handle, but it wouldn't budge. Slamming his fists on the door, he pressed his forehead against the metal surface in agony.

Kimberly stumbled to the table and climbed up onto it, lying on her back as her eyes closed and she fell asleep.

David scanned the room, looking for some sort of escape. *No windows or other doors. Ceiling looks solid with the fluorescent lights installed within its surface. There's an air vent, but it's too small to squeeze through.*

He approached Kimberly and stood over her surreal body, caked in dirt and scratches. He examined the giant mark on her cheek and the scratches across her throat and wondered what happened to her, knowing he had to get them out of this situation before it escalated into something worse.

He peered into her mess of hair looking for a hairpin of some sort. A raunchy stench filled his nostrils, and he pulled his face away in disgust. Holding his breath, he slid his fingers into the matted nest and pulled out a small twig. He tossed it to the floor and slid his fingers into her hair again, peering in. He saw a slimy glob of what looked like rotted fruit and quickly yanked his hands away, shaking his head. *Great, we're trapped!*

He reached into his jacket pocket and pulled out his cell phone, quickly dialing as he watched the door for any sign of security. His only hope right now would be Veronica, and that was if she answered. A beeping sound indicated he had no signal in the small room. He turned the phone off and returned it to his jacket.

The room was preventing him from using the phone, and security was probably on the way already, unless Bubbles was just playing a game with them. The thought struck him: *How did she know my name?* He assumed Amber could have told her, or maybe Bubbles really did have his wallet. *My ID and my bankcard are in there. I have to get them back. Why did she have to throw this girl into the mix? She hasn't done anything wrong…as far as I can tell.*

He walked over to the adjacent wall and sat down on the floor, resting his head against his knees. He could only hope for a miracle and wait patiently for an idea to come to mind on how they were going to get out of this mess.

4 Invitation To Escape

After pondering a way out of his makeshift prison and finding none, David pulled his face from his knees and stood to his feet. He glanced at Kimberly's lifeless body on the table. She was still asleep, out cold from her ordeal. Surprised that security hadn't arrived yet, he began to think that maybe this was all a prank, though he didn't know why anyone would want to pull a prank of this magnitude.

David took a seat on one of the aluminum folding chairs and leaned back. As he slid his jacket off, something fell out of the pocket. He draped his jacket on the back of the chair and leaned down, picking up a small red envelope. It was the invitation he had begun reading earlier, before his sister's call, before the breakup. He opened the envelope and slid the card out.

You are cordially invited…

White doily flanked the four inviting words. David opened the card, seeing first a crude drawing of a red rose, and then…

...to the blessed union of marriage between
Jerad Montlier and Carrie Green

on

Saturday, November 14, 1998 at 3 o'clock p.m.

This special event will take place at the Seventh Street Stalus in
downtown South Ryshard.

Reception to follow at the Montlier Estate.

He set the invitation on his lap and stared at it. He read
the words three times before he finally believed what he saw.
His heart raced at the mere mention of Carrie's name. *This
can't possibly be happening.*

For the past six months, he had wondered what happened to Carrie. After the incident that took place between
them during the shutdown of the LZR Project, he hadn't
seen or heard from her. He missed her, and seeing this invitation only tore open the scars that had just barely begun to
heal. It would be too awkward and painful to watch her marry another, especially Jerad Montlier. So why did she send
him this invite? She knew what David felt for her, so why
send a care package of bleach to rub in the wound?

David returned the invitation to his jacket. He mentally
closed up the scars that were beginning to reemerge, knowing he had to get out of the current situation before he could
do anything else. He had to worry about more than just himself right now; he had Kimberly to think about—the girl
who looked like she had been put through a meat grinder.

"Aahh!" She squealed as she tumbled off the table and hit

the floor. "Ohhh." Kimberly clambered to her feet and rushed to the wall. She glued her back to it and panted heavily.

David started toward her. "You okay?"

She held her arms out in front of her to keep him at a distance. "I…I'm okay. I guess I just… had another nightmare," she said as her gaze shifted wildly around the room.

"You're safe now."

"Where are we?"

"The mall. Do you remember what happened?"

She shook her head.

"Well, to make it short, we're stuck in this room until I can find us a way out or security comes for us." He took a seat on the table. "The girl at the customer service counter locked us in here. I'm not sure why, though."

Kimberly glared uneasily at him, running her hands through her long hair, trying to get the dirt clumps and small twigs out of it. Her fingers slid across her lips and found a splotch of blood, which she wiped away with the sleeve of her sweater. "How long have we been in here?"

He shrugged, unsure. "About twenty minutes."

"What day is it?"

"It's Tuesday night."

"Oh, no. What if they can't find me?" she mumbled to herself.

"Who's they?"

"No one."

"Look, if you're in some sort of trouble, I might be able to help you."

"I don't need your help, okay? I just want to get out of this room. I HAVE to get out of this room!"

"Okay, just take it easy."

Her eyes widened at him. "Why should I? I didn't ask to be trapped in here. They were supposed to meet me here in Lysallis."

"Who?"

"None of your business! I just want to get out of here."

"I'm working on it."

"Fine job you're doing!" She peeled herself from the wall and staggered to the door. She tugged on the handle and let out a loud sigh when it wouldn't budge.

"There's no escape. She locked us in here tight."

Kimberly yanked harder on the handle. "I have to get out of here!"

He heard the urgency in her voice but knew better, at this point, than to panic. "Save your energy. I tried looking for a way of escape. There are no windows, and the air duct is too small to fit through. Unless you have some hairpins I don't know about, we aren't getting out of here right now."

"Hairpins? I don't have any hairpins. Don't you have a phone?"

"My signal is blocked, probably by these walls. We have to be outside this room for there to be any chance of it working; otherwise, I would have called my friend to save us."

The lights in the room went out. Kimberly plowed into David, throwing her arms around him.

"It's okay. It just got a little dark."

She squeezed him tightly, pressing her face against his chest while he rested his chin on her head. He caught a whiff of her hair again and turned his head in disgust.

"I'm…I'm afraid of the dark."

"Oh." He glanced down toward the light shining through the wide crack under the door. The mall had closed, and it looked like security had either forgotten about them or never knew they were there. "Hey, I have an idea."

"What? To get out of here?" She pulled away from him.

"Possibly." He grabbed his jacket off the chair and shuffled through the pockets, pulling out his phone. "If I can fit this under the door, I might be able to get a signal in the hallway. I'll be able to reach Veronica, who can get us out of here." He approached the door and held the phone to the crack.

He dialed Veronica's number on the glowing green number pad, turned the phone's volume up to full blast, pressed the Send button and slid the phone under the door. He lay down on the floor and peered through the crack to watch as the phone skidded to a stop in the middle of the hallway. Then he listened closely.

Kimberly stood behind him, sighing loudly.

The phone let out a faint ring. Once...twice...then a third one, and he could hear Veronica's stifled voice.

"Veronica! Listen to me!" He knew if he yelled in the hallway, there was a chance security would find them, but he had to take that risk. It was their only hope of getting out of the mall. "I'm trapped inside an empty room in the Jewelplex Mall somewhere in the back hallway on the second floor! I need you to get me out! I'm in room 334!"

Muffled static buzzed from the phone, and then David heard the barely audible sound of a dial tone. "Well, that's it." He stood up, facing Kimberly. "That call was our only chance. I hope Veronica heard me."

"So do I. I'm starting to get claustrophobic."

David felt his way back to the table and sat down on it. "It seems we have some time to kill while we wait to be rescued.

Do you want to tell me what kind of trouble you're in?"

"It's a long story, and I'm worn out. Do you think we can save the small talk for later?"

He shrugged. "I just thought that if you told me what kind of trouble you're in or who you're trying to meet, I might be able to help you."

"Believe me, there's no way you could protect me from what made this mark." She sat on the table next to him and stared forward at the glow under the door. Her hand reached up to the mark on her cheek and quickly darted away after making contact with it.

"The least I can do is get you out of here, then maybe get you to a hospital or somewhere to get you cleaned up."

"Fine."

David made his way to the door and put his face to the floor, looking under the crack at his cell phone. "You know, I hope nobody heard me yelling."

"You didn't think about that before you did it?"

He stood up. "I did, but I figured it would be better to take that risk than to be stuck in here all night."

"Whatever."

"What is your deal? Do you want my help or not?"

She let out a long breath. "Yes. I'm sorry, I'm just...shook up."

"It's all right. It seems we've both had a bad day. I just want to get out of here and go home."

She rested her head in her palms. "I wish I had a home to go to."

"What do you me—?" The sound of footsteps echoed through the hallway. David rushed over to the door and peeked through the crack. His phone was gone. He stood up and stepped to the side of the door. The handle jiggled up and down. David stood ready in attack position to ambush whoever was trying to get in, though he didn't know how successful he would be without a weapon.

The handle turned and the door swung open with a creak, the hallway light revealing a slender-shaped silhouette. "David, are you in here?"

"Veronica?" David reached out, grabbed her wrist and pulled her into the room. The scent of raspberries filled the small area. He slowly shut the door to a crack. "Did anyone see you come in?"

"No, but we're going to have a heck of a time getting out of here." She leaned against the wall next to the door. "What are you even doing in here?"

"Long story. Some psycho girl locked us in here after Amber broke up with me and I forgot my wallet at the service counter."

"Amber broke up with you? Hmm."

David nodded, assuming Veronica had more to say but was holding back. "I know you didn't like her to begin with, so I don't expect you to have a whole lot of sympathy for me."

"I have sympathy for you, not her."

"Let's get out of here," David moved toward the door, about to pull it open to the hallway.

"I told you, that's going to be tricky."

"Why?"

"Because when I snuck in they started turning on the alarm system and locking the mall. I was right across the street at the gas station when you called me. I ran here so security wouldn't spot my vehicle."

"Ohhh," he moaned while he slid down the wall, sitting himself on the floor next to her. "I can't take much more today." He cupped his palms over his face and slid them down his cheeks.

"Neither can I," Kimberly added as she hopped off the table and approached the door, opening it wide so the expanse of light from the hallway illuminated her raggedy appearance.

"What are you doing?" Veronica asked, stepping into the light. David marveled—as he always did—at Veronica's sense of style. Her coal-black hair hung perfectly straight and tapered to the bottom of her neckline. She wore a brown turtleneck, black slacks and quarter-inch black heels. A tan suede purse—one David remembered her buying at the mall a few weeks earlier—hung from her arm. Veronica stood a few inches taller than Kimberly's head.

"I'm getting out of here," Kimberly said. "I've been through a lot. If you're going to join me, then go right ahead. If not, then stay out of my way."

Veronica shook her head. "You can't make it out of this mall without my help. I used to work security here, so I know how the system works. Most of the mall is filled with motion sensors, and a few areas are patrolled by a security guard, not to mention more than a dozen video cameras that are scattered throughout the building."

"I'm leaving."

"Look, you can't go out that way. We have to make our way to the front doors on the first floor in order to get to David's vehicle. If you go out the employee exit, we'll be stuck in the wrong parking lot, and security will catch us before we can escape. There are cameras outside the mall, and someone's watching those cameras all the time."

David stood up, put his jacket on and walked into the hallway. "Look, if you want to get out of here, listen to Veronica. As soon as we escape, I'll help get you a phone. Is that a fair deal? I think we all want to get out of here without any more problems."

Kimberly rolled her eyes and nodded, crossing her arms in a bratty gesture. "Fine."

"Maybe you can do something about that attitude while you're at it."

Veronica stood between them, glaring at David. "Let's just stop talking and get out of here, okay?" She handed him his cell phone, a red smile blossoming across her face.

He nodded, sliding the phone into his jacket pocket. "Yeah." He glanced at Kimberly as she huffed and turned her face away from him.

They started slowly down the hallway. Veronica leaned close to David's ear, glancing over her shoulder to confirm that Kimberly was following them. "Can she be trusted?"

"As far as I know. She isn't in much condition to cause us too much trouble anyway."

"Fair enough. Just don't let your guard down around her."

"I won't." He knew how protective Veronica could be sometimes, and he respected the fact that even after six months of being out of practice when it came to their adventures in the LZR Project, Veronica remained on her game.

They reached the end of the hallway and entered the food court. Darkness drowned most of the concourse, the Bravo's Burgers neon hamburger sign buzzing with a bright glow, the yellow and red light of the ketchup and mustard holding back the shadows. Through the windows to their right, David spotted the blue crescent moon hiding behind thin clouds.

Kimberly stopped and pointed toward the glass doors. "Why don't we just leave through there?"

"Just trust me, please," Veronica whispered. "I know this mall like the back of my hand. There are no security cameras here in the food court, except for the ones watching the doors leading outside. Once we make it to the escalators, the cameras scattered around the mall won't notice us in time to stop us before we reach the exit we're heading toward." Veronica motioned for them to follow her as she moved silently through the food court, stepping lightly on her heels, her dark silhouette like a mist of shadow evaporating into the night.

David followed, the neon burger light guiding his way. They stopped briefly at certain points, hiding behind tables and chairs to make sure no guards were close by. When they finally reached the end of the seating area, they rushed to the escalators. From the top of the escalators, David could make out a jewelry store on the bottom floor, a blue neon moon hanging over the entrance, illuminating the security fence that guarded its doors.

"We have a problem," Veronica whispered.

David turned and immediately realized Kimberly wasn't with them. "Where is she?"

Veronica pointed to the other end of the food court. Through the darkened concourse, David spotted Kimberly's figure running through the maze of tables back the way they had come.

"If she pulls on one of those door handles, the alarm will sound," Veronica seethed.

David grabbed Veronica's hand, her purse swinging wildly from her arm as they both ran back through the eating area, the clapping of Veronica's heels echoing loudly. "Guess we don't have much of a choice now, huh?"

"How the heck did you get into this mess, David? And who is that girl anyway?"

"I'll explain what I know after we get out of here. Right now we have to stop her before she sets off the alarm."

By the time they caught up with her, Kimberly was already tugging on the door handles.

"Stop!" David demanded.

Kimberly turned around, the unmarred side of her face catching the red and yellow glow of the neon burger sign. "Why?"

"You're going to set off—"

Before he could finish, Kimberly tugged on the handle again and sent a shrill alarm through the mall.

"I can't believe you just did that!"

"Stop right there!" A flashlight beam ricocheted off the walls of the food court. It reminded David of a spotlight in old prison-escape movies.

"Stand back." David motioned for the girls to clear away from the door as he turned and picked up one of the metal chairs. *Haven't done this in a while.*

"What is he doing?" Kimberly asked.

"He's getting us out of the mess you just made," Veronica replied bluntly.

David turned his head and threw the chair at the door. It crashed through the glass and tumbled across the concrete, landing outside.

David leapt through the opening with Veronica close behind.

"You broke the glass door?!" Kimberly screamed.

"Looks that way, doesn't it?" Veronica snapped.

A voice could barely be heard over the alarm: "I said stop!"

Kimberly bolted out of the opening as they all rushed down the stone stairs leading to the courtyard. When they reached the bottom, they ran through the courtyard toward the parking lot. The alarm echoed throughout the property, reminding David that his situation had gone from bad to worse. Reality sunk in that at any moment now, the police would be all over the mall like roaches, and the thought made him sick to his stomach.

When they reached the parking lot, David led them straight to a white four-door sedan resting under a tree. David pulled his keys out and quickly opened the driver's door. He slid in and unlocked the other doors. Then he turned the key in the ignition, wincing when the car only sputtered and spat. The girls scrambled into the vehicle as he tried starting it again, with the same result. "C'mon, you piece of junk."

"We need to get out of here." Veronica's breath rose into the air as she settled in the front seat, drawing the seatbelt across her chest.

"I know." David turned the key again, pumping the gas pedal as the car coughed and choked.

"Are those security trucks?" Kimberly pointed out the back window of the car at the headlights shining through the film of frost.

David glanced in the side mirror at the two security SUVs racing through the parking lot, bright green lights twirling madly atop their roofs. He closed his eyes and cursed under his breath, hoping the car would start this time. He turned the key again, and the engine stammered. He slammed his fists against the steering wheel as his gaze met the headlights reflecting off his mirrors. He turned the key again and, to his surprise, the engine roared as if it were a wild beast that had just been awakened from its slumber. He shifted the car into drive and slammed his foot down on the gas pedal. The back tires squealed and smoked, and the car lunged forward in a burst of speed as the SUVs caught up with them.

Kimberly quickly strapped the seatbelt across her chest and gripped the grab handle above the window. "We can't actually escape mall security, can we?"

David jerked the car in a tight left, the back tires sliding across the asphalt, shifting them into the direction of the main street. The SUVs replicated his move and continued behind him through the parking lot.

"We don't really have a choice, do we? If we don't lose them somehow, we'll be spending the night in jail for no real reason." The thought of being in jail, even for a split second, scared David. He had always been on the right side of the law, and to imagine what it would be like on the other side frightened him.

The SUVs crept closer, now only feet behind the escapees. David pressed down on the gas pedal as hard as he could, forcing the vehicle to go more than sixty miles an hour. "You might want to hold onto something."

"Why?" Kimberly asked, strengthening her squeeze on the grab handle.

"Trust him," Veronica replied.

David waited until the two SUVs were no longer directly behind him and slammed on the brakes. The car squealed and skidded to a halt. The smell of burning rubber filled the air.

White smoke surrounded them as the two SUVs performed last-minute maneuvers, flying past him in a confused panic. David waited until they had enough room to turn back around and come at him again, and then he stomped on the gas and sped toward them, darting between the two bodies of steel as he cleared their grasp and reached the end of the parking lot.

"Good move!" Veronica praised as he turned a tight right onto the main street.

Kimberly flailed around the backseat, squealing in terror. "Are you crazy?!"

"Now, do you have any clever ideas on how we're going to get away?" Veronica asked as David glanced in the rear-view mirror. He saw the blurred image of green lights once again. Along with the green lights, though, David saw white and blue—the lights of police cruisers.

"Yeah," David answered, "I do have an idea." He turned down another street, ran a red light and pulled into the Gas Guzzler station.

"Is stopping on our agenda?" Veronica asked.

"Well, stopping wasn't on my agenda," Kimberly answered. "Neither was running from mall security."

David stopped the car at gas pump number six and turned off the engine. He turned to Veronica with a cocky grin. "Get out your car keys and let's get out of here." He pointed to her red four-door hatchback parked in front of the gas station's convenience store.

She smiled brightly, obviously impressed with how well he paid attention to what she said. She unbuckled her belt, and they all hurried out and made their way across the station to the other vehicle.

David took a quick inventory of everything around them, noting a few cars near the pumps and another in the parking space next to Veronica's car. Nothing that posed a threat. *Good*, he thought, *this should be a quick getaway. I hope.* They hopped into the vehicle and Veronica started the engine.

The SUVs drove past the gas station, but the police cruiser swerved in, pulling up behind David's car at the pump. Veronica slowly backed out of the parking space as David and Kimberly watched the police officer open the cruiser door and point his gun at David's car.

"Out of the car!" the officer yelled.

The people pumping gas dropped to the ground, screaming.

Veronica drove onto the main street. "I tell you, that might actually be the closest you've ever cut it."

David glanced back at Kimberly. She was staring at her lap, shaking her head and biting her lip. "Head to my apartment," he said to Veronica, "She can clean up there, and then we'll decide what to do."

They drove down the street, the police lights and the alarm's scream trailing farther behind them.

5

Nocturnal Activities

Carrie Green sat at the dining room table, her scarlet silk dress flowing along her body like a current of wine. The sleeveless dress made her feel somewhat exposed to the gentlemen before her, but Jerad had insisted that she wear it. Jerad was particular about these things. A bright red solaris flower hair clip kept her long brown hair bunched on top of her head and out of her face.

Her gaze fixed on the white elephant bone plate in front of her, where she was tossing around a tender piece of steak smothered in a creamy brown glaze. The meal had sounded appetizing to her earlier in the evening, but now her stomach was feuding with the murky haze of cigar smoke that hung over the dining area like a cloud.

Jerad sat at the opposite end of the long table, smiling and laughing with his associates. The small, inverted triangle of hair under his lower lip, partnered with his jet-black hair combed back across his head, gave him the sophisticated look that went along with his wealth and helped him blend in with his colleagues. His body grasped a crimson silk shirt—which, surprising to Carrie, did not exactly match her dress—and raven-colored suit pants adorned his body. His silver belt tightened everything together like a braided whip, while sprits of Diamond Dust cologne fused with the smell of the cigars, creating a very bittersweet stench.

The ten businessmen who sat at the table—all wearing black suits and ties—were known as the Associates. They traveled here from different parts of the world, and each had the same motivation in life: wealth. Jerad owned the third largest corporation in Anaisha. His chain of companies, under the umbrella of Hover Incorporated, had proven to be one of the most valuable in the stock market for the last year and a half. The men sitting at the table were his most lucrative business partners, each one ruling his location with an iron scepter. They squeezed credits from their cities with a saturation of ads selling Hover products, provided economic stability with the employment of thousands of workers in each district and helped keep other smaller companies in check with Jerad's prominent name and credits supporting his business dealings.

Every now and then, Jerad paid for the Associates to fly to South Ryshard and have dinner at his home. Carrie had only attended one of these occasions before tonight, and she was quickly concluding that she neither liked them nor approved of the way Jerad treated her in front of his partners. He seemed inclined to ignore her, treating her like a side dish of vegetables instead of his fiancé. The attention he did give her was to solidify her position as his trophy, something Carrie did not approve of.

A large, bearded man in a chef's uniform knelt down and

whispered into her ear, "Dear Carrie, do you wish for me to bring you something else to eat?"

She set her fork down and settled her hands in her lap, staring straight down the table at Jerad. She debated on raising her voice loud enough for Jerad to hear over the noise at the table, but decided not to embarrass herself this evening. "No, thank you, Belgar. I don't have much of an appetite tonight."

"Very well. If you wish for anything, anything at all, I am at your service."

"Thank you, Belgar." She turned her head just enough to catch a glimpse of his warm brown eyes. "You're very kind, as always."

He bowed slightly and left the table, disappearing into the kitchen.

Carrie returned her glare toward the end of the table until she finally caught one of Jerad's glances.

Although his dark, hollow gaze overshadowed the dinnerware, he tilted his head to the right and smiled at her. "Princess, why don't you tell the Associates what I bought you for your birthday last week?"

Over the past few months, Jerad had made it a habit to buy her gifts for various reasons, most of which had nothing to do with a special occasion of any sort. Her birthday was significant—at least in his eyes, if not in hers—but buying her an automobile was a bit over the top. She felt repulsed by the way he showed her off with his wealth. Speaking with him about this irritating behavior had done her no good, so she had no choice but to resort to her own wiles.

Two can play at this game. "Oh, you must mean the drab, rundown Exertes vehicle that you bought me." She watched with satisfaction as he squirmed ever so slightly in his seat. The Associates sat with dull expressions on their faces, one of them twirling the end of his long, handlebar mustache. He reminded her of a famous deceased author, one whose name she couldn't remember off the top of her head.

She continued with her game. "Yeah, it's such an old model of the Stratas brand that I don't think that I'll be able to drive it for more than a week before it becomes just another passing fad." She flung a sarcastic smile Jerad's way, knowing that it would be the last countermove on her part this evening. Today had proven to be a long day—too long—and now she found herself worn out and ready for bed. "If you'll excuse me, gentlemen, I need some fresh air." Carrie set her napkin on her plate and stood up. She smoothed out her dress, still feeling somewhat bare without anything to cover her shoulders, and tossed one more annoyed glance at Jerad before leaving the table.

Carrie left the dining table, made her way through the living area and came to a set of glass doors that led to the backyard. Stepping outside, a frigid breeze swept across her, chilling her straight to the bone. As she approached the swimming pool, she inhaled the fresh air and did her best to exhale what she could of the cigar smoke she had ingested. Her lungs relaxed, thanking her for the reprieve, as did her somewhat ill stomach.

The glass doors opened behind her, and Jerad stepped outside, his silver cane in hand. When he approached her, she felt an unnatural warmth emanating from him, as if the sun had decided to rise in the night sky and strike her with its scorching rays.

"Sweetheart, you embarrassed me in front of my friends."

Carrie felt his large hands grasp the top of her bare shoulders. *Your hands are so warm.* She wanted desperately to explain what was bothering her: the fact that she knew nothing of her past. It was affecting her more than usual, but she resolved not to bother him with it. *Not tonight anyway.* Other issues needed to be cast off her chest.

"Those aren't your friends." Her voice came out soft and jittery as she stared into the dark pool of water. "They're your associates. And you know I don't like it when you show me off with your wealth, especially in front of them." She always felt somewhat uneasy bringing up these kinds of problems to Jerad. He had done so much for her—she didn't want to insult him by badgering him about his behavior in his own house. And yet, her guilt didn't outweigh the effect his condescending attacks had on her.

"I was simply trying to put on a show for the old beasts. I didn't mean to cause you any distress." He turned her around to face him, lifting her chin up.

She stared into his eyes, his bright blue eyes. So much familiarity seemed to be stored in those round spheres. Every time he shot his glittering glances her way, she melted in a way she couldn't explain. There was definitely something about him that she couldn't resist. Was it charm, chivalry, strength? She wasn't sure. Nor did she think it really mattered. He was all she knew. He was all she had.

He grasped her shoulders, the warmth from his hands flowing down her body in waves of heat. "I'm sorry. I didn't mean to hurt you." He successfully knocked her defenses down.

She broke into a smile and wrapped her arms around him. "I know. I love you, Jerad," she whispered in his ear as she lay her chin on his shoulder, grateful that she was wearing heels so she didn't have to stand on her tiptoes to reach his height.

"I love you too, sweetie," he said as he patted her on the back. "I love you too."

Carrie quickly emerged from her overly forgiving mood and pulled away from him, faking a smile, distressed that he rarely ever called her by her name. *For once, I want to hear the words, "I love you, Carrie."*

She decided to disregard her vexation and took what he said to heart. He did love her. What more could she ask for? Words were words, but his actions spoke volumes. The way he cared for her, the roof he kept over her head, the respect he showed her in regard to their sleeping arrangements.

Jerad leaned on his cane, a frown bleeding across his face. "Listen, I'm going back in. My leg is hurting, and I need to return to the Associates. Why don't you head to bed and we'll talk more in the morning?"

She nodded. "Yeah, I am a bit tired. It's been such a long day and—"

"Goodnight." He kissed her on the forehead and retreated into the house.

Carrie turned her back on him and glanced up at the cloudy sky. The wind swept across her again, hardening her bare skin into goose bumps. She struggled to hold in her tears. Her heart quivered thinking of Jerad. When he touched her, she felt warmth and what she figured had to be love. But when he left, when he was quick with his words and quick to leave her side, his actions stung her like a nest of wasps. He was a walking contradiction that messed with her whenever he was near.

Carrie sighed, deciding she was probably just tired and edgy about the upcoming wedding. That, combined with the desire to remember her past, made it difficult for her to make much sense of anything. She tried to let it go, put all of the forgotten past behind her, but now, with the wedding approaching, she couldn't seem to do it. It sat at the back of her mind like a stalled car with the hazard lights blinking.

It's only days until the wedding. All I have to do is keep busy, so I won't have a chance to dwell on such things. She still had a few things to tie up before Saturday. She had to choose the tablecloths and centerpieces for the reception. Because of Jerad's wealth, he had the means to get whatever he wanted at the very last minute, and that was usually how he played it with most things.

Fortunately, the maid had taken care of the invitations, taking that burden off Carrie's shoulders. Because Carrie could not remember anybody from her past, only Jerad's close family and some of his staff were invited to the event. *Strange that I won't even know most of the people at my own wedding.*

She glanced up, looking over the wall that surrounded the large garden area beyond the pool. Out on the horizon, she could see the glittering lights of the city, the stalus clock tower rising high above them. The tall shaft led up to a giant clock face that glowed blue against the backdrop of the skyline. Every time she stared at the clock tower, she felt as if she had some sort of connection with it. Yes, she was going to be married in that stalus in just a few days, but there was something else about it, something her mind wouldn't allow her to remember.

Carrie listened as the tower emitted its familiar gongs throughout the city…ten in all, she counted. *It's time to turn in and give my mind a rest. Tomorrow. Tomorrow I'll ask him about my past. If I show him how much this means to me, I know he'll help me.* She sighed and turned from the dark water and neon lights.

6 Intrusion

David and Veronica rested on the tan suede couch in the small living room of David's apartment while Kimberly showered. They kept the lights off in case the police or anyone else decided to show up, leaving only the glow of the blue night lights scattered throughout the apartment and the orange brightness of the porch light piercing through the cracks in the blinds.

David sunk back into the soft cushions and listened to the humming of the heater, closing his eyes for some much-needed rest. Everything going on—his car problems, bank issues, family dysfunctions and now running from the police—was starting to catch up to him. Mass chaos stood on his doorstep knocking, requesting to come in so it could hammer him into a breakdown. Weighing the heaviest on David's mind, though, was the infernal wedding invitation in his jacket pocket. Carrie had found a way back into the forefront of his thoughts—not a good thing considering how long it had taken him to push her into the darkened recesses of his heart and mind. *Why would she send me an invitation to her wedding when she knows full well how I feel about her? It doesn't make sense.*

He could still remember vividly the last time he saw her. The image was so burned into his memories that he would never be able to rid himself of it. He had been able to cover it up well enough to move on in the past few months, but this invitation had set that memory loose to wander from its cage. The last day of the LZR Project. The day everything went south…

David glided down the corridor that led toward the conference rooms, LZR Project staff passing him in the narrow hallway, smiling and nodding at the hero of the whole operation. He straightened his gray button-down shirt, making sure it was tucked into his black slacks all the way around his waist. He reached the frosted glass door of the third conference room and took a deep breath as he turned the handle and swung the door open.

Carrie looked up from the oak table with a wide smile on her face. "David."

He smiled nervously and took a seat across from her. Meeting her green gaze for only a moment, he suddenly lost his train of thought. He took inventory of her white blouse and whitish-green lipstick. Oh, how he wished he could kiss those painted lips. It didn't help that he was exhausted. He lacked the self-control to stay focused on what he wanted to say to her and the way he had rehearsed it a hundred times in his head.

"Veronica said you had something important to talk to me about."

He hesitated. Yes, he did want to talk to her. He wanted to tell her how he had fallen in love with her, how she had sway over him like nobody else. He had to word all this correctly or she might not understand him. "Yes. I did want to talk to you. I do want to talk to you. I—"

"What are you trying to say?" Carrie asked with a giggle. "I've

never seen you so fluttered before."

"Fluttered? Me? No, I'm not fluttered…whatever that means."

"You're not your cool, calm self. Is it because they shut us down? I thought we all talked about this."

"Well," he had to resist the temptation to change the subject, no matter how upset he was that the LZR Project was now defunct. "I am upset about that, but that's not what I want to talk to you about." He took a deep breath, his eyes wandering around the room as he started picking at his fingernails.

Her tone changed from happy to somber as she leaned back in the chair and gave a quizzical smirk. "What's the matter, David?"

He stared straight into her eyes, as if he were challenging the elusive Medusa to a staring contest. "I've known you for so long now. I've been through so much with you since the day we met back in junior high. I feel so close to you, as if you were family. I feel I know you like the back of my hand. You…" He paused for a moment, closed his eyes and pinched the bridge of his nose. He could feel his heart beating in his ears. He had to finish this, even if he did feel like he was going to collapse right here in front of her. He tried to focus on his scattered thoughts, pull them back into submission. One thought came to mind— I have to take the leap. *He had to tell her, once and for all.*

He opened his eyes, and his gaze fell on Carrie's lost expression.

"You're engraved in my mind," he continued. "I can't seem to go one day without thinking about you, without worrying about you, without…without wishing for more." He let the last few words hang in the air for a moment as her expression morphed from somber to something he couldn't pinpoint.

"What are you trying to say?" Her voice seemed lower now, and the bright smile she had on her face when he first entered the room was gone completely.

67

His heart beat faster, harder. He could swear it was going to jump out of his chest and fall right there on the table in front of them. But it didn't. No distraction came to save him from what was about to come out of his mouth.

"Carrie, I…I…I love you. I always have and I undoubtedly always will!" His voice raised with excitement as he released the words. "I am in love with you, Carrie Green. I can't hide it anymore. For the last few years, I've realized how much you mean to me. I've seen you date other guys, and I've burned inside with jealousy, wishing I could be that guy holding your hand or kissing your lips or holding you in my arms. I can't hold it back anymore, and however this affects our friendship is how it will affect our friendship because I can't go on knowing you any longer without at least telling you how I feel."

Carrie straightened up in the chair, her mouth wide open, a terrified look on her face. "What?"

"I love you."

"No."

"Yes."

"No. You can't."

His heart stopped beating for a moment. "Why not?"

"Because you just can't." Carrie darted up as David did the same.

"Carrie?"

"This is wrong. This is all wrong. I don't…" She stumbled toward the door, but David leapt in front of her, blocking her from opening it.

He shot a pleading look into her frightened eyes. "Carrie, I love you. I'm sure of it. You're the one I love. I'm…"

"Stop, David, stop! Please, I…I have to leave." Carrie's eyes began to water as she gently nudged him away from the door. "Please don't make this difficult."

He moved away from the door just enough to let her open it.

"Don't walk away from this. Please, I didn't mean to compromise our friendship, but I had to tell you. I had to get it out in the open."

"I have to walk away from this. If I don't...I have to."

"But...but I don't understand."

"You don't have to understand everything, David." Carrie opened the door and vanished into the hall. Wisps of her peach body spray lingered in the air like a mist of scented smoke from her burning tires.

"Carrie? Carrie!"

David opened his eyes. He found himself in the dark apartment, a sharp pain traveling from his stomach to his chest as he replayed the image of Carrie walking away from him. He pulled his body out of the cushions and noticed Veronica on the other end of the couch, filing her nails in the shadows.

"What's the matter?" she asked softly. "Besides the obvious."

He could hear the shower in the background, now that the heater had turned off.

"Besides the obvious? I don't know what else could be wrong."

"I know you better than that. There's something else on your mind besides Amber and the incident at the mall tonight. Can I take a shot in the dark?"

"Sure." His voice held all traces of exhaustion as he let the reply leave his lips in a surrendering fashion.

"It's Carrie, isn't it? I assume you got the same invitation I did. The one to the wedding?"

"Yeah."

"Strange that we don't hear from her for months and then all of a sudden she's getting married to one of the richest men in Anaisha, huh?"

He said nothing.

"So, what are you going to do about it?" She stopped filing and placed the cosmetic tool back in her purse.

"What do you mean?"

"Are you going to the wedding?" She stared down in her lap, inspecting her newly rounded fingernails.

"Why would I want to watch her get married?"

"There's a purpose to everything. You know, the most interesting thing about Carrie getting married out of nowhere is that it totally goes against her personality. She must have gotten really attached to this guy for her to make such a huge decision like that in a matter of months. I guess he realizes what he has and doesn't want to let her get away."

David ran his hands through his hair, reminded by the stickiness that came off on his fingers that he hadn't washed his hair in a couple days. He stared at the small night light under the computer desk in front of him, the blue circle reminding him of the moon. "Are you implying something? Like maybe I didn't take my chances when I had them?"

"I already shared my opinions with you a long time ago." She stopped playing with her nails and looked up toward David's stressed form.

"You still won't let me live it down, will you?"

"The whole time Carrie was with us, you and her showed every sign of wanting each other. She used to tell me how she felt about you, and I know you used to tell my brother how you felt about her. And, yeah, I'll come right out and say it even though I know I've said it before, but I think you let her slip right through your fingers."

"Wow, the truth hurts, I guess." The degree of his sarcasm shocked him. Veronica hadn't mentioned anything about Carrie in the last few months. Hearing it all now, again, felt to David like she was ripping his chest open and sprinkling sea salt on his wounds. "Look, there's no way that she felt the same way about me. I already told you that. It was simple infatuation. You should know that since she used to tell you everything."

"She used to go on and on about how much she was in love with you. Sometimes I couldn't shut her up."

David leaned forward and placed his elbows on his knees. *Had she loved me?* He either couldn't tell back then or didn't want to believe it. Things spiraled out of control with the shutdown of the LZR Project. On top of that, he picked the worst timing to tell Carrie how he felt about her. That moment in time hung at the top of his list of regrets. He shouldn't have told her at all, at least then she wouldn't have run away like she did.

He listened to the shower water. The ebb and flow of the current seemed to relax him a bit, but it didn't make up for the stress he had accumulated. "Then why did she leave, huh? Why did she take up and run instead of sticking with me if she loved me so much?" *There, I feel better now that I made my point about her. She left me, left me behind to rot.*

"I'm your friend, so I'm sorry I'm bringing all of this up now, but why didn't you chase after her if you loved her so much? After she left, you totally refused to listen to anything I had to say on the matter. You acted as if she never existed. That's why I haven't really brought her up since then. But I've been your friend for years now, and I can tell you that you two are so perfect for each other. Neither of you ever had the courage to tell each other how you felt. Well, until you did, and then she ran. She ran, David, because she was afraid that if she told you how she felt, it would ruin the friendship that you two had."

"Carrie was…extraordinary." He wrestled to hold the hurt inside. The strong feelings he felt for her were resurfacing and threatening to destroy him on their way up. "Why did any of us let her go?"

"I let her go because I did everything in my power to convince her to stay and work it out with you. She had pressures from her mom, the pressures of the LZR Project, and then she had the enormous pressure of you and her, and she couldn't take it anymore. I talked hours and hours to her about all of it, but she wouldn't listen. You can't force someone to do something they don't want to do, nor can you force them to listen to reason. What's been scary is not knowing where she's been this whole time. I'm just glad she's alive."

"So what's the point of dragging this out of me?"

"I guess I just see another opportunity."

"Opportunity? An opportunity for what? She's engaged. She obviously doesn't love me anymore. She's about to marry Jerad Montlier." He made sure to put bitter emphasis on "Montlier."

"I know for a fact that Carrie will always love you, no matter what. I mean, after six months of not contacting you, she sends you a wedding invitation? She's giving you an opportunity."

"For what again?"

"Right now, in the midst of this craziness, this chaos, it looks like an opportunity to get back what you lost."

"I'm afraid it's not going to be that simple. She's attached to someone else now, and I don't know how deep that goes." He leaned back in the couch, letting out a deep sigh.

"Follow your heart. It hasn't given up on Carrie, and I don't think you have either. Amber and you were attached, and look how quickly that changed. Carrie has only known Jerad six months, at the most. You've known her since eighth grade."

"I want her back, Veronica. I want Carrie back and I want her back to stay. But what if she really is happy with this guy? What if they are so much in love that it would be totally pointless to go to her wedding? What if—"

"David, the only way to answer a 'what if' is to match it with a 'try' and do something about it. Do you want this to be a regret, or do you at least want to try? Right now, it looks like you have nothing to lose and everything to gain."

Why does she always have to be right? "Well," he stood up and started pacing back and forth between the desk and the couch, adrenaline coursing through his veins as he let his thoughts run aloud, "if I'm ever going to have any chance with Carrie again, then I have to reach her *before* she marries Jerad."

A large grin swept across Veronica's face. "That's the David I know. Where have you been? Ever since Carrie left, you've changed. Now I can finally see hints of your usual reckless nature breaking through. I think we need to get to this wedding and crash the heck out of it."

David paced faster, tapping his chin with his forefinger. "Well, we have until Saturday, so that leaves us three days to get there. We can't take a plane, not with the cops looking for me. We can drive from here to the coast, and then we'll take a passenger ship to South Ryshard. It shouldn't take more than two days, which will leave us plenty of time to stop her."

"First things first. What are we going to do about Kimberly? And the cops?"

"Um…" He pondered for a moment. "After we get Carrie back, we can turn ourselves in and explain the whole thing. You and I know some of them anyway. I'm just afraid that if we try to turn ourselves in right now, we'll never make that wedding in time."

"I agree."

"As for Kimberly, we'll just get her home, wherever her home is, then we'll take off for the wedding."

"Good. Good plan. Let's hope for lack of complications."

"But we specialize in complications," he replied jokingly.

Veronica stood up from the couch. She smoothed down her slacks and straightened her turtleneck. She grabbed a small cloth hair tie from her pocket and tied her hair back into a ponytail. "I'll be glad when this ordeal is over. I'm just happy we finally found out where Carrie is. It's been killing me, not knowing where she took off to. I didn't realize she could be so reckless. You two are a perfect match."

"Thanks…I think."

Veronica set her hand gently on his shoulder. "It'll be all right, David. I'll be by your side the whole way. We'll get her back."

"I hope so." He rubbed his eyes with his palms, trying to wipe the weariness away. It was going to be a long trip for both of them, but hopefully well worth it.

The shower water stopped, leaving the apartment in complete silence except for the humming of the refrigerator in the kitchen. They suddenly heard jiggling of the screen door followed by violent pounding.

David glanced through the peephole. "It looks like…

Amber?"

Veronica stepped behind him. "What is *she* doing here?"

He unlocked the door and cracked it open to the screen. "Amber?"

"David? David, I need to talk to you." Her lips squished up against the dirty screen and then quickly pulled away, spitting into the air. "Yuck!"

Veronica laughed softly.

Against his better judgment, he opened the door and unlocked the screen. Amber stepped into the apartment as chilly air seeped in after her. He quickly shut the screen and the door.

"I don't think this is a good idea," Veronica whispered in his ear.

"Why is it so dark in here?" Amber asked.

"Because the police are after me. All because of our stupid little argument in the mall earlier today. You remember that, don't you?"

Amber sighed, sounding somewhat regretful for the events that had occurred earlier in the evening. "Look, I came over here to give you your wallet. I took it from the counter when you left the mall. I was going to keep it as reimbursement for my phone, but I realized that I couldn't do such a thing to you. So, here." She reached into her purse and pulled out a dark leather wallet, handing it to David.

He grabbed it from her and started tapping it against his palm impatiently.

"I also came here to apologize."

He stuck the wallet in his back pocket. The fact that she was solely responsible for the mess he currently found himself in danced around his head, stirring up frustration and anger. He took a deep breath and calmed himself. "So you feel guilty for taking my wallet but not for cheating on me?"

"You will not believe how sorry I am for *everything*."

"You're right, I won't."

"Look, I realize now that I was wrong. I was wrong to cheat on you, I was wrong to steal your wallet." She reached out and gently took his hand, drawing her body against his. "I want to be with you." He felt her warm breath against his neck as she began kissing it lightly. He closed his eyes while her kiss teleported him to another time, another place. A place where he could escape the haunting thoughts of Carrie, the mistakes of his past and the reality of his dismal life.

But then he remembered Carrie for what she was—not a haunting image, not a phantom that sought to make him suffer the rest of his life, but the girl he truly loved. The pain of what Amber had done to him slithered around his thoughts of Carrie, choking the life out of them like a mad boa whose only intention is to kill.

David's eyes flashed open, and he pulled away from Amber. "It's a little late to want to fix things now. You and I aren't together anymore, and now I have the cops chasing after me."

"The whole locking you in the room was a prank. The cops aren't really coming after you."

Silence fell among them. Veronica started to move, but David placed his hand on her arm to let her know he had things under control. She stepped behind him and glowered silently.

"The cops really are after us, since we broke a glass door and ran from security to escape the mall."

"What? What are you talking about? Why did you run? You're not guilty of anything." Amber paused and then, as if it was an afterthought, added, "We were going to let you out in the morning."

"Who's 'we'? And if you weren't going to let us out until morning, how did you know I was here at the apartment?"

"I'm sorry, baby. I want you back. I'll do anything." Her voice went soft and she started to whimper. "It was a mean prank I did, and I apologize. Please forgive me. I'm so sorry. I don't think you realize how sorry I really am. I did a horrible thing, and I don't want to be regretting it for the rest of my life. I just want us to be back the way we were."

David laughed under his breath. "That's a good one. That's a real good one. Like I'm going to take you back. It's not just the prank that bothers me, it's the fact that you cheated on me. Look, I really hope you're happy with him."

"But I'm not happy," she whined.

"You need to go, okay?" He opened the front door and then the screen, motioning for her to leave.

"David, I love you." Tears began to stream down her face.

The porch lamp let in enough light to allow David a glimpse of the black mascara traveling in little lines down her cheeks. He stared at her, his heart arguing with him about what to do. Veronica came up behind him and placed her hand on his shoulder, silently prompting him to turn Amber away.

"I'm sorry, Amber, but my heart belongs to someone else now, just like yours does. Guess you'll have to find some other jerk to be your puppet."

His comment brought a grin to Veronica's face.

Amber's face tilted up, her mask marred with black blots. "Someone else?" She sniffled. "How could there be someone else?"

77

"None of your business. Now, get out."

"Who is this other girl, David? Is it Veronica? I know you two are real chummy, but I didn't think it was like that."

"You don't deserve to know. Now please leave," he said as he motioned toward the open doorway. The cold air was seeping in like a pack of wild wolves, and he wanted to put an end to it and to Amber's unwelcome presence.

The door between the living room and the bedroom opened, and Kimberly walked out, drying her hair with a towel. She wore the same dirty jeans she had on before her shower, but now donned a red T-shirt that David had given her. "What's going on?" she asked.

Amber pointed and huffed at her. "Is this her? Is this the girl? This is the girl you love over me? You are such a back-stabbing jerk, you know that? We ended things only hours ago, and you've already replaced me? How dare you replace me! What is the meaning of this?"

David rolled his eyes. "Yeah, I'm really going to lose sleep over losing you." He gently shoved her through the doorway. "Just leave. I've had enough of your games for one night."

She stomped her foot on the ground as a look of shock spread across her face. "Wait…I know now. Why didn't it occur to me sooner? It's Carrie, isn't it? Of course. You couldn't get your mind off her when we were together and now—"

"Excuse me."

Everyone looked toward the doorway where a police officer stood. Amber backed into the apartment as the officer strolled through the doorway and shut the screen behind him. In the darkened apartment, David swore the man's eyes glowed a tint of red, but he figured it was just a figment of his tired imagination.

"Can we help you, officer?" Veronica asked as she walked over to the wall and turned on the living room light.

David noticed the officer had his hand on the holster of his gun, as if prepared for some sort of firefight. When his gaze met David's, he relaxed his hands to his side and left the holster alone, letting it hang off his waste at an angle. Clearing his throat, he said, "How are you all doing this evening?"

"Fine," Veronica answered.

"Good, good." He examined the room, taking in the small space. "I'm here tonight because I'm looking for a girl."

Silence and tension filled the air. David glanced at Veronica, who had her gaze steady on the man and the gun on his side. Amber inched quietly behind David, and Kimberly stood with her arms crossed, the towel atop her head.

David decided to break the silence. "Does this girl you're looking for have a name?"

The officer grinned. "Kimberly Sebastien."

Kimberly removed the towel from her head, and her wet hair tumbled down her back. She stepped in front of David and Veronica and set the towel down on the couch. "I'm Kimberly."

The officer took off his hat, revealing a burnished bald head. "I'm Officer Thana. I've been searching everywhere for you tonight. Your parents reported you missing hours ago." The man sneered and dropped his hand slowly to the holster again.

Kimberly stumbled backward, grabbing the back of the couch to balance herself. "Uh…"

Officer Thana reached out and grabbed Kimberly's arm, pulling her toward him. "It's me again, sssweetie!"

She broke from his grasp and stepped back behind David and Veronica.

Thana's eyes looked saddened, and he reached his hand out to take hers. "You need to come with me, hon, your parents are waiting for you at home." He pushed his way between David and Veronica.

"Hey!" Veronica shouted as she fell onto the couch.

"David!" Kimberly screamed. "This…this…this…"She scrambled around the officer and headed straight for the bedroom, Officer Thana hot on her heels.

A high-pitched squeal rang out from the bedroom and then a loud crash.

"Something's not right," Veronica said as she pulled herself up from the couch.

"Yeah, I know." David started toward the bedroom, Veronica in his wake. When they entered, they saw the officer standing over Kimberly's trembling body. She had fallen to the floor, David's dresser tipped over on top of her lower half.

"What's going on here?" David asked. When he received no answer from the officer, he stepped closer to the two of them. "I'd like to see your ID, please." When the officer continued to ignore him, David stepped even closer, his adrenaline rising to the occasion. He wondered if this guy was a real officer and what the deal was with treating Kimberly like she was a criminal. "You never really know what's out there nowadays. I just want to see your ID and make sure you're a legitimate officer of the law."

Before David could step any closer, the officer swung around and slashed at David's face with needle-sharp claws. David fell backward, his blood splattered in spots across the wall and carpet. "What?!" His cheek, where he had been cut, began to burn.

Veronica helped him to his knees, pulling his face toward her. "David, you okay?" She examined his cheek and then turned toward the officer. "What do you think you're doing?"

"It burns!" David shouted. "It burns!" The pain was unbearable, and he found himself plunging his face into the carpet, rolling the cuts along the floor to try and take some of the sting away. He caught a quick glance of the officer with his hand on his gun again.

"That's it!" Veronica lunged toward Officer Thana, but he was too fast—darting to the side and back around Veronica as she passed through the area he was in, almost tripping against the dresser.

"Ssstay out of thisss, Veronica."

"How do you know my name?"

Officer Thana grinned fiendishly. "I know you. I know all of you. Even Amber back there." He pointed to the front door as Amber stood, staring at him like a frightened deer, the front doorway half-opened before her. "It's quite foolish for you to interfere with my plans here. Kimberly isss coming with me thisss dark eve."

David managed to get to his feet, blood running down the side of his face. Although his vision was a bit blurred, he felt determined to save Kimberly's life and be rid of this crooked cop. "You aren't taking her," David growled.

Officer Thana grinned, exposing pointed teeth. "You will perish if you make the choice to come againssst me."

The living room light flickered off, taking the night lights with it. Only darkness enveloped them, the officer's eyes glowing a brilliant crimson.

"You won't be feeding on any of them tonight!" a woman's voice cried out.

In the front doorway, by the light of the porch, David could see two silhouettes—a man and a woman.

The officer hissed. "Not you again! Kimberly isss coming with me thisss dark eve, and you will not ssstop me!"

Without thinking, David thrust himself into the officer, nailing him in the abdomen as they both fell against the dresser and rolled to the floor. Kimberly screamed. David quickly got to his feet and grabbed her hand, pulling her out from under the furniture. Veronica helped him get Kimberly up, and then they fled the bedroom, making their way toward the front door. When they reached the front room, the two strangers were in the bedroom behind them.

"Go! Keep Kimberly safe." The woman's powerful voice shook the apartment walls. "We will meet up with you shortly."

"Time to go." Veronica grabbed her purse off the desk and took David and Kimberly's hands, tugging both of them through the doorway as a rumble shook the building.

"I can't leave those two with this guy, Veronica!" David shouted as he attempted to go back into the apartment. "We need to help them!"

Veronica swung around and grabbed his arm, yanking him away. "We can't in the condition you and Kimberly are in. We're leaving now!"

"At least let me grab a few things," he argued as she dragged them around the corner, toward the parking lot.

"There's no time, David." They reached Veronica's car. She dug through her purse for the keys. "In the condition we're in, we're no match for whatever that thing is. Maybe those two are real cops or something. Maybe even sentries. They'll handle him. The important thing is that we got Kimberly away from him."

Veronica found the keys and opened the car. She and Kimberly took the front seats while David slid himself across the back.

As the car started, David wiped his arm across his cheek, streaking blood across the sleeve of his leather jacket. He felt heat engulfing his face. Veronica backed the car out of the space as David stared through the back window and saw a red glow emanating from his apartment bedroom.

The back tires screeched as the vehicle lunged forward and sped through the complex, heading toward the small side street.

"Close call," David muttered.

"Too close," Veronica added.

"Are you okay, Kimberly?"

"Yeah," she replied softly.

Veronica turned the car's heater up. "Who was that? What was that?"

Kimberly shrugged. "Don't know. He's been chasing me ever since I left my uncle's house."

"Where is your uncle's house? We can take you back to him now…if you want." Veronica turned down Sage Street as David shifted across the seats, trying to get comfortable with the pain in his face.

"My uncle's dead."

"Oh."

"Can you go back to your uncle's house?" David asked. He moved his jaw around, noticing with some dismay that the more he moved his mouth, the more the pain seemed to spread to the other side of his face. At least the bleeding had stopped, but it was no comfort to David when he put his hand up to his wound and could feel deep canals in the flesh.

"My parents were killed when I was little," Kimberly whispered softly, "and earlier tonight, my uncle was murdered by the thing you saw back there. I can't go back home. I can't go back to that house." She shuddered. "There's so much evil there."

"Murdered? Are you serious?" Veronica drove the car around the corner and onto Common Street, in the direction of the freeway.

Kimberly bowed her chin to her chest. "I don't really want to talk about it."

"I'm so sorry to hear that," Veronica remarked. "Well, where do you want us to take you?"

"I...I don't know." Her voice trickled off at the end of her sentence. "Just drop me off anywhere."

Veronica glanced at David in the rearview mirror. She reached over, pulled some napkins out of the glove compartment and handed them back to him. "Do you need medical attention?"

David gently used the napkins to pat the blood from the scratches in his face. "I'm fine. Kimberly, do you have any friends or family we can take you to?"

"No. No, I don't."

Veronica glanced at David in the mirror again, her eyes telling him she was about to do something he might not like. "Would you like to join us?"

Kimberly turned, her eyes meeting Veronica's, then David's. "What?"

"We're heading to South Ryshard. You're free to stay

with us if you'd like. If you have nowhere else to go."

David knew Veronica was offering out of pity. She wasn't usually one to play babysitter. *The poor girl's better off with me and Veronica anyway. Besides, there's no time to sit and figure out who she's going to stay with when we have a wedding to break up.* David leaned back in the seat. *Perfect timing. My apartment is being torn to shreds, and I'm going on a journey halfway across Enera.*

"What's in South Ryshard?" Kimberly asked, rubbing tears from her eyes.

"An old friend," David replied before Veronica could go into any details he didn't want to hear right now.

Kimberly nodded. "My uncle…he gave me a phone number. I'm supposed to call it."

David crumpled up the bloody napkins and tossed them to the floor. Then he pulled his cell phone out of his jacket pocket and handed it up front to her. "Here."

Kimberly took the phone out of his hand with a half smile. "Thank you." After trying the phone number, she handed the phone back to David with a dismal look in her eyes. "Busy signal…again."

David shoved the phone back into his pocket. "You can try as many times as you need to." He lay down across the seats, the pain easing from his face, just barely.

"What about your apartment?" Kimberly asked. "What about that thing?"

"Nothing we can do about his apartment or that thing right now," Veronica answered. "If we return to the apartment when more cops arrive, it's only going to get ugly. Trust me, our best bet right now is to get as far away from here and that creature—or whatever it is—as possible."

85

"I guess I'd be safer staying with you guys. Not like I have anywhere else to go."

"Well, neither do we," Veronica replied as she drove onto the dark freeway and headed south. "You all right back there, hon?"

"Yeah, I'll be fine." David groaned. "Just great."

7

Road Hypnosis

Hours from sunrise, David drove across the border into Tindall. Veronica slept across the backseat while Kimberly dozed in and out of slumber in the front as the car rumbled down the dark and vacant highway.

The gas station break earlier had given David a chance to clean up his wounds and switch places with Veronica so she could rest. The driving seemed to relax his nerves. Maybe it was just because he loved being on the move, working toward a goal. He knew it had something to do with the fact that hope had sprung up in him, telling him, convincing him that he could stop this wedding.

As the radio broadcast a light-rock station, David found himself slipping in and out of memories from his past, stories that filled his mind and almost lulled him to sleep. They might have if it weren't for the slight burning sensation in his cheek keeping him at least partially alert.

A car commercial played, the narrator's voice a sultry female tone.

"Fast. Stylish. Savvy. The all new, 1998 Stratas Exertes luxury sedan. Power windows, all wheel drive and a V8 engine with enough horsepower to blow away the competition. We even have special deals if you want to purchase Hover-Technology on your new vehicle. Come by Dale's Luxury Dealership in Tindall today, and you can get a Stratas Exertes for only sixty thousand credits, fully loaded."

David remembered a time when he held Hover-Sheets in his own two hands, before Hover-Technology had been leaked to the world, before Jerad Montlier became a billionaire. That was years ago, and now Hover-Technology seemed to be around every corner he turned.

"Hi. I'm Victoria. I'm glad you have your radio set at ninety-nine point nine, Tindall's premier light-rock station. It's Wednesday morning, and starting at five-thirty, we'll have the Traffic Team update you on the highway situations. At seven, we'll start taking your early-morning music requests. And don't forget to join us for the Lunch Time Stress Break with a full, commercial-free hour of your light-rock favorites. For all of you lovers burning the midnight oil, here's a classic, "Love's Flame." Right now on ninety-nine point nine, KTND."

Immediately after the announcement, slow, rhythmic drums and piano notes that David knew all too well pushed through the car speakers and made him remember. Remember the past, remember Carrie…

Remember the night of the autumn dance their junior year at Lysallis High at the Tiffany-Briggs Hotel in the center of the city. It was then that he had the strongest feelings for Carrie. That's when he realized his feelings for her were real and not just inflated infatuation…

The necklace chain nestled into the curves of Carrie's neck like a silver snake. At the end hung a small crescent moon, its lustrous black shine matching the velvet dress that ended just below Carrie's knees. The green color that outlined the black moon brought out a sparkle in her emerald eyes, a sparkle that revealed her true beauty to the world tonight.

She pressed her face close to David's ear as they slowly danced in a circle to "Love's Flame." "David," she whispered, her warm breath falling across his neck like thick honey.

"Yeah?" he whispered in reply, feeling her soft skin underneath his fingertips as he moved them up and down her bare back in gentle strides.

"I...well...I want to tell you something. I...I don't know how to say this, but I guess I'll just say it the best way I can. We've been friends for a long time now, and I think we can be totally honest with each other. About anything. Don't you agree?"

"I do."

"Well, I—"

"Excuse me."

They broke apart to see who had the nerve to interrupt their dance.

A young man in a pinstriped suit stood before them, his hair parted in the middle, bangs dangling above his blue eyes. His gaze fell on Carrie like a wolf's when it finds a hare in the forests of Lindor.

"I don't mean to be rude, but I'd really like to have this dance."

David's reluctant agreement to let the man have his dance with Carrie remained one of David's greatest regrets. That night, the night of Lysallis High's autumn dance, the man they would later learn was Alex Waterford, took Carrie by force and left David behind to deal with an explosive and virtually no way of escape. As resourceful as David was, he couldn't save Carrie and stop the bomb at the same time. So he picked Carrie, tracking her and Alex through the hotel to the roof where the history of their relationship changed forever…

David burst through the door that opened out to the roof. The night air cooled the feverish temperature of his body, making him wish he hadn't stripped himself of his suit jacket. Looking out across the roof, he saw the skyline of neon-lit buildings, the blue Bank of Lysallis rising taller than all of them.

A whooshing sound crept up over the edge of the roof. A helicopter flashed bright lights and gusts of wind his way, forcing him into a crouch to keep from losing his balance.

David looked up and saw Alex in the back of the helicopter, Carrie at his side, the sound of the blades almost drowning out the man's sinister voice. "Looks like you lost something important tonight, David."

"It's not over yet," David mumbled to himself.

Alex pulled Carrie close and shoved a gun barrel into the side of her head. Her eyes lit up in ghastly fright.

David quickly analyzed the distance between the helicopter and the edge of the building. He took a few steps back, inhaling a deep breath. Below, in the bottom floor of the hotel, the bomb reached zero. He had nothing to lose now. Nothing to lose.

David would always remember that night, that moment in time when he realized he really did have nothing to lose. Carrie was all he had, and if she was taken from him, what good was he? That's what prompted him to jump onto that helicopter and fight Alex. A quick battle ensued—Alex proved to be more talk than action when it came to actual fighting—but at the end, after the hotel burst into flames and charred debris, Alex stabbed David in the stomach with a knife he managed to hide on himself.

Even on the floor of the helicopter with a knife sticking out of his stomach, David could remember the strained look on Carrie's face as she threw herself into Alex, knocking him out of the helicopter.

"David?" She cupped his face in her hands and kissed his lips. When she pulled away, her wide green eyes filled with tears. "Stay with me. Please, stay with me. We're heading to the hospital now. Just stay with me."

He realized then that he could never reveal his feelings for her. She almost lost her life because of him, and because of an old junior high classmate's obsession.

The yellow dashes in the road began to fade, and blackness filled David's vision. The car took the shoulder as the tires grumbled warning, waking David. He jerked the wheel, putting the vehicle back on the highway.

Veronica stirred in the backseat but didn't wake. Kimberly continued to sleep like a log.

David swore he was at that dance just now, had somehow gone back in time and experienced it all over again. But the reality was, he hadn't. His memories were plaguing him, like they always did when they came to the surface in cruel fashion. That wedding invitation had brought all of it back, had unlocked the doorway to the basement of his life. It was too late now. Carrie had left the basement and was wandering around his mind, tinkering with his heart like only she could do.

David glanced at the dash, at the glowing green dials and gauges. The gas tank registered a little over half full, which told him the car was getting decent mileage. They had filled up a little over an hour ago and at this rate, he figured they would have no problems getting to the shore with the funds and resources at their disposal.

"Why do...why are you going through Tindall instead of North Ryshard?" Kimberly's voice came out hoarse.

David glanced over and noticed the haphazard hair atop her head. "Have you ever been through North Ryshard?"

"No."

"It's a dump. It's safer going through Tindall."

"Oh." Kimberly sat up and yawned. "How long have we been driving?"

"A few hours now."

"I thought I was going to wake up and be in my bed...at my uncle's house...but I guess not."

"Why did that...thing...back there take such an interest in you? And why did it kill your uncle?" He glanced in the rear-view mirror at the set of shadows in his cheek. The wounds had swollen, but the burning sensation was slowly dying out.

"That's a long story," Kimberly whispered as she turned and stared out the window.

"We've got a long drive ahead of us."

"I just don't feel like talking about it yet." She turned from looking at the dark landscape and eyed the deep wounds in his face. "Are you going to be all right?"

"I've been through worse."

"I can't imagine."

"You'd be surprised."

"Would I?"

"Yes, I'm afraid you would. Who's at that number you keep trying to call?"

"I don't know. Every time I call, the line is busy. What

about you? Who was that girl at your apartment?"

"She's an ex. And she's going to stay that way." David smiled at Kimberly, but she was gazing out the window again at the starry sky.

"Whose wedding are you going to break up? Is it another ex of yours?"

David sighed. "No. It's the wedding of the girl I should have been with this whole time."

"Oh, I see. She's a regret. I hate those."

A moment of silence fell between them.

"I hate regrets too, but this is one that I'm going to fix."

"Who is she marrying?" Kimberly turned from the window to face the road ahead of them.

"Jerad Montlier."

"Jerad Montlier? Isn't he the guy who created Hover-Technology?"

"Yeah, don't remind me." David rubbed his eyes to erase the road hypnosis.

"I can drive if you want. I saw a sign back there for a gas station coming up at the next exit."

"Well, you seem to be in a better mood than you were earlier." Seconds later, David wondered if she would take that comment poorly.

"I'm sorry," she muttered. "I didn't mean to get testy with you. It's just been a really long night. Nothing personal."

He glanced at her. She had bunched herself in a ball on the seat and strained her fingers through her hair to straighten it out. "No harm done. It's been a rough night for both of us, I guess. I am getting tired, and this dark highway is starting to play tricks on my mind." He pulled onto the exit ramp and then turned down a road that led into a Fastie's Gas Station.

They stepped out of the car quietly, not wanting to wake Veronica, and walked into the gas station's convenience mart. The small bell above the door cried out as they entered, and under his somewhat drowsy state of mind, David recalled a story he heard when he was younger about a girl who was brutally murdered by her boyfriend. In the story, the girl came back to haunt the boyfriend who murdered her, and she would wail into the late night hour, her voice bringing agony to those who heard it. Why he suddenly remembered this grim tale—one his father used to tell him on camping trips—he didn't know, but he envisioned the sound of the bell mimicking the fabled girl's voice.

The mart appeared clean and empty, save for an old woman sitting behind the register. She wore a blue-collared shirt with the Fastie's gas pump logo over the left breast, and black slacks. She nodded kindly as Kimberly made her way toward the women's restroom and David began browsing through the coolers for something to drink.

"Lovely night," the woman commented from across the room.

David looked up over a shelf of potato chips and nodded. "Yeah, I guess."

"You from around here?" Her raspy voice grated the space between them, revealing that she was a chain smoker.

He didn't necessarily enjoy the fact that they were practically in the middle of nowhere in the middle of the night. "No, we're from Lysallis."

"Oh. That's quite a ways from here," she replied, pointing out the obvious.

He opened the cooler door and pulled down two black and red cans of Syn Soda. "Yeah. It's pretty far." He approached the front counter, and she began to ring up the cans.

Close up, David saw that her aging face sagged with wrinkles, and her eyes sunk into her head like the sockets were pockets for change. Yet her relentless desire to keep smiling made her appearance better than depressing.

Her gaze moved to David's cheek. "In a fight?"

"What?"

She nodded. "Your face."

He reached his hand up to his wounds, lightly grazing his fingers along the canals in his cheek. "Um...yeah, a fight."

"With a rake?"

"No."

"Looks like a rake did that. That or a giant pitchfork."

He pointed to the second can she hadn't yet rung up. "We really need to be on our way."

"Of course." She smiled again, her whole corpse-like face lighting up. "I'm just the curious type, I guess. It'll be two credits and sixty-seven coins for the goods."

David reached into his pocket and handed her a fistful of change. She sorted through it while he observed the small gray box on the counter to his right. The LCD screen on the back side of it glowed white, while the green scanning light radiated from inside the small slot in the front of the unit.

It was a card reader. David had never needed to use one, but he knew what they were there for. The small device would read a person's identification card by analyzing the DNA from the blood strip in the plastic, verifying—along with the photo on the card—the user's identity. The information taken from the card would be cross-referenced with Anaisha's database system, bringing up a digital picture on the screen that would authenticate the user. It was extremely successful in stopping identity fraud.

David counted himself fortunate that he had gotten his wallet back from Amber. It held his ID card, and the cards weren't easy to replace.

The woman nodded after counting out all the coins, scooping them into her aging palm as the register drawer popped open to receive them all. David picked the drinks up off the counter and started toward the door, glad to be done with that conversation.

"Keep Anaisha safe like you always have, David."

He paused and half-turned toward her, nodding. He found the fact that she recognized him but didn't make a huge public spectacle of it nice. Most people who recognized him either felt the need to berate him on the horrible job he and his friends did in the past or smother him with adoration and affection for being "Anaisha's greatest hero." He didn't really want to be a hero. He just wanted to live his life, and now he wanted to live it with Carrie.

The bell above the door shrieked as a man walked in, a young girl at his side and the stench of manure trailing in his wake as he passed David. The man wore a plaid red and black button-down shirt and raggedy blue jeans. A few strands of gray hair dangled out the side of his otherwise bald head. A white bandage ran across the top of his forehead, spotted in dark blotches of blood.

David left the mart without taking a second glance at the unkempt man, glad to be only passing through.

Kimberly exited the restroom and headed toward the coolers for something to drink. She had used the privacy of the dingy restroom to expunge the last of her tears. Now that she had slept a bit, she felt a little better, a little more emotionally stable. David seemed reliable in a pinch, and Kimberly felt somewhat safe with him. She wanted to say she remembered him from television a long time ago, but she couldn't place his face exactly. She didn't watch much television, but what she did watch could be blamed for contributing to some of her nightmares.

When Kimberly arrived at the coolers, she quickly found the Syn Soda and reached in to grab a can. She turned toward the registers to see a young girl—probably around the age of ten or eleven—standing before her, staring up with bright blue eyes from under a mop of curly blonde hair. She wore black capris and a black T-shirt, but the blonde hair brought out a peach tone in her skin, almost making her look like she was glowing.

"Hello," the girl said.

Kimberly smiled. "Hi."

Kimberly went to pass, but the girl casually sidestepped and blocked the way to the register. Kimberly went to go around the other side, but the girl just sidestepped that way as well, preventing Kimberly from leaving the cooler aisle.

"What are you doing?"

The girl's smile faded. Kimberly glanced up over the shelf of potato chips, and her heart suddenly tumbled into her stomach. A man with a white cloth wrapped around his head stood at the register. Kimberly took a second, more focused look at the young girl before her and fell to her knees.

"Daddy!" the girl shouted. Her bright blue eyes burned fiercely.

"No! No! Don't call him over here," Kimberly whispered.

"Why not?"

Kimberly didn't have a simple answer for that. She was sure this was the girl she spotted in the window of the farmhouse after Kimberly struck the old farmer in the head with a chunk of wood. How could she excuse herself for attacking the girl's dad—or guardian—when she was the one who had trespassed on their property?

"What's the matta, sweetie?"

Kimberly closed her eyes briefly and took a deep breath. She stood up and faced the farmer. She couldn't help but inch her gaze toward the white bandage running across the top of his head.

"N...nothing's wrong," Kimberly stuttered. "She, uh...she just wanted me to get her one of the cans from the top of the cooler." She looked to the girl, hoping she would play along. The girl smiled as Kimberly handed her the can of Syn Soda she had originally grabbed for herself. "There ya go."

The man grinned, revealing many gaps in his teeth. Each one reminded Kimberly of a black door that led to nowhere. "Thank ya much."

Kimberly nervously smiled back as the man took his daughter's hand and headed back toward the register.

Kimberly leaned back against the cooler door and let out a sigh of relief. At the far end of the store, through the glass windows, she could see David waiting beside the car for her.

All she had to do was wait for the man to pay for the soda and leave the store.

She watched carefully as the farmer pulled a wad of crumpled credits from the front pocket of his tattered shirt and dropped them down on the counter. The young girl glanced back at Kimberly, her blue eyes glowing like planets in the dark void of space. She tugged on her father's shirt, and the man bent down as she cupped her hand over her mouth and whispered something in his ear, all the while keeping a steady gaze on Kimberly.

Without realizing it, Kimberly knelt on the floor, peering around the end of the shelf, her heart beating vigorously in her chest. If the injured man found out who she was—

"What?! 'Twas you?!" The sound of feet slapping against the tile floor followed the words. Kimberly stood up straight as the man reached to his back for something. In fright, Kimberly stumbled backward and hit the tile with her butt. She waved her arms in front of her as the man pulled his hand from behind his back and swung a sawed-off, double-barreled shotgun toward her.

The young girl closed her eyes and tilted her head to the ceiling. Her voice pierced the air in hysterics, "Ahh!" She grabbed the sides of her head and fell to her knees, rocking back and forth. "This is the beginning of the end!"

***

David rushed through the front door of the mart. The bell cried out louder than before as the farmer swung around and pointed the shotgun toward him, freezing him in his tracks. "You best stay outta this."

David leapt quickly to the right, rolling across the floor as a double gunshot rang out and the window he had been standing in front of shattered, pieces of glass bursting across the hood of Veronica's car. David steadied his breath and tried to calm his racing mind enough to evaluate the situation. He didn't know what prompted the manure-scented man to pull his gun on Kimberly, but that didn't matter. David was lucky he had been eyeing the man to make sure Kimberly got out of the mart all right—otherwise she might be dead.

David made his way toward the end of the aisle, staying below the top shelf. He turned the corner at the end and shuffled past the end caps until he reached the coolers. Kimberly lay on the floor, the farmer's attention on the front of the store, where he must have thought David was.

"Help," Kimberly squeaked.

David grabbed her hand and pulled her up as the man swung around and caught them both in his murderous stare. "Oh, you both are gonna get it now!" He fired the gun, but only a faint click pierced the air they occupied.

Empty! David pulled Kimberly around the end of the aisle and dragged her back across the end caps and then down the first aisle toward the front of the store.

The man loaded the gun, giving David and Kimberly the chance to escape outside. They scrambled into the car as David fumbled with the keys from his pocket and shoved one into the ignition. The farmer appeared in front of them, the gun pointing directly at the windshield.

"Daddy! Daddy!" the young girl shouted. The farmer turned around briefly, his attention diverted long enough for

David to start the car.

"Hurry, David! Hurry!" Kimberly screamed.

"I'm trying!" As he threw the car into reverse and slammed his foot down on the gas, the tires squealed and spun. A second later, the car lunged backward. David spun the steering wheel, turning the car in the direction of the pumps. He shifted into drive and ran the car through the middle of the pumps as a gunshot rang out, blasting out the back window. Glass rained across the backseat, waking Veronica from her sleep.

"What's going on?"

"Stay down!" David demanded.

Veronica maneuvered around the broken glass, covering her head with her arms. David jerked the wheel right at the stop sign, tossing Veronica to the floor and hurling the vehicle onto the street that led to the highway.

"What is going on?!" Veronica yelled.

Kimberly gasped and waved her hands in the air in a panic.

David glanced into the rearview mirror as the red neon sign of the Fastie's Gas Station shrunk behind them. "I think you have some explaining to do, Kimberly!"

"Okay, okay! We're going to die, aren't we? We're going to die!"

"We're not going to die. Just tell me what's going on."

She took deep breaths and fanned her face with her hands. "That man…that man back there was a farmer I knocked out in the fields when I was trying to get to Lysallis. I didn't do it to hurt him really, I was just…startled. I guess his daughter recognized me back there and, well, he went berserk."

Veronica swept shards of glass off the seat and lifted herself back onto it. "I'm just glad you both got out of there alive."

"Barely," David remarked.

Veronica looked between the front seats at the dash. "You're going a little fast there, hon."

David glimpsed the speedometer and saw that the needle was approaching the eight-five line. "We need to get as far away from that place as fast as possible, in case that crazed farmer decides to chase after us. I'm just going to get us some distance and then I'll slow it down."

Bright yellow lights bounced off David's rearview mirror, hitting him in the eyes. Veronica turned around to see a pickup truck through the broken window frame closing in on them. "Step on it!" she shouted. As David floored the gas pedal, the car's engine hummed loudly and then kicked, their speed breaking ninety-two miles an hour.

David adjusted the dimmer on the rearview mirror, wondering how the farmer could have caught up to them in that piece of junk.

As the truck got within inches of their bumper, a shot rang out. The impact blew small chunks out of the top of the car's roof. Veronica rolled to the floor, glass crunching underneath her now huddled form.

Kimberly slid down in her seat, tears now streaking her face. She grabbed her seatbelt and yanked on it, the seats vibrating violently with the roaring fury of the engine.

David followed the yellow dashes on the road—all of which were melting together to form one long yellow line— as the car continued at ninety-eight miles an hour. The dashboard rattled and the doors jittered madly. The truck kept an impossibly equal pace just feet behind them. "I hope your car is built well, Veronica, because if it isn't, we're going to be scattered in every direction of the compass."

"This car is almost eleven years old, David! I don't think she *can* go much faster without splitting apart!"

"We'll just have to see." David planted his foot to the floor, causing the speedometer needle to race past the hundred mark. The needle dropped to zero, then bounced back up to a hundred.

Up ahead, a pair of headlights appeared over a small hill. The truck suddenly slowed down and backed off, but David continued speeding, the car rumbling on at a hundred and two miles an hour.

The headlights passed them, but then came to an abrupt stop and turned around. Orange and yellow lights flashed behind them, accompanied by an all-too-familiar siren.

Through the mirror, David could no longer spot the farmer's truck, only the police car. "Well, this is great." David applied the brakes and maneuvered to the shoulder, the engine making all sorts of jarring noises as the speedometer needle dropped.

Once the vehicle reached a dead stop, David slammed his fists against the steering wheel. "Just great!" Thick smoke poured out from under the hood, and the smell of oil filled the car. "This is just great. I don't know how this night could possibly get any worse!" he shouted, turning the car off and resting his forehead on the steering wheel. The police cruiser stopped behind them, the orange and yellow lights illuminating the dark road.

Veronica placed her hand on David's back. "Just take it easy. We didn't necessarily do anything wrong. We were speeding in self-defense, and I'm sure that after you explain that to the officer, he'll let you off the hook. Let's just hope word about our mall incident didn't get this far yet."

David lifted his head and watched through the side mirror as a police officer stepped out of the cruiser and started toward their car.

"Just stay calm," Veronica whispered, "and we'll make it out of this."

The officer tapped on the window.

"Here we go," David mumbled as he rolled the window down and smiled at the woman in black uniform.

"Well, good morning. Do you know how fast you were going?" Her voice came out like sandpaper rubbing against cement. Her short brown hair reached into the air, giving her the masculine appearance that would have caused Veronica to mistake her for a man. Up close, her face appeared young and her figure thin, but she looked as though she had been on shift through the night, thick bags hanging under her eyes like sacks of black ink.

"Look, I can explain everything."

The policewoman smiled. "License and registration, please."

David slowly reached into his back pocket and pulled out his wallet. He handed her his license. Veronica reached over Kimberly's seat and opened the glove compartment. She pulled out her registration papers and handed them through the window to the officer.

"May I ask why you don't have a back windshield?"

"I know it may sound a bit strange, but a crazed farmer was chasing us with his pickup and—"

The policewoman nodded and started back toward her cruiser. "I'll be right back."

David turned to Veronica. She shrugged. He glanced through the side mirror at the officer as she stood by the cruiser, talking on the CB. "I have a bad feeling about this," David murmured, shifting in his seat. He glanced down at the keys dangling from the ignition, panic creeping in. *All I have to do is turn the key, throw the car in drive and take off. I'm almost sure I could outrun this cop.* He squeezed his eyes shut and pushed the urge down. He had no guarantee the car would make it any farther, especially with smoke pouring out from under the hood. He had to be patient, maybe try again to explain things when the officer came back.

He opened his eyes and scratched his neck, feeling rough stubble beginning to form. His adrenaline reached a dangerous high, making it hard to discern between absolute right and wrong.

Veronica grabbed his arm. "She's a cop, not our enemy. They're on the same side as us, remember? Maybe this is our chance to finally explain what happened at the mall and clear our names."

He remembered the officer back at his apartment. That one wasn't on their side.

The policewoman returned to their car. David looked up at her with his best try at innocence.

She glanced down at the license in her hand and then at David. "What's your name, sir?"

"David Corbin."

She smirked and then looked at the license again. "Okay, let's try another one." Her gaze returned to David. "When were you born?"

"December 16, 1979." Knots twisted in his stomach.

"Get out of the car, Mr. Corbin." She said the name with

some sarcasm, which told him she didn't believe him.

"What?"

Kimberly slowly turned around and looked at David, her eyebrows raised in astonishment.

"You heard me. I said get out of the car. Now."

David pulled the handle and pushed the door open slowly. "Is there something wrong?" he asked as he stepped out.

"I'm placing you under arrest for criminal speeding and falsifying identification." She pulled a pair of handcuffs from her waist and grabbed David's arm, turning him toward the car forcefully. She pulled his jacket off and threw it on the roof and then began patting him down.

"Wait! What are you talking about? Falsifying identification?"

She slammed his body against the car and locked steel cuffs around his wrists. When she turned him around, she waved the license in front of his face. "This, Mr. Corbin, is a license for a Daniel Granger. If you're David Corbin, like you say you are, then how come you have someone else's ID?"

"That's not mine. Don't you recognize me? From the news? David Corbin? The Lazerblades?"

The woman shrugged. "I've heard of David Corbin. Can't say I really know what he's supposed to look like. Strange that you claim to be Anaisha's greatest hero, but you carry around an ID for Daniel Granger." She brushed the back of her hand very lightly across his wounded cheek. "And where did these scratches come from? Were you in some kind of fight?"

"Look, it's a long story, but there was this crazy farmer and—"

"You'll have plenty of time to tell your long story. Trust

me." She peered into the car at the girls. "You're both free to go, but I'm taking your friend with me." She handed the registration papers back to Veronica.

"Look, I honestly have no clue what's going on. I think my wallet was switched by someone. That's not my ID. I think that if you give me a chance to explain—"

"A chance to explain?" She glared at him. Her glossy lips glimmered in the police cruiser's headlights. "You can explain everything to me as soon as I get you to the detention facility." She grabbed David's jacket from the roof of the car and pushed him toward the cruiser.

***

Kimberly looked out the window at the dark brush and weeds under the moonlight. *I could easily hop out of the car. I could run into the hills, get lost and never be bothered by anyone again. All I have to do is open the door. So easy to just escape, get lost in the darkness.*

Emptiness covered her spirit like a black drape. Fear took hold of her, fear of that creature, that horrible man, fear of the day when he would finally catch up to her and devour her with his darkness. David wouldn't be able to stand up against him, neither would Veronica. Kimberly knew the man was out there, those red eyes watching and waiting, hungry for her blood. She would be a feast sooner than later.

Cold comfort wrapped around her bones. *Maybe it wouldn't be so bad, to end the pain and suffering.* Hopefully, it would be quick and without notice, when nobody was around to save her. No struggling. No, she wouldn't struggle this time. She would give herself over to the darkness and let it consume her whole.

Veronica crawled over the armrest into the driver's seat. "You're free to get out of the car if you'd like. Otherwise, you're coming with me." She shut the door and turned the ignition. The car groaned for a few seconds before finally sputtering to life. Kimberly thought for sure the engine would start smoking again or the car would simply crumble to pieces.

The police cruiser returned to the highway and drove past them.

"What are you doing?" Kimberly asked.

Veronica waited a few moments and then pulled her car back onto the highway in the direction of the police cruiser. "Following her. She'll lead us right to the facility, and then we can break David out."

"Follow her? Break David out?"

"Yeah. Something is definitely wrong with all of this."

"You're talking about breaking him out of a detention facility!"

"Like I said, I can stop the car and you can get out if you want. I'm not holding a gun to your head. But if you stay with me, I'm going to need your help to get him out."

Kimberly shook her head. *She's crazy.* Talking about breaking someone out of a detention facility was crazy. *Then again, I have nothing to lose, right?* Moments ago, she was ready to crawl into the darkness and die. She may as well give her life for something before that happens.

"Guess I don't really have a choice, do I? I either die in the fields or I die in a facility. Maybe a bullet in the head is better than sharp nails clawing through my skin."

"Don't be so overdramatic."

Overdramatic?

"You're not going to die. Trust me."

"But I don't even know you," Kimberly muttered softly as she balled herself up on the seat and returned her gaze to the dark landscape. *However this life is going to end, I hope it ends soon.*

***

About a quarter of a mile back, the farmer's pickup truck heaved down the highway, completing the caravan heading toward the detention facility. Olivia Coral stared out the window as the rolling hills passed. *It's time*, she thought. *It's time, and they aren't ready.*

8

Colors Of Morning

David's apartment lay in waste. Cracks and deep indents littered the walls, black burn marks marred the carpet, and the furniture had been used as makeshift projectile weapons. David's mattress leaned against the stove in the kitchen, his television set hung halfway out of the bathroom wall, and his computer—the same one he had relied on for years in his attempts to save the world—lay scattered in broken pieces all around the living room. Two strangers sat on a couch, which vomited stuffing from the gashes and tears it had accrued during the fight.

The two uncanny beings that had helped Kimberly out of a scrape more than once made quite a contrasting and conspicuous pair.

The male, when standing, reached almost six and a half feet tall. Short, brilliantly white hair covered the top of his round skull, styled in small spikes that, at first glance with a certain degree of imagination, could be mistaken for inverted icicles. He wore a bright white shirt, white pants, white boots and a long white trench coat that brushed the floor when he stood. On his back he carried a white leather sheath for his diamond-tipped, two-edged sword—his weapon of choice.

The female—a young and colorful complement to her blinding counterpart—stood a few inches shorter than him when she wore high heels, which was rare. Bright pink hair that could usually be found tied back in a long ponytail spilled across her shoulders. Her eyes were her trademark—and namesake—glowing the brightest turquoise hue anyone had ever seen. As if to intentionally oppose her partner's clothing color choice, she wore a black polyester short-sleeve T-shirt, black cargo pants and black boots.

The woman—Turquoise—examined the electrical burns that covered her right arm, eager for them to heal. It surprised her that she hadn't incurred more injuries in the scuffle. The demon hybrid had managed to rip an electrical line out of the wall and strike her with it. She couldn't remember feeling that much pain since dealing with the electroballs in her training class.

Her partner had been fortunate enough to avoid getting wounded at all and had even inflicted some damage on the hybrid, but not enough to stop him. He escaped just a little while ago, and they both thought it wise to allow their energy levels to return—and her arm to heal—before pursuing him again.

"I can't believe he got away again," Turquoise sighed, despair etching her words into the dead air of the apartment.

"Don't worry, we'll get him soon enough." The handle of the man's sword stuck out of the wood of the broken coffee table in front of them, and he stared at it with reminiscence in his eyes.

Turquoise glanced around the wrecked apartment. A poster hung crookedly on the wall to the right of them: *Super Spy 2: Wrath of the Arbitron.* A man in a black and white tuxedo posed with a gun in hand and a bunch of robots in the background. "But will it be soon enough?"

"Yes."

She locked eyes with her partner. "Cloud, I've never seen one of them that powerful before. What if we really can't stop him?"

"That's because you haven't dealt with one of the hybrids before. It's natural for them to evolve over time."

"It worries me."

"Well, stop your worrying. It does us no good. You and I will get him and find that timepiece if it's the last thing we do. It's our mission, simple as that."

"Simple?" She noticed the desperation in her voice, and it sickened her. She wanted to be stronger, both emotionally and physically, like him.

He smiled at her, his dimples marking the territory past the ends of his lips. "Yes." He laughed. "Yes, I guess nothing is simple with this plan. But that's the fun of it. We get to slay a hybrid and save the world. What more could you ask for?"

"Fun, huh?" It was probably just tiredness, but she felt agitated anytime he took things too lightly, as if killing these creatures was a sport.

"Lighten up, Turquoise. This is the first real mission you've been on. I can understand you being a little stressed; anxiety is normal for any first mission. But I've come to find in my years of doing this that stress only hinders your thought process..." he glanced at her arm, "and your healing powers."

"That hasn't been proven." She looked down at her arm, the surface of her skin bubbling and blistering. She was using a portion of her power to stop the pain, which was only prolonging the restoration process. Her mind wandered to Trinistar. What if she were still alive, here with them now? Would they have been able to kill that hybrid before it had another chance to escape? She wouldn't voice it, but Turquoise had already decided that once she finished this mission, she would hunt down Trinistar's killer and do what she had to do to bring justice to her untimely death. Trinistar had been her best friend in the Sector, if not her only friend aside from Cloud.

Turquoise caught Cloud glaring at her. "You're thinking of her again, aren't you?"

She nodded.

"Stop. We need to concentrate on this mission. I know you and her were good friends, but you need to let her go. She died. That's in the past, and we need to leave it there and move on." The cold tone in his voice led her to believe he was actually ordering her to give up the memories of her friend.

"I can't. It's not that easy."

"Look, someone or something killed her, and we could be next. We have to stay alert and focused, understand that?"

She looked straight at him, shielding her eyes from the rays of sunlight piercing through the shredded blinds. "Whatever you say. We better get going. We don't have much time before he catches up with the teens again. He already wounded David."

"David is strong."

"That he is."

"He's a good leader. They should be fine in his care."

"Yes." She nodded, glancing around the disheveled room. "They should be fine in his care." But even she didn't believe the words that ran off her lips. Turquoise knew David to be a resourceful leader, but he wouldn't be able to protect himself or his friends from the hybrid for very long. Thana was much too powerful.

"Are you strong enough to run?"

She nodded.

A moment of silence fell between them as Cloud stood to his feet, towering in the sun's rays. He bent down and pulled his sword out of the wooden table, sliding it back into its sheath. He reached out his hand toward her and smiled.

She grabbed it, and he helped her to her feet. "I'm worried about Kimberly." The heavy anxiety in her voice made her sound weak, which disgusted her. "She's a tough girl, has been her whole life since her parents died, but all that's happening to her all at once may be too much."

Cloud sighed, his head tilted toward the blinds. "Do I need to have them send me a replacement for you?"

Turquoise glared at him. How could he imply that she couldn't complete their mission? "No, Cloud. Why would you say something like that?"

He turned toward her, frowning. "You need to focus, understand? We can't be sitting here thinking of everything that can go wrong with the present situation. It's what it is, and we need to deal with it efficiently. Stop worrying about them and start figuring out ways we can get our hands on that timepiece."

The timepiece. Just another worry on her list. The small piece of crystal that had been taken from Kimberly was second on

Turquoise's priority list, the first being Kimberly's safety. Turquoise and Cloud had tried to "convince" the hybrid to tell them where it was, but he wouldn't breathe a word of it. They weren't able to keep him down long enough to find out if he had it on him. She knew they had to get that piece back if they were ever going to accomplish even half of their current mission.

"We need to find them." She stepped by Cloud, passed the kitchen and walked into the bathroom.

"Yes, I know."

She turned the bathroom light on, startled by the television embedded in the center of the shower wall. She shifted toward the broken mirror and saw a necklace dangling from the top right corner. "I'll take this," she whispered, gently pulling it off the edge.

She held the necklace in front of her for a few moments. The green line around the black crescent moon sparkled as it had the night Carrie wore it. The night of the dance, when Carrie had decided to tell David how she felt but never really got the chance. Turquoise placed the necklace in the small satchel that rested against her hip and walked out to the living room.

"I wonder sometimes if you're a little too sentimental," Cloud remarked.

"Sometimes memories are the only things that won't betray you."

He chuckled. "Touché."

"They're all on their way to stop Carrie's wedding. Knowing David, I'm guessing they're going to pass through Tindall instead of North Ryshard."

Cloud nodded. "Yeah, that sounds about right. David knows North Ryshard is too dangerous to cross through, especially in the timeframe they're operating in."

"So, let's get going." She patted Cloud on the back. "I'll feel a lot better once we've caught up to them."

"You sure you're healed enough to leave now?"

Turquoise took another glance at her arm. Her skin was void of the blisters and bubbles, and her arm was dark red. "Good enough."

9 Accusations

U p until now, the scenery David witnessed while cruising through Tindall with the female officer had been nothing short of dull. Rolling black hills in the distance, a dark sky overhead, twinkling stars barely visible through the glare of the cruiser window. But now, as the cruiser turned down an even darker dirt road and headed into the blackness of the night, he found the earlier scenery much more inviting.

Ahead of them about a half mile, he could see what looked to be the soft glow of lights. Their bright luminosity spilled across the form of a one-story building, which David took to be the facility. He had only once been in such a facility, and that time was brief and something he tried not to think about.

The vehicle stopped in front of a large security gate. The headlights leveled on a sign that read, TINDALL DETENTION FACILITY HUB 4 - OUTSKIRT.

A security guard approached the driver's door and nodded. "Officer Meldramine."

"Hi Walter."

"He's waiting for you inside."

Acknowledgement flashed in her eyes, but David barely saw it before the guard returned to the control panel off to the side of the gate and Officer Meldramine began fiddling with a stick of gum.

The gate slid open, traces of dirt rising up into the head-light beams. Officer Meldramine stuck the gum in her mouth and balled up the wrapper, tossing it into the cup holder. She drove through, waving briefly at the guard. David saw him nod before they entered the property, the road now paved and lit on both sides with small solar-powered lamps. The paved road led down beneath the rectangular building, into a small parking garage. Officer Meldramine parked the car in the closest spot near a pair of silver elevator doors.

After she turned the engine off, she sat in the seat for a moment, saying nothing, doing nothing but chewing her gum and staring at the wall of the parking garage.

David tried to shift his wrists in the cuffs, his skin getting raw from the heavy metal tightened around it. When the woman didn't move or talk for at least five minutes, David spoke softly, "You okay?" It was all he could think to say, all he could do to break the silence without being obnoxious.

She seemed to wake from her daydream and jolted out of the car. She moved David out and escorted him to the eleva-tors, prodding his back with her fingers as if herding him like a cow that had broken free from its caged farmland. She pushed a small triangular button in the wall. It lit up, and the humming sound of the elevator resounded through the garage.

David caught his reflection in the glossy surface of the

doors and recognized a blur of large scratches across his face. He could see the blurred figure of the woman behind him as well, a reminder that caused an aching in his heart for falling on the wrong side of the law. The fact that this wasn't his first time in this position only increased his disappointment.

A loud ding echoed through the garage as the elevator doors slid open. Officer Meldramine nudged him in and followed after, pushing a button on the control panel that triggered the doors to slide shut and the elevator to rise.

David glanced at the officer, but she promptly looked away, her eyes gazing here and there around the dingy and raunchy-smelling elevator. David wanted to talk to her, to launch into a quick synopsis of his situation. Instead, he reminded himself that the less he said now, the better. He had to conserve his energy, keep his wits—and whatever was left of his patience—about him. Tiredness swept over him, and his mind began to play games, telling him this was all just part of Amber's prank, even though he knew that was a stretch.

The elevator stopped at ground level. The doors slid open, and the officer led David through a dim hallway. He took note of his surroundings—patches of rust and grime littering the walls, black and brown splotches in the cement flooring. Up above, small light domes were embedded in the ceiling, giving the corridor an uncanny, intimate glow.

The two stopped at a large rusted door.

"This," Officer Meldramine motioned, "will be your new home for a bit." She pulled a ring of keys from her belt and, after wrestling with the key and rusty lock, opened the door.

She pushed David in. He almost tripped and then turned to her and scowled.

"Agent Parks will be with you in a few minutes to question you, so have a seat and don't do anything you might regret."

She left, shutting the door behind her.

Relieved that the room had more lighting than the hallway did, David found his way to a small aluminum table and chairs in the center of the room. He sat in one of the chairs, shook his head and took a long look at the grungy steel walls surrounding him. He shifted his wrists again, this time with minor panic in his movements. He had to keep the claustrophobia and full-blown panic at bay, or he would lose it. He hated being cuffed, being confined at all. He leaned back in the chair, confident that Veronica would be here soon to bail him out. She was the only one who could really help him at the moment, seeing she was the only one who knew he was here.

He closed his eyes and Amber came to mind. He studied her there, in his mind, where she couldn't move, couldn't flee from him. He studied her face, her body language, the tone in her voice that night at the mall. When she said she loved who-ever was on that phone call, her face seemed to indicate that she didn't mean it with her whole heart. As much as David felt hurt by her betrayal, something was nagging at him, some-thing about the whole situation seemed off-tilt.

He failed at trying to put the puzzle together in his mind. Pieces were still missing, hints that he was neglecting. He had the three-day break from Amber—the one she initiated, the unusual way she broke up with him, his missing wallet. It was all tied together somehow. Was another man really in-volved? If so, why would Amber steal David's wallet? Why have him locked up in the mall?

Maybe he was telling himself there was something more

because he wanted to avoid the pain of the breakup. His instinct, though, stepped in and reassured him that something more was going on. This wasn't just a prank. It couldn't be...

The scratches in his face itched, and the pain in his cheek returned in a current. His gaze wandered down to the grimy green tiles on the floor. A yellowish substance that David could only guess to be mold covered one in particular. Mold, which took on the shape of a dolphin, Carrie's favorite animal.

He wondered if Carrie was sleeping, if she was dreaming of him at all. He was still trying to figure out why she would contact him after all this time of silence and with a wedding invitation of all things. Something didn't seem right about it, but the only way he could get to the bottom of it was to get to that wedding before it was too late.

He played her final words to him over and over in his mind: "You don't have to understand everything, David." He remembered the look on her face, the frightened tone in her voice. He didn't think she would leave. He didn't think she would run away.

The steel door creaked open as David snapped to and looked up. A tall, thin man in a black suit walked in. He wore a blue, silk, button-down shirt unbuttoned at the top, exposing a chunky gold necklace.

"Ah. Hello, Mr. Corbin," he said as he shut the door behind him and strolled to the table. "I'm Agent Parks. Nice of you to join us this early in the morning." He took a seat in one of the chairs across from David.

David sized up the guy before he could speak another word. Parks had a lean figure but muscular arms. Even though Parks smiled, his eyes told David how tired the man was. Short, ruffled black hair covered his head, and stubble spotted his chin. Parks's slanted eyes and thin lips suggested to David that he might be from the Karyou region in the west—a rare find in this part of the world.

Parks dropped a manila folder on the table. "Well, where should I begin?" He opened the folder and started sifting through a stack of documents, flipping them upside down into another pile as he scanned them.

"How about you start by taking these cuffs off?"

Parks stopped flipping papers and looked up at David. "That wouldn't be a very good way to start our friendship. I think you know why you're here, and you should be surprised that you're not in one of the higher detention facilities."

"What are you talking about? For speeding?"

"Speeding?" He said the word loudly, as if trying to prove to David that he thought the idea ridiculous. "Do you take me for an idiot? You're not here just for speeding. You're here on charges of breaking and entering, theft, speeding, impersonation. I could go on, if you'd like me to."

"Theft? How am I in here on charges of theft?"

"The mall, David."

He looked at the man blankly.

Parks's face turned to stone. "All right. I guess we're going about this the wrong way. Let's start over. My name is Agent Ruinstar Parks. I am the chief agent for this detention facility, for the outskirts, the area you were speeding through. Now…" he sifted through the papers again. "Do you own a 1988 Stratas Cyclone, four-door?"

"Yes."

"Your car was pursued after you broke out of the mall

and escaped the scene of a crime. When Lysallis Police finally caught up with your vehicle, you were no longer with it. Now—and this is very interesting—when they investigated the mall, they found a broken glass door, an empty room with a broken lock and last, but not least, a very valuable piece of jewelry missing from the Moon Jewelers Jewelry Emporium."

"Are you telling me someone robbed the mall while I was trying to escape?"

Parks smiled.

"I was locked in that stupid room! How could I have stolen anything?"

Parks rubbed his palm across the stubble on his chin.

David took a deep breath. Then he let it out slowly and continued with his explanation of things. "I was locked in that room by a girl who went by the name Bubbles." David could already tell by the smirk on Parks's face that the man wasn't buying his story. "When nobody came back to let me out, I did what I had to do to escape the mall. That's why the glass door was shattered. I didn't stop to explain things to security because I was afraid they would mistake me for a criminal."

"You *are* a criminal! That's why you're here. Before you made your so-called escape, you broke into the safe at Moon Jewelers and stole a priceless rhodenine necklace. Then you escaped through the mall and took off in your white Cyclone. Now, if you're smart—which I know you have the capacity to be—you'll tell me where the necklace is. If you do that, I might feel inclined to bring the charges against you down a few notches. Quite a few notches, in fact, but only if you cooperate with me."

David glared at Agent Parks. "I did not steal *anything* out of that mall. I swear to it. You can check the security cam—" David stopped, remembering there were no cameras in the hallway or the food court. *And it would have been too easy to impersonate me for a jewelry heist.* He was trapped.

"Ah, you're at a loss for words. This means you know exactly what I've been talking about." Parks slid the folder to the side and propped his elbows up on the table. He leaned his face in close to David's, the pine-scent of some cheap cologne filling the space between them. "I want that necklace. Now you're in my district," he slammed his finger on the table, his words taking on a sharp tone, "and I can do or say or judge however I want to here. If I say you're innocent, you're innocent. If I say you're guilty...well then, you're guilty. If you give me the necklace, I can make your life a whole lot easier. If you don't, then I'm going to take you down a long, dark road that you may never return from."

"I didn't take any necklace." David found his voice calmer, more relaxed. He reminded himself to conserve his energy, especially now that escape was his only option out of this. Agent Parks had some side thing going on and wanted to pin it on David. David couldn't let that happen. He had a wedding to stop, and time was not on his side.

"Hmm," Parks muttered.

"I suggest you let me go. I don't really have time for this joke of an interrogation for a crime I didn't commit."

"You," he pointed his finger at David, sneering, "you don't have time for this? Do you think I do?" Parks stood up and began pacing, rubbing his chin. He stopped and pointed his finger at David again. "You're not going anywhere for a while...quite a while. You're being uncooperative and, on top of that, you have something that Lysallis Police sorely want back."

"I told you, I don't have any necklace. I didn't steal anything."

"Rhodenine, in its liquefied form, is Anaisha's rarest mineral, Mr. Corbin. I'm not sure if you knew that or not. They don't exactly teach you about rhodenine in your basic high school chemistry class."

Rhodenine sparked a red flag in David's mind, but he couldn't remember why it sounded familiar.

"There are only two known pieces of jewelry containing the liquefied mineral on this side of the planet. One of those two was in that jewelry store. Now, look. I know why you're doing this. I know why you stole it, and I know why you're being so difficult. I know that years ago, you and your little band of friends were off saving Anaisha from its dark criminal threats." He made his way around the table and leaned over David's shoulder, speaking in his ear. "You and your pals were in the spotlight non-stop. You were in newspapers, magazines and, if I remember right, even on a couple of talk shows. In fact, you did such a good job, you were going far above the efforts of the police or even agents like me in locking up the world's biggest and most dangerous criminals, especially Mr. Big.

"Well, it's been a while since we've had any major problems, and now you want your pretty little face back in the spotlight, don't you? And you'll do anything to get it there. Well," he rested his hands on the table next to David, "you're not going to get your precious spotlight. You're going to be kept here in this interrogation room until I feel it necessary to transport you to the prison, where you'll be held until I get that necklace, Mr. 'Daniel Granger.'"

David craned his neck to match his gaze with the agent's. "That's not my ID."

"That's one reason you're in here, but it's just one of many. I'll be back. I'm getting thirsty wasting my breath on you." He smiled sourly and glided toward the door. As he approached it, he turned back to David. "This will give you a minute or two to make up your mind as to which side of the law you're going to play on today." Parks left, slamming the door behind him.

10

Shotgun Breakout

Veronica parked the car on the shoulder of the highway about a quarter mile from the dirt road that led to the facility. The sun had broken through the sky, slathering its daylight across the green hills, lighting them up in a brilliant glow. Cold air swept in from the surrounding emptiness, but it didn't bother Veronica. She embraced the cold.

Smoke spilled from the hood as if the engine were a cauldron.

Out in the distance, between the highway and the Serlin Mountain Range, she could barely make out a nest of Anaisha Purifiers. The towering, purple-colored, air-filtration machines stuck up from the ground looking like cheese wedges, a half dozen in a group, all clustered together into the shape of a circle with only a few feet of distance between each of them.

Veronica loved that they were purple, her favorite color. If she were close enough, she knew she would be able to hear the melody the machines made while they constantly ran. Nobody had ever been able to figure out what the melody was—a musical number, almost fairytale-like in its enchanting tune—but it sounded beautiful to Veronica and always pleased her when she heard it.

"It's c...c...cold," Kimberly chattered softly as they walked down the highway toward the dirt path. She wrapped her bare arms around herself, goose bumps covering her skin.

"I know. It feels nice."

"Nice? Are you k...k...kidding?"

Veronica stuck her hands in the pockets of her slacks and fished around for her lip balm. She pulled out the small tan cylinder and rolled some across her lips. She offered some to Kimberly, who just shook her head, her face twisted in a scowl.

"What exactly is the p...p...plan here?" Kimberly asked.

Veronica stuck the balm back in her pocket, her fingers feeling the scar in her right thigh through the thin material of her slacks. The scar, given to her long ago by one of her own Scion blades in a battle against an enemy intent on killing David, reminded her why she was walking toward a detention facility, determined to break David out. The scar stood as a symbol to her—a lifelong symbol—that he was her highest priority. She had secretly vowed to protect him with her life, and she would keep that vow to her death.

"No real plan. Just run in, grab David and get out. Beat the heck out of anyone we run into, of course."

Kimberly stopped and gawked at Veronica. "Are you kidding me? We're going to be fighting? Those are police in there!"

Veronica turned to the girl. "You're welcome to stay here, on the side of the road, in hopes that when David and I get out of there, we'll be coming back this way. Which is to say we won't, because we have a wedding to stop."

"A wedding? How is that a priority right now?"

"Whatever David says is a priority, is a priority." Veronica knew there was something fishy about Carrie's invitation, but she wouldn't necessarily voice that concern to David. She knew he would want to stop the wedding for the simple fact that he still loved Carrie. Along the way, Veronica hoped to find some clue as to why Carrie was getting married so suddenly and to such a prominent figure. Most people knew not to mess with Jerad Montlier, and Carrie wasn't the type to go along with a man like that unless something more malevolent was at work, something blinding her or manipulating her.

Veronica continued toward the facility, urgency sweeping through her legs like the buzz of a tall cup of coffee. She really couldn't care less about this Kimberly girl. She found the girl whined a bit too much. Veronica would protect her of course—assuming the girl did what she was told to do. In the matters at hand, Veronica was an expert. More of an expert than her friends really knew, especially in the art of fighting.

They approached the dirt road on their right and started down it toward a large fence in the distance. Veronica counted one guard patrolling the gate.

"Follow my direction and we'll get through this just fine. You and I were just in a car accident and—"

"Car accident?"

"Yes, a car accident. The smoking engine will help us too." Veronica found walking the dirt road in her heels annoying. Potholes littered the uneven road, and giant rocks protruded from the ground. "Now, we were just in a car accident, and this facility is the only place in the area where we could turn for help."

Kimberly seemed to be considering this, her eyes wandering the ground, probably counting rocks or tracing the faint tire tracks in the dust.

"Are you with me?" Veronica asked.

Kimberly nodded and muttered what sounded like a half-hearted "yeah."

"Now, if they don't let us in, I'll take out the guard and you make a run—"

"What?!"

Veronica sighed. "I really need you to let me finish what I'm saying before you interject."

"You're talking about taking out the guard of a detention facility!"

"Yeah, so?" Veronica realized they were closing in on the fence. The security guard—aware of their presence—moved directly in front of the gate, his hand on the gun at his side. "Guard has no armor, a pistol, cargo pants and a jacket that might be bulletproof. Should be a breeze to take him down, but only if he doesn't buy our excuse. I'm sure the fence is electrified and surrounds the whole building, so don't try running toward the building until it's been opened."

"Guard? Gun? Electric fence?!"

"I wouldn't expect anything less at a facility. Actually, this is pretty light defense for a government building. Makes me wonder if other things go on here that the government doesn't want to be associated with."

"Guard? Gun? Electric fence?!"

"Would you shut up? It's not that big a deal. We used to handle these things—and much worse—all the time."

"We who?"

"David and I. And Carrie. And sometimes my brother, Sean. That's all neither here nor there right now, though. I have a plan, but I need you to follow my lead, okay? It's going to require a bit of improvisation."

Kimberly shook her head. "I don't know about this."

"We can do this."

Kimberly started gazing at the ground again, her eyes wide with fear and disbelief.

"This is the only way we're going to be able to rescue David. If you don't come with me, then I'm going to go in alone. I don't care about anything else right now except to save him before something worse happens. Who knows if that woman was even a real cop."

Kimberly's eyes narrowed a little and she nodded. "You're right. He saved me from the mall. The least I can do is repay the favor."

Veronica put her hand on the girl's shoulder. "See, that's the spirit. Don't worry, we'll be in and out of there in no time."

Kimberly frowned. "If you say so."

"You ready?"

Kimberly nodded.

"Just follow my lead." Veronica began to wonder if Kimberly would be able to make it through this part of the plan. It didn't really matter, Veronica thought, because as soon as the guard drew his gun from his holster and pointed it toward their feet, she knew they were past the point of no return.

"Halt!"

Veronica put her arms in the air, watching from the corner of her eye as Kimberly did the same. As they approached the guard, she saw that his face was red and white from standing in the cold.

"Don't shoot," Veronica whined. "Please, don't shoot! We're here looking for help."

The gun inched up toward Veronica's chest. "Get back! Now!"

Veronica took a step or two back, as did Kimberly in perfect sync. "We got in a car accident down the road from here." Veronica pointed in the distance to the smoking vehicle. "My friend here is hurt and in shock." She motioned to Kimberly, who had apparently turned to stone, her eyes fixed on the gun.

"This is a restricted area. Leave or I'll shoot."

"We were just in a car accident," Veronica pleaded. "My friend needs medical attention."

"What do you expect me to do about it?"

"We need a phone, so we can call for help."

"There isn't a phone for miles. Now, get lost!"

Veronica glanced at the building beyond the fence and back at the guard. "Isn't there one in there?"

"This is a secured detention facility. You two are not allowed inside."

"But who's going to help us? How are we going to get to the hospital? And our other friend is still with the car. Her head was cracked open, and she's bleeding to death."

The guard looked at her suspiciously. Then he glanced out in the distance at the car they had parked on the side of the road. "I didn't hear an accident anywhere near here. There's barely any traffic on this road at this time of the morning." He turned his attention to Kimberly. "And what's with her? She's white as a ghost."

"She's just afraid of guns, that's all. Like I said, she's in a bit of shock from the accident."

"I don't take any risks around here," the guard said as he inched closer to the control panel that operated the gate.

"Will you help us, please? I need to call for help, or I'm going to have my friend's death on my hands!" She glanced at the panel behind him. The little white box had a red and a green switch on it. *Simple.*

"Don't know what to tell you."

This guy is unwavering. "All I need is a phone. Do you have a phone we could use?"

The guard stared at her, his cheeks bright red.

"Look, maybe there's a phone in the building behind you. All I need to do is call for help. One little phone call and an ambulance will pick us up, and we'll be out of your hair." Veronica concluded that if the guard didn't give in the next minute or two, she would resort to physical prowess to overpower him.

The man sighed and lowered the gun. "There's a guard at the front counter. Ask him to use the phone." He reached behind and pushed the green button on the control panel, his eyes never leaving Veronica. The giant electrified fence split in half and slid open.

He pulled a walkie-talkie from his belt. "Carl, you have a girl on her way in. She needs a phone. Got in a car accident down the road." He placed the walkie-talkie back on his belt and motioned with the gun for Veronica to pass through the gate. "Your friend stays here."

"All right." She glanced at Kimberly, the girl's eyes staring straight ahead, unblinking. "I'll be right back."

Kimberly didn't talk. She didn't move. All she did was watch Veronica walk through the open gate and leave her with the guard. There was nothing else Veronica could do. It was probably just as well that Kimberly didn't come with her anyway. It could get messy, especially if Veronica had a tagalong with her.

The guard pushed the red button on the control panel, and the gate halves began to slide back into position.

A roar echoed from behind Veronica. At first she thought it was her imagination. Then she wondered for a split second if Kimberly had done something stupid and gotten herself shot. But it wasn't the blast of a gun. Veronica turned around to find a brown beat-up pickup truck barreling up the dirt road toward them.

The guard started firing at the truck. Kimberly stood there, frozen, staring at the oncoming death machine. Veronica slipped between the opening of the closing gate and grabbed the girl's hand, pulling her through the gate halves just before they snapped shut.

"C'mon! We've got to get into the building!"

"I…I'm feeling a little faint."

Veronica pulled her by the arm as they approached the blackened glass windows of the complex.

A loud blast roared around them—the blast of a shotgun—and the control box blew apart in a mess of sparks and smoke.

Veronica reached the glass double doors of the facility and yanked hard on one of the handles, swinging the door wide open as she dragged Kimberly through the doorway with her. They entered a lobby where a guard sat in front of a multitude of security monitors. A door to their left warned

AUTHORIZED PERSONNEL ONLY.

"Hey! Only one of you was authorized to come in here!" the guard shouted. Veronica reached the counter where the guard sat and faced a short, stocky man with a beard engulfing his face.

"There's a man outside with a gun! He attacked the guard at the front gate!" Veronica shouted.

The short guard quickly spun around toward the video screens behind him. He gasped as he watched the guard outside fall in a mist of blood.

***

David rolled his forehead around on the cold aluminum table, wondering how he was going to get out of his current dilemma. Any minute now, Parks would be back to interrogate him some more. David was out of energy, worn thin by the night's battles, lacking the patience and strength to deny answering questions he didn't know the answers to. He figured Parks wouldn't believe what he said anyway, so why should he waste his breath? All he knew was that he had to escape and get to South Ryshard. At the moment, Carrie's wedding was the only thing he had left to strive for. Behind his passion for her lay a debris-riddled wake of mistakes—the broken glass door at the mall, running from the police, speeding and letting Amber trick him. Hindsight was better than twenty-twenty this time around, but it wouldn't do him any good. All of that was done, and now he had to deal with it. It didn't help, of course, that an arrogant agent was mixed up in all of it.

The door creaked open as Parks strolled back in. He

slammed the door shut and took his seat. David lifted his head up and caught the man's grin as he set a white foam cup on the table.

"Did you miss me?" Agent Parks asked with a grin.

Like a hemorrhoid, David thought, but he didn't say that. Instead, he kept his mouth shut and let his brain work at finding a way of escape.

"Well, where did we leave off? Oh yes, I was going to ask why you created a fake ID for yourself."

Again, David said nothing.

Parks took a sip of water from the cup and ran his finger along the edge of it. "Ice cold." He locked gazes with David. "I want to know why you made a fake ID. Was it to buy weapons? Was it to throw the police off track? Or was it just for kicks? I know how some of you teenagers can be. You'll do anything to get attention with no regard for the consequences."

David looked up at the decaying ceiling. "I already told you, I didn't make the ID. My ex-girlfriend must have made it and planted it in my wallet in place of the real one. I'm sure it was all a part of her little prank. Speaking of which, is someone investigating where my real ID is?"

"Pretty elaborate prank." Parks leaned back in his chair and folded his hands behind his head. "Now, why would someone go to all the trouble to pull a prank like this?"

"I asked you if someone was investigating the whereabouts of my ID."

"We aren't on that subject yet. I ask the questions here, not you. I want to know why someone would go through all that trouble just to pull off a prank."

"How would I know?"

"I think I'm piecing this together pretty well now."

"What is it you've pieced together, exactly? You're blaming me for a crime I didn't commit. You keep asking why my ex-girlfriend would play a prank on me when you could simply arrest her and ask her yourself."

"I think it goes a little deeper than a prank, David. Did you ever…you know…hit your girlfriend?"

"What? Never!"

"Are you sure?"

"Positive. This is ridiculous."

"Where did you get those scratches running across your face? Did you hit her and she retaliated? Is this what the so-called 'prank' is all about?"

"I've never, ever hit Amber. These scratches came from some creature that showed up at my apartment after we left the mall."

"Creature? Your bedtime story gets more farfetched every time you tell it, Mr. Corbin. You sure it wasn't, you know, another personality? Maybe another side of you revealed itself when she made you mad."

"You aren't listening to a word I'm saying, and what you do listen to, you're twisting around into some sick fantasy. I didn't steal from the mall, I didn't create that ID and I have never hit my ex-girlfriend!"

"So, you still refuse to cooperate, well—" The door swung open. Officer Meldramine stood in the doorway, panting.

"We have a problem."

"Sandra, can't you see I'm in the middle of something here?"

"There's a disturbance in the lobby. Some crazed psycho—a farmer I think—has gone wacko on a couple of girls and our guards."

Parks ran his hands up his face and through his hair as he turned to David with narrowed eyes. "You and I will finish this in just a moment, so don't go anywhere." He got up from his chair and followed the woman out of the room, the door slamming shut behind them.

"Where am I going to go?" David muttered, his sore wrists reminding him of his bondage. *Farmer? Two girls?* He could only assume it was Veronica and Kimberly, and if that was the case, he had to help them.

***

Kimberly and Veronica took cover behind the short security guard, who stood beside the window, gun in hand, watching the man in the pickup. "Where's my backup?" The guard shouted.

The farmer hopped out of his truck, a sawed-off shotgun in his grip. Veronica eyed the little girl in the passenger seat, wondering why she didn't flee from the vehicle while she had the chance. Then again, where would she go? They were miles from anything but hills and Anaisha Purifiers.

Kimberly shivered with fright. The guard noticed and gave her his best grin through his bushy face. "Don't worry, girls, this is one-way, bulletproof glass. He can't see in, but we can see out. Look, you two should probably get into the hallway until this matter is taken care of." He motioned to the door labeled AUTHORIZED PERSONNEL ONLY.

"I can help you," Veronica offered.

The man shook his head. "I don't need help. It's just a

138

farmer with a gun. I have a gun too, and I bet I have better aim." He unlocked the door with the set of keys around his wrist and opened it, motioning for them to go in. "Stay in here until I come back and tell you it's safe."

Veronica took Kimberly's arm in hers and tugged her into the hallway. The guard closed the door, sealing them inside.

They slowly made their way down the dimly lit corridor. Veronica checked each door they passed in hopes of finding one that would open up to David, but all of them were locked. "We need to hurry," Veronica whispered, "before someone finds us snooping around back here."

"Like me?"

They spun around to find Sandra behind them. She aimed her gun at Veronica's head. "You two are in big trouble."

Veronica stared down the barrel of the gun. "So are you."

"How so? I'm the one with the gun."

Veronica wondered if she could take the gun for herself. The narrow corridor would amplify the difficulty of a struggle, especially with Kimberly in the midst of it. The walls looked steel, meaning they might be able to deflect a bullet and send it on a wild ride.

"Come with me," Sandra said. Veronica decided to follow her for the moment, hoping she would lead them to David. Sandra led them to a door at the end of the hallway and, after unlocking it, motioned with her gun for them to enter.

Inside stood an aluminum table and a few chairs scattered about. A white foam cup sat idle on the table.

"You two make yourselves at home," Sandra said as she pushed them farther into the room and slammed the door behind her. It was then that Veronica spotted David hiding in the corner, where the open door had been. Before Sandra could turn around to follow Veronica's gaze, David rushed up behind her, throwing his body into hers. They both toppled to the floor, where Sandra's face landed, and her gun slid underneath the table. She threw David off and scrambled to her feet.

"You—" She yanked David up by his shirt and slammed him against the door. A loud clang echoed through the room. "I'll kill you for that!"

Veronica dove under the table, grabbing the gun, while Kimberly glued herself to the wall, her eyes wide with fear.

"I'm gonna—"

"Let him go!" Veronica shouted. The woman turned around, the gun now aimed on her. Blood ran from her nose where it had impacted the floor.

"Screw you," Sandra muttered as she grabbed David and slammed him against the door again.

The sound of the gun being cocked got Sandra's attention. She turned from David, wiping her bloody nose on the sleeve of her uniform as she sneered at Veronica. "Put the gun down."

Veronica smiled. "Let him go or I'll put a bullet between your eyes."

Sandra laughed. "Are you kidding me? I'm a police officer! Even pointing that thing at me is going to get you locked up for the rest of your life."

Veronica glanced over at Kimberly. The girl had her hands over her face, shielding herself from viewing whatever was about to happen. Veronica wasn't prepared to actually kill this woman—especially not in front of Kimberly, who had probably already seen enough violence for one day—but she would follow through with her bluff if Sandra didn't let David go. "I'll tell you one more time. Let him go."

Sandra stared at her, blood dripping from her top lip. She used her sleeve to wipe some of it off.

"I'm looking for an excuse. Give it to me."

Sandra had the front of David's shirt balled up in one fist. She pushed him up against the door and let go of his shirt, her eyes still on Veronica.

David motioned to the cuffs around his wrists. "Unlock them."

Sandra grabbed the key ring off her belt and unlocked the handcuffs. The metal braces fell to the floor with a clang. David walked past her and joined Veronica's side, rubbing his wrists. Veronica noticed deep red rings where the cuffs had been.

Sandra stood there, keys in hand, her eyes like those of a tiger whose cubs had just been stolen. "You three will pay for this. When I catch up to you, you'll pay. I promise you that. You'll all pay."

"Whatever," David replied. "Right now, I have somewhere to be. If you do end up catching up with us, then maybe we'll go through this stupid charade again, but you and Agent Parks seem to have a problem listening to anything I have to say. I didn't steal that necklace. I didn't hit my girlfriend—my ex-girlfriend. I didn't do anything wrong."

Veronica wondered what he was referring to. A stolen necklace? Who in their right mind would think that David would ever hit Amber—or any girl for that matter?

"We'll be the judge of that," Sandra growled.

"Not this time." David motioned for her to give him her keys.

Sandra sneered. "You're fighting a battle you can't win,

David. I'll find you, and when I do, you'll pay for what you've done here."

"Give me your keys."

She tossed them to him in an underhand throw. He motioned to the cuffs on the floor. "Pick them up and place them on your wrists."

Sandra did as she was commanded to do. When the cuffs were secured around her wrists, David approached her and tightened them.

"That's too tight!"

"No, they're perfect."

"Don't try following us," Veronica warned as she moved toward the door. Kimberly slowly pulled herself from the wall, her eyes averting Sandra's killer gaze. The threesome opened the door and left the room. David shuffled through the woman's keys and found one to lock the door.

He turned to Veronica and smiled. "Thanks for the rescue."

Veronica shrugged. "You already knew I was going to come break you out."

"True." He turned to Kimberly. "You okay?"

She nodded.

"Follow me. We'll get out through the parking garage," he explained, leading them to the elevator. As they traveled down toward the garage structure below, Kimberly's face twisted into something that Veronica could only describe as a mix of fear, panic and maybe a touch of psychosis.

"What's the plan?" Kimberly finally asked. "How are we going to get out of here? How are we going to get away from this place?!"

Veronica waved her hand at the girl. "Calm down, will you? The hard part is over. We just have to stay under the farmer's radar, and getting out of here will be easy."

"Calm down? Calm down?! You almost killed a cop back there!"

Veronica shook her head. "I wasn't really going to kill her."

"Veronica would never do that," David added.

Veronica was glad he still believed the best of her, but it wasn't true. If Sandra had made the wrong move, Veronica would have killed the woman. Put a warm bullet in her head, regardless of how David felt about it. If the woman didn't take advantage of the chance for peaceful means and crossed the line, Veronica was willing to go the rest of the way to ensure David's safety.

The elevator stopped. Before the doors could slide open, David pushed the STOP button. "The plan right now is to get to South Ryshard by any means possible."

Kimberly let out an irritated sigh. "You aren't at all worried about clearing your name? Are you kidding me? A wedding should be the least of your priorities right now."

David shrugged. "There's not much else I can do right now. I tried to explain myself, and they don't want to listen. I think something else is going on with all of this, but I'm not sure what yet. This isn't just about a silly prank Amber wanted to pull on me. Until I can find more answers, I have to do what I can, which is to head to South Ryshard and stop the wedding."

Kimberly's mouth hung wide open. "You're serious?" She turned to Veronica. "He's serious?"

Veronica grinned. "He sure is."

"You both are crazy. I don't know how I got stuck with the two of you, but you're both just...just...out there." Kimberly seemed absorbed with her own thoughts, her eyes shifting toward the floor of the elevator. Then she looked up at both of them. "Let's get out of here, and then I want you to drop me off at the nearest town. I really have to get a hold of the number my uncle gave me. That's *my* priority right now."

David shoved Sandra's keys into his pocket. "Have it your way." He looked to Veronica, his eyes asking if she was ready with the gun in case officers waited outside the elevator. She nodded, holding the gun toward the doors.

David pulled the STOP button out, and the doors slid open to a vacant parking garage, two police cruisers in the otherwise empty space. Kimberly and Veronica stepped out as David pushed the STOP button in again, preventing the use of the elevator from anyone above.

When they exited the elevator, Veronica, against her better judgment, almost dropped the gun in a nearby trash receptacle. She felt it necessary to continue to honor the agreement she had made with David, Carrie and Sean—an agreement not to use violent means to get things done. Their group, the Lazerblades, had been an example of peace. Guns were never their weapons of choice, and Veronica didn't want to open up a violent can of worms by shooting someone in front of David or Kimberly. But without the gun, Veronica feared they may not be able to escape the building. If she tossed the gun and had to resort to physical violence to protect David, she worried it may force her to reveal the dark arts she had perfected years ago—something David knew nothing about.

Instead, Veronica held the gun close to her thigh, forcing herself not to use it unless absolutely necessary. When she turned from the trash receptacle, she noticed David and Kimberly staring at someone, a young girl with bright blonde hair—the same girl Veronica had seen in the farmer's truck.

"David?" Kimberly whispered.

"Yeah, I see her."

"Who is that?" Veronica asked.

"Not sure."

"She's the farmer's daughter," Kimberly answered.

David stepped toward the girl. "What are you doing here?"

Kimberly's eyes searched the garage, no doubt looking for the farmer. "Where is he? Where is your daddy? Is he here with us? Is he here to kill us?"

Veronica wanted to put a muzzle on Kimberly, shut her up for a while. Before they had even stepped out of the elevator, Veronica had already scanned the garage and found nobody, not even the young girl. The farmer wasn't here right now. Veronica decided to chalk up the mystery of how the young girl appeared out of nowhere to a mistake of observation on her part, not something supernatural.

"Who are you?" David asked.

"My name is Olivia. I'm here to guide you and your friends."

"Guide us?"

Olivia nodded. "I have to get you to the place I see in my visions. I don't know where it is exactly. I just know I have to get you on the right path to lead you there."

"She didn't talk like this back at the gas station," Kimberly whispered.

David took a few steps back from the girl. She put her hand out to stop him, the bright blue color of her marble-shaped eyes suddenly turning green. "You can't leave yet. I have words for you, from the visions. I'm sorry, but I don't know what they mean."

David shook his head. "I don't have time for this. We're in a building swarming with crooked law enforcement, and your crazy dad is up there killing people."

"The mark of love in the hands of the Protector is the key to the truth, but in evil hands it is the end, the destruction of this world."

"I don't know what that means."

Olivia shrugged. "Neither do I. We'll see each other again. You'll understand much more later. All you need to remember is that honey mixed with dirt is not the way. Only honey mixed with honey will keep honey pure."

Her eye color shifted from green to yellow. Veronica wondered what the girl's babbling meant. *Honey? Dirt? The Protector?*

"Did anyone else see her eyes change color?" Kimberly asked.

Olivia smiled. "Anything is possible in this life as it is in the next."

"We should really be going." David motioned to the ramp leading out of the parking structure.

"Not yet!" She thrust her hand out again. "The message is not finished yet! David, Veronica and Kimberly, the path ahead is treacherous and deadly. It is not a path you have chosen on your own, but it is the path that has been chosen for you. Deception and chaos lie ahead for all of you, but you must not give up. You mustn't. If you do, all will be lost."

Olivia's voice went into a soft whine as she dropped her gaze to the floor. She fell to her knees and placed her palms out against the ground. "All will definitely be lost. You are the last and only hope, though I wish it weren't so. If you fail…it will be just like what happened on—"

"Last hope for what?" David interrupted, irritation in his voice. "What are you talking about?"

Her head tilted up. "You'll find out…soon. You'll find out very soon."

Veronica glanced over her shoulder at the open elevator. Something told her to get out of there, to get them all out of there. "We have to go. Now."

Olivia got to her feet, her eyes widening. "Deception and chaos…Chaos? You need to leave quickly! Go out the front and follow the street back to your car."

David pointed to the ramp. "That's where we're going, in one of these police cruisers. There's a gunfight upstairs, and we don't really want to be in the middle of it."

"The gunfight is over…for now. My dad is looking for me. You mustn't take the ramp. Head back up using the elevator you came down on."

David turned to Veronica for her opinion. She had no clue which way would be safest to go. The ramp could very well lead to the same trouble they encountered in the building. But she wasn't all that sure her vehicle would start again either. "You lead the way, and I'll follow."

David glared at Olivia. "You better be right."

"The visions are never wrong…just my interpretation of them sometimes." She looked up at Veronica. "And you must leave the gun here, in the garbage can you were going to throw it in."

How did she know?

David led them back to the elevator. Reluctantly, Veronica dropped the gun in the trash, completely bewildered. Had Olivia read her thoughts? How did she know Veronica had a gun? If it had been anyone else asking her to toss the only physical weapon they had, she would have refused outright. But something about Olivia, her tone of voice or her innocent smile, convinced Veronica that she meant them no harm. Not intentionally anyway.

Once inside the elevator, David pulled the STOP button out as Veronica took one last look at Olivia. The girl trotted through the garage and up the ramp that led outside. The elevator doors shut, and the compartment rose with a hum.

"Who was she? Who was that little freak?" Kimberly paced the elevator. "I can't...I can't stay in here much longer. I have to get outside, I have to be someplace with open space."

Great, Veronica thought, *stuck in an elevator with a claustrophobic*. "What did she mean by her riddles? 'Honey mixed with dirt' and something about our 'paths' and the 'destruction of the world'?" Veronica asked as she leaned against the wall. "Sounds like someone's been getting some high-end drugs from her daddy."

"I don't know," David answered. "But we don't have time to sort through it right now. This place is crawling with trouble, and we need to get out fast. If she's right about the gunfight and her dad—which I doubt she is—we shouldn't have too much difficulty getting down the street to your car."

"First, we have to get out of this building," Veronica reminded him.

The elevator stopped. David pushed the STOP button again and looked at the girls. "I'm not so sure this is a good idea, going this way."

Veronica shrugged. "We don't really have a choice. Either way we go is a risk."

Kimberly cowered in the corner of the elevator. "If we run into the farmer, I'm done for. That man is crazy. He wants to kill me!"

David shook his head. "There are three of us. He won't get a hold of you without going through us first."

Veronica sighed. "It'll be all right. David and I will protect you. Just do what we say, and we should be able to get out of this building unharmed."

"Should?" Kimberly squealed.

David pulled the STOP button out, and the door panels slid open to the hallway. Silence. The doorway that Kimberly and Veronica had entered the hallway through earlier sat at the end of the corridor, the path to it unobstructed.

"That's it." Veronica whispered. "That's the door to the security lobby."

"I have a bad feeling about this," Kimberly said as she grabbed David's arm.

"It's natural, once you've been around us enough," Veronica remarked. They stepped into the hallway and slowly started toward the end.

"You!"

Kimberly let out a yelp. Veronica and David swung around to find her in the farmer's grasp, his shortened shotgun pressing into her chest.

"Let her go!" David shouted.

The farmer took a few steps back and then wrapped his other arm around Kimberly's neck, placing her in a headlock. The gun barrels moved down into her ribs. "War's my daughtar?"

"She was in the garage when we last saw her. Please, let her go," David pleaded.

"No. She's caused me some trubble! Now, I've gotta re-tern tha fava'.''

"No, you don't. Please just let her go. She didn't mean you any harm. We don't mean you any harm. We just want to get out of here, okay?"

"Not okay." The man started walking backward, toward the opposite end of the hallway. "An eye far an eye. Isn't that tha way of your world?" He cackled, the gaps in his teeth showing like little black holes. "You don't understand what's at stake, now do ya? I can't let her go any farther. She *has* to die!"

The man suddenly stumbled on his own feet and wavered back. Kimberly's eyes opened as he released his grip on her and fell against the wall, dropping the gun to the floor. She darted from him and continued past David and Veronica. They followed after her. Veronica realized it would be better to escape than to try and subdue the man.

"No! She can't leave here! She has ta die!" the old man wailed as he slowly gathered to his feet.

Veronica kept her focus on the door ahead. Her shoes clacked loudly in her ears, her heels growing sore from her adventures. The hallways seemed to stretch for miles and miles, and it made Veronica wonder if this was all just a nightmare. Would she wake up soon—now maybe—in her warm bed? She feared the impending gunshot that would ring out and the injury that would follow if they didn't escape before the farmer had time to recuperate.

"Go!" David shouted.

Kimberly reached the door first, fumbling with the handle, trying to open the locked panel. David flipped through Sandra's keys, trying his hardest to find the one to unlock the door.

"Hurry!" Veronica shouted. The farmer was on his feet, shotgun in hand.

"I'm trying!" David stuck a silver key in the slot and turned it, unlocking the door.

Kimberly plowed through the doorway, almost knocking David and Veronica over. Veronica rushed through, almost tripping on the guard's body lying on the floor in a pool of blood.

David entered behind them when a gunshot rang out. Veronica spun around so fast, her head almost jerked off. David tumbled to the floor, moaning in pain, blood seeping from his arm. Crimson drops splattered across the walls and the floor. She rushed to his aid, pulling him up to his feet as the farmer barreled through the corridor.

"C'mon, hon, we have to get out of here now or never!"

"Give me your keys, and I'll get the car!" Kimberly shouted.

With no time to think about whether or not the girl would leave them here and run off on her own, Veronica pulled the car keys from the pocket of her slacks and tossed them to Kimberly. The girl vanished out the front doors as Veronica followed far behind, lugging David beside her and out of the building. They found the pickup truck, seemingly abandoned, both doors wide open. She debated on seeing if they could take it out of here, but something told her it wouldn't be a good idea.

David stumbled and fell on the cement path. Veronica pulled him up and glanced up to see Kimberly reaching the road the car was parked on. Veronica heaved David to the fence, which was mangled and torn, and glanced back to make sure the farmer hadn't left the building yet. *No sign of him.*

David groaned.

"Stay with me. Stay with me! We just have to make it to the car."

The car was coming to her. Kimberly managed to get the vehicle started and pulled up just beyond the broken fence, skidding to a stop, providing a cloud of dust just large enough to cover Veronica and David as she shoved David into the backseat.

Another gunshot. The passenger window shattered, but Veronica had arched her body over David and shielded him from most of the glass.

The car's tires grabbed the dirt road and kicked the vehicle forward as it lunged toward the main street.

Kimberly held the wheel tightly as she sped back onto the highway and headed in the direction they were going before making the eventful pit stop at the detention facility. "Where's the nearest hospital?"

Veronica tried to think, but the blood soaking her backseat turned her stomach into knots. Not because it was blood, but because it was David's blood. She should have let him exit the hallway first, then she would have taken the blast instead, like she was destined to.

"Veronica?! Hospital?"

"Keep going south, and when you see Highway 7, go west into North Ryshard. You should hit a hospital minutes from the border."

"No," David muttered.

"Sorry, sweetie, but we have to. We can't risk waiting to reach one of Tindall's hospitals. Besides, there's too much heat on us now." She moved her hand through his bangs and stared into his eyes. "Just relax. We'll get you the help you need." She reached over the front seat and opened the glove compartment. She pulled out a wad of napkins and pressed them against his bleeding shoulder and back. "Boy, you really got nailed this time. Just stay with me, okay? At least until we get to the hospital."

11

Battles of the Heart & Mind

The silver chain flowed across the delicate curves of her neck like a slithering silver snake. At the end dangled a small oval capsule, its lustrous black shine matching the black velvet dress that fell just below her knees. The glowing green line that wrapped around the center of the capsule brought out a glow in her eyes, a glow that revealed the true beauty that lay dormant within her, buried underneath mountains of lost memory and foggy visions of a past that may or may not have occurred.

Carrie smiled at the necklace in the dresser mirror. Jerad had given it to her shortly after they met. He told her he wanted her to wear it all the time, a visible token of his love for her. So she made it a point to always have the necklace on—while she slept, when she ate, even in the shower. All the time and everywhere—except in the swimming pool. Carrie couldn't bear the thought of the pool chemicals destroying her lovely token, but she didn't dare tell Jerad that she took it off even for that reason for fear of hurting his feelings.

Carrie turned from the dresser, her fingers mindlessly checking her head for the six or seven bobby pins holding her hair up. Satisfied that each was in its place, she sighed and took a seat on the edge of the bed to slip her black-strapped heels onto her feet.

Excitement coursed through her veins at the thought of having the whole day with Jerad. No work, no interruptions. Just lunch, wedding talk and maybe a movie, all with her future husband. She planned to use the time to question him about her past, at least to learn what he knew of it, maybe even persuade him to help her dig up some of it.

She stood up and shifted her feet in her heels until they felt semi-comfortable. Then she glanced in the mirror once more, double-checking her hair to make sure there weren't any wild strands trying to escape the holds of the bobby pins. She grabbed her black purse from the dresser top and left the room.

As she made her way through the living room, her attention turned toward the flat-screen television embedded in the wall above the fireplace. The stock market channel was on, as always. Syn Soda stock was rising again, which came as no surprise to Carrie. Jerad, in his attempts to teach her about stocks, told her the story of how Sunshine Cola almost put Syn Soda out of business years ago, had it not been for an unexplainable turnaround in Syn Soda's popularity in a matter of weeks. Sunshine Cola shut down, and Syn Soda took a monopoly of the cola industry.

She crossed to the dining table expecting to find Jerad eating breakfast or reading the daily news but instead found a note and a red long-stemmed rose on the glass tabletop.

Carrie set her purse down and picked up the flower, sniffing its sweet vapors. It was by far one of her favorite scents, one she never tired of. *How thoughtful of him.*

She lifted the note from the glass:

My Princess,

I regret having to postpone our date, but something came up within the company that has to be taken care of swiftly. I had to leave town for the day, but I will return tonight. Plan on dinner around 8. Love you, Jerad

Carrie set the note down, sniffed the rose again and did her best to stop a frown from forming on her face. But her heart sank to the floor, despite her best efforts to stay positive. All she wanted was a day with her future husband. One day, just the two of them.

This was the third date he had broken in the last week, the third in a line of "company emergencies." His associates needed immediate guidance on how to sell new Hover products, or a factory in Tindall or Mecca needed assistance with broken equipment, or some urgent meeting somewhere required Jerad's physical presence. The excuses—and she did believe them to be excuses—were endless. She figured Jerad was either a workaholic or simply didn't enjoy being around her as much as she enjoyed being around him. She refused to completely believe the second theory and decided he was just addicted to work.

She set the rose on the table as Belgar, in his white chef's uniform, glided through the doorway between the kitchen and dining area. He stopped a few feet from her, glancing first at the contents on the table and then at Carrie's forlorn expression.

"Dear Carrie, I assume Jerad will not be joining you today?" His deep, familiar voice brought some comfort to her ailing heart.

She looked up at him sullenly and shook her head. Her eyes began to water, and she looked back down at the table to avoid his stare. "No, Belgar. My fiancé won't be joining me today."

After a brief moment of silence, Belgar, in his usual low tone, said, "I'm sorry to hear that."

Carrie shook her head. "It's not your fault. It's nobody's fault. It's no big deal."

"No big deal? Who are you kidding, dear Carrie? Were you not the one telling me yesterday that you were looking forward to the time with him today?"

Carrie stared down at the note. Jerad had printed perfectly on the paper, almost as if he had typed the note. But the ink glimmered with the natural light coming through the windows, proving to her that he had indeed written the note in flawless script and recently.

She mustered enough strength to say, "I was looking forward to today." Then she looked up into Belgar's dark brown eyes and held her finger under her nose, trying her hardest to hold in the tears. "I'm fine. Just forget about it. It's not like it hasn't happened before, right? I should be used to it by now."

"Well, I have errands to run today, if you would like to keep me company for a while." Without waiting for an answer, he disappeared into the kitchen.

"No," she answered loudly as she glanced back down at the note. She picked up the rose and breathed in its sweet vapors again. "I think I'm just going to take some quiet time for myself, you know, now that the Associates are gone and Jerad is away."

She heard water running in the kitchen. Belgar reentered the dining room with a skinny glass vase. "Very well." Carrie handed him the rose, and he dropped it in the vase. "I will have my cell on today if you need me, dear Carrie. You call me, and I'll be here in a flash." He stroked his beard and then pointed his finger at her. "I mean it."

She smiled weakly. It occurred to her that Belgar seemed to be there for her more than Jerad was. "Thank you," she said with the most sincerity she could muster.

Belgar placed the vase down in the center of the table.

"Can you please throw this away for me?" She picked up the note and handed it to the burly man.

He hesitated for a moment, staring down at the piece of parchment in her trembling hand. She didn't know if he was looking at it in spite or if he was deciding how to dispose of it. He finally took it from her and crumpled it in his massive hands. She noticed an edge in his eyes, one she couldn't easily discern. Was he angry at Jerad's behavior toward her? Carrie found it cute that Belgar would show disdain toward a man for treating her unfairly. It reminded her of someone who used to watch over her in the same manner, someone from her past.

Belgar stared toward the floor, his face scrunched up, his brow furrowed in displeasure.

"Thank you," she said.

He broke from his trance and nodded to her. "Anytime."

Carrie left the dining room, tears streaming down her face as soon as she entered the living room. She frantically wiped them away with the sides of her palms as she hurried toward her bedroom. *Don't be a fool and cry over this, Carrie. He runs a business, and the business just needs him more than you do right now. That's all.*

She entered her bedroom and shut and locked the door behind her. Her room, with its dim lighting, four-post bed, dark-stained furniture and scented candles, served as a sanctuary of sorts when she felt down. She sat on the edge of the bed and began loosening the straps of her heels, freeing her feet from their leather restraints. When she moved up farther on the bed to rest, she noticed a small brown package lying on her pillow.

That maid is a tricky one, she thought, *sneaking the mail in here while I was out of the room.* Carrie couldn't remember seeing the maid at all that morning and had wondered if the woman had called in sick. Carrie picked up the package and observed her name and address in cursive on the front, but no return address, which made her curious.

She lay back against her pillows, comfortable in her quiet space, and began ripping the brown paper off, revealing a green, leather-bound book. She tossed the wrapping to the floor and examined the item. The worn cover was blank of any illustrations or words, aside from her full name, which was engraved in the bottom right corner in gold letters. Opening the book, she found tattered pages covered in scribbled words and dates. It was a journal, this much she surmised, but she wondered if it was hers. All indications pointed to the obvious conclusion, but who would have mailed her own journal to her?

She went to the first page:

Monday, August 24, 1992

Dear Diary,

Today was the first day of eighth grade. I met a strange kid in my Enera Language class. His name is David Corbin, and he's actually kind of cute. He dropped his pencil on the floor and when he bent down to pick it up, he bumped his head on the table, and I just laughed. Maybe that was mean, but it was funny. He looks a bit like that boy who was in the newspaper a while ago for saving his sister from Mr. Big. This can't be the same boy. He seems shorter than the one who was in the paper.

A drawing of a red, three-wedge pinwheel lined the edge of the page—the same mark that marred her back shoulder blade.

Was this really her diary? Why would someone go to the trouble of writing a fake diary and trying to pass it off as hers?

The name David Corbin seemed familiar, but it just teetered on the edge of her mind, not trying too hard to reveal itself. Just like the name Mr. Big. She knew him to be a criminal—she knew that much from the mentions of him on the news. He was currently locked up in a penitentiary, serving a life sentence. But who put him there? The Lazerblades had, she knew that, but who exactly were the Lazerblades?

Carrie flipped through the diary, glancing at entries, pulling out tidbits of relevant information, like time spent with David Corbin and a best friend named Veronica. The diary made mention of another boy named Sean, probably Veronica's twin brother from what Carrie could gather. The entries spoke of their time together chasing Mr. Big. *How ridiculous!* How could she have been involved in hunting one of the world's most notorious criminals? The news occasionally mentioned that the Lazerblades had done these things, but she knew she couldn't have ever been tied with the Lazerblades at any point in her life.

The tales she glazed over revealed wild stories about their battles with Big, all the ways he escaped and all the ways he pulled the wool over their eyes. *Pure farce*, she told herself. *Pure farce*.

Then Carrie came across an entry that fully convinced her the diary was fabricated. The entry made mention of a time machine created by someone they knew as Professor Grey—a name that rang no immediate bells for her. David had somehow used the time machine to go into the future? Carrie found herself unable to contain the giggles she had been holding inside. The journal indicated that David wanted to use the machine, but she could find no entries stating whether he actually did or not. It didn't matter. *Time travel is impossible.*

One long-winded entry she stumbled across went into some detail about how David had saved her life. She skimmed the entry, reading bits and pieces of how David rescued her and Veronica at the top of a clock tower where they were both being held by a woman known as Tabitha Rose. Tabitha was a traitor, at one time helping them in their escapades against Mr. Big and then turning on them in an attempt to kill Carrie and Veronica. *How rich. I suppose all good stories have to have a traitor.*

One particular entry caught Carrie's attention above the others, though, because of the emotions it stirred in her…

Wednesday, November 11, 1992
Well Diary, tonight my mom and I got into a pretty heated argument. She told me she wanted to go out to a nice dinner, just the two of

us. But when we got to the restaurant, all she did was rip into me about David. A clever ambush by a despicable woman. She gave me a speech about the potential I have and the mistake I am making by heading into these adventures with David instead of focusing on my academics like I should be. She even went so far as to scold me for leaving in the middle of the night to help David and Veronica stop the assassination attempt on Senator Anderson's life. I am sick of this! What is her problem with me being around David? He is a hero of all things, and she told me tonight that I'm not to see him anymore. Well, that isn't going to happen. Looks like I'll just have to start doing things behind her back. Daddy doesn't seem to have any issue with David. Maybe that's why Mom doesn't want me around him…

She set the book on her lap and buried her face in her hands, trying her hardest to remember. Remember the past, remember David and Veronica. An image of their blurred faces crossed into her memory, but when she tried to focus on them, they vanished, leaving behind a mist of disappointment.

I helped save President Anderson? Impossible. Carrie shook her head. "No way," she said aloud. There was no way the diary could be real. The stories inside it were too farfetched, too unreal. If the stories were facts, where were the people who were mentioned in them? Where was Veronica now? And David? If Carrie had such strong feelings for him, why wasn't she with him now instead of with Jerad?

Her fingers skipped through more of the diary, telling herself over and over that it was all a fictional concoction. But her curiosity burned inside her like a blazing forest fire, prompting her to read on, to ingest more of the elaborate stories, to read about an orphan girl named Jennifer—a girl whom David fell in love with at some point and made his girlfriend. Carrie later learned that Jennifer was Mr. Big's niece, and the union between Jennifer and David caused quite a stir in their close-knit circle of friends. Jennifer eventually vanished in the middle of the night, leaving behind a note for David stating she found her real parents in Crystal City and was heading there to be reunited with them.

Carrie read stories of grand adventures, tribulations and trials, but had no memory whatsoever of them, just vague images of a boy named David. A boy she had apparently fallen in love with at one point.

Carrie decided to put the diary away and rest her mind, which was blurring at a dizzying speed. Enough curiosity remained in her to read one more entry, and that entry answered one of the questions that had been running through her mind this whole time: What happened between her and David? If they loved each other so much, what could have stopped them from being together?

Saturday, November 18, 1995
Dear Diary,

Last night was the autumn dance…and the turning point between David and me. I am writing to you from the hospital room where David is being held. He's sleeping right now. He's going to be all right, but I was so scared when I saw that knife go into his stomach. I've never really seen him this hurt before, even after all the adventures we've been through. And he almost died tonight. I don't know how to sum up the evening. I don't know if I could. I'm not going to try. All I know is that I can't ever tell David how I feel. He was almost killed tonight because of me. If we were ever to be together, I know his life would be in more danger than it already is. I need to keep us as friends and not let it go any further than that. Not now. I am going to rest. This chair I'm in isn't the most comfortable, but I'll manage. David's parents should be here in the morning to pick him up. Tonight may be one of the few times I actually get to sleep beside David Corbin, my forbidden love.

Goodnight Diary.

She closed the book and placed it on her nightstand. As much as she wanted to believe it was a piece of fiction, something in her gut told her it was all real. The adventures, the romance, even the time travel…it had all really happened.

Then it struck her that Jerad might know about these events. She could ask him this evening, and maybe his answers would shed some light on what was going on. But first she needed some time to rest her weary mind.

12 Confrontation

Turquoise and Cloud reached Tindall Detention Facility Hub 4 shortly after David, Veronica and Kimberly escaped the crazy farmer and the detention agents. Turquoise's heart sank when she saw the destruction before them. The electrified gate was torn down and strewn about the driveway leading up to the building. On the ground, on his back sprawled a lifeless guard with bullet wounds in his chest.

"What happened here?" Turquoise's voice snuck out with a squeak.

Cloud shrugged. "Something bad."

They entered the main building. A trail of blood streaked the floor from the front doorway to the security door. A guard lay on the floor just outside the security door, his clothes soaked in red, his face pressed against the tile in a pool of blood.

Turquoise hunkered down on her knees and stretched her neck out, sure that she was going to throw up.

Cloud ran his fingers along the crimson marks on the floor, examining the blood like a detective would. He glanced back at Turquoise with a look of annoyance. Then he stood to his feet and skimmed the area.

"This blood isn't all from that guard. Someone else was injured here."

Turquoise stood to her feet, the nausea in her stomach subsiding. She took a deep breath and leaned against the window overlooking the driveway. She didn't want to appear weak in front of Cloud, but she couldn't easily control her nausea. All of this was easier for Cloud, since he was experienced and seasoned.

Turquoise knew there was more here than just carnage. Something lingered in the air, something fouler than the smell of death, and it made her stomach twist in knots. Turquoise found herself on her knees again.

Cloud grabbed her shoulder."Let's see what we're dealing with here." He helped her to her feet.

She took a few deep breaths and steadied herself again. "What if the blood is from one of the teens?"

"Could be."

"What?"

"Would you calm down?"

Turquoise steadied herself. "Sorry."

Cloud put his hands out toward her. "Just…take it easy, okay? It looks like most of the blood is the guards', but it seems to me one of the teens might have been shot as well. The blood is somewhat fresh, so they couldn't have gone too far."

"We need to find them, Cloud. What if it was Kimberly? What if she's the one who was hurt?"

"We need to check out the rest of the building before we go on a manhunt. We have to see if Thana is anywhere around here. If he is, we need to kill him now before he can go any farther. I don't sense him at all, so this should be quick and easy."

Turquoise thought about using her powers to reach out and see who was hurt and if they were all right. But if she did that, she might not have the strength to fight Thana if he was indeed here. "I feel an evil presence here."

"Hmm," Cloud let the comment slip from his lips as he rolled his eyes away from her.

"I know what you mean by that."

"What?"

"Is there something you want to tell me? Is there something I said that you don't agree with?"

"No. I just noticed that you feel an evil presence almost everywhere we go. You were recorded stating that you felt an evil presence at least ten times during our training sessions, when nothing was there. I can't tell if you're just oversensitive or too green in your gifting."

Turquoise sulked. How could he think her too green in her gifting? Or oversensitive? "I think that thing is here. We need to find it and kill it once and for all. Those poor teens are already in a mess trying to stop that wedding, and now they have a demon hybrid chasing them—it's too much."

"I'm telling you Thana isn't here. Why would he be here? If he was following the teens, then he would have taken off after them when they left the building."

"He's probably waiting here for us." She closed her eyes and took a deep breath. Her senses came alive to the evil presence she felt in the building. She could smell his decaying human flesh. She could see him dragging his claws across deteriorating metal. She could hear his incessant laughter, wheezy and jovial. His deadly essence wrapped around her like a blanket of thorns. Red eyes peered out of the darkness and searched the horizon for the teens, for Kimberly, for Turquoise.

She opened her eyes. Before her, the security door stood open.

Cloud came to her side and motioned with his finger to his lips for them to stay quiet. She knew the gesture had a double meaning—he didn't want her freaking out and blowing their element of surprise.

Cloud pulled the long sword out of the sheath on his back and led them into the hallway. Turquoise checked the door handles of each of the rooms that branched off the main corridor, finding all of them locked. She trailed Cloud, his sword out in front of him, the metal glimmering in spots. Turquoise knew the corridor was too narrow to battle in. Cloud wouldn't be able to move nimbly with his giant sword, and she wouldn't have much of a chance to use her powers. Thana would easily be able to tear them limb from limb, leaving a mess across the walls and floor.

Cloud stopped near an open doorway and waited for Turquoise to catch up. He held the sword out in front of him as he slowly turned into the room. Nothing but tables and chairs graced the otherwise empty space.

Turquoise saw a foam cup sitting idly on the table. "Where is he?" she asked.

Cloud didn't answer. Instead, he left the room and made his way toward the elevator, Turquoise following close behind. She knew Cloud didn't believe her gift worked, so maybe he was just checking out the building to humor her.

He pushed the small button near the elevator, and they waited.

A soft hum told them the elevator was rising up the shaft.

Turquoise wondered if the elevator held Thana. Maybe he would leap out and gut the both of them when the silver doors opened. She tried to shake the horrible thought from her mind to avoid falling into anxiety-ridden despair.

She stepped back from the elevator as a ding echoed through the corridor and the doors slid open to reveal empty space. Turquoise caught her breath, and they stepped inside. Cloud pushed a button, causing the doors to shut and the elevator to descend.

Turquoise wanted to say she was worried about the teens, worried the most about poor Kimberly, but she said nothing. She just held her breath while the elevator hummed toward the garage floor. She sensed Cloud staring at her from behind, but she didn't acknowledge him. He didn't understand her fully and underestimated the power of her gift. She knew for a fact that Thana was down here, that he was waiting for them in the deepest part of the building, but the only thing that would convince Cloud of that was for him to see Thana himself.

The elevator stopped, and the metal doors slid open. Turquoise wanted to shut them, to head back up to the surface and escape this place. She wanted to find the teens, to run far away from the demon hybrid, but she knew if she did, Thana would eventually catch up with all of them. Thana would find Turquoise in her sleep, when she was clutching the small teddy bear that Trinistar had given her before she was murdered, and would slice her up and scatter her remains across all of Anaisha. No, she couldn't go out like that. She would much rather go out fighting, go down striking back at her enemy.

Chills crawled across her skin as she stepped out of the elevator.

Cloud glanced briefly around the parking garage before setting the tip of his sword to the ground and rubbing his palm around the handle. "Told you. Nothing here. Nothing to worry about."

Turquoise wasn't so easily convinced. She examined the garage carefully, peering around pillars, searching under a police cruiser—the only vehicle in the garage. She felt the presence so strongly, but her eyes deceived her.

Cloud sighed loudly enough for Turquoise to get his point. "Let's go. If we hurry, maybe we can catch up with the teens before Thana does." Cloud started back toward the elevator.

Turquoise stood frozen near a pillar, her senses in overdrive. "He's here, Cloud. I feel it the strongest now."

Cloud turned around. "Turquoise, there's nobody—"

"Heh, heh, heh, heh, hehhh…"

Cloud swung his sword up in front of him. Turquoise stretched her arms out, ready for a fight.

"Heh, heh, heh, heh, hehhh…" The sound carried through the garage, echoing off the pillars, the vehicles, the walls. The sound seemed to come from all directions and from no direction. It confused Turquoise and even Cloud, who turned around a few degrees every so often as if he knew where the voice originated.

"Thisss…" The voice hid behind a pillar to Turquoise's right. By the time she turned, it had moved directly behind her and leapt to the pillar on her left. "Thisss isss where it endsss."

Cloud and Turquoise spun and saw Thana standing in front

of the elevator. He still wore the police uniform, only now it was ragged and torn from the battle at the apartment. He was slowly losing his human form, looking more like a beast than a human. Human skin peeled from his hands and face, and his eyes glowed with a shade of crimson. Jagged, sharp teeth like the glacier cliffs of Arstic lined his sinister grin.

"You're right. It's time to finish this," Cloud remarked.

Turquoise bent her arms inward, charging up her Fury. She knew this would be a fight to the death. Both parties wanted to end each other's opposition.

"Where are the teens?" Turquoise asked.

Cloud pointed his sword at the creature. "Where is the timepiece?"

Thana grinned. "I can't tell you that."

"You will tell us by the time this is all over," Cloud threatened.

"When thisss endsss, ssso do you." Thana suddenly lunged at them.

Turquoise snapped her arms out, emitting a powerful gust of air that thrust Thana into the elevator doors with a loud thud. His body dropped to the floor, leaving behind an imprint in the metal doors. Turquoise marched toward him, her arms outstretched.

Thana staggered to his feet and shook his head. "A missstake, girl." He thrust his own hands outward. The force of wind picked Turquoise straight up off the ground. She hovered in the air for a moment, disoriented by the creature's power. He moved his arms back and forth as she coasted over him and collided, back first, into the elevator doors. Her body tumbled to the concrete with a moan. She propped herself up with her arms and stood with her back against the doors, staring at the creature. *How did he do that? He didn't have this power back at the apartment.*

Cloud charged toward Thana, swinging his sword down at him.

Thana swiped his hand through the air, and claws struck the sword, cutting the blade in half. The top half of the metal bounded across the garage with a clang while the bottom half of the sword fell out of Cloud's hand and skidded across the floor. Thana thrust his arms out again, sending a burst of air toward Cloud, who careened backward and hit the ground like an airplane in a crash landing, tumbling across the pavement and slamming into one of the pillars as concrete dust rained down from the ceiling.

"Cloud!" Turquoise ran to Cloud's side and helped him up.

He brushed himself off and pulled her close. Blood dripped from his lip. "Listen to me. The first chance you get, you need to escape."

She gazed into his blue eyes and shook her head. "I'm not leaving you."

"You will."

"I can't leave you! I can't! You're all I have." Fear swelled inside her like a helium balloon, but she knew she had to be strong. Without Trinistar, it was just the two of them. If she left Cloud, how would she deal with what was to come and handle what needed to be done?

Cloud pulled her closer to him. She smelled rotten meat on his breath and fought not to vomit. "Listen to me. Listen very closely, because this is an order. You're going to run for the elevator."

"But I can't—"

"You'll run to the elevator, and I'll be right behind you."

She felt tears forming in her eyes. She didn't know why she suddenly felt so much emotion. This wasn't the first time they had fought this creature, but something inside her told her this was the end. She couldn't discern if it was a prophetic feeling or just tiredness and fatigue from their battles, but she couldn't shake it. Despair threatened to consume her like maggots.

"Run for the elevator. I'm right behind you. I just need to distract him long enough to get us out of here."

She reluctantly nodded. "Okay. Yeah, okay." She wiped the mist from her eyes. "But you better be right behind me."

"I promise."

Turquoise stepped back a few feet and then started off in a dash.

"Oh, no you don't!" Thana reached his claws out in a desperate attempt to attack her as she rushed by him. The nails grazed her arm, shredding part of her short sleeve and her bicep before she slammed herself into the elevator doors. She slapped her hand on the button and turned to see Thana shifting his attention to Cloud. The doors opened, allowing Turquoise to step back into the elevator. She glanced down at her arm and saw a set of bloody scratches in her flesh. They burned, but they weren't enough to slow her down.

When she looked up, she saw Thana staring at her, a wide grin on his face. "Poor girl." He clapped his hands together, causing the elevator doors to jiggle and slam shut, a distorted ding echoing through the garage.

"No!" Turquoise shrieked as she gripped the small crevice between the doors and tried to pull the halves apart. "Cloud! Cloud!" She pounded her fists against the metal. She couldn't leave him there on his own, not without his weapon. She stepped back, reaching her arms out toward the doors and pulled her arms apart. The doors jiggled but wouldn't open. She tried again, mustering all of her strength for the task, but it was no use. The doors only rattled, taunting her.

She put her ear to one of the doors and closed her eyes, listening to the battle while also quieting her spirit. She heard nothing for a few moments. Then she made out a moan and a groan here and there. It sounded like the battle was moving around the garage, giving her hope that Cloud was still on his feet and able to fight.

"Ahhh!"

Turquoise pressed herself against the door. "Cloud?"

A giant force slammed against the steel panels, knocking Turquoise back. "Cloud?" She heard what sounded like metal striking the door, small grooves pushing through to her side of the elevator.

"Ahhh…aahhh…" Cloud's voice trailed off.

"No!" Turquoise screamed.

She heard Cloud's body slide down the doors. She closed her eyes and tried to get a hold of herself. *C'mon, Turquoise, remember your training. You have to stay calm, you have to stay focused. Pull together, girl, please pull together.*

Thana pulled the elevator doors open but frowned when he found nobody inside. "Where did the hero go?"

"Right here!" Turquoise shouted as she swung down from the open ceiling of the elevator. She glided over the beast, landing behind him, then turned swiftly and struck her arms out as a gust of wind pushed him down into the box. She clapped her hands together, and the doors slammed shut.

"Cloud," she whispered as she examined his lifeless body lying on the floor near the elevator. Giant gashes ran across his once flawless face. She noticed a gaping spot of blood in the center of his chest. The red ooze stained his white outfit. "Nooo," she sobbed, tears streaming down her face. "Why? Why did you have to die? You were supposed to escape with me...you and me, Cloud. We were supposed to get out of here together."

She could feel her own life ending here in the parking garage. He had been a mentor, he was like a brother, and now he was dead. If only she had protected him and fought like she had been trained to, maybe they wouldn't have separated and he might still be alive. Her eyes flooded with more tears as she choked on her breath, sobbing convulsively at the death of her partner.

A static ding rang out, pulling her attention toward the elevator. The doors were open, but she saw nobody inside. She approached, looking up to see the hole she had swung down from in the ceiling and the shaft beyond it. Thana had fled. What worried her was where he was going. She wiped her eyes on her arms, knowing she had to go on. Defeating Thana fell on her shoulders now, and she wasn't about to let Cloud or even Trinistar's death be for nothing.

She pressed her lips against Cloud's cold forehead. "May I finish what the three of us started." Her hand found its way into the inner pocket of his trench coat and pulled out a small, square, plastic case the size of her thumb. Her pink nail popped it open, revealing a tiny data chip nestled inside. With some satisfaction, she closed the case and slid it into her satchel.

She stared at Cloud for what felt like hours. *It's a shame you had to die. You're a much better fighter than me.* Her arm smeared her remaining tears across her cheeks, cooling them off. She walked to the half of the broken sword with the handle and picked it up off the floor. She gazed at the etchings of wild wolves around the silver handle. Wolves had always been his favorite animal. She waved the weapon in the air, watching the light bounce off the edges of the sharp, jagged metal. *This'll do the job. That thing's killed Kimberly's only guardian, and now, Cloud. Who knows if it killed Trinistar as well? I'm not going to let it kill anyone else.*

She slid the sword into her belt and made her way out of the facility.

13 Recovery

David woke to a blur of bright white. He quickly shut his eyes and then slowly opened them again, adjusting to the fluorescent lighting overhead.

"David? David, are you awake?" Veronica hovered over him, her hair dangling above his chest, freed from its hair tie restraint. "You okay?"

"Yeah. I think so," he mumbled, lying still to give himself a second to return to reality. "Where am I?"

"We're in a hospital in North Ryshard."

David attempted to sit up and felt a sharp pain shoot through his right shoulder. He fell back to the bed's surface and cringed. "What's wrong with me?" he whimpered.

"Don't worry," Veronica said as she took a seat at the edge of the bed. "They took the pellets out. You had a few of them in your shoulder blade." She turned to her left, where an aluminum dish sat on the nightstand. She picked up a small metal ball from the dish and showed it to David. Tiny spikes lined the outside of the blood-stained sphere.

"That was inside me?"

Veronica nodded, setting the piece of ammunition back in the dish. "They pulled out half a dozen of them. Doctor said you might have scarring."

Scarring was the least of his worries. David was grateful to be alive. A few times back at the facility he thought he might be dying. He never wanted to go out by being shot in the back. Maybe in a giant firefight or an epic sword battle or something of the sort, but never by being shot by a crazed farmer.

"Where's Kimberly?"

Veronica pointed to the other side of the room, beyond the curtain that draped around his area. "She's resting. They gave her an ice pack for her face and some antibiotics."

David put his hand to his face, touching a large patch over his wound.

"Yeah, they put some special ointment on your gashes. Said you should heal ten times faster than if you didn't treat it at all."

"What time is it?"

"It's about," Veronica glanced at her watch, "three in the afternoon."

The curtain opened as an elderly man in green doctor's scrubs walked in. He pulled the curtain back into place and smiled warmly at David. "Mr. Corbin, how are you feeling?" The man's voice sounded raspy, but somewhat jovial. He checked the small monitor beside the bed and nodded, slowly and carefully taking out the small needle that penetrated David's arm.

"I…um," David watched as the sharp object exited his skin and was tossed into a small red container on the wall. He hated needles more than anything and felt glad that he had been unconscious most of the time this one had been inside him.

"Don't worry, you won't need to have anymore sharp objects injected into you." The doctor kept a gentle tone, acknowledging David's phobia. "Luckily, you didn't lose a lot of blood. Besides the ammunition we pulled from your shoulder blade, we disinfected the deep cuts in your face and treated them. So, they should heal without any problems, but I don't know if you will have scarring or not."

"Doctor, how is Kimberly doing?" Veronica asked.

He turned to her and smiled. "She's just fine. She had some scratches on her neck and bumps and bruises over her body, but we took care of them. As for that bruise on her face, we'll have to give that some time to heal. Seems she was hit pretty hard. Do you know what hit her?"

"Not exactly." David kept an innocent composure as he answered the question. He didn't have the time or the energy to explain everything that had happened. *Would the doctor believe us if we told him that some red-eyed creature with claws the size of kitchen knives slapped the heck out of her?*

The doctor moved the curtain away. "We'll need to keep you here one more night, Mr. Corbin, just to make sure you're in good health when you leave. I'll check back on you in a little bit." He walked out, shutting the curtain behind him.

"One more night?" David started to turn out of the bed.

"Where do you think you're going?"

He swung his legs over the edge of the bed and touched his bare feet to the cold tile. "I'm getting out of here."

Veronica grabbed his legs and turned him back under the covers. "You're not going anywhere. If the doctor says you stay here one more night, then you stay here one more night."

"You know we won't make it in time if I have to spend the night here."

"Yes, we will. I'd rather cut it close and have you in good health than risk you getting injured anymore. We stay here tonight. I promise you, we'll still make that wedding."

Reluctantly, he pulled the covers up over his gown and leaned back against the bed frame. He didn't like being confined in bed. Because of the urgency of the wedding, it seemed as if he had a giant clock in his head counting down the hours, the minutes, the seconds that he had left to claim Carrie as his own. He knew if he missed this chance, if he let her marry Jerad, that he would regret it for the rest of his life.

Veronica grabbed his hands and rubbed them gently between her palms. "I promise you, we won't let Carrie marry him, okay? I want you two to be together almost more than you two want to be together. Just rest up now while you can, save your strength for the rest of our journey. We're still a long way from South Ryshard."

David nodded. "Fine."

"Besides, Kimberly needs her rest too. You've both been going nonstop."

David gave up trying to convince Veronica otherwise. He knew he could keep going as long as necessary, until he had Carrie safe in his arms. But he agreed to listen to Veronica. She was on this journey just as much as he was, and if she felt it best to stop and rest for a bit, then he would do so. Reluctantly.

"Now," Veronica reached over to the nightstand and picked up the white phone, handing it to him. "I think it's time we contact our families and make sure they're all okay. Who knows where that beast went or what happened to the two strangers who helped us out."

"Okay."

"I already called my mom and dad and told them I'm going to be out of town for a few days."

"You're lucky. Your parents don't ask a million questions when you tell them something like that. My mom acts like a news reporter half the time."

Veronica dialed David's mom and handed him the phone. He took it from her, taking a deep breath that he exhaled into the receiver. The phone rang. Pain echoed throughout his back. He rolled his shoulder around slowly, making sure he was still intact. From his shoulder to the middle of his back felt numb, like he had been sitting against a block of ice for the last hour.

A soft voice answered the other end of the phone. *"Hello?"*

"Mom?"

"David?"

"Yeah. Just wanted to touch base with you and make sure you're doing okay."

"I'm fine. Where are you?"

"Well...that's a long story. Let's just say I'm going to be out of town for a bit. Don't worry, I'm fine."

"Don't worry? Really? How many times have you told me that before?"

"I lost count."

"Where are you?"

"North Ryshard."

"What are you doing all the way out in North Ryshard?"

What am I doing in North Ryshard? "I'll be back soon, Mom." *No better way to avoid an argument than to avoid the question altogether.*

"Can you tell me why you're in North Ryshard?"

"I'll explain everything later. Just know that I'm safe and I'll be home soon. Is Dad there?"

Silence.

David caught Veronica staring at him. She smiled when he made eye contact with her and then she turned away, fiddling with her nails, scraping some brown nail polish from her middle finger.

His mother sighed heavily. He wondered if she would hang up abruptly. She had done it before, when conversations became unbearable or touched on subjects his mother wanted to avoid. *"Your father is on a business trip. He's in Mecca for some political rally."*

"Oh."

"I'll let him know you called. Just stay out of trouble, please."

"I will." He knew it was a lie, but there wasn't much else he could say without having to extend the conversation further than desired.

Without saying another word, his mother hung up. David struggled to place the phone back on the nightstand. Veronica grabbed it midway and set it down as David leaned back and rubbed his eyes.

"You okay?"

He nodded.

Veronica smiled. "Good. You should rest some more. I'll be right here with you all night. We'll leave first thing in the morning."

"First thing."

She nodded. "First thing. I promise. I'm going to check on Kimberly. You get some rest."

David relaxed his head on the pillow and stared at the ceiling. "Thank you, Veronica, for coming with me. I couldn't do this without you."

"That's what friends are for, right? Besides, if you two don't get together this time around, I'm going to pull my hair out."

"You and me both. Do you think you can get me some pain pills?"

"Yeah. I'll ask the doctor." She left through the curtain.

David turned on his unwounded side and let his mind wander to his family affairs. His father, the photographer, was in Mecca? That was pretty far for someone to go to take pictures. And why didn't his mother go along with him, like she used to? David remembered the times he ran around Enera, saving the world, while turmoil brewed beneath the surface of his parents' relationship. He never confirmed if their problems, their arguing, bickering and fighting, had anything to do with him and his running around, fighting criminals, or if their marriage had just gotten old and stale. They had gone to counseling in the last year, and David thought he had seen improvement in them before he moved out to live on his own. Maybe he was wrong.

Nothing I can do about that right now.

He figured Veronica was right about his needing rest, so he closed his eyes and shut out the rest of the world.

14

Deception

A gent Parks and Officer Meldramine drove through Tindall in the police cruiser.

"Where do you think they went?" Sandra asked, turning the radio down, tired of driving. Nothing but rolling green hills and black asphalt for hours, and they hadn't received any leads on where the trio of teens had escaped to.

"I don't know exactly. If they survived that farmer's attack, then they could end up at a hospital, at a friend's house, anywhere. They're cunning. All of them. Especially David." Parks rolled his window down and laid his arm on the edge of the door, letting the cold air blow through the car.

"Hey! Can you roll that back up, please?"

"I'm warm. I just want it down for a minute, so I can cool off a bit."

"You're warm? How could you be warm? It's almost forty degrees outside."

"Just shut up and drive, okay?"

A ringing sounded inside the car. Sandra and Parks both

glanced at each other, shrugged and then looked around the cruiser to find where the sound was coming from.

"It sounds like a phone," Parks said.

"Yeah. But where's it coming from?"

Parks craned his head down between the front seats and found the ringing. He lifted the black leather jacket that had been sitting there and rummaged through the pockets, pulling out a small cell phone. He looked down at the green display. "Cybil Corbin?"

Sandra nodded. "That's David's jacket. I left it in here after I arrested him. Must be his phone."

A shrewd grin spread across Parks's face as he flipped it open. "Hello?"

"Hello? David?"

"Um, yes," he feigned.

"David, where are you? Mom says you're in North Ryshard?"

"So?"

"What the heck are you doing out there? Do you know how dangerous it is there? And you're giving me the lectures on drugs? Do you think—"

"Um, I gotta go. I'll call you later. Bye." Parks shut the phone. "Looks like we're headed to North Ryshard."

"North Ryshard? Why North Ryshard? That's out of our jurisdiction."

"Well, Sandra, this has become personal. There are really only two reasons why someone from Lysallis would want to go to North Ryshard, and that's either because they're trying to get some cheap drugs or they were forced to go to a hospital." He let a sigh of satisfaction creep out, like a hunter who had just discovered where his prey was hiding.

"Yes, sir," Sandra replied.

The phone rang again. Parks slid the phone into the pocket of his suit jacket, ignoring the call. "Two can play at this cat-and-mouse game."

Sandra continued down the long stretch of highway, the freezing air pulling up the hair on the back of her neck. *This is going to be a long one*, she thought. *Long and cold.*

15

Memories & Matters

Carrie awoke to find she had fallen asleep on the bed, still wearing the black dress she had put on for her day with Jerad. She turned over toward the clock to see that it was a little after five in the afternoon. *The sun is going to be setting soon.* She felt fatigued from the midday nap, not really wanting to get up, but knowing it would be pointless to go back to sleep. *Maybe a dip in the spa will feel nice.* Carrie realized she probably had plenty of time to do anything she wanted. Regardless of when Jerad said he would be home, he rarely ever came through on time with any of his promises. The evening was hers.

She slid out of bed and sluggishly wandered into the bathroom. She came out dressed in a black two-piece swimsuit with a towel draped over her arm. When she entered the main hallway, the silence caught her off guard. *Belgar must still be out on his errands.* She was accustomed to having Belgar around for most of the day, when he didn't leave briefly to purchase groceries. During most of the week, the maid was around; whether she was seen or not was a different story. But with the house completely empty—no Jerad, Belgar or the maid—Carrie felt a sense of loneliness.

Opening the door to the patio, she braced herself for the cold air that swept over her. She hurried to the spa, setting the towel down on one of the lounge chairs while she unhooked the back of her necklace. She wondered if Jerad would even come home tonight. If not, she would enjoy the time alone instead of resorting to sulking about it all evening.

She set the necklace on the towel and glanced over the wall at the city beyond. Skyscrapers shimmered in the sun's orange and red glow like lit matchsticks huddled together. The clock tower stood in the distance, rays of sunlight ricocheting off the face, turning it reddish-purple.

A cold breeze chased her into the steaming spa. As her body lowered into the hot water, she reached out and pushed a small button along the rim of the spa and activated rumbling bubbles. The jets crossed through the water, tickling her in spots and massaging others. She took a seat on the underwater ledge and closed her eyes, allowing the cool breeze that had chased her in to coast across her face, the only part of her body exposed above the water.

When she opened her eyes, she saw the sky laced with puffy clouds draped in hues of yellow and orange. She felt her mind relax, as if a huge weight had been suddenly lifted off it. She could remember things…some things.

David. His eyes. She thought of his green eyes as she held onto the side of the spa and closed her own. Looking into his eyes had the power to calm her. Peace and security rested in David's eyes. She could lose herself in them so easily…

Carrie opened her eyes and sat up in the spa, shocked at the clarity with which she was able to remember him. Him and his entrapping eyes. Was it possible the diary could really be hers? Was it possible she had at some point known David Corbin?

She closed her eyes again and let her mind wander in hopes of remembering something else, something more substantial than a young man's eyes. *A dance.* David held her close to him while they danced to the slow song they had waited for the whole night. So much warmth in his embrace. She wanted to tell him her feelings that night, how much she loved him, how much she wanted to be in his warm embrace for the rest of her life.

But something interrupted their evening. A stranger. He put a gun to her head and forced her to the roof of the building. She dropped her necklace along the way, so David could find her. On the roof, the night air chilled her to the bone...

A biting breeze nipped at Carrie's face and woke her from her memories.

She opened her eyes to the gray clouds above. *It might rain soon.* She swished her hands around in the water and pushed herself to the other side of the spa. She tried to keep her body below her neck under the water, to stay warm. She dreaded getting out of the spa. For now, she was warm and wanted to stay that way. To her right, the palm trees swayed to the rhythm of the breeze moving through the yard.

She gazed down at the swirling, bubbling currents and tried to force memories of her parents. Nothing in regard to a house fire came to mind, nor did anything in reference to her father. She did remember her mother, though. The yelling, the fighting, the arguments—all flashed through her mind like the files in a library catalog.

In the bubbling currents, she saw the house she used to live in. *How do I know I used to live there, though?* A one-story home painted white with a dark blue trim. She lay on the front lawn, staring up at a black sky, wondering what to do about David's confession earlier in the day. He told her he loved her. She ran from him. *Why would I do that?* Her mother walked out of the house looking down at her, her bright blonde head blocking Carrie's view of the darkness…

"Young lady, have you decided what you want to do with your life?"

Carrie fought to hold back the urge to yell. "No, Mom. I have other things on my mind right now."

"Oh, do you now? Precious little Carrie has other things on her mind right now?"

"I'm asking you nicely, Mom, to back off. Please, leave me alone."

"Young lady, let me tell you what you should *be thinking about right now. Your future. Instead, you keep hanging out with these 'friends' of yours, 'fighting crime' and getting your name plugged in the newspapers. Where has it gotten you, young lady? Nowhere. Now your little crime-fighting company is closed down, and what do you have to show for it? Nothing. You keep making stupid, googly eyes at this David loser who's been in your life I don't know how long now, and it's just been a big waste of your time and mine. You act so immature sometimes, you know that? Why don't you go back to junior high if you're going to keep acting like this?"*

"Stop, Mother! I've asked you nicely, and I'm not going to ask again. Just leave me alone."

"Leave you alone? How dare you talk to me like that! I am your mother! You better straighten yourself up and start acting like a lady. You should be in college, taking courses on business or law, not galli-

vanting around town with a bunch of losers."

"I am eighteen years old now, Mom. I can do what I please, understand? I will do as I please!"

"No, you won't! Not when you're under my roof! You will do as I say, is that clear?"

"Then I don't need to be under your roof anymore!"

Carrie returned to reality, emotions of rage and frustration bubbling to the surface of her memories like the water she soaked in. *Is that argument the reason I left? Left to go where? Haven't I lived in South Ryshard my whole life?*

She gazed through the turbulent water to the dark purple tile of the spa floor. The way the water rippled and caused the violet hues to come up through the water reminded her of shimmering crystals, like ones she had seen before. Those towering walls of amethysts in the cave she entered while in Crystal City. She was sent there to find a sindaris stone, but a run-in with a gypsy turned her whole life upside down…

The old woman in the city told her about this cave. The Cave of Visions, she called it? The old gypsy lady said, "Whatever a person sees in the crystal shards is what is to come in the future."

Carrie reached out to touch the amethyst wall that towered in front of her. A soft hum pulsed from it as she pulled her hand back and took a step away from the mammoth shard. An image of herself appeared in the surface. Her reflection wore the same tattered brown cargo pants and white T-shirt she was currently wearing.

"Hello?" she asked the image, feeling somewhat embarrassed to be talking to her own representation.

Carrie watched as David appeared near her reflection. He wore a gray button-down shirt tucked into black slacks. She had always thought him handsome in that shirt. He handed her reflection a rose and started talking, but Carrie couldn't hear what he was saying. Her reflection took the rose and said something to him, and they suddenly kissed each other.

Carrie turned away from the crystal shard and glanced around the room, not seeing the image in any of the other crystals. When she looked back at the reflection, she saw David on the ground, covered in blood. Her heart skipped a beat, and she turned away to collect herself.

When she turned her attention back on the reflection, her image knelt over David, tears pouring out of her eyes.

That last vision burned its way into her memory. She broke free from the daymare and found herself staring down at the frothy surface of the spa water. Goose bumps rose across her shoulders. She lowered them back into the hot water as chills ran up the back of her neck.

She wanted to remember everything, but she couldn't, not all at once anyway. She wondered why she was suddenly re-membering some things and not others. This wasn't the first time she experienced something like this. Each time she took a swim in the pool or a dip in the spa, she found it easier to recall parts of what she at first believed to be false memories, something out of her imagination. But connecting what she was now remembering to what she read in the diary…she be-lieved the diary could very well be hers, as could the memories. What caused her memory to return remained a mystery. May-be it was the fact that she was relaxing her muscles, relaxing her mind in the spa. Maybe it was the extreme temperature flux between the chilly evening air and the steaming spa water.

She needed to ask Jerad about her past. Surely he would know something. Someone had to know something. The house fire story was still up for debate. She could neither recall it nor prove that Jerad was lying to her. She had done her fair share of research through news articles. Nothing about a house fire or a young woman with limited memory.

Carrie stared up at the dark clouds filling the sky. One of the passing clouds resembled a large, dark dolphin. This pleased her and made her wonder why. *I love dolphins*, she decided.

Carrie grabbed the side of the spa and lifted herself out. Chills broke out across her flesh. She quickly grabbed the towel, being careful not to lose the necklace. She draped the towel around her body and rushed into the house, a faint ache swelling in her head as she made her way to her bedroom and entered the bathroom. She turned the light on and shut the door, not sure when anyone else would return to the house. She slid the glass shower door open and turned the knobs.

After setting the necklace and towel on the sink, she slipped off her bathing suit and stepped into the shower. The warm water covered her body like a blanket, snuggling away the faint headache till it was no more.

As Carrie bathed, she wondered about everything she had experienced today. So many doors had suddenly been unlocked, so many paths revealed. But the one she wanted to travel down the most was the one that would hopefully reveal what happened between her and David. The diary entries told her she had once been in love with him. *But why not now? Why can't I remember a house fire or Jerad rescuing me, or even how I got here?*

Carrie finished her shower, turned the water off and stepped out, wrapping a dry towel around her body. Standing before the foggy mirror, she rubbed a circle so she could see herself. She stared at her eyes, suddenly remembering more slivers of her past. More of her mother's yelling. Doctor visits. She turned her right shoulder toward the mirror so she could see the red three-wedged pinwheel design on the lower part of her shoulder blade.

She remembered seeing the same shape at the bottom of each of the diary pages. *A birthmark? A discolored scar? Were the doctor visits for this abnormality or something else entirely?*

"My lovely flower, why aren't you wearing your necklace?"

Carrie turned around to find Jerad standing behind her, decked out in a black suit and black tie. The chill of cold silver settled around her neck. *How did he get in here without me hearing him?* Hints of his Diamond Dust cologne intermingled with the strong scents of cigars as he grasped her bare shoulder and smiled at her.

"You're home early," she said.

He leaned both hands on his cane. "I promised you we would spend some time together this evening."

"Yes, of course," she answered, a wide grin leaking across her face.

He pulled her close and kissed her. She closed her eyes, enjoying the warmth of his lips against hers, his wandering hand touching her bare skin. Her body melted in his grasp.

She pulled away somewhat abruptly and looked him in the eyes. "I need to get dressed." She said it with a deliberately stern tone in her voice, knowing she had to stand her ground and make sure things didn't go further than this, especially not when she was half-naked.

Carrie gently nudged him out of the bathroom, smiled

and closed the door between them. She found herself carefully locking the door, hoping he didn't hear her doing it. She didn't want to be overly rude about her intentions. "What do you have planned tonight?"

His voice, faint through the door, seemed to have traces of disappointment in it. "Well, I was thinking we could have Belgar cook us a nice meal and then we could tie up some of these last-minute wedding plans together."

"Belgar isn't here yet, is he?"

"He knows to have dinner ready by seven."

Carrie couldn't help but be overjoyed at the thought. *A whole evening, just the two of us.* She couldn't remember the last time they had spent an evening together, alone, and she was happy to see him putting forth effort toward their relationship.

"I can't wait," she replied, biting her lip.

"I'm going to change into something more comfortable."

Carrie stared into the mirror, admiring the large grin on her face. He had the ability to make her happy; it was just the frequency he had to get right. *Tonight,* she told herself, *I'm going to get some answers from him. Answers about my past that will hopefully give me a clearer view of my future.*

16 Rude Awakenings

"Hello, Mr. Corbin."

David slowly opened his eyes, not to the fluorescent lights from before but to the soft glow of the emergency lighting above his bed amid surrounding darkness. In front of him, in the shadows, two figures sat in chairs. David found his hands handcuffed above his head to the metal bed frame. He wiggled into a somewhat comfortable position to give his shoulder some slack. The pain was minute, almost nonexistent, and he remembered taking some painkillers Veronica brought him before everything went dark.

"Glad to see you're awake."

"Who are you?" David asked.

"I'm insulted you don't recognize my voice." The man bent his head down into the small area of light.

"Parks?" David wanted to struggle out of the cuffs, but he calmed his panic for the moment and tried to give his wrists as much room as he could to avoid breaking open the cuts from wearing them earlier.

Parks leaned back in the chair, back in the shadows, and sighed. "I wanted to get you some flowers and a get-well card, but the gift shop had a poor selection."

"How sweet of you," David said. "But I think I'd like to be out of these cuffs more than I'd like a card from the likes of you."

"You're under arrest for all the things I charged you with earlier. We'll add escaping custody and attacking an officer on the list while I have your attention." He returned to the light. His beady eyes motioned to a gun in his hand. "I warned you."

David wondered where Veronica was. He assumed the second figure in the darkness—which his eyes were beginning to adjust to—was Sandra Meldramine. "Where's Veronica?"

"She headed to the cafeteria to grab a cup of coffee. She was getting drowsy sitting here staring at you. Don't worry, though, Sandra here will be heading down there in a minute to take care of her. I find it interesting that you show more concern for her than for yourself right now."

"You don't want to know what will happen to you if you hurt her."

"Hey!" Parks shouted, his partner still sitting motionless beside him. "If you haven't noticed, bright boy, you're not in a position to make threats. Now…" he scooted the chair into the light, moving closer to the bed. He moved the gun within an inch of David's nose. "I need you to answer some questions for me."

David would have been intimidated if it weren't for the fact that he had dealt with Parks' kind before. "I'm not sure why you have it out for me, but you don't scare me." David realized if he kept Parks and his partner busy up here, Ve-

197

ronica might have more time to figure out what was going on.

Parks squinted and tapped David's nose with the tip of the gun barrel. "Really?"

"Really."

"I'm losing patience with you." Parks leaned back in the chair. "If you don't make the wise decision to cooperate with me, then your other friend, Kimberly, is going to die a very mysterious death."

David said nothing. Instead, he did his best to stay calm, to try and figure out a way to get that gun from Parks and get out of the cuffs.

"Do you understand everything I've been saying? I have control of whether your good friend, Veronica, and your sidekick, Kimberly, live or die. The very last thing you want to do is tick me off."

Sandra moved her chair into the light next to Parks. The way the shadows played on her face made her eyes seem hollow, giving her the look of a ghoul.

Parks set the gun down on his lap. "See, Kimberly is safe and sound—right now anyway—on the other side of the curtain, sleeping peacefully in her little bed. She struggled a bit when we crammed the sleeping pills down her throat, but she managed to cooperate once they kicked in. If she ever awakens from her deep slumber will be up to you. We have plenty more pills where those came from."

David became aware that he couldn't reach the gun on Parks's lap, not even with his foot, and with Sandra there, he had no chance to get hold of it before she pulled her own gun out and put a bullet in him.

"So, now that I have your undivided attention, I'll start

with the questions. What was that farmer doing at the facility? Is he a friend of yours?"

"Did he look like a friend of mine?"

"What was he doing there?"

"I don't know."

"You don't know?"

"Are you telling me your little police force couldn't handle a simple farmer?"

Parks nodded.

Sandra stood up and leaned in close to David. Thick bags hung under her eyes, which seemed to twinkle a bit from where she stood under the light. "We'll forgive you for your sarcasm. The farmer really isn't that important. What we really need to know is where that rhodenine necklace is."

"I already told you I didn't take the necklace. I don't even know what necklace you're talking about."

"You and your friends thought you had me back at the facility, didn't you? You thought you were a tough guy, huh? Well, you messed up. I told you I'd catch up to you. I told you I'd make you pay. Now, if you want to put all this behind you, wipe your slate clean and be rid of us for good, just tell us where the necklace is."

"I don't know."

"I'm having trouble believing you," Parks said as Sandra sat back down in the chair. She reached into the front pocket of her police uniform and pulled out a pack of cigarettes. She popped one in her mouth, igniting it with a silver lighter she pulled from her pants pocket. She sucked on it for a few seconds and then blew a stream of white smoke directly into David's face. He inhaled, an itch forming at the back of his throat.

Sandra smiled. "Since you aren't going to cooperate, maybe we'll have to give you an incentive to answer our questions." She took the gun from Parks and held it up for David to see. He could have grabbed it from her had he not been cuffed to the bed. "I just want you to see the weapon that's going to kill Veronica. She's in the cafeteria, Agent Parks?"

He nodded. "She is."

Sandra blew a ring of smoke that encircled David's head.

"If you lay a finger on Veronica, you'll regret it to your grave!"

Parks swung his pointer finger back and forth like an upside-down pendulum. "Don't raise your voice. The doctors know you're a suspect. I told them to leave me alone while I question you. They won't be coming to your rescue. Don't waste your breath, or I'll get tired of hearing it and waste it for you."

David pulled on the cuffs, curious to see if the bed frame would easily come apart, but it wouldn't budge. He suspected that the painkillers were wearing off, since his shoulder was beginning to feel sore.

"I'll be back with some incentive," Sandra said, cigarette hanging from her mouth, smoke billowing from it as if she were a dragon readying itself to devour an innocent animal. She left through the curtain. David listened to her footsteps as they crossed the tile flooring and vanished as the door shut behind her.

Parks sneered. "Nothing you can do now, Mr. Corbin."

"If that changes, you'll pay."

"I'm getting really tired of your smart mouth, you know that? I didn't want it to come to this, but you've left me no other choice." Parks left through the curtain and began rummaging through counter drawers and bottles on the other side of the room. "I had the doctor leave me a little present. All I have to do is find it."

Panic coursed through David. A window to his right would have offered a solution, had he not been in cuffs or uncertain of what floor he was on. There was an emergency button under his bed, but he couldn't reach it in his current position. Even if he did and someone came to the room, Parks would end up subduing and/or killing them as well.

"You know, I do have some respect for you, David. I really do. Don't think just because I've placed you under arrest that I don't appreciate your...what's the word...moxie? No, I think that means courage more than it does style. Hmm...flair? Maybe that's it. I really like your flair, your antics. I mean, robbing a jewelry store wasn't enough, was it? You had to go off and add a number of other fun little things to your list. You're someone who has to constantly outdo himself, and I like that."

Despite the pain growing in his shoulder and back, David pulled with all of his strength at the cuffs, hoping to break the bed frame or maybe slide his sore wrists out of the cuffs.

"Shh." A soft voice filled his ears. He glanced around but didn't see anyone. *"Relax, David."* The voice sounded familiar, but he couldn't figure out where it was coming from. *"David, relax, please."*

David stopped tugging and let his arms hang. He suddenly felt his whole body relax and the panic subside. The pain in his shoulder vanished and he had to fight to keep himself from falling asleep.

"See, I have to outdo myself every now and then, just to stay ahead of the game," Parks continued. "That's why when it comes to making an example of you, I'm going all the way. Maybe next time, those who wish to follow in your footsteps and disobey the law will think twice before they do it in my district."

"You must hurry." The cuffs released and David's hands fell out of them. *"Take the stairs, David."*

Incredible shock overtook David at how he had become free. He couldn't see anybody in the room with him, at least not on his side of the curtain. And that voice…seemed to be inside his head.

"Hurry!"

David slowly and quietly slid out of bed, feeling somewhat naked in his gown. The floor felt cold against his bare feet as he tiptoed through the side curtain where Kimberly slept. He gently shook her, his heart racing, wondering when Parks would return from finding his "present."

Kimberly turned over onto her other side and yawned. *No,* David thought. *You have to wake up!* He tugged her side and pulled her toward him, shaking her vigorously as her eyes slowly opened. He pulled on her arm, dragging her body toward the edge of the bed.

"This is where it ends, David," Parks said from across the room. "You aren't getting out of this hospital alive. Who's going to help you? Who's going to save the day if it's you who's been captured? Quite ironic if you ask me. You should have thought about hiring a bodyguard or something."

"Shh," he whispered, holding his finger to his mouth as he helped Kimberly out of bed. When she finally stood to her feet, she swayed to the left, and David had to catch her and set her straight.

"Mmm," she moaned softly before David quickly put his

hand over her mouth. Her eyes shut.

David took his hand off her mouth. She randomly tossed her arm in the air, slapping him on the shoulder and causing his pain to reappear. He took her arm, placed it around his neck and then headed toward the door.

To David's right, on the other side of the room, he could see Parks using a syringe to pull a liquid substance from a small vial he had found. With his back to them, he didn't see David and Kimberly sneak out the door and enter the hallway.

David went as fast as he could down the half-white, half-pale-green corridor toward the stairwell, carrying most of Kimberly's weight along his side. The pain in his shoulder drifted in and out, but he ignored it long enough to stay focused on the stairs, on escaping.

Doctors and nurses loitered near the counters, preoccupied with their computers and other patients. Nobody stopped David and Kimberly from reaching the door that had a picture of a flight of stairs on it. David pulled it open and started down the stairwell with Kimberly in tow.

***

Sandra stepped out of the elevator into a crowd of groaning patients. She glanced at her watch and saw that it was only a quarter past ten at night. Somehow she thought it was later. Doctors and nurses passing through the hallway nodded to her, acknowledging the police uniform she wore. It felt good. She thrived on the respect others gave her—it came close to making up for the lack of respect she received from Agent Parks.

She overheard a nurse ask about the commotion on the

seventh floor and reported that security was on the way to check on it. Sandra threw the thought to the back of her mind and decided to hurry so she could help Parks with whatever trouble David might be giving him.

Hustling past a collection of signs that indicated the way to the gift shop, florist and cafeteria, Sandra turned and passed through a set of double doors into the cafeteria. To her surprise, she only found two older women attendants behind the serving counter, one replacing the macaroni and cheese and the other brewing fresh coffee.

A solitary cup of steaming coffee sat in the middle of one table. "No," Sandra whispered.

"Hey, Officer!"

Sandra spun toward one of the hairnet-clad women.

"If you're looking for the young girl, she left about two minutes ago, back out those double doors you came through."

"Thank you much." Sandra tossed a fake smile at the lady and entered the hallway. "Guess we'll have to do this the hard way."

***

David and Kimberly reached the third-floor landing, continuing down the stairwell. David's shoulder throbbed now, but he knew he had to press on if he wanted any chance of staying ahead of Parks and warning Veronica. Not that he was overly worried for Veronica. He knew she could take care of herself, had even saved his life on more than one occasion.

"David!" Veronica turned the corner of the stairwell below them.

"Boy, am I glad to see you."

Kimberly wobbled back and forth, her eyes heavy from the drugs running through her bloodstream.

"What's wrong with her?"

David moved Kimberly down a few steps and passed her off to Veronica. "Apparently, Parks crammed a bunch of sleeping pills down her throat."

"Great." Veronica shifted her purse to her left arm and supported Kimberly with her right. "We have to get out of here, pronto. That cop woman is looking for me, and I'm pretty sure you made Parks mad by escaping."

David moved his shoulder around a bit, trying to adjust to the pain seeping into his muscle. "How did you know?"

"I overheard a security page on the intercom."

"I don't always tell you this, but I'm happy you're as observant as you are. Now, let's get out of here." David started down the stairs in front of them, Veronica following behind with Kimberly at her side.

They reached the bottom of the stairwell, and David peered out the small window in the door overlooking the lobby. "I don't know where Sandra went, but the exit is right there." Veronica glanced to where David was pointing toward a set of automatic doors on the other side of the lobby.

A shrill alarm blared through the building. Bright lights flashed through the stairwell, indicating a fire alarm.

David heard choice words leak under Veronica's breath.

"Pretty…lights and…mmm," Kimberly mumbled as she leaned against the wall.

David smiled, pointing out the window as people began to file out of the hospital like a herd of cattle. "We can use this. Now's our chance to get lost in the crowd and make our way out without those cops seeing us." A sharp pain shot through his shoulder, sending his arm into a spasm. "The painkillers have worn off."

"Hang in there," Veronica said softly. "We're almost out of here." She hoisted Kimberly's arm around her neck. "Let's do this."

David slowly opened the door, and they stepped into the lobby. "Make a run for the door." He glanced at Kimberly, her eyelids bouncing up and down as she struggled to stay awake.

The threesome started into the crowd, the current of people emptying from the hallways and side rooms becoming a bit more turbulent. An elderly man collapsed over his crutches. David stopped to help him back to his feet.

"Thank you," the man said.

"Don't mention it. Just get out of the building."

Kimberly groaned. "Where's my puppy wuppy? Puppy… wuppy…"

"Well, well, well." They turned to the right. Between the steady stream of people, David could see Sandra standing in a doorway, her gun aimed on them. "This time, you three aren't escaping. I still owe you for what you did to me back at the facility."

At the sight of the gun, the crowd spiraled into chaos, shoving each other down, stampeding toward the exit. David grabbed Veronica's hand, and they all made a mad dash toward the automatic doors.

A shot fired, and one of the glass panels in front of them shattered. Screams filled the air as people stumbled over one another. David, Veronica and Kimberly staggered out the front doors.

The cold air swarmed up David's gown, making him wish he had grabbed his clothes on the way out. Veronica lugged Kimberly's body across the front lawn as they entered the hospital parking lot.

"Where's the car?" David shouted, his eyes scanning the lot for her little red vehicle. The fire alarm cried out into the night sky as if the building itself were alive and wounded.

"I don't remember!" She sweltered with frustration as a bullet pinged off a piece of metal, sending them all to the asphalt behind a parked vehicle.

"How do we get out of here without your car?" David asked.

Kimberly began to shiver, her eyes rolling to the back of her head.

"Just look for it!" Veronica shrieked. "I don't remember where we parked; I was too busy trying to keep you alive!"

David huffed. "We're going to have to steal one then, just until we're safe."

"H…he…ey…," Kimberly groaned.

David snapped his head toward her. "Not now, Kim!"

A disheveled woman in a plaid button-down shirt and frayed jeans ran past them, screaming, "The building's on fire! The building's on fire!"

"You g…g…uys…," Kimberly fought to get each breath out as her eyelids clapped open and shut, "This…" She flung her arm up and slapped it against the side of the car they were hiding behind. It was Veronica's car.

Veronica unlocked the car with the keys from her purse and then unlocked all the doors so David could lift Kimberly onto the backseat. David crawled over the middle console and fell into the passenger seat, the pain in his shoulder flaring up again, as if someone's hand were inside his body, picking and prodding the muscle and bone like guitar strings.

Veronica backed the car out of the space, careful not to hit any of the hospital staff and patients filling the lot. David gazed out the window and caught one last glimpse of Parks and Sandra, both standing on the hospital lawn, watching the car pull forward toward the main street.

David leaned back in the seat and closed his eyes, hoping they would make it to the wedding on time and that all of this wasn't for nothing.

17

Answers & Questions

As the fireplace embers crackled and snapped, Carrie and Jerad sat on the couch in the living area discussing plans for their upcoming wedding. Carrie browsed the pages of *Lisa's Linens*, a two-inch-thick catalog that rested heavy on her lap. For the past hour, she had garnered no luck in getting Jerad to agree with her on any details for the wedding, leaving her frustrated. Either he had already lined up certain aspects without her knowledge, or he shot down each idea that she brought up.

"What about purple?" she asked, exhaustion showing in her voice. She was looking at a page full of tablecloths in varying shades of violet. It wasn't her favorite color, but she figured it might be a nice compromise.

"No. Purple is too…feminine."

"Feminine? It's a wedding."

"Yes, my wedding. Purple is out of the question. What about black?"

"I've never really cared for black."

"How do you know?" Jerad asked, surprise in his voice. "What does that mean?"

"Your memory. How do you know if you've ever liked black or not?"

"I don't like it right now. What about green? Green would look good with the white place settings."

"We'll do red. Red tablecloths. That's final."

"Is it?"

Jerad stared at her with an expression she hadn't ever seen in him before. His eyes reflected swirls of orange and yellow from the fire, and she thought she saw him grinding his teeth. Out of curiosity, she glanced down at his hands and noticed one of them starting to curl up into a ball. A few minutes later, his hand relaxed, and she found him staring out the window behind them, toward the swimming pool outside.

Carrie had suspicions before tonight that Jerad had a violent side, but she could never furnish her own proof to that effect. He had a temper, she knew that much, but he usually only expressed it with a red face and balled-up fists. *Is it normal for someone to get so angry so easily? Over a wedding detail?* She wondered if he wanted to hit her.

Jerad turned back toward her, his fingers playing with the triangle of hair under his lip. "We'll do green, if that's what you want."

Carrie nodded. "Thank you." *Now on to other matters*, she thought. She grabbed Jerad's uncurled hand and massaged it gently in hers. "I wanted to talk to you about something."

"Yes?" he asked, his eyes lighting up with curiosity. Carrie guessed he thought she might be referring to sex.

"It's about my past. About my memories."

210

"Oh." He pulled his hand out of hers and turned his head toward the window again.

This isn't going to work, Carrie realized. She would have to show him the diary, show him proof of what she wanted to discuss. Otherwise he wouldn't take her seriously. "I'll be right back. I have something to show you," she said as she rushed off to her bedroom. She swung the door open, allowing light from the hallway to chase the darkness within, and rustled through the bed sheets to pull the diary out from under her pillow. She hugged the small book briefly, appreciating how much it meant to her. It was the only link to her past, the only record of what may or may not have happened in another age, and she was about to share it with the man she loved.

She returned to the living area to find Jerad prodding the burning logs with an iron poker. Carrie flopped down on the couch while he placed the poker next to the fireplace and limped back to the couch himself.

"What is it you want to show me?" Jerad asked as he nestled in next to her. His eyes appeared warm and friendly, until they gazed down on the book in her hands and then suddenly narrowed with suspicion.

"You know how I've been asking you a lot of questions about my past?"

He hesitated and then answered, "Yeah."

A large grin spread across her face as she placed the book on her lap. "This came in the mail for me today. I don't know who sent it to me, but I think it's my old diary. From when I was younger!"

"What do you mean it came in the mail?"

"I found it on my bed this morning. There's no return address on it, but I read a bit of it earlier and it seems to have helped jog my memory more than anything else I've tried."

Jerad fiddled with the patch of hair under his lip again, this time combing it with his finger, a thoughtful expression dancing across his face. He reached his hand toward the book. "May I?"

Carrie handed it to him.

He flipped the book open and started browsing, his eyes squinting at certain pages. Carrie couldn't read his reactions, and this disturbed her. She figured Jared would be excited for her, happy that she had finally remembered some of her past—even if the majority of it was about someone she used to be in love with.

After a while of reading, Jerad shut the book hard and held it to his chest. He looked up at Carrie, his eyes filled with darkness, the flames no longer dancing in them. "Baby, I need you to listen very closely to me, okay? This book of lies…" he held it up for her to see, but out of her reach, "is not going to help you with your memory. If anything, it's only going to make things worse."

"What are you talking about? If it's really my diary, how could it make things worse?"

"Trust me." He tossed it into the fireplace.

Carrie dove for it, but Jerad had already anticipated her move and reached out, grabbing her and pulling her back to the couch. She watched the green leather cover twist and bend in the heat. The pages lit up and burned, as if the flames wanted to do away with the book that had already unlocked some of the doors to Carrie's past.

At a loss for words, Carrie just stared at the fire, her heart sinking with the destruction of her diary.

"Didn't you and I agree to leave your past in the past?"

Jared asked.

Her dreams, her answers erupted in a blaze, and she found she couldn't turn away from it, as if a long-lost friend was disintegrating in the fireplace, crying for help. But she did nothing, nothing to salvage the book, nothing to put a stop to the murder.

Carrie turned toward Jerad, his eyes lacking any hint of remorse. "How could you? You destroyed my only link to the past."

"I did it for your own good, sweets."

"I don't believe that. I don't believe that at all. That was my diary. Those were my entries, my stories of a past I can't even remember."

Jerad tilted her face toward him. "Are you happy with me? Are you looking forward to us being married, of us being husband and wife for the rest of our lives?"

"Are you asking me if I love you?"

"Stop looking at everything under a microscope. That diary could have been nothing more than a prank, a fake, a forgery. Why would you base your happiness on that? You and I are going to be married in only a few days. That's what's important right now. What is the use of clouding everything with your past, a past that may or may not even be true?"

As hurt and frustrated as she was, Carrie realized he could very well have a point. "But who's to say it was fake or real? You glanced at it for a few seconds. I read full entries, and those entries brought memories back to my mind. The handwriting in there was mine—or a very, very close replica." She wondered if he saw David's name in there at all. It would be hard to miss—he was mentioned in almost every entry.

"Don't wish on stars that have already fallen, my love.

The past is back there, behind us, in the past. Don't dwell on it and ruin what we have to look forward to. Believe me, anyone could have made that diary. Maybe someone is trying to trick you into believing all that stuff."

But why? She wanted to ask him that, but suddenly felt exhausted. *Where will my answers come from now? I can't leave my past in the past. It's easy for Jerad to say that because he knows what his past holds, and what he's leaving behind. I don't. I have no choice. Now he just destroyed the only key to my past.*

Jerad leaned over and placed his warm hand on her cheek. He stared into her eyes and smiled. "I love you."

Hearing his words, feeling his touch, she melted inside. They kissed, and the passion she felt made her forget his faults. The fire within herself was all she could think of now.

His hand wandered across her sweat pants, moving from her knee up toward her thigh. Desire burned within her. She wanted him in every way possible—to kiss him, to touch him, to sleep with him, to lose herself in the moment. She rested her back on the couch as he hovered over her, his hand making its way up her t-shirt.

Carrie's eyes shot open and she scrambled across the couch.

He wiped his lips on his arm. "What are you doing?"

"I can't do this," she whispered. "I can't go that far yet."

Jerad sighed loudly, clearly frustrated. "We were just kissing."

"Your hands…I know it will get to a point that I can't control."

He said nothing, just shrugged.

"I've told you before that I don't want to sleep with you until we're married."

He stared out the window.

"It's nothing personal. I just…I have beliefs, ones that you have to respect."

"I do." He turned toward her, his fist balled up on his leg. "I'm sorry."

Carrie scooted across the couch to embrace him, but he darted up and grabbed the iron poker, jabbing at the pile of diary ashes, causing the brittle shards of burned paper to scatter throughout the fireplace.

18

Turquoise Rain

Turquoise arrived at the hospital an hour and a half after David and his friends had escaped the chaos. During that time, a small fire had broken out, causing the hospital staff and patients to flee the building and seek refuge at another medical facility, leaving the building abandoned and flooding. Turquoise wasn't surprised that nobody had thought to turn off the water. Many people in North Ryshard really only cared about one thing—themselves.

Turquoise walked slowly down the dim hallway of the seventh floor, her feet sloshing through water that flooded the dark corridors. Emergency lighting spread a minimal glow here and there, but not enough to take away the fear Turquoise felt being alone in the hospital and without Cloud or Trinistar at her side.

Turquoise pushed her wet hair out of her face and tied it back in a ponytail, leaving a few stray strands loose. The scratches in her arm hadn't healed yet, mainly because Turquoise was saving her energy for the fight she expected to face here in the hospital. The beast, the demon hybrid, had killed her partner, leaving her alone. Alone to fight the forces of darkness, alone to find the timepiece and complete the mission that she, Cloud and Trinistar set out to complete. She didn't expect the demon to go any farther before attempting to take her out, now that she was so vulnerable.

Peering in the rooms that broke off the main hallway, she sensed the teens had been here, on this floor. She remembered the training simulations in the Sector. The demon hybrids were formidable foes, creatures neither bound by the weaknesses of regular demons nor fragile like the humans. But the Sector's programs obviously weren't up to date on the true abilities of these specimens, neglecting to educate her on the finer points of their ability to evolve, to grow stronger and more cunning.

Turquoise stopped in front of the room she knew the teens had at one point occupied. She entered, spotting a pair of handcuffs dangling from the headboard of the bed. She had focused all her energy to free David and, until now, wasn't a hundred percent sure they had escaped the hospital.

She made her way back into the hallway and continued toward the end of it, waiting anxiously for her energy to return to full measure. She found it difficult to keep her thoughts straight on the mission and not allow them to drift toward the past, toward the good times she had with Trinistar before everything changed, before death took its toll and Turquoise saw yet another ugly facet of this life. Trinistar had been more than a friend, she had been the first person to accept Turquoise for who she was, what she was—a freak with super powers. That's what it all boiled down to. And when the Sector took her in, she didn't think she had anyone who understood her, really understood where she came from.

But Trinistar did. And now she was gone. Cloud was gone. *Is this all a dream?* The water pouring from the sprinklers, showering her in cold water—*is it real?* The dark rooms—*what awful things are waiting in the shadows for me? Will I forever be trapped in this nightmare?*

Turquoise shook the thoughts from her mind and scolded herself for dwelling on such things. It was her job now to get her hands on the timepiece and finish this mission. She felt she might also be the teens' only chance at surviving the mess they were walking into.

She reached the end of the hallway and stretched for the handle to the stairwell door when her senses flipped into overdrive. She spun around, the smell of decay, the image of ugliness telling her that Thana occupied the hallway with her.

Through the mist of water, she could make out Thana's silhouette standing in the middle of the hallway at the other end.

Turquoise extended her arms to her sides, wiggling her fingers. She felt her Fury charge up, but she also sensed the air fill with an energy she hadn't felt before. It tickled her nose and buzzed the back of her neck. It was electric, and it was flowing through the air, through the water at her feet.

"Heh, heh, heh. You're all alone." Thana stepped forward from the shadows at the other end of the hallway, his shape moving through the pillars of emergency lighting to reveal a shape more deserving of Thana's character. The police uniform he had used to pass off as a human authority figure had torn in spots. His face didn't look all that human anymore, his eyes glowing crimson red, his head a bulbous lump instead of the shiny round it had been back at the Stalus.

Thana stopped at the halfway point of the hallway, his breath wheezing in and out of his lungs. A gun hung from each hip, snug in its holster. The fact that he had acquired weapons on his journeys told Turquoise that he might be getting weaker from the battles, having to resort to archaic mechanizations rather than the powers instilled in him.

Turquoise set her palm on the sword handle sticking out of her belt. Although a pulse pistol would have been a much better weapon considering the situation and the fact that she was alone, she had been trained in hand-to-hand, melee combat, such as sword or knife fighting.

"Prepare yoursssself to passs into the ground, Turquoissse. You have put up sssuch a remarkable ssstruggle, but it will all be over in a matter of momentsss."

"For you."

"I am forced to kill you before I can move on to dessstroy Kimberly."

"You're not killing her. You're not killing anyone else."

"I sssee you have taken it upon yoursssself to sssee to my demissse. Cloud failed. David wasss no match for me."

Turquoise took her hand off the sword handle and stretched her arms out again. She paused to take inventory of her surroundings. The stairwell door behind her—an escape, if she needed one. The rooms off to the sides, all of them filled with items she could use to kill this thing, assuming the broken sword in her belt failed to do the trick. The narrow hallway left very little room to fight in, but the broken sword would work best here.

Determined to defeat the demon hybrid before her, Turquoise started in a light jog and then broke out in a full run toward Thana. He did nothing to move out of the way, and that would only work to her advantage. When she closed most of the space between them, she pulled her arms back, ready to thrust her Fury at him with everything she had. If she could bring about the most damage to him in the beginning, it would make the battle that much easier to get through and ensure her victory.

The impact felt like a cinderblock striking her chest, knocking her into the water. Not sure what hit her, she rolled onto her stomach and lifted her head out of the water, spitting the dirty liquid out of her mouth. She gulped in some air and choked on it, the sudden pain in her chest making it hard to breathe.

"Conssssider that a free lessson in what happensss when you are hasssty."

Turquoise struggled to her feet, bent over and coughed up blood. The red ooze slid from her mouth and dripped into the water at her feet. She realized he had shot her in the chest with one of his guns. Now she had a nice hole in her lung, and she found the very act of breathing to be nearly unbearable. The pressure in her chest squeezed her lungs together like balloons being twisted into animal shapes. She fell to her knees and closed her eyes, doing her best to fish the bullet out with her mind and heal her wounds. When she opened her eyes, satisfied that the hole was patched and she would be able to continue this battle, she noticed Thana's hands resting on the holsters of his guns.

She stood to her feet and held her hand out. "Hold on a

sec. Who said anything about weapons?"

Thana stared at her, his red eyes glowing like embers in a dying fire. Then he pulled the guns out of their holsters and dropped them in the water. He lunged toward her and threw a punch, but she grabbed his arm and used all her strength to swing and release him into the other end of the hallway. He collided with the stairwell door.

Struggling to his feet, he smiled at her, teeth stained in blood. He dug his claws into the wall behind him and pulled the door off its hinges, throwing it at her. She watched carefully as it skated across the water like one of the flat rocks Turquoise remembered skipping off her family's pond when she was younger. She leapt in the air as it approached her, planning to land on it and use it as a weapon against him. But the speed at which it was thrown was faster than she had originally calculated. Her feet made contact with it, but the door slid right out from under her. She fell to the floor headfirst, hitting the back of her skull against the tile beneath the water.

Turquoise moaned, holding the back of her head, grateful the water cushioned her fall. *Can't make that mistake again.* When she looked across the way, she saw Thana charging toward her, pistols in his hands. *I thought he dropped those!* Bullets filled the hallway, but not before Turquoise could put her arms out and erect a pink shield around her to absorb the ammunition.

Thana stopped a few feet from her, sliding the guns back into the holsters at his sides. "Impresssive."

She lowered the shield and rose to her feet. *He's trying to weaken me by making me use my powers. I have to get closer, start getting some real hits in.* She kept her gaze on his hands, on his guns. She should have known he wouldn't fight fair. He was part demon after all.

The guns went up again—so did her shield—as bullets filled the space between them but disintegrated into the surface of the shield. The guns returned to their holsters, and her shield came back down. Turquoise wondered how long this was going to continue. *Why doesn't he just attack me without the guns? Why is he keeping his distance?*

A piece of the debris splashed into the water near her feet, causing her to glance up and observe the ceiling crumbling from the water damage in the floor above. She wondered how far down the hallway the damage went, if she could run backward and avoid what was about to fall. She couldn't take the risk to look, though, not with Thana standing there, feet away, his guns waiting to be pulled from their holsters again.

She erected a pink bubble over her head as chunks of ceiling came crashing down around her. As she released the shield, three or four bullets struck her in the abdomen. Turquoise fell to the flooded floor, clutching her wounds as her blood tainted the water around her with dark streams of crimson.

Thana approached her, guns back in their holsters. "Thought you had me, didn't you?"

Turquoise struggled but managed to stand to her feet. She bent over moments later, the pain in her stomach forcing her to her knees.

"Thisss isss no place for you, Wedge. Kimberly isss mine. Her sssoul isss my property, and there isss no need for you to go any further in your feeble attemptsss to ssstop me."

Turquoise took light, airy breaths, her mind racing to figure out how she could survive this. She closed her eyes for a moment and attempted to push the bullets out of her stomach when she felt Thana grab her drenched hair and pick her up off the ground. The sharp pain around her skull brought tears to her eyes.

"Good hasss no chance in thisss world of wicked. Your kind isss outnumbered. The humansss are outnumbered. It'sss time for all of you to give up."

Her lip quivered, and her eyes slowly opened. *Can't let him finish me. Not like this.* She reached down to the sword in her belt, her hand wrapping around the wet handle, the pain in her stomach pulsing through the rest of her organs. Looking into those glowing red eyes, Turquoise managed to grin slightly. "This is for Trinistar." She slipped the broken sword out and struck it into Thana's chest.

He released his grip on her and she dropped to her feet. "Wha—?"

He gripped the sword handle with both of his large hands while Turquoise scrambled through the water toward a door at the other end of the hallway. When she reached the doorway, she collapsed to the floor, swallowing a mouthful of water. Thoughts of her training came back to her, but none of it had really prepared her for a battle like this. Most of her simulations were in virtual arenas with both opponents in full health and with weapons of equal power.

Turquoise turned to see if by some stroke of luck, Thana was dying from the stab wound she inflicted on him, and instead watched as Thana tore the tattered police uniform from his body and dropped the rags into the water. His red eyes glared at her, glowing like the ends of lit cigarettes. The emergency lighting illuminated his disfigured body as the red demon flesh bulged and his thick veins pulsed with a dark energy. Thana, now hunched over like a wolf, growled at her.

Her training had definitely not prepared her for this. The realization struck her that she could very well die here and now, ill-prepared, alone and weaponless—aside from her Fury, which was weak to begin with.

Turquoise crawled into the nearest room and managed to use the door handle as a crutch to get to her feet. She shut and locked the door and then stammered to the bed, tossing herself on it, curling her body in agony. She closed her eyes and fought to regain health. Concentrating all of her effort on her abdominal wounds, she felt the bullets passing through their canals, back out the way they had entered her body. Turquoise lifted her shirt as each bullet slipped out of her stomach and dropped on the sheets, staining the bed in blood as the wounds began to seal themselves.

She lay on her back wondering where Thana was. With a sense of hope, she considered that maybe he had left to chase after the teens. This, of course, would give her time to heal so she could figure out a way to destroy him once and for all. Her body began to shiver, her wet clothes chilling her flesh. If Thana found her now, she knew she would be finished.

Shielding her face with a pillow, Turquoise raised her arm up and thrust a burst of air at the lights above her bed. They vibrated and shattered, raining shards of glass around her. In the cloak of darkness, she heard the pitter-patter of Thana approaching her room. She imagined his sharp teeth and glowing eyes, his form stripped completely of all human skin and nothing more than raw demon flesh—it frightened her, but she told herself she couldn't be afraid. Not now.

She knew she had to kill him. Kill him here and now, at

least try, even if it meant her own death. Turquoise tossed the pillow into the water surrounding her bed and leaned back against the headboard.

She let memories of Trinistar fill her mind. The girl's smiling, angelic face and her optimistic personality. She had been a sister to Turquoise, the only sister she had known, and Cloud had been a brother. They were her siblings. Her deceased siblings, all because of the demon outside her door. She had to kill him or she would be killed.

Her body healed in those few moments. Using most of her power, she sealed her wounds enough to stop the bleeding and most of the pain. Her eyes adjusted to the darkness and her ears sensed movement just outside her door. She concentrated on what the room looked like in the light—the counters, cabinets and curtains in front of her. Over in the far right corner sat an oxygen cylinder she could use.

Turquoise rolled off the bed as the door flew off its hinges and careened through the curtains, crashing into the wall at the other side of the room. The metal loops that held the curtains scattered through the air, ricocheting off objects with a tinny clang.

Peering over the mattress, she watched the creature's still silhouette in the doorway. She slowly climbed back onto the mattress, sopping curtain in hand, and stood atop the bed, waiting for Thana to stop moving.

She closed her eyes and drew every ounce of Fury she had left, thrust her arms out and pushed the curtain forward, wrapping it around him. He struggled, clawing and snapping his jowls at the fabric, trying desperately to free himself. Quickly, Turquoise tore loose one of the curtain rods just as

Thana's claws shredded through the curtain. He lunged at her, knocking her to the floor.

She pushed the bar up in front of her, holding him back with it. She thrust the pole toward him, knocking him backward just enough to allow her room to get to her feet. She twirled the rod in her hands so the end pointed toward him. "This has to end here, Thana. I can't let you leave here alive, not after all the people you've killed."

"Killing me will do you no good in your quessst. There are so many more like me—thousssandsss who are already sssurfacing on thisss planet to dessstroy the humansss once and for all."

"That's impossible. There can't be thousands like you. You're rare, a special breed, and once I kill you, I'll make sure whatever is left of your breed is destroyed as well." She swung the rod out, striking Thana in the face, knocking a portion of his teeth out and spewing blood from the impact.

Turquoise jumped into the air and struck the pole down across Thana's skull. She heard bone crack and a groan from the hybrid. She landed on her feet just as he grabbed her leg and swung her toward the window across the room. She hit the glass, cracking the surface with her back, dropping the rod into the water. Claws struck her, carving a bloody stream across her forehead. She stumbled backward, bumping into the glass again as Thana lifted her by her shirt. The wound in her head burned like fire, and warm, thick blood coated her right eye, sealing it shut for the moment.

Thana opened his mouth, cracked and blood-stained teeth lining the inside of his gums. The stench of rotting flesh reached Turquoise's nose and forced bile up her throat. She swallowed it, the tart taste causing her to wince. She remembered the oxygen cylinder in the corner to her right. She slid her hand into her satchel, feeling for one of the explosives she carried. When her hand finally wrapped around the circular metal disc, she turned the bezel just slightly, pressed the button in the center of it, and pulled it out of the bag.

Thana thrust her backward into the window, adding more cracks to the already weak surface of the glass. Turquoise dropped the explosive from her hand as Thana slammed her into the window yet again. Her body broke through the glass this time and slipped from his grip. She grabbed hold of the ledge just as a bright orange and yellow burst of color filled the room with a flash of intense heat. Flames exploded out the broken window like a dragon's breath, frying her hands.

Turquoise held onto the ledge with all her might as the windows above and below her shattered, raining glass down the side of the hospital like crystallized snow. A squeal, like a live pig being barbecued, echoed through the atmosphere as another explosion blew out the corner of the building to her right. Brick and drywall vaporized into a black smoke as the scent of burning flesh—a demon's skin being consumed by mortal fire—wafted into the air around her.

The squealing grew louder as something swept across the top of Turquoise's head. Thana grabbed her legs as he fell, his flesh melting in a ball of flames. She tightened her grip on the ledge and kicked her legs, trying to shake loose the unwanted stowaway. She saw his charcoaled arm break off, then a leg. A husk of what he once was, Thana continued to hang on for his own life as Turquoise risked a hand away from the ledge and pointed it down at him. She thrust a burst of air at his face, flinging him from her legs and hurling him toward the pavement below.

Thana's body cracked open on the asphalt, scattering black debris into the wind. Turquoise grabbed hold of the ledge with both hands and pulled herself up, back into the room. A large chunk of the corner had been taken out by the oxygen cylinder, giving full view to the night sky and empty parking lot below. Small flames flickered here and there, burning themselves out in cabinets and patches of wall.

She fell to her knees, her strength gone. Her eyes grew heavy, especially the one coated in blood, but she fought to keep them open. In training, she had been warned to fight off sleep immediately after a battle, especially one that took a lot of mental and physical strength. There was always the chance that other enemies waited nearby to attack her when she slumbered.

Turquoise doubted that other demon hybrids lay in wait, but she wanted to take no chances. She scooped water up from the floor and splashed it in her face, rubbing gently at the blood-soaked eye. She rinsed her forehead, grateful her healing powers had been able to at least stop the blood flow. She could feel the cut above her eyebrow, unsure if it would heal without a scar.

"That was for my friends," she whispered. "That was for my friends and for me." She stood to her feet and made her way back into the hallway. She began swishing her hands around in the water, searching for Thana's officer uniform, wondering if by some chance she could find it.

She felt a wad of clothing under the water and pulled it up. A bulging lump in one of the pants pockets told her she had finally gotten hold of the item she had been fighting for all along. Tugging the timepiece out of the pocket gave her a flood of relief. She sat down in the water, letting the cold liquid submerge her waist in a blanket. Turquoise held the small, hexagon-shaped crystal in her palm, staring at it under the emergency lighting, watching the different angles of the crystal capture the light and send it back to her in dazzling, multicolored fragments.

How many people did he kill for this?

19 Evanescence

erad's silver cane tapped against the stone steps as he descended the staircase that led underneath the house. A lit cavern met him at the bottom, blue fog hovering in the room. He glanced to his left and strained to look through the dissipating haze at the many bookshelves lined up along the walls. The shelves contained ancient texts from sources that Jerad knew very little about. Most of the volumes weren't his, and some were even written in languages he didn't understand.

In the center of the room, toward the back, a long glass tube came up out of the floor and connected to the ceiling. The figure of a thin female, asleep and naked save for thin strands of blue cloth running across her chest and between her legs, floated in the midst of bright orange liquid. Long black hair floated above the woman's head, caught by the bubbles dancing in the liquid. Her arms hung at her sides, almost thin enough to be mistaken for broomsticks, while her face appeared spotted and wrinkled like a bad piece of fruit.

Jerad tapped his knuckles on the glass.

The woman's eyes burst open, glowing blue pupils meeting his. The haze shifted around the room and disappeared into the walls. "What is it, my love?"

He smiled. "Everything is going according to plan. I just want to see your beautiful face once more before I turn in for the night."

She smiled, flashing bright white teeth against her pale complexion. "Did you destroy the diary?"

"Yes. The little wench started remembering things."

The woman shook her head slowly. "Do not worry. The rhodenine will prevent her memory from coming back. Just make sure she keeps that little treasure around her neck."

"Yes, of course."

"You will also need to keep an eye on your helpers around the house. I suspect your maid and your cook are not all that they seem to be."

Jerad nodded, rubbing the patch of hair under his lip. "Yes. I've had my own suspicions about them."

"Very good."

He placed his hands on the gemstone cresting the cane and looked at her with anxious eyes. "Are you almost healed, my love?"

She nodded slowly. "Soon. Very soon. A little more time is all I need to get back to my original self and be at your side."

"I love you."

"I know, Jerad. I know. Soon, you and I will have that book in our hands, and we will destroy Anaisha with it, just as I helped destroy Earth."

"Yes." He stroked his chin. "Earth." He placed his palm

on the glass, the cold surface relieving his sweaty palms. He always got nervous around her.

She slowly raised her arm, placing her own palm on the glass to mimic his. "Soon, my love. You and I will be together. When I am at full health, I will lead my great army across the land to destroy the life on this wretched planet once and for all."

"Soon." He removed his palm and turned, walking back toward the stairs as the blue mist reappeared in his wake.

20
Breakfast Of Champions

D avid, Veronica and Kimberly sat in Charlie's Diner, exhausted from the night's activities. They had driven for a almost three hours to get out of the vicinity of the hospital only to end up in a small dump of a town that had no more than a gas station, a rundown thrift store, a train station and this diner.

Luckily, the thrift store carried jeans, T-shirts, hoodies and sneakers for David and Kimberly to change into, seeing how hospital gowns were not the current trend in fashion. Even Veronica had changed into jeans, sneakers and a purple hoodie, trading out the sophisticated look of her slacks and turtleneck.

There weren't many safe spots in this section of the region, but Veronica had managed to steer them clear of unsafe areas she apparently knew about. Old, abandoned business towers and dilapidated apartments with a resident here or there surrounded the diner. David was sure that other people occupied the business towers, but he had no reason to wonder about that any further. The goal was to rest briefly and then move on toward South Ryshard.

Kimberly slept on her side in the booth across from David and Veronica, the sleeping pills she had received at the hospital still working through her system.

"What's our next step?" David asked before taking a sip of his coffee. The air outside was cold enough to freeze Old Man Winter himself. David just wanted to snuggle under warm covers somewhere and sleep until he woke and realized this whole mess was just a bad dream brought on by some spoiled meat he ate at Bravo's Burgers.

Veronica's eyes wandered around the diner, no doubt searching for any trouble that may want to brew around them. "We should head south to the ocean. We can take a passenger ship from there to South Ryshard."

David scratched an itch on his cheek and found the patch still there, covering his wounds. He pulled the corner away from the skin and peeled the bandage off his face. The underside had five lines of red running parallel to each other. He rolled up the bandage and flicked it underneath the table.

Veronica grimaced. "Hey! That hit my leg."

David frowned. "Sorry."

"It's okay." Veronica turned to look out the window.

"I'm beginning to think this is a hopeless cause. I mean, maybe this whole thing is just stupid. I've been shot, Kimberly's almost been killed a half dozen times and, well, I don't know. I don't even know what I'm saying, what I'm doing." He set his forehead on the cold laminate of the table and sighed.

"It's only stupid if you think it is, David."

He looked over at Veronica, who still stared out the

window. He caught a glimpse of the corner of her eye, and at that angle, he saw a depth in it, as if she was retelling herself a story about these streets, maybe one of their adventures together. But was there something deeper, something she wasn't telling him?

Veronica broke from her retrospect and turned her gaze toward David. "I think we've come too far to go back now."

"I just think maybe this isn't meant to be." He leaned his elbows on the edge of the table and dropped his face in his hands. A sharp pain in his shoulder caused him to lean back against the plastic seat of the booth. The pain shifted to soreness.

"Why do you think that? Just because we're running into trouble around every corner?"

David nodded.

"You don't think some things are worth fighting for? Is Carrie worth fighting for?"

He sighed. "Of course she's worth fighting for. But every step we take forward, we get knocked back two. The law is after us, some creature is on the loose in Lysallis, and we have a pair of cops out to kill us."

A glimmer arose in Veronica's eyes. "We're only hours from the coast. From there, it's a short journey to South Ryshard. Then just hours to Carrie. Hours. Are you telling me you want to head back now? It's a more difficult journey home than it is to Carrie—especially with the law chasing us."

David leaned his elbows on the table again, careful of the shoulder wound, trying to maneuver into a comfortable position that would cause him the least amount of pain.

Veronica went back to staring out the window. The building across from the diner gave David an eerie feeling, the way it rose into the darkness above them, the windows filled with tattered curtains, like eyes from a sinister entity.

David glanced down at his plate of half-eaten pancakes. "What if we don't make it to the wedding on time? What if I get there and make a fool of myself for nothing? What if she really is in love with Jerad? What if—"

"What if we don't? What if you do? What if she is?"

David fell silent, caught off guard by Veronica's blunt reply.

She regained the seriousness in her eyes as she stared at the alley across the way.

"If we get to the end of this road and it's all for nothing,… I don't know what I'll do."

"Yes you do. If things don't work out, we'll go back to Lysallis, satisfied that we at least tried."

"I don't know if I can do that."

Veronica turned to him, disappointment in her eyes. He hadn't seen her disappointed in a long time, not the girl who always seemed to look at the bright side of things. "You've changed, David. For the worst. You haven't been yourself since they shut down the LZR Project or since Carrie left. I remember your reckless days, when you ran after right and wrong without a second thought of the consequences or the outcome. That was one of your strengths."

It pained him to hear her use the word "was," as if that was a facet of his character that he no longer possessed. He had changed, and not into something he was particularly proud of. Recklessness had been his partner, his brother at one point. Now, he held back, afraid of what might or might not happen. Hesitancy had become his sister, and she was becoming a burden on him.

He turned his attention toward the television hanging in the corner on the other side of the room.

"*Coming soon to theaters across Anaisha:* Super Spy 3: The Coming Apocalypse. *When we last saw Secret Agent Timothy Philips, he destroyed the evil robot army of Arbitrons. What he didn't know was that his arch-nemesis, Mr. Vile, escaped the maximum-security prison with a plan to destroy all of planet Niox. Now, in the third installment of the* Super Spy *series, Agent Philips must stop Mr. Vile and his henchman before all of Niox is destroyed forever. In theaters November twentieth.*"

That's next Friday, David thought. *I wonder if I'll be able to see it with Carrie.* He pictured a nice quiet date, just the two of them. No crooked cops, no crazed farmers, no mythical creatures. He'd do the old stretch-and-yawn move to get his arm around her. *Yeah, that would be nice.*

The bell above the front door clanged as David and Veronica turned to see a thin woman with bright pink hair enter the diner. She carried an unsteady gait, one that caused her to stumble slightly, but she caught herself before colliding into one of the tables.

"I don't like the looks of this," Veronica whispered.

The woman leaned against a table and scanned the diner, her gaze falling on David.

"Why is she staring at me?"

Veronica took a sip of her tea. "Don't know. She's quite a colorful one, isn't she? Turquoise-colored eyes, pink hair. She looks pretty beat up, though."

"Are her clothes burned?"

Veronica nodded. "Sure looks that way."

The woman stumbled toward their table, taking a seat at the

end of the booth Kimberly lay across. "I found you. Finally."

Her soft voice made its way through David's memory. He pointed his finger at her, but before he could say anything, she nodded and put her finger to her bright pink lips, motioning for him to keep it down. "I was the one at your apartment that night. I was the one who helped you out of the cuffs in the hospital."

"Yes," David replied. "Yes, I recognize your voice."

She smiled. "I'm glad you're both okay." She glanced down at Kimberly. "Is she all right?"

Veronica took another sip of her solaris tea, her eyes scrutinizing Turquoise. "She'll live."

The woman nodded. "Of course." She turned back to David and Veronica. "I'm Turquoise. I've been following you three since Lysallis."

"Why?" Veronica asked.

"It's a long story."

"Did you kill that thing back at my apartment?" David felt somewhat hopeful.

Turquoise stared at him for a moment, saying nothing. He swore he saw her lips trembling but then realized the caffeine from his coffee had started to kick in.

"He's dead," Turquoise whispered. "I killed him."

"What about my apartment?"

Turquoise shook her head. "Not much left."

David slapped his palms down on the table, rattling the salt and pepper shakers. "Great! Now I have nothing to go back to."

"Well," Turquoise reached into her satchel and pulled out a necklace, handing it to him, "you have something."

David took the silver chain, letting the black crescent moon dangle in front of him. "The necklace?"

238

Turquoise nodded. "I thought you might want it."

"What about your friend?" Veronica asked, taking another sip of tea.

Turquoise shook her head. "He didn't make it."

David set the necklace on the table, staring at it. "I'm sorry."

"Somehow, I knew it was coming. He'll be missed, but I refuse to let his death be in vain."

Silence fell across the table like thick fog. David shifted uncomfortably in his seat. The soreness in his shoulder had spread to his back.

Turquoise reached into her satchel and pulled out what looked like a piece of crystal and set it down on the table in the middle of them. "This is what I've been fighting for. This is why my partner and I were after the creature at your apartment, the hybrid."

David reached out and picked up the clear object, holding it in his palm. It felt significantly heavier than it looked, and inside, he could see an emerald core that reminded him of Carrie's eyes. Gazing deeper, he realized that the emerald was actually a small clock. Different angles of the outer shell transformed the light it reflected into varying shades of blue, purple and red.

He suddenly comprehended everything Veronica had been telling him. Emotion stirred within him while he stared at the emerald there in the center of this strange device. In that emerald, in Carrie's eyes, he saw the future he desired. Marriage to the woman he loved, the woman he had always loved. Her embrace held compassion, undying love, unsurpassed beauty— and it was all his to fight for. His to obtain. As if looking straight into Carrie's eyes, the emerald seemed to cry out to him, pleading with him to love her with everything he had, everything he was and was going to be.

"That," Turquoise said, pointing to the crystal, "is what this whole mess is about."

Veronica took the item from David's hand and examined it closely. She didn't show any signs of falling deep within it, like David had. She set it down on the table and took another sip of tea.

Turquoise picked up the crystal. "This is the key that will unlock Anaisha's future."

David rubbed his eyes, feeling the coffee buzz through his bloodstream. The caffeine woke him up some. "Anaisha's future?"

"Yes." Turquoise set the crystal on the table again, very gently, as one does when they are afraid to break something fragile. "The world is headed for disaster. I don't know all the details, but I do know the planet is in danger of falling into the hands of an evil force. This timepiece is the key to stopping that from happening."

"How so?" Veronica asked.

"I'm not sure. I just know it was the first step in my mission."

"And the next step?"

Turquoise looked at Veronica, hesitating to say anything more. David felt the coffee buzzing through him full-blast. His mind awakened, but his body still wanted to sleep, to slumber there at the table while Turquoise and Veronica talked into the night.

Turquoise looked at David when she spoke. "The wedding you're on your way to stop? Well, that's my second goal. To stop the wedding of Carrie Green and Jerad Montlier."

"Why?" David asked, sitting up in the seat.

"I don't know exactly. I've just been told the main objectives, not the details."

"Who do you work for?" Veronica asked, finishing her tea. She looked on Turquoise, her eyes full of suspicion. David couldn't blame her. She tended to be suspicious of anyone new, but that was because of all the times in the past she hadn't been and paid the consequences.

"I work for an agency that sent me out to retrieve and protect this timepiece. I learned a few days ago that Kimberly and her uncle were targets because they had it. Cloud, Trinistar and I were assigned to find her, protect her and obtain the timepiece. But things ended up getting a lot more complicated than that. I was instructed that after finding the timepiece, I needed to move on to step two, which is to stop the wedding. As fates would collide, you are on your way to do the same."

"But you don't know why?" David asked with some anxiety in his voice.

Turquoise shook her head. "No, David, I don't. If I did, you would be the one I would tell. I was thinking...maybe we can team up together, since we're all after the same thing. Help each other out."

The more help, the better. David glanced at Veronica, who stared out the window again. Since she posed no objection to Turquoise's proposal, he nodded to Turquoise. "Okay."

Turquoise grinned, leaning back in the seat while exhaling a long sigh of relief. "Good. I think we can do this if we do it together."

Veronica turned from the window and glanced into her empty tea cup.

Turquoise glanced down at Kimberly again. "Are you sure she's going to be all right?"

Veronica looked up. "She's been through a lot in the past couple days. I don't know how much more she can take in the state she's in, but she's alive. As soon as those sleeping pills exit her system, she should be good as new—well, as good as when we crossed paths with her."

"Poor girl. None of this should have happened to her."

Veronica picked up the timepiece, examining it again. "What does this do? There's a clock in the center and three small holes around the top of it."

"I'm not sure. Cloud was my team leader, so only he knew the details of our mission. And even he only received limited information.

"Hmm."

A blonde-haired waitress approached the table, taking the plates while gawking down at the crystal timepiece. "Can I get you guys anything else?" Shades of red blush highlighted her cheeks while a thick frosting of pale foundation covered the rest of her face.

Veronica glanced into the empty tea cup again, debating if she wanted more. "I'm good," she answered, sliding the cup to the waitress.

"If you need anything, just ask. I'll have your check for you in a few minutes."

"Do you know where the closest hotel is?" Turquoise asked.

"Well, the one we had in town burned down a few months ago. The next one is about fifteen miles north of here."

"That won't work," Turquoise mumbled.

David fought to keep his eyes open, his body and mind

warring against each other. He didn't care where they slept. As long as he could rest, he could pull himself together.

"We need to rest here, in this town," Veronica replied. "I don't care if we have to sleep at this table, but we can't go any farther without some rest."

"Well, the owner of the diner is out of town for a few days. He's got a room in the back with a few beds that he uses for himself and any friends that pass through. I could let you stay there 'til morning, 'til the next shift comes in."

"That would be great," Veronica said.

"You guys just have to be out by nine tomorrow morning."

"Fine with us," Turquoise agreed.

"Great, I'll run these dishes to the back and get you settled in. The only people here are me and the cook. I don't want anyone on the next shift knowing I let you stay here. I could get fired for it. And this being one of the only places in town to work, that wouldn't be a good thing." She left to the back.

"Poor girl," Turquoise whispered.

"What do you mean?" Veronica inquired.

David turned toward the television again. An infomercial for a liquid solution that could weld metal together played on the set.

"She's been abused," Turquoise explained, her eyes on the path the waitress took to the back. "Probably by her husband or boyfriend."

"Abused?" Veronica asked. "Like physically?"

Turquoise nodded. "She has bruises along her wrist from someone grabbing it. She also has a small trace of a bruise under her eye that she's tried to cover up with makeup. Not to mention the nail marks in the side of her neck from someone trying to choke her."

Veronica's eyes widened. "Wow!"

"The Sector trained me to observe the smallest of details. I guess I do it now without even trying. I feel somewhat sorry for her, being stuck in this town with an abusive partner. I don't know how people live like that."

Veronica stared out the window again. "I guess fear just takes hold, and people sink in it like quicksand."

"Yeah, fear. I guess fear gets to people in different ways."

David watched the wind whip stray newspapers around the dark street outside.

"It does," Veronica said. "It's a part of life, though. Overcome your fear to get to the next goal."

"Or the next mission," Turquoise added.

Silence fell among them. David took another glimpse at the television, the host spraying the miraculous liquid on two pieces of touching metal. The metal melted just enough to meld the two pieces together. He remembered seeing something like that so long ago. His mind slowed, and he felt his eyes close, darkness engulfing him for the night.

21

Bounties & Badges

Agent Parks and Officer Sandra Meldramine pulled into the parking lot of Charlie's Diner just before sunrise. Parks pulled his pistol from the holster under his arm and double-checked the ammo inside the clip. He then began to pet the gun, as if it were a live animal resting in his hand. "I really hope we find those brats in this town. I have to find that necklace before someone else gets their hands on it."

"Look, can we avoid making a scene here?" Sandra pleaded. "This town is not one of my favorites."

Parks stopped stroking the gun and turned his face to her, the lighting from the Charlie's Diner sign casting a red glow on his cheeks and forehead. "We're going to find those teens."

"I know," Sandra said. She sighed softly, hoping Parks wouldn't catch on to her attitude. She was growing tired of his increasing obsession with David and his friends. "I just don't see what's so important about this necklace."

"You don't need to know why the necklace is important.

Your job is to help me get it. And we do that by finding those teens and squeezing the information out of them. Even if it means killing David."

Sandra shuddered at the thought. It was one thing to intimidate, another thing completely to kill someone. She could kill a criminal who endangered her life or someone else's, but not a group of teens. Sandra glanced down at her watch, checking the time by the red glow of the sign. The sun would be rising soon, and with it, a new day. "If you kill David, you'll never find the necklace."

"I'm getting that necklace one way or another. If he gets in the way, that's just his tough luck. He's not going to have the last laugh by escaping my custody three times in a row."

Sandra peered through the diner window. Inside, the waitress lay back in one of the booths, resting. "There doesn't seem to be anyone here but the waitress and maybe a cook."

"We'll see about that." Parks opened the car door. "Let's go."

Sandra followed him into the diner.

The waitress slowly got to her feet, pulling her blonde bangs from her eyes. "Good morning." She turned toward Parks and Sandra, and her eyes suddenly widened with a look of fear. "Ruinstar?"

"Trixie," Parks groaned. "Long time, no see."

The waitress stepped back toward the counter, rubbing her wrist. "That's not my name anymore. I go by Brook now. How did you find me?"

"I wasn't looking for you, but it's nice to know this is where you work now."

Sandra noticed the waitress trembling and figured she had at one point been Parks' punching bag. "How do you two know each other?"

"Well," Parks frowned, "we were a couple once. Now I don't know what we are." He moved closer to Brook, her body trembling worse with each step he took toward her. He reached out and grabbed her bangs, running her hair through his fingers. Brook's head twitched in reaction.

Parks let go of her hair, a hurt look in his eyes. "What's the matter? Are you afraid of me? I thought we were happy together, Trixie. Why are you scared of me?"

He went to grab her hair again, but Brook slid back along the counter, out of his reach. "I…" She took a deep breath, but couldn't seem to get any words out.

"Can we find out about the necklace and get moving with this please?" Sandra asked.

Parks nodded. "Very well. Listen, Trixie, did a group of teenagers come through this diner at all?"

She hesitated, then shook her head and frowned. "No."

"No?" He drew closer to her, his hand moving toward the gun under his arm. "Are you sure about that?"

Brook moved along the counter a few more feet. Sandra noticed a pie case at the end of the counter, a knife gleaming under the glass dome. She wondered if that's what Brook was moving toward. If that was the case, Sandra would let the waitress get her hands on the weapon, give her a fair chance to use it against Parks.

***

Turquoise stood silently behind a wall in the kitchen, observing the scene in the dining room. As much as she wanted to intervene, she didn't want to reveal her presence unless she had to. The waitress had helped her and the teens, and for that, Turquoise would make sure nothing happened to her. But Turquoise wasn't confident about going up against the crooked agent unless absolutely necessary.

"Now, now, Trixie," Agent Parks coddled. "I want you to answer my question, and this time, I want you to tell me the truth."

Brook reached the end of the counter and shoved her hand underneath the glass dome, pulling out the knife. She swung it in front of her, the silver glare flickering light across Parks' face as he leapt backward.

"Whoa, Trixie!" He put his hands up. "I'm not the enemy here, those kids are. Now, just tell me where they went before someone gets hurt."

Brook jabbed the knife toward him, slashing the air in front of him in an X motion. "You stay away from me!"

"Oh, no," Turquoise whispered as she snuck through the kitchen. Her mind immediately registered that the cook was missing. She told herself he was probably outside smoking or asleep somewhere in the building, ignoring the facts she knew to be true—the cook wasn't a smoker, nor was there anywhere else to sleep in the building other than the small room she had come from and the dining room.

Turquoise was about to charge out of the kitchen area and attack Agent Parks when she felt a cold piece of flat metal press against the back of her neck.

"Don't move, Turquoise. I'm not here to kill you, but I will if I'm forced to." The rough voice tumbled into her ears, freezing her in her tracks. She stood close to the stoves, her eyes able to see over the appliances through to the dining room. Brook continued swinging the blade at Parks while Sandra stood, doing almost nothing to stop the situation.

"Who are you?" Turquoise whispered.

"I'm no one important."

Turquoise felt the hand reach to her hip and rifle through her satchel. She went to turn but couldn't. Her limbs suddenly went numb, her legs giving out underneath her as she collapsed to the floor. Her cheek hit the tile hard, mashing her teeth into her tongue. She tasted blood. Her face froze, her eyes staring at the blue cabinets in front of her.

"The front of my gun barrel is coated with antractat. You're paralyzed, temporarily. Long enough for me to inspect this timepiece of yours to make sure it's real."

Turquoise paid close attention to the situation in the other room, even though she was fighting her own battle, trying her hardest not to panic.

"So are you going to tell us where the kids are?" Parks asked.

"No!" Brook screamed. Turquoise heard a scuffle but couldn't be sure of what was happening.

"Stay down, Trixie! Lick the floor for all I care, just stay down while I decide where to put the bullet."

"Parks!" Sandra shouted.

"Don't worry about the waitress." The voice above Turquoise sounded almost compassionate, but she knew better than to trust her first impressions about someone she didn't know. Two soft whizzing sounds coasted over her, and then silence filled the dining room.

Minutes passed, and Turquoise felt more and more uneasy, unsure whether her attacker had plans to kill her. She allowed herself to remember Trinistar and Cloud, even her short interaction last night with David and Veronica. These were people she enjoyed meeting, enjoyed allowing into her life, and if things were going to end now, like this—without even giving her a chance to defend herself—then she would accept it as best she could. She had done her best, had given her all. Obtained the timepiece, destroyed the demon hybrid. Those were high marks on her career, but she was most proud of keeping Kimberly safe up to this point.

"This is a fake? I don't believe it." The stranger picked Turquoise's limp body up and pressed her against the wall, holding her there.

She came face to face with her captor and immediately recognized him. His long, black trench coat, short black hair and five-o'clock shadow…Drather. He was a mercenary and a bounty hunter, one of the most successful and notorious in the land. She had heard a few stories about him, none of them really all that believable. She wondered if the scar running down the side of his neck was really from taking down a hydra beast.

Knowing that he spent his time looking for the timepiece only proved to her how valuable it really was.

His brown-eyed gaze retained her turquoise stare as he held up the small crystal with one hand while pinning her against the wall with the other. Her legs buckled, but he had her pinned. She felt the weight of her body working with gravity to pull her back to the floor.

"This," he started, "is a fake. How do I know? Well, the words 'Made in Mecca' are engraved on the bottom of the emerald clock inside it, something you obviously didn't notice. Losing your touch?"

As much as she wanted to answer him, she couldn't. Her lips refused to move, and drool leaked out the corner of her mouth.

"Guess this is going to get more interesting. I don't really have time for all of this, but I guess it's just a career pitfall, huh?" Drather tossed the crystal to the floor. It shattered, pieces scattering across the kitchen tile. He glanced at the large gash above Turquoise's eye. "Nasty wound. I'm assuming you finally killed that disgusting thing?" He grinned again, this time as if he was happy with her progress thus far. "About time."

He leaned over and grabbed her waist, slinging her over his shoulder.

A fake? How can it be a fake? There's no way. I killed Thana for it. I didn't go through all of that for nothing, did I? Fear surged through her. She couldn't move, couldn't speak, couldn't escape. Her body just hung over Drather's shoulder like a helpless ragdoll. *What is he going to do with me?*

Drather carried her to the small room and flipped the light switch on. The beds were empty, of course.

"You got them out earlier, didn't you?" He sighed as he walked through the kitchen and into the dining room. Turquoise saw Brook sitting in a booth, hiding her face with her hands. The bodies of Parks and Sandra lay unconscious on the floor.

"You're smart, Turquoise, I'll give you that. You better hope I find those kids, and then you better hope they have the real timepiece. 'Cause if they don't, they'll be finding themselves another Wedge to protect them." He walked out of the diner with her over his shoulder.

Drather stopped and glanced down at the police cruiser in the parking lot. "We don't want them getting to the teens before I can, do we?"

251

22 Lost & Found

C arrie lay in bed, staring at the ceiling. *Today's Thursday. The day after tomorrow is the wedding.* She hadn't slept well at all. The night riddled her mind with doubts about her soon-to-be husband. She rolled onto her side and stared at the clock for a long while, her brain trying to register the numbers her eyes saw. It was almost seven in the morning. *Jerad's still sleeping, if he's even here.*

She slid out of bed, smoothing her red silk nightgown in places it had bunched up while she slumbered. She crept to the doorway and peered into the hallway. *Deserted.* She snuck slowly and silently across the tile, making her way to the living area. She found the house silent and still, giving her more time by herself, more time to unlock the mysteries surrounding her lost memory.

Carrie approached the fireplace and sat in front of it, crossing her legs on the carpet. She wondered what she expected to find. The fire had to have decimated the diary—she saw the fire destroy the small book with her own eyes.

But she felt drawn to the fireplace, had even dreamed of it during what precious time she had slept last night.

She slid apart the metal curtains guarding the fireplace and gazed in at the mountain of white ash. No sign of the book on the surface. She reached her hands into the fire pit and shuffled through the ash, hoping to find something salvageable, maybe the book's spine or a piece of the cover. Something—she didn't care what. A piece of the diary equaled a piece of her past.

Her hand came across a chunk of debris. She pulled it out, white ashes scattering around her as she set the item on her lap. It was the core of the book, the diary itself, still intact somehow, the cover charred and pieces of the spine gone. Her gold name had turned black. Opening what remained of the book, she found curled paper fragments burned and beyond recognition. She could have sworn she witnessed the destruction of this last night. But here, on her lap, sat the diary. At least part of it.

As she flipped through the brittle book, she stumbled across a brilliant white page, unmarred by the fire. No burn marks, no charring around the edges. *Strange,* she thought. She managed to find a few other unscathed pages like that in the diary, causing her to question what she actually witnessed last night.

Carrie started reading in chronological order:

Wednesday, October 14, 1992
Dear Diary,

Today David, Veronica and I returned from Solaris Island. We went there looking for treasure, but we got stranded in the middle of the island and it took us a while to find our way to the shore.

I'll admit it was beautiful. My feet are sore, though, and I think something really nasty bit me in the leg because I have a bruise the size of my fist. The nights were chilly there, but the days were breezy and somewhat warm. We had to eat coconuts that David picked from the trees. It's so funny every time I think about it, but David was climbing this one tree and as soon as he got to the top, he lost his balance and fell. He's okay, but a little sore.

The very best part of the whole trip, though, was the dolphins. I got to play with dolphins! It was so cool. David found a group of them hanging around the shore, and he called me over because he knows I love dolphins. We petted them, and then they played with us a little in the water before swimming away together.

I hope I never forget that for as long as I live. Is there another man out there who would share a special moment like that with me?

Anyway, we ended up finding the treasure…after a couple days of wandering the island. There wasn't much of anything but a strange necklace. It was just a little black capsule-looking thing with a green neon line glowing around it. It hung from a silver chain—a pretty cheesy-looking silver chain. I don't know how the green line glows without a battery. When we got off the island, we put the necklace somewhere safe, at least until we can find out how much it's worth. It could be from an ancient civilization that used to live on that island!

David is my Prince Charming. I can't stop thinking about him! I think I'm falling for him more and more every day I spend with him. My mom didn't appreciate the fact that I was missing for a few days. I guess a good portion of Lysallis was looking for us. My mom told me I wouldn't have gone missing if I wasn't hanging around David.

Whatever. Little does she know, I wasn't in any hurry to get home. The island was nice while it lasted.

Goodnight Diary. And sweet dreams—of David :)

Thursday, December 3, 1992

Dear Diary,

Today we went to Professor Grey's house to show him the necklace we found on Solaris Island. He checked it out and said that it contained a mineral in it called rhodenine. (I think I spelled that right). He says the capsule can cause the person wearing it to lose their memory. Creepy. I'm glad none of us wore the necklace. I can only imagine what would happen if David or Veronica had put it on. Would David actually forget about me? I don't really want to think about that.

We decided to let Professor Grey keep the necklace for his experiments.

Goodnight Diary.

Carrie stared down at the page for a moment, her thoughts racing like a bullet train through her head. She stood to her feet and paced the living area a few times before finally taking a seat on the couch. She grasped the necklace, pondering what she just read. It was a gift from Jerad. *This can't be the same necklace. Just coincidence.*

She read the last salvageable entry:

Saturday, December 26, 1992

Dear Diary,

This has been a horrible week. We found out that a few nights ago, the necklace we had given to Professor Grey was stolen. Professor Grey's brother and his wife were murdered. I can't believe that little necklace would draw so much evil. Nobody is sure who did it, but Professor Grey is pretty shaken up. He won't speak to anyone. I feel so bad for him.

I am tired, Diary. It's pretty late, and David and Veronica are coming over for lunch tomorrow so we can all figure out how to help

Professor Grey.

Goodnight, Diary…

Carrie shut the book and tossed it at the fireplace. It managed to make it into the fire pit, causing ashes to spin up and land around the carpet. Carrie turned and gazed out the window at the swimming pool outside. She rubbed the necklace in her hand, wrestling with the truth of the matter.

If the diary really was hers, then all the pieces had finally come together. She had no memory of her past because of the necklace. Jerad had given her the necklace, and he was constantly becoming more guarded about her unveiling her past. *But why would Jerad want me to lose my memory? Isn't he in love with me, or is it all a front? A front for what?*

Sadly, she realized she had no way of telling if the diary was really hers or if the writings within it were really true.

She glanced down at the black cylinder hanging from her neck. She determined she *could* test if the diary was real, if what was written was really history that she had been tricked into forgetting. Carrie reached to the back of her neck and unclasped the necklace. She let it slide down her nightgown and fall into her lap.

Staring at it, she concluded if Jerad found out—if he did indeed have wicked plans—he might hurt her. *Well,* she thought, *he can try. But I have to risk it, have to confirm once and for all.*

Carrie picked up the necklace from her lap and shoved it into the couch cushions.

A door slammed shut in the main hallway. *Belgar? Jerad? The maid?*

Feet slapped across the tile, and Belgar entered the living

area, dressed in a black robe. "Carrie? What are you doing up this early?" He rubbed sleep from his eyes and let out a rumbling yawn.

Carrie wondered if she could trust Belgar with what she had found. She decided to keep it to herself. "I was going to check Jerad's stock, see how many points it's risen since yesterday."

"Well, I can make you some breakfast if you'd like." He smiled warmly and then turned toward the fireplace, noticing the ashes all over the carpet. "Looks like we'll have to get the maid in here to clean up this mess."

"Actually, I think I'm going to head back to bed. I didn't sleep well last night, and I need my rest."

Belgar glared at her for a moment. Carrie expected him to say something about his suspicions, but instead he nodded. "Oh yes," he said, "I understand. Get your rest. If you require anything, dear Carrie, I am a beckon away."

Carrie smiled and went to her room, closing the door behind her. She stared at the bed, her mind racing. *What if Belgar is in on it too? What about the maid? Ah, stop jumping to conclusions!*

Carrie settled under the sheets, closed her eyes and let her mind reveal the truth in everything.

23 Windmills

*T*wo coffins.

"It's okay, Kimberly, it's okay to cry. Let it all out."

His soft voice eased her pain a little. She looked up to find Uncle Grey in a black suit, looking down on her with a mournful countenance. She turned back to watch the two brown coffins lower into the ground, their surfaces littered with roses, pictures and trinkets.

Tears streamed down her face like drops of dew down the side of a vase. She clasped her hand over her chest and took a deep, pulsing breath. She felt Uncle Grey's hand rest on her shoulder as the crowds of people surrounding the burial hole blurred in her watered vision.

Kimberly wiped the tears from her eyes, pain crashing against her heart like ocean waves. Why did her parents have to die? Why did they have to leave this world so soon, when she had so many questions? They never told her what would happen if they died. They never told her who she could trust.

Uncle Grey knelt to her eye level as the coffins disappeared into the ground behind him. "Listen, Kim." His warm eyes beckoned her from behind his spectacles. "Mommy and Daddy are gone, but that doesn't mean you are. They wanted the absolute best for you, sweetie. I can't promise you that I can give you their best, but I do promise I'll give you mine."

A steam train's whistle screeched through Kimberly's dreams like a scream she couldn't silence, starting slowly and rising higher and higher until the sound disappeared.

"Ahh!" She jolted awake, gasping for air.

David turned abruptly. "You okay?"

His voice coaxed her back to reality. She took a moment to gather her surroundings. She found herself in a seat between David and Veronica on what she figured was a train. She turned and nodded to David and then leaned back in her seat, sighing with relief. David's face was refreshing, especially after the nightmares she had crawled out of.

"I feel...sick." She rubbed her upset stomach and turned to her right to see Veronica fast asleep. "Where are we?"

"On a train headed south to the shore. We narrowly escaped the diner and managed to outrun that crooked cop and his insane partner. Don't worry, though, we're safe here." He shifted in his seat, moving his arm into a more comfortable position.

"Diner? How long have I been out?"

"Since last night. When we left the hospital, you passed out in the car and haven't really woken up since. Parks and that woman cop showed up at the diner, so Turquoise woke us up and got us out of there."

"Turquoise?"

"I think it would be best if you just relaxed. We're going to be on this train for a while." David closed his eyes.

Kimberly looked around the cabin, relieved to see only the three of them in the small section of the train. She wanted to be far away from everyone but her friends, at least until she could get her mind straight.

She turned and glanced out the window to the left of David. The brown and green hills raced past them while the bluish sky hung overhead. "Hey, David?"

He opened his eyes, and she could see hints of tiredness and irritation in them. "Yeah?"

She knew she should probably leave him alone. He had already saved her life on more than one occasion, and he probably needed his rest. "Never mind."

David sat up in his seat. "What is it?"

"I just…I just wanted to know why I've been out so long."

"The crooked cop drugged you with sleeping pills back at the hospital."

"The last thing I remember…that police woman was holding my mouth open while that guy shoved pills down my throat."

"If he had stuck any more in there, you'd be dead right now."

"Oh."

David closed his eyes again, settling his arms on the armrests and wiggling his nose as if it itched.

Kimberly studied a poster on the wall in front of her, a picture of an Anaishan Sentry pointing at her with the blue-and-green-striped Anaishan flag behind him, the words "Here for your safety and protection" printed in large font underneath.

"Is that…that creature dead?"

"Yes."

Finally, she thought. *That thing won't be chasing me anymore.* "Thank you. Thank you for not leaving me behind."

"I would never leave you behind."

"I don't understand."

David sighed, opening his eyes again, clearly irritated, probably from the lack of sleep.

"I just…" Kimberly didn't know why she was so talkative all of a sudden. She wanted to let David sleep, but now that she had slept, had trudged through her nightmares, outlived that horrible monster, she wanted to converse with someone. "I don't know why you and Veronica would stick your necks out to save me."

She thought she saw David smile briefly. "It's what we do."

"Nobody has ever shown that much concern for me. Nobody but my uncle, anyway."

Silence fell between them for what felt like slow-moving hours. Kimberly noticed David gazing out the window of the train.

"My parents were murdered when I was younger. After that, my uncle took me in, and we lived together until he was killed the other night. Since my parents' death, I haven't been able to connect to anyone. I haven't had any friends. I don't trust people…know what I mean? How can I? Everyone I love is killed, so why would I want to pull anyone else around me? Just so they can die too?"

David continued to stare out the window. At first, Kimberly wondered if he was even listening to her, but then he turned his head so his right eye was staring at her.

"I'm sorry for your loss. I've lost people I loved, all in the name of justice. I don't know how to console you, because I've never lost my parents. My uncle passed away a couple years ago from alcoholism. Beyond that, I manage to get close to those who hurt me. Traitors have been in my midst, enemies in my arms. But that's life." David turned to look out the window again. His words seemed to linger in the air for Kimberly to review. They were powerful, they were a part of him, and she realized he had shared in her pain at some point or another, even if his parents were still alive.

"I've been running from everyone and everything for so long now. I don't think I can run much longer."

"Well…" David said, still gazing out the window. Kimberly caught sight of a rickety windmill in the distance. "Whatever we face now, we all face together."

She felt grateful for his honest, open friendship. But she wondered, feared really, if and when the time came for her to face whatever was chasing her, if David, Veronica or anyone else would really be able to save her.

24 Determined

Turquoise sprawled across the backseat of Drather's car, motionless but awake, while he drove them south on the highway. She kept her eyes closed, concentrating on everything around her. The sounds outside—the rustling of the weeds, arguing from shacks they drove past, the wind howling with anger at the evil that was leaking into their world. The scent of manure, the feel of the heater blowing on her from the front vents.

She tried her best to reach out mentally to the teens, but the throbbing pain in her forehead prevented her from focusing her power to that high of a degree. So instead, she worked on trying to move her hands. The poison Drather had injected in her was strong, but she had no idea how long it was meant to last.

"I think it's fair that you know what you're getting into. That timepiece is the most sought-after object in Anaisha right now. Whoever has it is supposedly one step closer to world domination. I know, I know. Sounds a bit cliché. And it is. I doubt it has that much power. But what is one man's—

or woman's—treasure is another's junk. I may not care about the timepiece—what it is anyway—but I do care about how much it's worth to others."

Turquoise sensed they passed a grocery store, run down by the years in North Ryshard. She wondered if Drather might stop to get her food or drink. She felt incredibly thirsty, though she figured that was an effect from the poison.

"I admire your tenacity," Drather said. "I even admire your soft spot for the kids. But I think you should leave this timepiece business to the professionals. You were hired to find it and protect it. Others are after it for their own reasons. My reason? Credits. That's all I care about. You're in it for the world. You're a wannabe savior, and as respectable a title as that may be, it's not realistic.

"I'm going to get that timepiece from the kids. Then I'll be on my way. You don't need to follow me. You just let me do what I do best, and you'll live to see another day. I get my credits, you get your freedom and the teens go back to their humdrum lives, filling in the gaps with college, parties and meaningless relationships."

Turquoise didn't know why Drather thought the teens had the timepiece. She had no way to argue with him over it either, not that he'd believe her. She just had to focus on staying calm until she saw her opportunity to escape.

She felt the car slow.

"Looks like we're just in time," Drather remarked as he pulled into the parking lot of a train station.

Turquoise closed her eyes and focused all of her energy into her hands, trying to make them move at least a little bit. Her fingers started to twitch…then her wrist. The motion slowly returned to her limbs as she flung her now movable arms toward her satchel. She wriggled her hand into it, grabbing hold of a vial she had put into the bag for an emergency such as this.

"Now," Drather said as he opened his door, "you stay put. I'll be back shortly." He left the car, not even bothering to check on her condition. Turquoise wondered if that was a side effect of his ego or if he simply underestimated her abilities.

She slipped the small vial full of white liquid from her satchel and fumbled with it for a few moments before finally managing to get the cap off, revealing a small needle protruding from the top of the opening. More feeling swept through her arms, allowing her to position the needle directly over the crease of her arm. She shoved the needle under her skin, the prick forcing a slight flinch.

As the healing elixir emptied into her bloodstream, Turquoise wished with all her might that she would be able to reach the teens in time. Whether or not they had the timepiece didn't matter at this point. Their survival was essential to the fate of Anaisha.

25

Shades of Gray

As the train pulled into the station, David continued to stare out the window. Part of him didn't want to leave the safety of the train. Part of him wanted to sleep, wanted to forget all of this. But he couldn't. Although he wanted to stop the wedding between Carrie and Jerad because of his love for Carrie, the fact that Turquoise had been assigned to stop the wedding only increased his resolve to do so. He had to get to South Ryshard. He had to put a stop to whatever was going on down there before Carrie did something she might ultimately regret.

"Who is that?" Kimberly asked, peeking over his shoulder out the window. Even though she didn't point, David already knew who she referred to. A man in a black trench coat stood on the edge of the platform, his eyes scanning the train exits.

"He doesn't look friendly," Veronica said from behind them.

"No, he doesn't," David agreed. "C'mon, let's get off the train, but make sure he doesn't see us."

Against his better judgment, Drather boarded the train. He presumed he would have seen the teens get off, but after the train had finished unloading its passengers, he waited and waited, with no sign of them. He realized they could have gotten off another way, but thought that unlikely. There weren't many exits they could have escaped through without him spotting them. The only conclusion he could draw, then, was they were still on the train.

He pulled a metallic card the size of an ID from the inside pocket of his trench coat. The front of the card was actually a small monitor showing a wire frame display of the train. He moved through the train, watching the card for small pink spots—people—but with no luck. Somehow, he had lost track of the teens and the timepiece.

Drather kicked a nearby seat and shoved the card back in his pocket. Cursing to himself, he pondered his next move. He still had Turquoise at his disposal, and dispose of her he would if need be. He couldn't care less about a single Wedge. He needed to finish this job and be on his way. He had been hired to destroy the timepiece, but how could he if he had no idea where it was?

This meant he had to go to Plan B.

He made his way to the end of the passenger car and opened the door that led to the engine. In order to accomplish Plan B, he knew he'd have to do away with all of the teens—especially David—before they had a chance to get in the way. He didn't like the idea of killing people unless he was forced to or unless it was necessary to accomplish his mission. He found this to be somewhat of an extenuating circumstance. He would get paid big credits for this job, and he needed them to continue funding his personal aspirations of vengeance.

"Train is leaving in three minutes," the loudspeakers blared.

Just enough time, Drather thought.

He reached into his coat and pulled out a small, circular, black disc. He hesitated, the splinters of his conscience that were still alive begging him not to do this. But he had to stick to his plan. To carry out Plan B, he had to do away with the teens here and now. He knew they had to be close—or hiding in the train somewhere that his tracker, which was known to be faulty on occasion, couldn't pick them up.

Drather pushed a button on top of the disc and stuck it on the coupling between the car and the engine. He turned his face away as the disc popped and the couplings separated, their ends nothing but melted steel. He pulled out a silver disc from his coat, turned the bezel halfway around the disc, and stuck it on the outside wall of the separated passenger car.

He glanced across the way to the platform and saw people boarding the train, others gathering to see their loved ones off on their journeys. Fighting his conscience, Drather pushed the button and leapt off the car, fleeing the coming disaster.

***

As soon as they saw Drather vanish from the train, Turquoise, Veronica, Kimberly and David stepped out from the awning that covered the main ticket booths and restrooms and onto the train platform. The train whistled loudly as giant puffs of steam curled out from beneath the engine.

David wondered where the black-clad man had disappeared to and what he was doing here in the first place. He meant to ask Turquoise, but she insisted they focus on steering clear from him until she could tell them his story at a later time.

"We need to go," Turquoise said.

The train started forward, but before the four of them turned to head out of the station, David noticed all of the cars separated from the rest of the train, left behind as the engine moved down the tracks.

"That can't be good," David whispered.

Turquoise saw the cars and grabbed David's hand. "We have to go. Now!" She pulled David toward the archway that led out to the dirt lot surrounding the station, Veronica and Kimberly following close behind.

As soon as they were a good distance from the station, David ripped his arm out of Turquoise's grip. "What is going on?! Why were those cars left behind?"

"Drather," Turquoise answered. "The guy in black. I think he put a bomb on one of those cars, to destroy the station and kill you guys. That was probably his intention to begin with—find the timepiece and kill you three."

"Bomb?" David turned to face the station. "All those people. We have to get them out of there!"

Turquoise grabbed his arm and yanked him in front of her. "Listen to me. We have to get out of here. That bomb was meant for you three. And if the bomb doesn't kill you— or if he doesn't think the bomb killed you—then he'll find another way to do so."

"We have to save them," David whispered.

Veronica put her hands on his shoulders, her hazel eyes pleading with him. "She's right, David. We have to get out of here. Our safety is what's important right now. We're the only ones who can help Turquoise stop that wedding."

David shoved Veronica out of his way as he ran toward the station.

"David!" Turquoise shouted. He ignored her cry, his mind racing, trying to cope with the fact that a bomb was about to go off. As he passed under the archway, he began yelling and screaming at everyone lingering on the platform. He pleaded with people to leave, to flee the station, using the words "bomb" and "die" as much as he could, hoping panic would spark and everyone would flee the area.

Most of the passersby took off running, stumbling and screaming in response to David's warning, but some remained on the platform, staring at the isolated train car, wondering what it was doing there all by itself.

David caught the gaze of a small boy who held his parent's hands as they stared at the train car. The boy frowned as he looked back at David, as if he knew what was coming, knew what was about to occur and was powerless to do anything about it.

Veronica ran across the platform, shoving people toward the archway without explanation.

David knew they were out of time. Something inside him told him the timer was about to reach zero.

The explosion rocked the ground, an orange fireball blasting up into the air and out to the sides, blowing the train cars in all directions. David expected to be catapulted through the air, his body ripped to shreds by the impact of

270

the eruption. Instead, Veronica tackled him to the ground, using her own body as a shield to protect him from the blast.

When David looked up, when he realized he wasn't dead, he found Turquoise off to the side, arms extended, a thin pink shield up over their section of the station platform. Turquoise had managed to capture their area in a protective bubble of sorts, saving him, Veronica and herself, along with some of the stray people who refused to listen to David's exhortations of impending doom.

David struggled to his feet, the tackle bringing more pain to his already aching shoulder and back. He helped Veronica up as Turquoise fell to her knees and closed her eyes. Fear rushed through him. Fear at what had become of all the people outside the protective shield. If Turquoise hadn't come back into the station, he would more than likely be dead now, as would Veronica. David turned to look through the archway and noticed Kimberly standing in the dirt lot, hands cupped over her mouth.

"You okay?" Veronica asked, brushing herself off. Smoke drifted across the platform, draping the station in haze.

He nodded, but he wasn't okay. He wasn't okay with the death toll that he knew could have been prevented had Turquoise thought to rescue everyone in the time it took the bomb to count down to zero. He wandered in a daze over toward the edge of the platform, which was buried in charred wood and twisted metal, and stood, staring at the slouching train cars, which had become nothing more than a steel skeleton.

As much as it pained him to do it, David looked around, taking in the charred bodies strewn about. Everyone outside that shield, everyone who ignored David's cries died, blasted to a crisp by a mercenary's bomb.

One of the bodies caught his attention. It lay draped over a section of the train car's wall that had made it to the platform. The form, small and crooked, hung at an angle that wasn't natural for the human body. *The little boy.* David fell to his knees.

He heard Veronica calling his name, but her voice soon faded behind the sound of his sobbing. The scene flashed in his mind—the little boy's face looking back at David, frowning, seemingly knowing what was coming. His parents, standing idle, ignoring everything David tried to tell them. Had they been too mesmerized by the stationary train cars? Why else would they have stood there, their son between them, oblivious to the chaos?

Someone shook him, and he looked up to see Veronica standing over him, her hair dangling in her face, her eyes asking him to get up, to come back to reality. But he didn't want to. He couldn't. He thought of the rest of the bodies lying across the platform and wondered how many lives had been halted because Turquoise decided to run instead of fight. Flee instead of save.

He managed to turn his head enough to see Turquoise on the ground, her body curled into a fetal position. Veronica helped David to his feet. He rushed over to Turquoise, grabbing her by the shoulders, pulling her up in his arms.

"Who are you? What gave you the right to let these people die?!"

His rage came out in a flood, tearing through his veins like a surge of electricity. He had little to no desire to stop it, just let it flow through his body and mind, his mouth an outlet for the surge.

He shook Turquoise. Her eyes bobbed open and then shut. *Is she sleeping? Did the shield take all of her energy, leaving her drained and incoherent to the rest of the world?*

Veronica pulled Turquoise out of David's hands and set her on her back on the ground. Then she stepped in front of David, her eyes full of fire. "What do you think you're doing?"

"She did it, Veronica! She's why these people died! She's why that little boy is dead!"

Veronica grabbed his arms and shook him, then she slapped him in the face. "Come to your senses, David! She just saved us. She saved us and the rest of the people who were behind the shield. You can't blame her for what happened to everyone else."

Turquoise stood to her feet. "I'm sorry, David. I'm sorry about that little boy. But we couldn't do anything for them."

David tried to charge past Veronica, but she held her ground and nudged him back.

"You!" David screamed. "You wanted to run! You wanted to leave while everyone blew up! I had to come in here and warn everyone. I had to try and save these lives that you just let go up in smoke!"

Turquoise crossed her arms, tears streaming down her face. "You don't understand what's going on here, do you? You don't understand what's at stake. You, Kimberly, Veronica and I are the only ones left to stop that wedding. If we don't do it, Carrie will marry Jerad and then—"

"And then what? And then what? You don't even know what will happen. *You* don't even know what is going on!"

"My life is this mission, do you understand that? My friends have died..." she wiped her tears on her arm and snorted. "My friends…they're dead. I have nobody. Nobody to help me, nobody to show me what to do. It's just…just me."

David closed his eyes and forced his tantrum down a few notches. He took a deep breath and let it slowly slip from his lips, exhaling the chaos and confusion he felt.

Veronica touched his back and whispered softly in his ear. "It's okay. Just breathe, David. We did what we could. She did what she could."

When he opened his eyes, he saw Turquoise walking through the archway. He could see Kimberly in the distance, through the smoky haze, on her knees in the dirt parking lot, crying.

Veronica grasped David's hand in hers. "Let's go. We need to get to the shore before the ship leaves or none of us will be able to stop that wedding."

David went with her through the archway, trying his best to put the deaths behind him. Those they did save stared at them as they left the station. "This is getting to be too much." Up ahead, Turquoise tried to comfort Kimberly, who seemed to be in a state of shock.

David let his mind wander as Turquoise broke into one of the vehicles parked in the lot and hotwired the car. When the engine started, Veronica helped David into the backseat with Kimberly, her eyes glazed over in a sort of thunderstruck state.

Veronica took a seat in the front with Turquoise, who drove them away from the station. When they reached the main street, David closed his eyes and allowed sleep to overtake him.

***

Drather returned to his car, a tower of smoke rising from the station behind him. As he approached the vehicle, he peered in the back window and didn't see Turquoise. He opened the back door and found an empty vial of antitoxin on the seat. He wasn't surprised. He had made the decision to hurry and find the teens rather than to secure Turquoise, who was supposed to be paralyzed.

I should have taken her bag, he thought, sighing. *Time to raise the stakes and bring balance back to this whole mess.*

Drather pulled his cell phone out of his trench coat pocket and dialed.

"Hello," a calm, deep voice answered.

"This is Drather."

"Ah, yes. Our conscience-driven mercenary. What can I help you with? Did you find the timepiece?"

"I want the bounty raised," he said, casually leaning against his car. He watched the dark smoke swirl in the distance like dancing ghosts. He thought he saw faces in the smoke, the faces of those he had just killed. *Just my imagination*, he told himself.

"Well, I sure hope you have a good reason for wanting the bounty raised."

"Things have gotten out of hand. More out of hand than what you've agreed to pay me for."

"I find this hard to believe. This was supposed to be a simple task for a famed mercenary such as you."

"I'm resorting to Plan B."

Silence. The faces in the smoke moved their mouths, saying things to Drather that he could not hear.

"Where is the timepiece, Drather?"

"The one I found was a fake. I have no idea where the real one is, so I'm going to Plan B. The plan you set up."

"Hmm."

Drather shuffled his feet, kicking up a small rock that was halfway buried in the dirt. He didn't want to look at the ghosts, didn't want them making him feel guilty for what he did. His ends justified his means. They always did.

When his contact said nothing for two minutes, Drather decided he didn't have time to deal with this. "I want a higher bounty now or I quit. The agreement was for fifty thousand credits. I want that changed to a hundred thousand, upon completion of Plan B."

"Eighty. If you succeed."

"I said a hundred. A hundred or I turn around and disappear right now. Don't think for a second I'm bluffing either."

More silence. The ghosts left, but the smoke formed a dark steeple, high into the sky.

"Very well. Please remember what we instructed you to do. Use the right equipment, specifically the stuff we gave you, and don't kill any bystanders. We are a committee of peace, not war."

"Of course you are. Make sure you have my credits waiting for me when I'm done."

"Good luck."

Drather closed the phone and rubbed his grainy chin. He knew that if Turquoise had escaped, then she probably helped the teens escape too. *I have to beat them to South Ryshard.*

26 Morning Shift

"**W**ake up."

Parks opened his eyes. A large man in a dirty apron stood before him. "Who...who are you?"

"John. I'm a waiter on the morning shift."

Parks sat up to find himself in bed. His head began to swim, and he closed his eyes to keep from blacking out. "Sandra?" he grumbled, opening his eyes and turning toward the other bed.

She rolled over on top of the covers, her uniform unbuttoned, her feet bare. "What?" She opened her eyes. "What's going on? Where am I?"

Parks spotted his shoes and socks on the floor, near the foot of his bed. He grabbed them and started putting them on. "We're in the diner, remember?"

"You guys sure have been out for a while," John said.

Parks saw a goofy grin on the guy's face and wanted to wipe it off with a few bullets. Instead, he glanced at his watch and realized it was approaching one in the afternoon. "Where's Trixie?"

"Who?"

"Brook? She goes by Brook now."

"The girl from the night shift? She wasn't here when I got here at nine. I found the place unlocked and you two on the ground in the dining room. I brought you both in here." John chuckled. "Customers tend to get freaked out when they see bodies lying on the floor in the middle of a diner."

Sandra sat up, found her shoes and socks and started putting them on. She glanced down at her open shirt and then glared at John. "Who unbuttoned my shirt?"

"I wanted to make sure you were comfortable, that's all. You were running a slight fever when I brought you in here."

"Did you call anyone?" Parks asked.

"No. There's no police station or facility for miles. You guys had a pulse, so I let you rest."

Sandra rubbed her neck. "What hit us?"

"Don't know," Parks grumbled, rubbing a sore bump on his own neck. "Must have been some kind of tranquilizer. Where did those brats go? I know they were here." Parks stood to his feet and drew his gun.

"Whoa, man. Just take it easy."

Sandra shot up from the bed and grabbed Parks' hand, forcing the gun to his side. "Take it easy is right."

Parks stared into Sandra's eyes for a moment, the desire to put some bullets into her unattractive face nearly overriding any common sense he had left. Reluctantly, he slid the gun back into the holster under his arm.

"They probably headed toward the shore," Sandra said

as they walked out into the dining area.

"Then that's our next stop."

As soon as they walked outside, Parks saw their cruiser slanted at a right angle. Scanning the side of the car, it became obvious that someone had slashed both tires beyond repair.

Curses flowed from Parks' mouth as he kicked the side of the car with his foot and began beating on the windows with his fists. "Those wicked kids!"

For minutes, he continued to beat the car, putting whatever dents or dings he could into its surface with his bare hands. Sandra did nothing to stop him, though he wished she would so he could have an excuse to beat on her. After he exhausted himself, he began to pace the length of the car, his mind racing for a way to get to the teens and show them a lesson once and for all.

"We'll have to get to Detention Facility 7 somehow," Parks started. "They'll have a chopper there. We can use it to catch up with them."

"Are you sure it's wise to keep wasting our time chasing after a bunch of street urchins? We've been on their trail for what feels like forever. Maybe it's time we just forget about them."

Parks leapt in front of her face, snarling like a wild animal. "We are going to find those brats and do away with them! And we're going to find that necklace too, and nothing…I mean… nothing…is going to stand in my way. When they draw their last breath, you're going to be there to help me dig their graves."

"I don't have time for this." Sandra started to turn around when Parks seized her arm and forced her back to him.

"You aren't going anywhere. You work for me, remember?" He shook her violently. "Remember?!"

Sandra pulled her arm free of his grip. "I remember!"

"Good. Good, you'll do good to remember."

"I go as far as the shore, if that's where they're even headed. If we don't get them there, I'm outta this game."

"You're out of the game when I say you are. Don't forget about your son, Sandra."

She scowled. It pleased Parks that his words had gotten through to her. She knew he had control of her son's fate, so she would do good to remember that he was in charge.

"Where do you think your little ragdoll waitress went?" Sandra asked him.

"Don't know. But after we take care of these kids, I'm going to make it a point to pay her a little visit. Teach her what happens when you try to pull a fast one on ol' Parks."

"Whatever."

"Jealous?"

Sandra scoffed. "Not in the least! I just think you overkill the whole vendetta thing. Scaring those kids is one thing, but trying to kill them? And now you want to teach the waitress a lesson?"

John stepped outside, a smoking cigarette hanging from his lips.

Parks drew his gun and pointed it at John. "Give us the keys to your car. Now!"

The waiter raised his hands in the air. The cigarette dropped to the ground as he fumbled into his pocket for his key ring. He handed it to Parks and then stepped slowly back into the diner as Parks holstered his gun.

"Trust me, Sandra. I can be your best friend or your worst enemy. Do your best to stay my friend." He opened the door to the cruiser and pulled David's jacket out. "Is that clear?"

"Yeah," she replied. "Clear."

"Better be crystal, Sandra. Better be crystal." He slapped the waiter's keys in her palm and pointed to the red car parked next to theirs. "Take the wheel."

27 Endangered Memories

When Carrie opened her eyes, the clock's red numbers told her it was 6:30 p.m. She slowly sat up in bed, rubbing her eyes, her temples throbbing with a migraine. As disappointed as she was with sleeping away the whole day, she admitted she could probably slumber for another three or four hours, at least to shake off the pounding in her head.

She slid her legs off the bed and sat at the edge for a moment, waiting, hoping for the pain in her head to subside. Then she made her way to the mirror, squinting in agony as the throbbing traveled to her neck. In her reflection, Carrie noticed the absence of the necklace and suddenly remembered the diary.

She closed her eyes as images of David and Veronica passed through her memory so clearly that she swore she had just seen them in person hours ago. She remembered leaving Lysallis—spurred on by David's confession of love, remembered her mother—her mother's face turning red when she yelled at Carrie to forget about David and get a life, struggled to remember her childhood but realized her head ached even more when she tried to conjure up memories that far back.

Jerad. She couldn't recall him saving her from a fire. She couldn't remember anything about him that went back beyond meals and conversations she had with him weeks ago. Carrie decided she'd give her mind a bit of time to heal. It had only been hours since she ditched the necklace, but already she was seeing proof of its forgetful power.

One question popped into her mind and, after one or two attempts at dismissing it, refused to leave. *Who sent me the diary? Was it David? Maybe Veronica?*

In the mirror, Carrie noticed she looked nineteen. No longer old, no longer mature beyond her years. She was beginning to feel like herself as more pieces of her past fell into their hidden places in her memory. Carrie placed her hand over her chest, thoughts of David surfacing like air bubbles in a lake. He was the one she loved. Not Jerad.

The impact of this realization almost sent her into a dizzy spell. She leaned forward and grabbed the mirror to keep from falling over. Maybe Belgar had some medicine she could take for her head. She knew she wouldn't last the rest of the evening if the pain kept up. As grateful as she was for the memories, the bittersweet balance of the migraine almost brought her to tears.

Carrie precariously made her way into the hallway, careful not to go too fast or make too sudden a movement for fear of blacking out. When she reached the living area, she settled down on the couch, aware of the necklace buried underneath the cushion. She wondered if the cushion would be enough of a barrier to stop the necklace from messing with her mind.

The house, quiet and still, seemed unusually empty for the late hour. Usually Belgar was back—if he had left to accomplish errands—cooking dinner by now. No Jerad. No maid. No Belgar. Carrie felt the silence weighing on her like a wet blanket. She grabbed the television remote and cycled through various channels. She had no desire to check stocks or watch an action movie. Seeing houses built for the poor appealed to her, but when commercials came around, she couldn't help but channel-surf again.

She stopped on channel twelve, which was right in the middle of a newscast. A young, brown-haired newswoman stood in front of what looked to be a mall.

"Three teens broke into the Moon Jewelers Jewelry store and stole a priceless necklace Tuesday night. But that was only part of their rampage across Enera. After authorities pursued the suspects, finally catching up with them in Tindall, the three teens were arrested and placed in a detention facility. They escaped hours later, killing guards and officers in the process. It is believed they are now at large somewhere in North Ryshard. Reports tell us they are armed and extremely dangerous.

"If you cross paths with these villainous individuals, contact authorities immediately. Two of the three are highly recognizable. Known in the past as the Lazerblades, the powerhouse of heroes who helped the Enera government take down mega criminal, Mr. Big, through means of the LZR Project, David Corbin and Veronica Amorou have now crossed over to the other side of the law and are on the run. A third, Kimberly Sebastien, is reported to be assisting them in their crimes.

"We'll bring you more news as we get it. I'm Janet Doyle for

Action Twelve News."

The screen switched to another woman, a bit older than Janet and dressed in a bright yellow blouse. She sat at an anchor desk, colored sheets of paper in front of her. *"Thank you, Janet. This just in: An explosion at a train station in North Ryshard has killed more than fifty people. Here's James with more details on that…"*

The pain in Carrie's head spiked, moving into her eye sockets, buzzing through her sinuses. She rolled off the couch and hit the floor, grabbing her temples. Memories rushed through her mind. Memories of David.

They met at Lysallis Middle School, eighth grade, Basic Enera Language class. A classroom full of students materialized in her mind, but only one stood out. *He sat in the row to the left of me, his brown hair scruffy and disheveled. Quiet and shy. He dropped his pencil on the floor, and after he reached down to pick it up, he hit his head on the desk.*

"Are you all right?" she asked, a giggle in her innocent voice.

Carrie broke from the memory and felt pain rushing through her entire skull. "Ahh!" She screamed, rolling around on the floor. She felt something warm on her lips and wiped away blood with her arm. "What's happening to me?!"

She sat up, burying her head in her arms, blood oozing from her nose and streaking her bare skin. Almost unbearable pressure blanketed her whole face, pushing on her sinuses, squeezing her temples like a vice.

Seconds, minutes, hours later—she wasn't sure of time anymore—the pain settled, even vanished, leaving her on the floor, on her side, blood marring the carpet. The news story came back into her range of hearing, as if she had been off on

285

some island somewhere, away from the world, closer to herself.

"Authorities are investigating a possible connection between the TransEnera North Ryshard Station catastrophe and the teens. We'll give you more details as the story unfolds."

"Thank you, James. We just received word that a 25,000-credit reward is being offered to anyone with information leading to the capture of David Corbin, Veronica Amorou or Kimberly Sebastien."

Carrie's pulse slowed, and she felt the veins in her temples expand.

Where is David? That was the only question on her mind now. *Is he really a villain now?* Her diary recorded stories of their adventures as heroes of Anaisha, not criminals. *Why would David and Veronica be on the run?* There had been no indication in the diary, at least in the portions Carrie read, of anyone named Kimberly. But that didn't really matter. What mattered was finding the truth in all of this.

Carrie looked down at the bloody mess around her. Streaks of crimson marred the otherwise immaculate white carpet. Jerad could come home at any time, so she had erase any signs of her blood or he would ask questions she didn't want to answer. Until she could figure this all out, she knew she had to play along with Jerad. She supposed—didn't know, though—that he was a dangerous man. All indications pointed to his wanting to keep her memory from her. *But why? There has to be something back there, something in my past that is a threat to him.* Until she figured that out, she couldn't let on that she suspected anything. And if he asked her about the necklace, she would have to tell him she lost it.

28 Relics Of The Past

W hen Turquoise pulled into one of the last parking spaces in the expansive dirt lot, David couldn't help but sigh with relief. They had finally made it to the shore, despite their misadventures and the wounds to his shoulder. Those wounds, he noticed, were beginning to hurt again. As much as he wanted to take some pain medication, he didn't want anything that would cause him to lose his alertness or edge. He was having a hard enough time getting back into things—it had been more than six months since his last so-called adventure—and he didn't need anything making it harder on him now.

Everyone stepped out of the car, the cool evening air sweeping through the lot, gently twirling the dirt into small twisters. In the distance, on the other side of the lot, a line of multi-deck passenger ships sat docked, preparing for the final departure of the day. The sun was busy setting in the west, casting orange and red paint across the sky, giving the white ships a brownish hue. White ship lights twinkled in the dazzling dusk scene.

"We made it," Veronica stated, relief in her voice.

Kimberly wrapped her arms around herself, the wind growing colder as the sun approached the horizon. David stared at her until her eyes met his. He hoped to see something in those eyes, some sort of normalcy, a human glimmer that would tell him she was okay after what happened at the train station. Nothing resided in those eyes but ghosts, phantoms, which to David resembled wisps of a young boy dying in a fireball.

David looked away from her and wondered how much longer he would be able to hold onto his sanity.

"Okay," Turquoise said, motioning for them to follow her through the parking lot toward the shoreline. "We have just enough time to make it to a ship before they all head to South Ryshard."

As the group started walking, David noticed they were some of the last people in the parking lot. They had about a half mile ahead of them. Most of the vehicles they passed weren't anything fancy—old, derelict. On his left, David saw a beat-up, brown car leaning on two flat tires. He swore he smelled urine, but that could have been his imagination.

"This looks more like a junkyard than a parking lot," David groaned.

Turquoise nodded. "I know. This lot's supposed to be for people who take the ships to South Ryshard and then come back at some point. But some people don't come back, and their cars just sit here, taking up space."

"Why wouldn't someone come back from South Ryshard?" Kimberly asked.

"They find something there they can't live without,"

Turquoise answered. "Credits. Clubbing. There's a lot there you can lose yourself in."

It dawned on David that Carrie may have had the same intentions when she fled to South Ryshard. Maybe she wanted some time alone—from him and from her overbearing mother. If that were the case, it was easy to see how she might have simply found herself "stuck" in South Ryshard. Especially if she made the romantic acquaintance of someone as rich as Jerad Montlier.

Turquoise suddenly signaled for them to take cover behind a blue school bus. Without asking questions, they did, but David didn't know why. He had been too busy daydreaming to pay attention to their surroundings. He figured if he was going to be out in la-la land, maybe it would benefit him to take some pain pills.

As soon as they were all hidden behind the side of the school bus, Turquoise peered over the hood. David walked the length of the bus and took a peek around the back. About a dozen vehicles away, toward the shore, officers scouted the area.

Just what we need right now, David thought.

"What's going on?" Veronica asked, shoving herself close to David so she could see what he saw. The warmth of her body insulated him from the cold wind.

"Just more trouble," he replied.

"I see them. We'll have to be careful." Her warm breath fell across his neck, tickling the hairs there. He suddenly felt safe, protected. *Have I always felt this way around Veronica?* He couldn't recall. It was a strange feeling. He was so used to being the protector, but around Veronica, at least right now, he felt like she was protecting him. *That's silly.* He had always been the leader, been the shield to their little ragtag group.

His brain, tired and worn from the journey, felt fuzzy. He couldn't think straight, couldn't decipher what they were supposed to do about the officers standing between them and the ship they absolutely, positively had to get on right now.

"Under the bus," he heard Turquoise say to them. Veronica and David dropped to the dirt and shuffled underneath the large vehicle. When Turquoise and Kimberly joined them, David heard the officers saying something indescribable as their footsteps closed in toward the bus.

David found himself wondering how far he was willing to go to get to Carrie. *Will I hurt or kill the officers if needed in order to get on that ship? Maybe*, he thought grimly. He wasn't sure. He couldn't go back into those confining cuffs. He couldn't go back to that interrogation room. Whatever the cost, he had to stop that wedding.

The police—two males and a female—passed the bus, their footsteps heard at the end of the vehicle. With cars on both sides, the officers would have to peek under the bus in order to see them. Hopefully, the officers hadn't caught sight of them before Turquoise scrambled them under here.

David stared at the rotting underside of the school vehicle, Veronica lying next to him. Moments later, he watched Turquoise slide out from under the bus and followed her lead with Kimberly and Veronica.

"We need a plan," Turquoise mumbled. She reached into the satchel that hung at her side, fumbling around for who knew what. David didn't really care, as long as it could get them to the ship before it left.

While he waited to see what Turquoise had up her

sleeve, he caught Veronica staring at him. Her hazel eyes watched him, studied him. *What is she thinking? What is going through her mind that she doesn't care to share with me at this moment in time? Does she have secrets there, hidden behind those eyes, like locked doors, the keys of which are in places I don't have access?* He had always known Veronica to be candid with her opinions, but some things she wasn't so candid about, like experiences in her past, her family...anything that had to do with romance. She kept those things from others, hidden in the closets of her mind.

Turquoise pulled a small disc from her satchel and walked around to the front of the bus. David turned toward the side of the vehicle, aware of the insane irony he was dealing with. The words LYSALLIS HIGH SCHOOL were printed in big, black lettering. This bus looked very similar to the one that he, Carrie and Veronica had ridden here on a school field trip years ago. That was when David saved Veronica and Carrie's lives.

He saw Veronica staring at the bus. With what was left of the setting sun, David swore he could see a glistening in her eyes.

Turquoise returned, hurrying. "We'll have about ten seconds once I set the bomb. As soon—"

"Bomb?!" Kimberly shouted.

"Yes, bomb. I'll place it on the engine, should give us a nice explosion—enough of a distraction to get us across the lot. There's nobody in the lot but us, as far as I know, so this should be relatively safe. We just need something to draw the officers' attention away from us."

"Let's do it," David agreed.

"As soon as I set it, we need to run as fast as we can to-ward the ship. No looking back, no stopping for any reason."

Kimberly dropped to the ground and sat with her legs out in front of her. "I don't feel so good."

Veronica picked her up under the armpits and pressed her against the bus. "I know you're having a rough day. I get that. But we have to make it to that ship, okay? Not just to stop the wedding, but to save our lives. If those ships leave without us, we'll be stuck here, and those cops will no doubt arrest us."

"Fine!" Kimberly shoved her hands into Veronica's chest, pushing her away. "Just get out of my face."

"We need to do this now." Turquoise turned the bezel on the disc, pressed the button in the center, and slapped it on the hood of the bus. "Go!"

Ten. David counted in his head as they ran down the aisle, the ship directly in front of them at the very end. He felt his mind reawakening.

Nine. The pain in his shoulder spread across his back again. He pushed himself, though, determined to get to the ship, to save his group and Carrie.

Eight. They passed a sports car, the Stratas Runner, something he had asked his parents for on his eighteenth birthday. Instead, he had gotten the rundown Cyclone that now lay in the hands of the Lysallis Police.

Seven. David felt his adrenaline peaking, and he found himself speeding ahead of Kimberly and Veronica. Turquoise kept a good lead, one that David couldn't catch up with no matter how fast he tried to run. He was still a bit out of shape, so the cramp sprouting in his side did not surprise him.

Six. "Hey!" The voice came from his left, but David knew

he didn't have time to look to see who it was. He figured a police officer had spotted him. That was okay. A few more seconds and they would be in the clear.

Five. "C'mon!" Turquoise shouted, waving behind her for them to somehow catch up. The cramp in David's side blossomed into something almost more painful than his shoulder. He felt like he was falling apart, his body screaming at him to stop, to give up, to give in. He couldn't.

Four...

Three...

The ship whistles blew, echoing through the dusk air to announce the final boarding call.

Two...

One...

A tremendous boom rocked the ground they ran across. David kept on his feet, Turquoise just feet in front of him, Kimberly and Veronica still behind him. The reflection of flames flickered off the windows of the vehicles they passed.

Another boom startled David. *Of course*, he thought, *a chain reaction.*

They approached a crowd of people loitering around the dock to watch the ships leave port. Most were facing the group of runners, their eyes lit up by the explosions, their mouths open in awe.

Another boom. Then another. The sound and succession reminded David of cannon fire. One by one, vehicles exploded with the sounds of shattering glass and colliding debris. Two officers moved into position ahead of them, at the end of the aisle.

"Officers!" Turquoise shouted, pointing her finger back

at the explosions. Another boom echoed, as if on queue.

The foursome stopped in front of the police officers. David did his best to hide behind Turquoise as she spoke to the officers. They seemed to be preoccupied with the fireballs behind them, paying little attention to who stood in front of them.

"Officers, there…there were men back there trying… trying to kill us." Turquoise tried to catch her breath as she got the words out. David peeked around her and spotted the ship at the front of the line moving slowly away from the dock. "They tried to kill us…but…we escaped. Some of our friends might have…they might have gotten caught in the explosion. Help them, please!"

The police officers glanced at each other and then dashed toward the fire.

Turquoise led David, Kimberly and Veronica through the crowds of people as the ship whistle echoed through the air again. The second ship in line began to pull away from the dock as the first one entered deeper water.

Kimberly stumbled on the dock and fell to her knees, vomiting across the wood. Those standing nearby gasped and stepped back in disgust. She coughed and then collapsed. Turquoise reached down and lifted Kimberly into her arms, bolting for the other end of the dock.

An old man sitting in a wooden booth near the last ship waved them toward him. "Hurry up, young 'uns! Ship's 'bout ta' leave!"

When they reached the booth, Turquoise gestured for Veronica to reach into her satchel. "Should be a wad of credits in there. Give it to the man."

Veronica reached in and pulled out a large roll of paper

credits. The man's eyes lit up. Veronica began to pull the papers apart, but Turquoise shook her head. "All of it. Give it all to him."

The man took the credits with a smile. "Room tickets are only ten credits each, but I've ne'er been one ta' turn down extra."

"Make sure we're not disturbed," Turquoise said, her glance catching his like a bear trap catches a leg. "Catch my drift?"

The old man nodded, stashing the credits somewhere under the counter. "I catch yer' drift. I catch it well and good. Four rooms for you travelers."

"Good."

The man turned behind him to a wall lined with nails, key cards hanging from each one. He pulled four off and handed them to Veronica. He glanced at Kimberly briefly. "Rooms are straight up tha' stairs."

Veronica took the keys. Turquoise shifted Kimberly's unconscious body in her arms and nodded at the old man. "Thank you."

He gave her a wide smile, revealing large gaps in his teeth. "No, no, sweet'art. Thank you."

Turquoise started up the stairs leading into the ship. David glanced back at the blazing lot. Cars continued to explode, people fled the docks and the police buzzed around in a panic. He couldn't have come up with a better plan himself.

He turned and started up the stairs behind Veronica. *We escaped. Now it's time to save you, Carrie. Just hold on. I'm coming.*

The ship's whistle sounded again as the four of them entered the ship. The transport vehicle cut through the dark waters to take the young travelers toward their final destination.

29

A Hero's Call

David stood at the edge of the bed and brushed the hair away from Kimberly's face, glad to see her still breathing.

"She'll be all right," Turquoise said softly. "I think her body's just trying to get rid of the last of the pills. I doubt that run helped."

"At least we're safe now," David whispered.

Veronica stood up from the edge of the bed and turned toward David. "I'm going to get some rest."

"Yeah, I could use some too," he replied.

Veronica ran her hand through David's hair. He looked up and saw her smiling warmly at him. "Get some sleep. Things will look different when you wake. That's what my dad used to say."

"Sure."

Veronica left the room, leaving behind a void that awed David. He squeezed the bridge of his nose and told himself it was just his emotions spiraling out of control due to his lack of sleep and overdose of drama.

He stood and headed toward the door. "Night, Turquoise."

She grabbed his arm and gently pulled him around. "I need to talk to you, David."

Sighing, he sat down on the edge of Kimberly's bed. "Yeah?"

Turquoise pulled a wooden chair in front of him and took a seat. Her long pink hair fell in front of her face, draping her turquoise eyes. "I know all of this nonsense about the timepiece and the wedding and everything is sort of confusing, and I'm sorry for that. There's a lot more going on here than just a wedding and a piece of lost crystal."

"What do you mean?"

"If Carrie marries Jerad…well, that's it then. It could very well mean the end of things. The timepiece is indeed half of the equation to saving Anaisha. Carrie is the other half. I don't want to worry the others too much, but you…you can take it, David. You can handle this, I know you can."

He looked away from her, toward some paintings of the desert. Kimberly stirred on the bed and then fell back to sleep.

Turquoise reached out her hand and gently grabbed David's chin, turning his face back toward her. "Please, listen to me."

"I'm listening."

"You're tired. You're worn out. I understand all of that, because I feel the same way. But once again, just like in the past, it's up to you, David, to save this world."

He laughed. "That's what I did in the past. The time for those things is over. I've gotten over it. I just want to save Carrie and go somewhere safe where we can spend the rest of our lives together."

Turquoise shook her head. "I hate telling you this, but that's not how this is going to play out. You're a born leader, and you always will be. You can't run from that. When you, Veronica, Carrie and Sean were a team, you were the leader. Not necessarily because you wanted to be, but because it came naturally to you. They looked up to you."

"Sean didn't."

"He's an exception. Pride was his enemy, and he fed into it. But David, that's all in the past. Right now, what I need from you, what Anaisha needs from you, is your strength, your leadership. If Drather didn't get the real timepiece from us, I'll bet he's going to go after Carrie."

David straightened his slouching body. "What?"

"There is a resistance group, a small one, that believes nobody should interfere with Anaisha's present or future. They probably hired Drather to find the timepiece and destroy it. That way nobody could get their hands on it and use it.

"There is another group...a terrifying group...whose desire is to find the timepiece and Carrie and somehow get hold of a power that could destroy this world. Jerad is part of that group."

"Jerad?"

"Jerad was prompted to marry Carrie. I don't know why, though. You see now why we have to stop this wedding? There is no choice in the matter. This is where you and I are now—on the same side with the same goal. And we're the only ones who can do it. Nobody else is going to step up, and there isn't time to call on others for help. It's just the four of us to stop this event before it happens."

"What was he hired to do? Just marry her? For what, sex? Credits? Why?!"

"Calm down."

"No! No, I'm not going to calm down! This is ridiculous." He clenched his fists and slammed them down on the edge of the mattress. Kimberly stirred again but quickly fell back to sleep.

"David." Turquoise reached her hand out to calm him. "David, I need you to keep your cool. I know it's been a while since you fought to save Anaisha, but I need you right now. I need you to stay calm, I need you to keep yourself on the same level as me so we can get through this together."

"I don't even know you, Turquoise. Who are you? What is your part in all of this? Why should I even trust you? For all I know, you could be leading us into a trap."

She stood to her feet. "I'm what they call a Wedge. I was born with…well, powers, for lack of a better word. I can use Fury—a name I gave one of my powers, which is really just air manipulation—and I can heal myself. I can reach out with telepathy and help others. I was sent by the Sector, the headquarters for Wedges, to find the timepiece and stop the wedding. The Sector wants peace. I want peace. Cloud wanted peace…"

A moment of silence fell between them as David saw her eyes peeking out from behind the pink drapes of hair. Her turquoise eyes looked like small, tropical oceans with sharks of agony and grief underneath their surfaces.

She looked directly at him, pushing the hair behind her ears, out of her face. "Why did you stick your neck out for Anaisha so many times before, David? Why risk your life for

Carrie, for Veronica or for Sean? You took bullets for them. You sacrificed your life for them—and for the world—on more occasions than I can count."

"That was in the past."

"The past?" She glared at him. "Really? You and Veronica have been protecting each other as if you were brother and sister. And you've been watching over Kimberly as if she was a cousin you just started to get to know. You and I fight for the same reasons, David. Our lives mean nothing if we can't live them in peace. And this world will not live in peace unless evil is destroyed."

David fiddled with his hands.

"We have to stop this wedding. No matter what. A union between Carrie and Jerad will only end in destruction. I've been trained to stop this from happening, and I promise you I won't give up until she's safe or I'm dead."

David looked up into Turquoise's eyes again, but she was staring at the floor. Her hair had fallen back over her face and swayed in front of her like the beaded curtains of a gypsy's shop.

"Before that day in the conference room, I had never told her how I felt about her. I never told her how much I loved her, or that I cared for her more deeply than I had for anyone else in my lifetime. I never kissed her. I always wanted to grab her in my arms and kiss those beautiful lips…and now, it's too late."

Turquoise pulled her hair back behind her ears and stared him straight in the eyes. "It's not too late, not yet. We still have time, David. We have until Saturday. Actions will speak louder than words. If this journey doesn't prove to her

300

that you love her, I don't know what would."

"We have to save her, Turquoise. We have to. We can contact her, right? We can call her and tell her what's going on. We can send a message through telegram, we can—"

"No. No, we can't. She's surrounded by too many enemies right now. Jerad keeps close tabs on her, and if he suspects anything, he may move his plans up. Besides, I have people on the inside keeping a close eye on her."

David decided she was right. If Jerad found out they were on their way, he would move forward with whatever diabolical plan he had.

"Get some rest. You'll need it for tomorrow. I'll keep an eye on Kimberly." Turquoise smiled confidently at him, her pink lips curling into a wide crescent that put him somewhat at ease.

David stood and headed toward the door, knowing sleep would do him a world of good.

30 Visions

*D*ark clouds rolled overhead, and a cold, chilling wind skated between the buildings. Flakes of snow rained down from the ceiling
of black sky, blanketing the apartment complex in white.

David walked across the gel-like floor of the dark living room. A
gust of wind blew through the blinds, carrying with it a sense of fear and
dread so powerful, it paralyzed him. A glimpse of a shadow moving at
his side broke him from his frozen state, but when he turned his head,
he saw nothing out of the ordinary. He saw another shadow out of the
corner of his eye, but again, nothing when he turned to face it.

He turned toward the bedroom door in front of him and came face
to face with a pair of glowing white eyes. Hollow eyes, like those of a
dead man long since buried under the ground, eyes seeing nothing but
darkness and decay.

A deep voice moved through the apartment. It originated from
whatever being owned those glowing eyes, and yet the sound of the voice
seemed to come from everywhere. "You are too late. She is dead."

Although he didn't want to ask, although somehow, deep inside, he
knew of whom this creature spoke, he asked, "Who?"

"Oh, you'll see soon enough." The man or beast or whatever stood in front of him, visible only by a pair of glowing eyes, giggling as a school child would when being tickled by a parent. "You arrived late, too late. And now, for that mistake, she has left this world with no way to say goodbye to you."

The eyes vanished, leaving nothing behind but the echo of the words spoken moments before.

Lights flickered on behind David, illuminating the kitchen. When he swung around to see who had turned them on, his attention focused on a small envelope sitting on a round wooden table. He now recognized the apartment, realized where he was. But when he tried to conjure up the name of the person who lived here, his mind blocked it, stopped his tongue and froze his memories, preventing him from calling forth that person.

He reached out and picked up the envelope. On the front, written in thick black ink, he saw the word "DRATHER." David ripped the end of the envelope open, and hundreds of credits drifted into the air like the string on a kite. He watched as they hit the ceiling and passed through it, one long continuous flow, as if the envelope was a black hole of sorts, giving way to an unending supply of credits.

Without even thinking about it, he pulled a lighter from his pocket. When he turned it over, he saw the words "The Prestige Hotel" etched in the side, as if someone had carved it with a dull pocketknife. He rolled his thumb across the flint wheel and sparked a flame, which he held up to the constant flow of paper credits. The flame ignited the bills, and a stream of fire flowed up into the ceiling and vanished with the credits it was attached to.

Screaming outside pulled David's attention toward the sliding glass door on the other side of the living room. He heard a man and woman arguing, then what sounded like a whole group of people. They were all yelling something, but David couldn't make out the words, as if they spoke a language he neither understood nor had ever heard before.

For a reason he wouldn't remember past this moment, he turned toward the bedroom door, the one the glowing eyes had stood in front of—or guarded. The burning credits continued to flow from the envelope to the ceiling, leaving David amazed that the ceiling didn't catch fire. Although something told him the ceiling wasn't even real, so why would it?

When he grabbed the knob of the bedroom door, he felt something cold and slimy. Turning his hand over, he saw spots of blood on his palm. His heart beat harder, so hard he could almost feel it burrowing out the front of his chest. He placed his jittery hand on the gold-plated, blood-covered knob again and turned, pushing the door open. The door free-floated through the room, as if it was never on hinges to begin with, and then disappeared into the shadows of a corner.

Light from the kitchen spilled across the carpet, revealing a trail of blood from the threshold to the bed. His eyes caught the edge of the mattress, where the light barely reached. Two legs dangled over the side, the rest of the body hidden in shadows. The smell of something rotten and possibly dead filled his nostrils, causing him to step back a foot or two.

Outside the sliding glass door of the bedroom, he could clearly make out a patio covered in snow so white it almost blinded him. It reminded him of the glowing eyes, the eerie entity that had visited him just minutes ago.

A man dressed in black clothing stood out there, shaking his head. When he spoke, David could hear him clearly, even though the sliding glass door was shut between them. "I'm sorry," the man said. "That's all I can really say. She died because you don't know when to give up, when to back off, when to surrender or when to call it quits. To turn in your chips and walk away with what you had left would have been best for you, but you didn't do that. You continued to fight, to move forward with a stubborn will that cannot be easily broken. Because of that will, because of your selfish, hard-headed will, she had to die. There was no

304

other way to stop you."

With a ferocity, a burning rage he had never felt before, David exploded toward the man…

"David? David?" The voice echoed in the air around him. "David? David, wake up."

His eyes shot open, and he sprang from the bed, gasping for air. When he came to his senses, he realized he had been dreaming. Turquoise sat on the end of his bed, dressed in a white T-shirt and black cargo pants. Her brilliant pink hair flowed down her back.

"You okay?" she asked.

David had to force the other half of his mind to detach from the dream and reenter this reality. It took a few minutes to mesh the two worlds together, but when they collided and finally became one, he took a seat on the bed and did his best to slow his breathing down.

"Was it a nightmare?"

David shook his head. "More. More than a nightmare."

"What do you mean?" Turquoise stood to her feet and stretched.

It had to be more than a dream. It felt so real. The apartment— David realized he couldn't remember much about the apartment, nor could he put his finger on why it had been so familiar to him in his dream. He covered his eyes and shook his head. "I…I dreamed of credits…and glowing eyes…and that guy, Drather."

"Drather?"

David nodded, pulling his hands from his face. When he looked up at Turquoise, she had her hand to her chin and was

305

studying him. "Yeah, Drather," he said again. "He killed someone. Someone important to me, but I don't know who. A girl…I know that much. It was a girl. Those legs, they belonged to a female."

Turquoise continued to study him, her eyes narrowing. She simply replied with, "Hmm."

Soreness throbbed in David's shoulder, but he didn't say anything about it. The last thing he wanted to do was take another pain pill. He had taken half a pill before bed and thought that could have been the reason for his terrifying dream. He suddenly realized he wasn't wearing a shirt and blushed when he reached for his T-shirt lying on the floor. After he slipped it on, he noticed Turquoise staring off toward a wall, her eyes glazed over in heavy thought.

"What?" he asked her.

She broke from her trance and shook her head. "Nothing. You don't know who the girl in your dream was? No clue?"

David shrugged. "I don't know. What if it was Carrie?"

"It was just a dream."

"How do you know?"

"You should go back to sleep. You need your rest. I'm staying up to keep watch." Turquoise left the room.

David had a feeling there was more she wasn't telling him, but he figured it was probably just her opinion and not any secret knowledge she possessed. How could she possibly know anything about his dream? His nightmare? And how could he possibly go back to sleep after that?

31 Escape

Carrie woke numerous times in the middle of the night. After tossing and turning, her head ached more than ever. Her memory returned to her in sonic waves that blasted through her mind, bringing visions back. Visions of the past, of her adventures, her parents, David, Veronica, Sean, even Mr. Big and his criminal network and the chaos he had once inflicted on Anaisha. All of it came back in a flood of pain.

When she woke at six, she couldn't go back to sleep and decided to get up for the day. She sat up slowly, rubbing her aching temples.

David...I love him.

Veronica...my best friend.

My parents...they love me, despite how they treated me.

Jerad...I don't love him. He lied to me...lied about there being a fire...lied about my parents dying...lied about everything.

She remembered everything.

Carrie was born and raised in Lysallis. Lysallis was her

307

home. *Not this extravagant house, not with Jerad, not in South Ryshard.* She met him in one of the office buildings in the center of the city when she first arrived in South Ryshard for an interview. He happened to be there, talking business with her potential boss. He asked her out, gave her the necklace as a gift and stripped her of her memory, her identity even. *But why would he lie? Why go through all this trouble? What is he after?*

She finally remembered her past, and she knew she had to escape her present. *There won't be a wedding. I have to get out of this place. I have to reach David and tell him how I feel about him. But isn't he a wanted criminal now? Didn't I hear his name on the news just yesterday?*

The urgency to flee overrode the pain in her head and made it easier to move around, to do what she knew she had to. She crawled out of the bed and straightened her nightgown. She guessed Jerad was probably gone as always or fast asleep. This would give her time to pack a few clothes and grab something quick to eat. *I'm starving.* She knew her best bet was to get out of South Ryshard before he caught on to what she now knew.

She quietly opened the bedroom door, careful not to make a single sound that could wake Jerad, the cook or even the maid, if she was around. To Carrie's surprise, she came face to chest with a large man dressed in a black sweater and black pants. His square, chiseled face squeezed into a smirk as he positioned the thin microphone branching out from his right ear toward his mouth.

"She's up," he said into the mic. His hand moved to a firearm that rested on his side.

"What's going on here?"

The man moved toward her, forcing her to step back into the room. When she got near the bed and the man stood in the doorway, blocking it completely, he pointed his finger at her. "We've been ordered to keep you in your room until Mr. Montlier gets home."

"What? That's nonsense!"

"I'm just following orders."

"I don't take orders from my fiancé."

The man motioned to the gun at his side. "Will you take orders from a man with a gun?"

She said nothing to the obvious threat.

"That's what I thought. Now, stay in here and keep quiet. As long as you cooperate, I won't be forced to hurt you in any way." He backed across the threshold and closed the door.

Carrie stood fuming, her arms crossed, her blood boiling. She wanted to run, to flee as fast as she could. *I could probably outrun this guy, but how many more are in the house?* If there were more and they were all armed, she knew she wouldn't be able to outrun a bullet.

Instead of running, Carrie took a deep breath and turned toward the mirror. *Just calm down, Carrie.* She had to think clearly, completely, before making a move. If Jerad wasn't home, she had time. *Why would Jerad trap me in here, unless he knew? Unless he found out about the necklace?* How he knew didn't matter. What did matter was getting out of the house and finding David. That was Carrie's very first priority.

A plan sprung into her mind, a juvenile one that she wasn't all that proud to execute. Regardless, she knew her only way out of this place was to get her hands on a weapon.

Carrie opened the door and came face to chest with the

guard again.

"What did I just tell you?" His hand went to the firearm again, this time peeling up the strap that kept it in its holster.

"I need to use the bathroom."

He grinned. "Please. Do I look like an idiot?"

"I just woke up. Is there anyone in this world who wakes up not having to go to the bathroom?"

The man thought about that for a second, his eyes steady on Carrie, his hand on the firearm strap. "You have five minutes," he finally said, moving to the side.

Carrie entered the hallway and started toward Jerad's bedroom when she felt a tight grip wrap around her arm and pull her backward, almost to the floor.

"Where do you think you're going?"

Carrie straightened up and brushed her nightgown down. "To the bathroom."

"Bathroom is over here." The man pointed behind him.

"That one...gets clogged too easily. Unless you want to call a plumber or have Jerad's hallway full of toilet water, I'll need to use the one in Jerad's bedroom."

He frowned. "Five minutes. If you're not out in five, I'm coming in after you."

"I'll look forward to that," she said sarcastically as she entered Jerad's bedroom and closed the door, locking it behind her. She flipped the light switch on, illuminating the large room. She had only been in Jerad's bedroom once or twice before, and his sparse decorations still amazed her. The walls stood bare, and the furniture pieces consisted of plain wood—no stain, no gloss. The carpet had been dyed black, and red sheets with black swirl designs covered the bed.

Carrie dashed toward Jerad's dresser, quietly pulling the drawers open one by one. She rummaged through socks, underwear, pants, belts, but turned up nothing in the form of a weapon. *He has to have something in here. He has to protect himself with something.*

She moved to the nightstand, pulling its drawers open, finding nothing but a black metal box locked with a digital password screen built into the lid. Knowing she didn't have the time to hack it, she scanned the rest of the room, wondering where else he might hide a weapon. She reached her hands under the pillows, the bed sheets but brought them out empty.

This is my only chance!

Under the bed, nothing.

She found the walk-in closet full of Jerad's tuxedos, suits, jackets and fine nightwear. Toward the back, she parted a group of jackets to reveal a plain white wall. To her right, she parted more jackets, finding nothing but white wall again. Up on the top shelf sat shoeboxes full of dress and casual shoes that looked like they had never been worn.

But no gun. No knife. No weapon of any kind. If she were more skilled, she could probably use a hanger or a shoe as a weapon to bludgeon that idiot guard, but once again, she didn't know how many there were or what kind of firepower they were packing.

"Hurry up in there!"

Right then she noticed a glimmer in the corner of her eye. When she followed it, she found a small switch plate behind some of the jackets. Carrie pressed it. Nothing happened. She pressed it again. Nothing. *That button has to do something!*

Then a faint hissing sound filled the small space, and the

back wall sunk back and slid to the side, revealing a dark stairwell. A cold draft burst out, engulfing her in goose bumps. She grabbed one of Jerad's suit jackets and slid it on, tightening it at the front to keep from freezing. Then she stepped into the stairwell. Her foot found the first step, and chills danced up her legs. She started down the steps, one by one, determined to find a way out of the house.

At the bottom, darkness gave way to a blue mist that drifted through a cavernous room. Peering through the haze, Carrie saw bookcases lining the walls, each one filled with shelves of texts. She moved through the mist, reaching out to it, grabbing at it with her hands. It felt as if she had taken hold of a cloud, but when she looked at her hands, she only saw a thick coating of moisture on her palms. Carrie looked up and saw the mist parting near the center of the room.

There, in the middle of the cavern, stood a long glass tube reaching up from the floor and connecting to the ceiling. A woman floated in the midst of orange-tinted liquid, her shriveled body bare except for strands of blue cloth that ran across her chest and between her legs. Her eyes were shut, but Carrie sensed she was neither sleeping nor dead.

Something pounded on the door upstairs. Carrie's five minutes were up, all too quickly. She couldn't help but stare at the woman in the tube, her hair lifting with the air bubbles that snuck from her mouth. *How can she breathe in—*

The woman's eyes opened, exposing glowing blue pupils that seemed to pierce the glass like laser beams. "Death," she uttered, her jaw opening wide to reveal jagged, yellow teeth inside, "to the Lazerblades. Death to them all!"

"Wha—" Carrie dashed into the stairwell, heading up as

312

fast as she could, fear moving her feet, terror igniting her steps. She ran as fast as her legs would take her, stumbling once but catching herself as the blue haze followed her up toward the surface. She bolted out of the closet and caught her breath before scrambling to push the switch that retracted the wall back to its normal position.

A lingering cloud of blue mist hovered around the entrance to the chamber as pounding sounded on the bedroom door. "Hey! If you're not out in ten seconds, I'm coming in!"

She hung Jerad's jacket up and hurried to the door, fumbling with the lock, opening it in a state of minor panic.

"Fall in?" He grabbed her arm and threw her down the hallway. Her knees caught the floor, and she winced at the way the tile tore her skin. The man lifted her by the arm and pushed her through the open doorway to her bedroom, where she tumbled across the carpet.

"You stay in here or I'll put a bullet between those pretty little eyes of yours!" he growled before he slammed the door.

Carrie buried her face in the carpet and cried. Her memories, her fiancé turning into her enemy, the ghostly woman in the basement. It was all too much, and she suddenly felt the fragile toothpicks of her strength snap under the weight of it all.

Death to the Lazerblades? Isn't that what the woman had uttered, her foul mouth opening to form the words? What does it mean? The Lazerblades was the name of their group, years ago—back in her memories.

Her tears stopped, and in their place, she felt the heartache of isolation. *Where are my friends now? Where is David? And what is Jerad going to do to me when he gets back?* She decided that she would fight. She would fight back and force the answers she wanted out of him. She stood to her feet and began to search the room, looking for anything at all she could use to fight him with.

Candles. She could burn Jerad's house to the ground. That would alert the police, but if she couldn't escape the house in time, she would burn with it.

She could ambush Jerad when he came into her room...*but how?*

The bedroom door opened, and Carrie turned to see the maid enter, shutting the door behind her. She looked directly at Carrie and put her finger to her mouth, motioning for Carrie to stay quiet. The maid placed a stack of towels on the bed and then took a glance at the door, probably to make sure the guard wasn't trying to keep tabs on her.

"We need to get you out of here," the maid whispered as she turned back toward Carrie. The woman looked much younger than Carrie had originally thought. Carrie had only seen the maid on a few rare occasions, and even then, the woman liked to wear scarves over her head—like the black silk one she wore now—concealing most of her face. Carrie decided she couldn't even call the maid a woman, more like a young girl. Her flawless face framed her golden brown eyes, which held so much energy and vitality.

"Who are you?"

"Angel."

"You're the maid."

"Sure I am." She pulled the silk wrap off her head, unveiling short red hair, and set it on the bed. "You'll need that. Go ahead and get that nightgown off." Angel then started to untie the white apron from the front of her black maid uniform.

"What are you talking about?"

Angel set the apron on the bed. "I don't have time to explain everything to you. You have to trust me. Jerad knows what you did with the necklace, and he's going to make you pay for it when he comes back."

"How did he find out?"

"Please. You didn't think a multibillionaire would let you in his home without some sort of video surveillance, did you?"

Carrie had been stupid, and the realization left a bitter taste in her mouth.

Angel grabbed her by the shoulders and stared directly into her eyes. "Listen to me. You have to get out of here before Jerad gets home. There's so much at stake right now, but it will have to be explained to you later. Right now, you're going to get out of that nightgown and put on my maid uniform."

"Where is Belgar? Is he working for Jerad…you know, not just as a cook?"

"Belgar is dead. They buried him in the garden about a half hour ago. Didn't do a good job of it either."

"He was my friend," Carrie muttered.

"He was my friend too, more than you'll ever know, but right now my job is to get you out of here. Stop wasting time and take off that nightgown."

"Where will I go? I want to find David, but I don't—"

"David is on his way here, to rescue you. But he isn't going to make it in time, so…" Angel sat Carrie down on the bed and put the apron and scarf in her lap, "you're going to have to dress like me and sneak out of here." Angel began unbuttoning her uniform.

Carrie slipped the nightgown off over her head and took the uniform from Angel. When she had it buttoned up and Angel had the nightgown on, Carrie noticed they were both about the same size and the clothes fit on each other almost perfectly.

The maid wrapped the apron around Carrie's waist and tied it in the back. "You must not speak to those men out there, understand? You can't give them any reason to think you're Carrie Green. Just take these towels," Angel placed the stack of towels in Carrie's lap, "and head out to the pool area. Once you're out there, jump the wall and head for the city." Angel slipped off her white tennis shoes and gave them to Carrie, who put them on her own feet.

"I went into the basement. I saw—"

Angel shook her head. "Don't. I know what's down there. Just forget what you saw. It'll be taken care of soon."

"What do—"

"Enough with the questions." Angel wrapped Carrie's hair in a bun and draped the scarf over her head, tying it at her chin. "Get out there and get as far away from this place as you can. David will find you; just find a safe place to lie low."

"What about you?"

Angel smiled. "Don't worry about me. I can take care of myself. Now, take those towels and go. Some of Jerad's men aren't the brightest, so you should be able to get past them with no problems." She nudged Carrie toward the bedroom door. "Once you're over that wall, run as fast as you can."

Carrie nodded. "Thank you."

"I'll see you again soon. Just keep your head down, your voice silent."

Carrie shifted the towels in her arms and opened the door as the maid went quickly to the bed, out of the guard's view. Carrie stepped into the hallway, leaning her face toward the towels.

"Does Jerad pay you by the hour, maid? What is taking you so long today?"

Carrie stayed silent as she made her way toward the living area. *What I wouldn't give for a chance to punch you in the face and shut you up for good.* Two men guarded the glass doors to the yard. They eyed her suspiciously, firearms on their hips. She was grateful she hadn't flown off the handle and tried to take them out in a desperate and suicidal escape attempt.

She entered the living area, passing the couch, thinking of the necklace and where it was now. *Maybe I can grab it and take it with me as proof of what Jerad tried to do. I could take it to the authorities and use it against him.*

No, she told herself as she approached the doors leading to the patio. *If he knew about the necklace, then surely he has it back in his possession now.*

"Where you going?" one of the guards asked before she could open the door leading outside. Carrie pointed toward the swimming pool.

The guard glanced at his watch. "It's not even eight yet. Jerad said you usually clean the pool around nine on Fridays."

Another guard slapped him on the shoulder. "Man, she's the maid. The maid! She gets things done early on Fridays so she can partay all night. Know what I mean?"

"You know, you've really been gettin' on my nerves today."

"I'm just saying, man, she's probably got plans. If I had plans on a Friday, which I alllways do, I make sure to get my work done early so I can have more time with the ladays."

The guard who had stopped Carrie motioned toward the

317

pool. "Go ahead."

The other guard slapped her in the rear. "You know where to find me if you want me to show you a good time tonight, know what I mean?"

Carrie refrained from breaking the man's arm and beating him with it and simply nodded as she opened the door and passed through to the patio outside.

32 Eternal Friendship

David stared at the sunlight reflecting off the ocean water, the movement of the waves washing away the nightmares that had haunted his slumber. He found the smell of the ocean waves refreshing, and it made him wish he could stay out here on the open water forever.

Dolphins dodged in and out of the ship's wake, as if they were doing a ballet just for him. Or maybe they were doing it in memory of Carrie. David pulled the crescent moon necklace from his pocket and stared at it, remembering the past.

Veronica approached his side, munching on a granola bar. She offered him some, but he shook his head and continued to stare out at the ocean. The sound of the pulse engines turning the ocean water into energy to propel the ship lulled him into a relaxed state of mind, almost making him want to head back to his room to sleep some more. If only he could sleep past the nightmares.

"How are you holding up?"

"I don't know," he replied. "I don't know about anything

anymore. I received a wedding invitation, and since then, my whole life has turned upside down. I've lost my apartment, most of my things, my girlfriend—where does it end?"

Veronica took a bite of the granola bar and stared out at the ocean. "I don't have an answer for that."

"Hmm."

For a long moment, they stared at the ocean together, seagulls cawing above their heads.

"I miss the way things used to be," David whispered, more to himself than anyone specifically.

Veronica nodded. "I know."

"I…I want for things to be the way they once were. You know? I know it sounds crazy and maybe even a bit hypocritical, but I miss having Mr. Big and his goons to chase around. Yeah, things were tough, but…I don't know, there's just something missing now. Something is missing, and I can't figure out what it is."

"Friendship."

He turned to her. "Friendship?"

Veronica finished the granola bar and stuffed the wrapper in her pocket. "Everyone left after the LZR Project shut down. Sean, Carrie…"

"But you and I—"

"I know." Veronica dropped her gaze to the deck of the ship. "You and I, friends. I know."

He turned back toward the ocean, shoving the necklace in the pocket of his jeans, debating whether he should try to get a bit more sleep or grab some coffee to keep going. He knew things were only going to get more difficult. Their ragtag group was about to go up against one of the richest men in the world, with nothing more than unpracticed skill.

Veronica put her arm around David's shoulder. Her embrace, the very act of her touching him seemed to set him at ease. She always had that ability, and until this moment, David thought it was because she was as close to him as a sister.

But now, looking into her eyes, those hazel eyes that shimmered green and gold in the sunlight, he felt a connection with Veronica, a connection that allowed him to see her on a deeper level than he had ever seen her before. She wasn't just a sister, she was a friend. She wasn't just a friend, she was someone who gave her unyielding loyalty to him. If he could place his life in anyone's hands, he could set it in hers. She always had his best interests in mind, always put his happiness before hers.

She was always there, no matter what.

Veronica looked into his eyes, and a warm grin came over her face. "We're going to save Carrie. I promise you that. No matter what, we'll get her back. No matter what, I'll be by your side when we do."

He gazed out at the ocean again. A cool breeze brushed over them. "You're really the only one I trust with my life."

She drew close to him, and they both stood there for what felt like hours, watching the dolphins, enjoying the crisp ocean air.

33 Run!

Carrie ran as fast as she could through the flowered fields behind the house. She headed straight for the street ahead, the one she knew would lead her directly into the heart of South Ryshard. There she could find refuge in some building or shop and come up with a game plan.

The morning sun had begun rising in the sky, drenching the day in bright light. It was symbolic, she supposed, since it really was a new day for her. With her memories intact, she felt new life breathed into her, and it pushed her forward, away from Jerad, away from the lies, away from the terror she had seen in the basement.

Carrie reached the street and stopped for a moment, resting her hands on her knees as she bent over to catch her breath. The maid uniform felt itchy, but she felt happy to be dressed in something other than that skimpy nightgown.

She looked up at the buildings just across the bridge that led into South Ryshard and couldn't help but feel waves of relief wash over her. She was just a stone's throw away from freedom.

The cars passing along the bridge didn't seem to notice her as she stood there, panting. She wanted to run across the bridge as fast as she could, but her exhausted lungs told her how incredibly out of shape she had become since living with Jerad. She remembered being athletic in her prime, exercising regularly, eating healthy. She had been a vegetarian, which explained why she lost her appetite whenever she was served meat.

A police car drifted off the road into the gravel of the shoulder she was loitering in. *Just my luck!*

The driver's side door opened, and a tall, dark-skinned officer stepped out. He pulled his drooping pants up, readjusting the belt around his waist, his eyes scanning Carrie and then turning their gaze up toward Jerad's house on the hill.

"Morning, young lady."

"I'm so glad to see you!" She pulled the scarf off her head and tossed it to the ground.

The officer walked lazily toward her, his eyes scanning her again. His quaint mustache drooped down the sides of his lips and touched the bottom of his chin. He scratched it with one hand while he hung the thumb of his other hand off his belt loop. "Just do me a favor and be quiet for a second, okay?"

Carrie didn't know how to respond to that.

The officer stopped in front of her, his eyes glancing up at Jerad's house again. "What are you doing here on the side of the road?"

"I've been living at Jerad's house and I…"

The man looked at her with astonishment. A small grin snuck into the corners of his lips but quickly faded. "Jerad Montlier?"

"Yes. Up on the hill."

"I see." He pulled a pair of cuffs from his belt and motioned with his hand for her to turn around. "Make this easy, okay, and you won't get hurt."

"What?" She saw the cuffs dangling from his hand, and dread mixed with panic. She eyed the bridge, wondering if she could make a run for it. Her knees were still recovering from the jaunt down the hill, but she believed she could make it across the bridge quickly. Then it would just be a matter of getting lost in the city.

"Turn around."

She shook her head, unable to wrap her mind around what was happening. As she considered her situation, that she had coincidentally run into a crooked cop connected to Jerad somehow, Jerad's black limo drifted along the shoulder and stopped behind the police car.

Jerad stepped out, dressed as sharply as ever in a black suit and black tie. He made his way toward the two of them, a slight limp in his walk. He glanced at the street, at the bridge, at the hill leading up to his house.

"Officer."

The dark-skinned man nodded to Jerad. "Would you believe my luck?"

Jerad smiled, his eyes locking with Carrie's. "You are a very lucky man, Officer Reins. I just barely called in her escape five minutes ago."

"I was heading over to start a perimeter around the house, and she just happened to be standing here on the shoulder." He grinned at Carrie. "As if she was waiting right here for me."

She glimpsed the bridge again, intent on making a run for it. She would die trying, she knew that. Anything was better than going back to that house. She feared that Jerad may have other means to take her memory away, and then what? What would happen if she forgot all of this and was back at his side, no recollection of how truly sinister he was?

"I see that look in your eye, young lady. It'll serve you no good. I'm gonna put these cuffs on you…gently. And then you're gonna go with Mr. Montlier here. Don't make this harder on yourself than it has to be."

Carrie barely turned her body in the direction of the bridge, but before she could take a single step forward, the officer grabbed her by the hair and threw her on the ground. Her jaw hit the gravel, snapping her teeth down. She felt the weight of the officer on her back as he cranked the cuffs around her wrists.

The man's warm breath fell in her ear. "I told you not to make this hard on yourself." Then he pulled her to her feet and nudged her toward Jerad's limo.

She dug her feet into the gravel and began to scream, but this only made Jerad join in the effort to capture her. He grabbed her feet, and they carried her wriggling form to the limo, where they shoved her into the backseat. Jerad slammed the door, and the locks engaged.

Carrie thrashed across the leather seat, trying her hardest to pull her wrists through the metal handcuffs. Jerad entered the driver's seat and waved to the officer, returning to his cruiser. The engine started and Jerad turned his head so he could see Carrie. "You made a mistake taking that necklace off, my dear."

"I'm not your dear! You're going to pay for this! I swear you're going to pay for this!"

Jerad pulled the car onto the main street. "Your empty threats mean nothing to me. Since you've decided not to be a willing participant, I'm forced to play another hand." The separation glass slid up between Carrie and Jerad. The air vents rumbled to life as a white fog seeped out across the leather seats.

No, not gas! Not gas! Carrie took a deep breath and held it in as the white mist covered her face. Each second she held her breath felt like an eternity. *Just hold it until we get to the house. When Jerad thinks you've been knocked out, you can make another run for it. Just hold on.*

Pressure squeezed against her lungs. Her heartbeat slowed. Her chest tightened as the car slowed down, an attempt by Jerad to buy more time before reaching the house up the hill.

Just hold on. Just…just…

Carrie gasped, inhaling the white cloud. Her eyes fell heavy, and she could do nothing to stop her face from hitting the window before she tumbled to the floor of the car.

34 Haunted

"**K**imberly, can you get the door?" Uncle Grey shouted from the hallway. "I have to use the restroom!"

Kimberly set the television remote down on the folding table and hopped out of the recliner.

The doorbell rang again.

"I'm coming!" she shouted.

She moved through the dark living room and approached the front door, peeking through the peephole as she did whenever anyone knocked on their door. A stocky, bald-headed man stood on their porch, staring in at her with beady black eyes. He scowled, and the way his face twisted with the expression caused her to hesitate a moment before finally unlatching the lock and opening the door.

"Can I help you with something?"

He stared at her for a long, silent minute, his eyes gazing deep into hers. Black holes. That's what she thought of his eyes. Little black portals with nothing behind them but the Depths.

"No, you can't." His hand moved fast, clamping around her neck and squeezing before she could get a scream out.

"H…he…" She grabbed his arm with both hands, trying her hardest to pull free from his grip. "H…h…"

"Silence." He forced his way into the living room and pushed her into the wooden hutch. She fell to the floor. As he held his hand out and motioned toward himself, the hutch separated from the wall and came down on Kimberly, dishes and glassware crashing into the floor around her.

Blackness surrounded her. As she lay there, she felt a giant shadow hand reach up out of the carpet and wrap itself around her neck. She tried to gather enough strength to crawl out from under the furniture, but the hutch seemed to grow heavier and heavier with every second that passed, almost as if it was trying to push her into the floor. The grip of the hand finally cut off her airway, and she felt like she was drowning. Another hand wrapped its long, shadowy fingers around her waist and began pulling her into the floor.

Her flesh moved into the floor, but her spirit and soul refused to move with it. If it was possible to be in two places at once, she presumed this was how it felt.

"Kimberly!" Uncle Grey lifted the hutch off her and helped her to her feet. "What happened?"

"Ahh!" She sucked in a mouthful of air and looked around for the shadow limbs, but found none. "A man!" she shouted. "A man broke into the house. He's here, he tried to kill me!"

Uncle Grey pushed his glasses closer to his face and hurried to the kitchen. He pulled a glass paperweight out of the freezer and handed it to her. "Take this, Kimberly. Take this and keep it safe." He pulled out his wallet and shuffled through the papers in it, handing her one of them. "Take this too." She stuck it in the same jeans pocket she used to hold her cell phone. "Call that number as soon as you can. The person who answers will help you, but you will have to trust him with your life. Do you understand? I don't have time to explain, dear. I love you." He *kissed her forehead. "Now, go!" He moved her toward the front door.*

A gust of wind whipped at her back as Uncle Grey lifted off the ground and flew into the wall, shaking the whole house. When she turned back, she found the intruder, the man with the beady black-hole eyes, rushing toward her. He slapped her across the face and ripped the paperweight from her hands.

She fell to her knees, her face on fire. The man pulled Uncle Grey out of the wall and threw him to the floor. Kimberly heard her uncle's body snap, the bones breaking at the mercy of the invader's strength. Then the man turned toward Kimberly, his face filled with an evil grin. "You're next!"

She ran, her feet scrambling over the carpet like it was dry sand near the ocean. She screamed at her feet, her legs, to move, to move faster, to get away. They cooperated just enough to get her out the front door and down the cement driveway.

When she turned back, she saw the evil man pursuing her. She screamed, her eyes frantically searching for a neighbor or friend outside, someone who would hear her screams and help. "Help! Help! Somebody, help me!"

The sky above her swirled into a mess of red and orange, turning everything around her into a scene of blazing fire. Something fell from the sky, crushing a group of houses down the street, casting debris through the neighborhood. When she looked up, she saw something falling toward her. She couldn't discern what it was, but the big, black object resembled a meteorite.

The houses around her started to open their window eyes. Huge, glowing red eyes. Fangs sprang up in the doorways, and the nightmarish creatures uprooted themselves from the foundations and began moving toward her.

Kimberly Sebastien felt her mind split apart.

When she turned back, the evil man stood there, within inches of her. "You can't run from me. You think I'm dead? I'm not dead,

Kimberly. I can't be killed. I'm coming after you. We're coming after you and your friends. All of you will perish as millions before you."

Kimberly struggled through the mound of covers, gasping for air. She lifted herself out of them and took a deep breath. Something was still chasing after her. The scary thing was that she didn't know what it was or how soon before it caught up to her.

35 South Ryshard

he passenger ship reached the shoreline of South Ryshard around six in the evening. The four travelers stepped onto the wooden dock amid a small crowd of passengers and those waiting for their friends and loved ones. Dark clouds had formed over the city, signaling an impending storm.

David smelled rain, and he took a moment to breathe it in. Standing on the dock, knowing they had finally reached South Ryshard, he couldn't help but smile. It was a brief smile, as was the smell of rain.

Veronica pointed out in the distance to a tall clock tower. "Remember?" she asked.

"Yeah."

"Looks like they've rebuilt it since we were here last."

David closed his eyes, remembering the clock gears, the silly grin on Tabitha's face, the sound of the tower exploding, crashing down on those who were inside the attached stalus. What had been a field trip quickly turned into a bloodbath and a fight for their lives. He opened his eyes, and they all started toward the street that met the dock.

Up above them, David saw a golden archway. Etched into the side were the words: "In the Pursuit of Wealth and Pleasure." He remembered passing under the arch when they came here years ago. Before that field trip, he didn't know what the big deal was about South Ryshard. Now he knew better.

The surface of the city contained shops and office buildings. Beyond the city, across the main bridge, lay suburban neighborhoods, both ritzy and rundown. But underneath the streets, in the very core of South Ryshard, sat the bars and clubs that made the city famous. Everything seedy, everything taboo took place underground, hidden from daylight, safe in the darkness. People could party all day and night without ever being interrupted by the rising or setting of the sun, or by the Anaishan Sentries who had no jurisdiction underground.

Kimberly walked beside David, her head down. He heard Turquoise mentioning earlier how Kimberly had experienced nightmares most of the night. It seemed everyone was struggling internally with the events taking place.

Turquoise led them toward the line of taxis waiting to take people into the heart of the city. Along the curbs, tall trees rose high into the sky, the leaves of which were turning a brilliant greenish-purple color. He had only seen this type of tree—the calipso—once before, in a remote part of Merena.

"Number twenty-four," Turquoise said, pointing to a hover-taxi with the numbers printed in bold on the door. "That's the one we want."

As they crawled into the vehicle and started toward their next destination, David tried to remember what Turquoise had told him about her plan. Turquoise had a contact in one of the hotels in the city, the hotel manager, who had supplies for their rescue mission. They headed to the hotel, but David felt the desire to skip the hotel and go straight to Jerad's house to pull Carrie out. The wedding was tomorrow, and David was very unsure about the contacts Turquoise had inside Jerad's place. Apparently, both of the contacts had gone silent, so nobody knew if Carrie was safe or not. She and Jerad could already be married for all David knew. The thought terrified him.

After arguing with himself in his head, he decided to put his trust in the plan. Veronica had approved it, and so David, trusting her with his life, went along with it.

At the hotel, they would formulate an assault plan to take down the wedding tomorrow and rescue Carrie. Although David was opposed to using guns, he felt his morals sliding away from that stance. He did his best to keep his beliefs intact, though, since they seemed to be the only part of his past that hadn't changed yet.

But he admitted that the world was changing. Violence seemed to be the answer to everyone's problems lately, and David wondered how long he would be able to keep from succumbing to the same mentality.

They entered the main city, passing business and banking buildings and shops with names like "Tattoo Palace," "Kiki's Lingerie," "Augustine's One-Stop Sports Shop" even "Black Hole Arcade." David thought it strange to see so many chain commercial buildings towering over the city of industry, residing next to small entrepreneur businesses that still had their owners' names attached to them. The merging of the two entities made for a very interesting empire.

The taxi pulled next to the curb of a tall hotel building, and the four travelers got out. David examined the building and the immediate area, keeping his eyes peeled for any signs of trouble. For all he knew, Parks or a slew of other characters could be just around the corner, waiting to attack them when their guard was down. *It would be easy*, David thought, *with the tired state I'm in.*

He followed Turquoise, Veronica and Kimberly into the hotel lobby. A large sign over the front desk read "The Prestige Hotel," triggering his terrifying nightmare and the hotel name on the lighter used to burn the floating credits.

Coincidence, he thought. *Just a dream.*

A man behind the counter, dressed in a silver suit, nodded to Turquoise. His eyes burned bright orange.

Turquoise approached him, glancing around to make sure none of the people passing through the lobby were eavesdropping on them.

"The days are evil," the man said.

"Full of trouble and strife," Turquoise recited.

The man's tense shoulders relaxed, and he let out a sigh of relief. Reaching into his inside jacket pocket, he pulled out a keycard, handing it to her. "Take this. Room 1003. Please, be careful."

She took it and nodded. "I will. Thank you." She turned and led everyone to the elevator. They took it to the tenth floor, where they entered room 1003 using the key card.

"Yuck!" Kimberly shouted, her face twisting into a grimace. "Stinks of cigarettes."

David found the yellow walls and long crimson curtains

to be a depressing decorating choice. A small black laptop sat on the table on the other side of the room.

Turquoise made a beeline for the laptop. "There's some food in the small fridge over there." She pointed to the short hallway between the main room and the bathroom.

Kimberly headed toward the bathroom. "I'm taking a shower."

"I'm going to rest." Veronica took off her hoodie and lay down on one of the beds, her back to David.

Turquoise opened the laptop and pressed the power button. Nothing happened. She checked the side of the unit and noticed the system was missing its battery. She rushed across the room, almost knocking David over. "I'll be back. I have to talk to the manager." She left.

David stood there, staring at Veronica. He could see the strap of her bra through the thin T-shirt, along with the faint lines of scars crisscrossing her back. She never told him how she got those scars, and he never really asked. He just remembered her wearing a thin shirt, like the one she had on now, a while ago, and Carrie asked her what had caused the marks on her back. Veronica shook her head and smiled. She always smiled. Smiled and said not to worry, not to concern themselves with her, that she was okay and just wanted to enjoy the company of her friends.

But those scars came to his mind on occasion, peaking his curiosity. He had a hard time comprehending the fact that she had endured something that looked like it had been incredibly painful but refused to tell her friends about it— her best friends.

"Do you mind turning on the television? Some background noise might help me rest."

"Yeah," David replied. "I can do that."

He looked at the small nightstand between the beds but saw no remote. Then he opened the top drawer. Inside, he found an item that had, up until now, only existed in his nightmares. A small white lighter sat inside a glass ashtray. The lighter had "THE PRESTIGE HOTEL" printed on its side.

Veronica rolled over to face him. "You okay?"

David nodded, picking the lighter up out of the drawer and shoving it into his pocket without Veronica seeing. "Yeah, I'm good." He pulled the remote out of the drawer and shut it.

Coincidence, he told himself. *But what if it isn't?*

36 Runaway Emotions

K imberly stepped out of the shower, draped a towel around her and rubbed some of the steam from the mirror. Staring at herself, she wondered when her life was going to come to an end. *Should I end it myself, finish things on my own terms?*

She tilted her face this way and that, watching it catch the light, wondering if anybody out there would find her mess of a life beautiful. A zit made an appearance in the crevice of her nose, and she wondered if she should pop it now before it had a chance to get worse.

Yes, I could end my life now, before things get worse. Put myself out of this misery. Death followed her everywhere she went. First her parents, then her uncle, and all those people at the train station. All those people…

The faces flashed in her mind like old photographs. She closed her eyes and yanked at her hair, hoping to make the pictures stop. She bit down on her lip until she tasted blood. Kimberly couldn't get the images to go away, couldn't get the sound of the train car exploding or the screams she heard right after, to leave her ears.

Tears spilled from her eyes, and she sank to the floor, leaning her back against the cabinet. *I miss you, Uncle. I miss you so much. When will I see you again? When will I get to watch television with you and go fishing with you again? When can I watch you draw up the blueprints to your experiments again? When...*

An exhausted sigh left her lips, and she stopped crying. *Be strong, Kimberly. Be strong. You made it this far!*

But how much farther could she go? Where could she go? She was hitching a ride with people she barely knew, people who would eventually leave her or die at her side, like everyone else in her life. Maybe she could leave them, run far away so they could live their lives like they were meant to. David had saved her life, as had Turquoise and Veronica, and she owed them that much, owed them the chance to live in peace.

Then she remembered the phone number her uncle had given her. She could try it once more, give it one more shot. Maybe it was a number to someone in the family, someone else who could take her in. If she couldn't get a hold of them, if the number refused to allow her access to this one person her uncle trusted with her life, Kimberly would have to run. She would have to run far away from here, far away from those who had saved her life.

Kimberly dressed in a soft white bathrobe that hung from the back of the door and left the restroom. She found David watching television; a commercial for Syn Soda happened to be playing. A little girl danced around on a grassy lawn, a tan dog playfully skipping around her in the background. The same catchy tune Kimberly had heard one too many times echoed from the television's cheap speakers while the girl on the lawn grinned. *"Syn Soda is the best! Syn Soda beats the rest!"* The girl stopped dancing and held up a black bottle of the world-famous cola. *"Syn Soda makes me happy."* She smiled while the dog began happily ripping up the lawn behind her.

The commercial ended, and a woman wearing a black tube top and short black skirt appeared on the screen, standing in front of an empty hallway lit up with blue neon. Rapid drumbeats pounded through the television's speakers.

"Bored tonight? Wishing for something more than the same, dull thing, every…single…day? Then come to the party. Come to where the mystery and allure are always at an all-time high." The woman's index finger summoned the viewer into the screen. She began swaying her waist to the rhythm of the dance music in the background. *"Join me at South Ryshard's premiere club, Expired Reality. This, my good friends, is the place where all your dreams come true. And I do mean all of them."* She blew a kiss toward the screen. *"If you're looking for a fun time tonight, come on down. We're located underneath Seventh and Penny Streets."*

Veronica got up from the bed, eyeing the robe Kimberly wore. "Do they have another one in there?"

Kimberly nodded.

Veronica locked herself in the restroom. Kimberly took a seat on the edge of the bed opposite David, facing him. Although she wanted to try the number her uncle had given her one more time, she was afraid nobody would answer and she would have to keep to her commitment to run. She didn't want to run, not really, but it was the only option she felt she had to keep her curse—or whatever it was—away from

David, Veronica and Turquoise.

She eyed the phone on the nightstand, refusing to give in to the urge to call. Instead, she turned to David and smiled. "I…I wanted to thank you for all your help. For saving my life."

David fidgeted with the remote, picking at the small circular buttons. "No big deal."

"It is," she insisted. "I wouldn't be alive right now if it wasn't for you. You saved me in the mall, and you've protected me this far, even though you've had so much happening yourself." She got up and sat on the edge of David's bed next to him.

"I wasn't going to leave you behind," he replied casually.

"How's your shoulder?"

A smirk formed on his face. "I'll live. I've been in worse shape than this before."

She looked into his eyes, his green gaze mesmerizing her. She suddenly found him attractive, as if blinders had been pulled off her eyes so she could see what really sat in front of her. "I…If things don't work out between you and Carrie…" Kimberly suddenly regretted her words.

"Nothing is going to happen to Carrie. I won't let it," he snapped, staring her square in the eyes.

Kimberly's heart stuttered at the passion burning in his eyes. They almost glowed with ferocity. In them she saw madness, determination. Maybe even a hint of hysteria. Kimberly found herself somewhat frightened to know David was a man who wasn't about to let anyone or anything stand in his way of true love.

But true love didn't really exist. *Does he know the consequences he faces if he fails?* "What if you risk everything to get her back and you find out she doesn't love you anymore?"

David stared at the floor. The television was airing an episode of "Peter's Alibi."

"I know she still loves me," David said softly. "I know it. I can feel it, like I've always been able to feel it. Each time I breathe, each morning I open my eyes, all of it is for her. She's the one I'm meant to be with. I bet my life on it."

"I'm sorry. I didn't mean anything...I..." Kimberly shut her mouth, ashamed of the way she was acting. *What right do I have to play temptress? Am I jealous? I want someone to feel that passionate about me. I want him to feel that way about me. I want to sink into his arms. The way he held me in the mall, I want him to hold me like that again. I feel so much pain, but there's so much healing and warmth in his embrace.*

"Have you tried that number?"

Yes, the number. It's time to roll the dice and see how my life is going to play out. She stood up and approached the phone. "I guess I got so caught up in the fact that we finally made it here that I completely forgot." She picked up the phone and dialed.

Ringing.

The other end clicked. *"Hello?"* a deep voice answered.

Excitement flowed through Kimberly. "I can't believe I finally got through to you."

"Who is this?"

"My name is Kimberly Sebastien. My uncle, Howard Grey, gave me your number. He's...he's been killed. He told me to contact you, said you would help me."

David's eyes widened.

"Where are you right now?" the voice asked.

"I'm at The Prestige Hotel in South Ryshard."

"I'll be there soon. Just stay put. I'm coming to you." The line clicked and went silent.

She hung the phone up and noticed David staring at her with wide eyes.

"Grey, your uncle, was killed? Professor Howard Grey?" He almost choked on the words.

"Yeah. Right in front of me."

David shook his head. "How?"

"That creature at your apartment killed him. It slaughtered him and then came after me. Uncle handed me some kind of crystal thing before the creature took it from me. I guess he'd been doing some research on it." She turned away and stared at the floor. "I don't understand why he had to die."

"Are you really his niece?"

She nodded.

"Professor Grey used to work with our team. He invented a lot of the weapons we used." He bounced his pointer finger up and down toward her. "Wait a minute, I remember you now. I remember when we used to go over to Grey's house. You were that little girl who always stayed in your room because you were too shy to talk to any of us."

Kimberly gasped. "That was you? That was you who came over, visiting my uncle all the time?" She closed her eyes, placing her face in her palms. "Of course. That was you!" Her eyes snapped open. "I remember you now. You and Veronica and Carrie and Sean."

David sighed. "We were good friends with your uncle." He stood up and put his arm around her, pulling her close to him. "I'm so sorry to hear of his death. I'm sorry all of this has happened to you."

Kimberly rested her head against his chest, sinking into the safety of his embrace. Had she known he was the boy she had a small crush on when she was younger…

The shower water stopped, and Kimberly took a deep breath.

***

"Who was that on the phone?" Sandra asked, flying the chopper over the chilly water below.

"That was Kimberly, one of the brats," Parks said. "Stupid girl doesn't know she was calling David's phone."

"Where are they?"

"The Prestige Hotel in South Ryshard."

"So we'll head there, arrest David and his friends, and put them on trial for the stuff they put us through."

Parks grinned. "No. No, that's not what we're going to do. We're going to play a little game first."

Sandra gazed out at the cloudy reflection on the water, wondering how she could get out of this. Parks was taking things too far now, and she didn't want to be part of his little game anymore. At first, it was about a fake ID and a necklace. Threatening a few kids was okay, but now she knew, beyond the shadow of a doubt, that Parks was out for blood, willing to kill anyone who stood in his way. And that was too high a price, even for her.

37 Hope

"Wake up, Carrie."

Her eyes slowly opened to darkness. A light flickered on. She looked around and found herself on the floor of Jerad's garage with her hands tied behind her back, not with the cuffs but with hard plastic, which was cutting into her wrists. She still wore the maid uniform, which had been her best and probably only chance at escape.

"You coming back to our world?"

She squinted as the lighting in the garage reached full illumination. Jerad towered over her, leaning on his cane. Behind him sat his collection of exotic cars. Along the walls, dozens of glass cabinets held his priceless artifacts and antiques. She remembered coming into the garage once, but Jerad didn't like her being there. These were his valuables, his life's treasures.

Jerad knelt down to her. "Whatever you were trying to do this morning, you better never try after we're married."

Carrie spit in his face. "I'm not marrying you."

He pulled a kerchief from the front pocket of his suit and wiped the saliva off him. He very slowly, deliberately, folded the kerchief in fourths and stuck it back into his pocket. His movements reminded Carrie of an animal that, knowing its wounded prey is at its disposal to do anything it wants with, takes its sweet time, prolonging the moment of impending doom.

"You are marrying me. Tonight." Jerad stood up and strolled past his cars, running his fingertips across the hoods. "You see these cars? Each one is an expensive luxury I enjoy in this life. I enjoy each one of them because I have worked hard for them. You don't get anywhere in this life without taking it by force. I wanted power and fame, so I took them. I didn't get them. They weren't given to me freely. No, I took them by force, and now they are mine." His eyes met hers. "And now, I want you."

"Too bad."

He shook his head, smiling. Then he strolled casually to one of the cabinets along the wall closest to her and tapped the glass with the tip of his cane. "I also own many artifacts, some which are from planets you will never visit. Some have come across my hands from other realities, ones you will never know. And some…well, some came to me by other means. The violent means I spoke about just a moment ago. My cane, for one, is used to compensate for an injury I incurred when I was younger. But you see the gem here at the top? It's one of Anaisha's most marvelous treasures." He knelt to her level again, showing her the dazzling cobalt gemstone at the top of his cane. "It is a pain stone, extracted from the depths of Anaisha long, long ago. This blue stone will inflict enormous pain on the individual struck with it, because it is a poisonous stone. It bleeds an evil serum through the many small pores in its surface when it is struck with mighty force."

"I'm not marrying you. Your little toys don't scare me."

"A toy? No, it's no toy. It is an unorthodox weapon, but it is no toy." Jerad stood up and leaned his hands on the gemstone.

"Did you hear me, pig? I'm not marrying you, so you may as well just let me go."

"I buy myself these luxuries with credits. My wealth is a direct result of my success. And I am successful because I am smart. A lot smarter than what you take me for."

"I don't love you. I'm not marrying you. You tricked me. Lied to me!"

"Love? How dare you assume a man of my stature would marry a commoner, especially one as young as yourself, for love. What do you think would possibly compel me to fall in love with you in the first place?"

"No." Her eyes widened, refusing to be put off by the bright lighting, probably a side effect of the gas. She used her strength, what little she had, and rose to her feet. She leaned back against the wall, the wind taken from her. "How dare you think someone like me would want to love someone like you. Who do you think you are? Wealth doesn't make you anything but greedy, selfish and more undeserving of the love I have to give."

"Please. You talk as if love has a value, which it doesn't. But regardless of your thoughts on love, I will admit that you aren't as predictable as I first thought you were. You did find out about that necklace, although you had some help on that one. The diary. But you made a mistake in thinking I wouldn't find out about it." Jerad smirked. "And your friend, Belgar. Boy, he really got in my way when I brought my men in to watch over you. Don't worry, though, he's safe and sound in the dirt—or afterlife—whichever one you believe in. Now if I didn't need that meddling maid, she'd be in the same soil right now."

"My friends are on their way to save me, and they won't be showing you any mercy." The very thought of David gave Carrie hope that she would be rescued. She knew what he felt for her and how determined he could be when he wanted something badly enough. He would save her, and they would finish off this creep before he could do harm to anyone else.

Jerad laughed, tapping his cane on the floor. "That's rich." He brought the cane up horizontally and pushed it into Carrie's neck, pressing her against the wall. "Your friends are headed straight into a trap. Don't think for a second that I didn't anticipate their foolish actions."

Carrie struggled to push the cane off her neck, gasping for air, but Jerad pushed harder, cutting off her airway.

"You aren't going to be rescued this time. David is going to die. Veronica is going to die. Even Sean. All of you." He released the cane, and she dropped to the floor, choking on air. "Face your reality. You are mine now. I own you. And in just a couple hours, you and I are going to be married. After that, we'll move on with my plans."

"Plans? What plans? I wouldn't marry you if—"

Jerad's hand struck her cheek. "Next time, it will be my cane that strikes you. You may have gotten your memory back, but you still have no clue what's going on."

Carrie's jaw burned from the hit, but she still managed to

347

make eye contact with Jerad. "David is going to kill you, with my help of course."

"I'll return in a bit, and then we'll move forward." Jerad turned the lights off and entered the house, slamming the door behind him.

Carrie sat in the darkness, alone with the cars, the artifacts and her fears. She moved her jaw around, trying to shake the sting of the slap, but only made it hurt more. She struggled to get out of the plastic binds, but it was no use. She lay down on the cold concrete and closed her eyes.

You're my only hope, David. Rescue me like you have so many times in the past.

38

Seeing Through The Wool

Turquoise carved a path straight through the hotel room and to the laptop, completely ignoring David and Kimberly, who were sitting on the beds, watching the television. She reached the computer, crammed the battery she received from the hotel manager into the back compartment and turned it on.

David moved off the bed and approached Turquoise. Her leg jittered, and she tapped her finger furiously on the surface of the small table.

"What's the matter?"

The operating system welcome screen came up, and Turquoise typed in the required password. Then she shoved the small chip she had taken off Cloud into a slot in the side of the laptop. She felt David's presence there, peeping over her shoulder. She wanted to tell him to scram, just for a moment, just until she could figure out what was going on. But she didn't. The last thing any of them needed to be doing right now was snapping at each other.

A red three-wedge pinwheel design slowly materialized in the center of the screen. Turquoise double-clicked it with the mouse, and it morphed into a black document icon labeled "PERFECT SPIRAL MISSION OBJECTIVES."

"What is that?" David asked, leaning over her shoulder so much that if she turned her face, she would run into his ear.

"It's a data chip I took from Cloud when he died. It contains all of our mission info." She double-clicked the document icon, and another password screen popped up. Turquoise typed in the password she had received before leaving the Sector and leaned back in the chair, waiting as an hourglass appeared on the screen.

David no longer leaned over her. He gazed out the window. Turquoise took a deep breath, steadying her heartbeat. The hotel manager had told her a message was on its way from Jerad's house, sent by either Belgar or Angel. Until she received that message, received some kind of confirmation that Carrie was safe, she wouldn't be able to relax.

The hourglass disappeared, and the computer screen filled with a white background, followed by black text:

-PERFECT SPIRAL MISSION-
SPIRAL TEAM:
TURQUOISE WEDGE
TRINISTAR WEDGE
CLOUD WEDGE (ACTING LEADER)

OBJECTIVES:
Active Objective - Guard Carrie Green from harm
•OBTAIN CRYSTAL TIMEPIECE

- STOP WEDDING OF CARRIE GREEN
- JOIN UP WITH WEDGE GROUP 324 FOR FURTHER INSTRUCTIONS REGARDING RETRIEVAL OF THE CODEX OF RA'F

"What is that?" David asked, pointing to the last line where it read, "The Codex of Ra'f."

"I was never told the exact details of our mission, such as why we have to get the timepiece or why exactly we have to stop Carrie's wedding, just that we need to do those things. But I was never told I'd be going after the Codex of Ra'f."

"What is the Codex of Ra'f?" Kimberly asked, moving off the bed.

Turquoise shrugged. "I really don't know. I've heard of it, that it has special powers that can stop evil from consuming Anaisha, but that's about it."

"Where does Carrie fit into all of this?" David asked.

"I don't know that either." Turquoise clicked on the "X" in the upper right corner of the screen. The window collapsed and brought her back to the desktop where the black document icon sat, staring at her. "At least we know we have to stop this wedding. I don't have a clue where the real timepiece went, but I'm sure that as long as we stop the wedding, we'll put a dent in what needs to be done."

David pointed to a very small, red pinwheel spinning in the bottom right corner of the screen. "What is that?"

Turquoise should have seen it before, especially with her powers of observation. *I must be tired*, she told herself. *Or distracted.* As she clicked the pinwheel, the screen went black and then began to fill with lines and lines of small, coded

351

text. The computer hummed loudly as the coded text morphed into understandable letters and numbers, and then words and sentences.

File#54637845643 - Cloud - Account Balance
(as of Monday, November 9, 1998): 340,000c

Recent Payouts:
Wednesday, October 28, 1998 -
50,000c - Drather - Rhodenine Necklace
Wednesday, November 4, 1998 -
50,000c - Drather - Trinistar
Saturday, November 7, 1998 -
50,000c - Drather - Trinistar

Tasks
•Murder Trinistar   COMPLETE
•Make prepayment to Drather to steal Rhodenine necklace from Jewelplex Mall   COMPLETE
•Obtain Rhodenine necklace   COMPLETE
•Obtain Timepiece
•Murder Turquoise Wedge
•Stop wedding of Carrie Green
•Use Carrie Green to obtain access to Ra'f Gaul Temple
•Murder Carrie Green
•Obtain Codex of Ra'f

Turquoise felt her heart plummet into her stomach. "This can't be Cloud's chip."

David stepped away from the table, running his hands

through his hair. Turquoise sensed the sudden anger in him, fostered by the frustration that had already been building up in him during the journey here.

"There's no way Cloud would have done these things," Turquoise whispered. "I bet...I bet the card is a fake."

"You just said that you pulled the card off Cloud's dead body. How can it be fake?"

Turquoise didn't have an answer for that. Maybe someone planted it on him, so she would think he was a traitor. *No way would he betray me.* Turquoise closed her eyes and let what she just read sink in. Slowly, pieces began to fit together. As much as she wanted to believe that Cloud would never do something malicious, the evidence, the information on the chip, actually made sense.

Trinistar died that night at the hotel by an accidental drowning in the swimming pool. Turquoise found it hard to believe then, but she had nobody to pin the murder on. Nobody but Cloud. And since she never had an inkling of suspicion toward him, he never became a suspect.

But it had to have been him. He filed the final report stating Trinistar died of accidental causes. And when Turquoise asked him where he was that night—seeing how they were all in separate locations in the hotel—he hesitated and then told her he was at the bar. When they arrived at the hotel, Turquoise remembered seeing a notice near the phone stating that the bar, lounge and restaurant were closed for repairs until further notice.

Cloud killed Trinistar.

She opened her eyes and scanned the computer screen again. Cloud wanted to use Carrie to access the temple housing the Codex of Ra'f. But if that were so…that would mean Carrie was the Ancient Key—the only person able to enter the temple. *Carrie is the Ancient Key?*

David leaned his head in front of the computer screen, his eyes wide and full of determination. "We're leaving. We have to get Carrie out of there, now!"

"What's going on?"

Turquoise peered over the laptop to see Veronica standing at the edge of the table, dressed only in the white bathrobe, cleaning out her ear with a cotton swab.

David raced around to the other side of the table, shut the laptop and drove a glare deep into Turquoise's eyes. "We're going to find Jerad's house, and we're going to pull Carrie out of there, right now!"

"I'm still waiting for word from the hotel manager on Carrie's status. There's a chance she's not even in the house right now." Turquoise opened the laptop, but when the screen came back up, she saw a flashing message on it:

Urgent Message--------
Wedding has been pushed up to tonight-------
8:00 p.m.---------
Seventh Street Stalus----------
Black SUV in front of hotel-------------
7:40 p.m.--------------

"Looks like you're going to get your wish, David," Turquoise mumbled. "He pushed the wedding to tonight. We do have to leave, and now." She glimpsed down at the clock in the bottom right corner of the computer screen and realized they had a little over an hour to stop the wedding. *Plenty of time.*

Kimberly and Veronica glanced at each other in their bathrobes and raced off to the bathroom to change.

The phone rang, but Turquoise didn't care to pick it up. She had all the information she needed, and if the manager wanted to get a hold of her, he would have to do it via the computer. He had a vehicle prepared to meet them out front in a little more than twenty minutes. That left them twenty minutes to drive the small stretch to the Seventh Street Stalus. They could do this. She knew they could do this. She just hoped David kept his head screwed on straight through it all.

***

David rushed over to the phone, his adrenaline at an all-time high. What he had seen on the computer screen was enough to convince him that this was a life-or-death situation now. Apparently, Carrie had become a sought-after object, and although he didn't completely understand everything going on, he did understand that Carrie's life was in danger.

He picked up the phone, expecting the front desk. "Hello?"

Nothing.

"Hello?"

David waited expectantly, listening for breathing or some other indication that someone was on the other end, but he heard only silence. He hung up the phone. He turned around to see Turquoise staring at the computer screen.

"We have to go," Turquoise said. "Now!"

"What are you talking about?"

"I just received a message from the manager. Parks is here, in the hotel. He has Anaishan Sentries with him."

Kimberly and Veronica left the bathroom, dressed in jeans and hoodies. David grabbed his black hoodie off the bed and slipped it on, zipped it up and flung the hood over his head. "I can't take on a whole group of sentries."

Veronica sat at the edge of the bed, slipping her sneakers on. "Sentries?"

"Parks brought them with him." David rifled through the other drawers in the room, hoping to find a weapon of some sort. All he found besides the ashtray from earlier was a phone book and an instruction card for the television remote.

Turquoise slammed the laptop shut. "I'll run ahead and take out who I can. You need to get yourself and the girls out of here. An SUV will be waiting for you out front. The wedding is at eight at the Seventh Street Stalus on Penny Street. I'll meet you there." She rushed out the door, leaving the three of them in the hotel room.

David ran to the door and peered out into the tan-carpeted hallway. The corridor was clear all the way to the end, where brown elevator doors stood shut. David waited a minute or two, his panic forcing him to think those doors would open and cough out a squad of sentries, guns blazing. He finally turned back into the room.

Veronica had her purse strung over her shoulder. "How did Parks find out we're here?"

"I'm not sure, but I didn't think he'd come all this way to find us." David started into the hallway with Veronica, heading toward the elevator, hoping to take the stairwell down to the lobby. If Turquoise was smart, she would have taken the stairs as well, meaning their way should be clear through that area.

Kimberly caught up with them, grabbing David's shoulder to slow him down. He spun around, pulling himself out of her grip. "What? We have to get out of here!"

"I got a hold of that number last night, the one I was told to call. A man said he was going to meet me here."

"Fine, let him find us. We can't stick around this hotel much longer or we're going to find ourselves—" David nudged Veronica and Kimberly toward the wall as he moved to the one opposite. He heard the creaking sound again and pointed to the ceiling.

"We're right over them. Dropping down to suspect level in ten seconds."

Sentries! He glanced down the hallway, knowing they couldn't hit the stairwell or the elevator now. If the sentries above them knew where they were, no doubt they would have already blocked all escape routes.

The ceiling creaked louder, and then a body fell through, landing feet first on the floor. When it stood to face David, his fears were confirmed. An Anaishan Sentry. He stood at least seven feet tall and wore shiny blue armor, a blue helmet covering his face.

"Hi."

The sentry reached his arm out and grasped David by the throat, slamming him against the wall. "David Corbin has been apprehended."

David grabbed hold of the thick armored arm, but found it immovable. If the sentry didn't release his grip soon, David knew he would pass out—maybe even suffocate.

"Let him go!" Veronica screamed as she leapt on the sentry's back. She grabbed hold of the helmet and began to twist and pull.

Kimberly took off running down the hallway in the opposite direction of the elevator.

"David Corbin, you are under arrest. Anything you say or do will be held against you—"

"He can't say anything when you're choking him!" Veronica popped the helmet off and slid down the sentry's back.

The man's square-shaped head turned toward her, a stone, soulless gaze in his eyes, which were glazed over in white. He reached his other arm out toward her but only gripped air. "Veronica Amorou, you are under arrest."

David felt the sentry's grip loosen just enough for him to gasp for air. He kicked his leg out, hoping to score a shot in the sentry's groin, but only struck metal there.

Veronica leapt toward the wall, kicked off it and swung the helmet at the sentry's skull. Bone cracked and blood splattered through the air as the sentry released his grip and collapsed to the floor.

David fell to his knees, sucking in what air he could.

Veronica dropped the helmet and glanced down the hallway. "Where did Kimberly go?"

He pointed down the corridor. "That way."

"We have to find her."

David stood up, rubbed his aching neck. "We have to get out of here. If Kimberly wants to run off on her own, that's her choice. We have a wedding to stop, a life to save."

Veronica frowned. "I'll search for her. You get out of this hotel as fast as you can and get to that wedding."

"You have to be kidding me. I can't do this alone!"

"I'll find Kimberly and meet you at the Stalus. We didn't

protect her up to this point to let her get hurt now."

"She ran off! We didn't tell her to run off!"

"I know, I know. But I'm going to do this. You have to get out of here. They're after you."

David looked down at the broken sentry at his feet, blood from the man's head soaking into a large puddle in the carpet. David felt grateful there had only been one sentry. But that one sentry had already reported back to the others, and it wouldn't be long before more came swarming after him, with Parks at the helm.

Veronica grabbed his hand, squeezed it and then started down the hallway. "I'll see you at the Stalus. I promised you I wouldn't leave you to do this by yourself."

He watched her until she was almost at the end of the hallway and then he started in a run toward the stairwell at the other end, quickly mapping things out in his mind. He knew he was on the tenth floor. He knew Turquoise had gone ahead, on an unknown route, to take out what resistance she could. He would have to chance taking the stairs down to the lobby.

39 Flip

7:17 p.m.

Kimberly's paranoia grew, consuming her as she ran down the main hallway of the tenth floor and into another one that branched off from it, looking to find another elevator. Minutes earlier, she had come across one, but it was guarded by a sentry, so she had been forced to continue her frantic search. She didn't know why she was having such a hard time navigating this one floor of the hotel, but it felt like her mind had been jolted by a shock of electricity and was trying to function while it tried to repair its frazzled nerves.

While she ran, while she escaped, she contemplated—or tried to—her reason for leaving David and Veronica, especially when they were in trouble. *I had to get away.* That was the only thought repeating in her mind. *I couldn't help them, and I couldn't just stand there and watch them die.*

Kimberly glimpsed over her shoulder to see if anyone was following her. She stopped in her tracks and took a double glance at the hallway behind her. It stretched farther than she could see, in both directions. She closed her eyes and wondered if she was suffering from more side effects of the sleeping pills. When she opened her eyes, the hallway had returned to its normal length.

She started running again, the only sound echoing in her ears the one her jeans made rubbing together at her thighs.

"Gotcha!"

Kimberly stopped so fast she almost lost her balance, grabbing the wall for support. Officer Sandra Meldramine stood in front of her, gun pointed straight at the girl's face.

"Where are your friends?"

Kimberly's eyes traveled down the barrel of the gun, and she suddenly found herself at peace. This was it, this was the way she would leave this world. Whoever was on the phone who told her he was coming to meet with her was a liar. She had run from the only ones able to protect her, leaving them to fend for themselves. It was all over now. She found comfort in the fact that she would die by a bullet rather than being torn to shreds by the creature with the red eyes.

"Hey!" Sandra shouted. "Where are your friends?"

Kimberly shrugged.

Sandra holstered the weapon and grabbed Kimberly's arm. "C'mon, we need to get you out of here."

"Out of here?"

"Yeah. We need to get out of here before Parks or a sentry finds us."

The clattering of metal reverberated down the hallway. Sandra pulled her pistol from the holster and aimed it at the sentry turning the corner a few rooms away from them.

He stopped in the middle of the hallway, his blue helmet turning from Sandra to Kimberly. Sandra moved slowly in front of Kimberly, positioning the gun on the sentry.

"Sandra Meldramine, officer of the decorated order of police, you are under arrest for drawing a weapon on an Anaishan Sentry. Under section four of article ten in the Anaishan Penal Code for Suspect Behavior and Actions, I am going to take you in to be detained until a court date has been designated for you."

"I'm not going anywhere."

The sentry started to move toward Sandra. She fired the gun, the bullet ricocheting off the blue armor and hitting the wall to the right of them. She fired two more shots, pushing Kimberly back as she did so, giving them more room to run.

Kimberly didn't know why Sandra, the woman who had shoved the pills down Kimberly's throat at the hospital, was all of a sudden helping her. Kimberly was about to turn and run when a blur moved past her and ran into the sentry, knocking him through one of the hotel room doors.

Parks stood to his feet and brushed himself off. He adjusted his tie and flapped his jacket, spitting on the sentry, whose helmet had fallen off in the tackle. "Stupid fools think they can replace us." Parks pulled his gun and fired a shot straight into the sentry's exposed head, blowing brains and blood across the carpet.

"What did you just do?" Sandra looked away from the mess, holding her stomach as if she was about to throw up.

Kimberly refused to look away, something in her mind shutting down, her body failing to listen to her screams for it to run.

Parks turned toward them, menace in his eyes. "I've been wanting to do that for a long time. Stupid things think they can replace us? Replace that!" He fired another bullet, spreading the sentry's face across the wall. "Yeah!"

"Parks!"

He laughed, shoving the gun back in his holster. Then he rushed toward Kimberly, grabbed her by the neck and slammed her against another door. "You're going to come with me, and I don't want any more trouble out of you."

"Let me go!" Kimberly struggled, seeing a look in Parks's eyes she hadn't seen in anyone else before. Insanity. She had seen terror, fear, evil, passion. But not insanity. She remembered in school, years ago, a teacher reading from a book and quoting the author saying, "Insanity is the crossing of the line between being in control of oneself and giving that control to the darkest, most innate parts of the mind and soul."

Sandra pulled her gun on Parks. "Let her go."

He looked at Sandra, his eyes glazed over in a shadowy film. Kimberly felt something else at work in the hallway, something unnatural. The red eyes—those red eyes that had chased her, the source of those eyes, the very structure attached to those eyes was somewhere close by, somewhere within reach. She felt sick and wanted to throw up, but if she did that, Parks would surely shoot her out of annoyance.

"What are you doing, Sandra? Put the gun away. Put it away now."

"No. Let her go or I'll shoot you."

"You don't have it in you to shoot an agent."

"I swear I'll do it. I'm done being your puppet. I'm done with the charades, the games. You have something wrong with you, something seriously wrong with you, and I don't want any part of it anymore."

"My puppet? If you haven't forgotten, I saved your son. I

363

did!" He spit when he spoke, and his eyes widened as if the balls were trying to leap out of their sockets. "If I had turned him in when I should have, he would be in prison right now."

"Let her go." Tears streamed down Sandra's pale cheeks.

Parks let go of Kimberly and stepped toward Sandra. "You can kiss our deal goodbye. Your son is going away for life. For the rest of his life!"

"They're all humans! My son, David, Veronica and Kimberly. They're humans, Parks. You've been screwing with them the whole time, and I can't be a part of it anymore."

"Screwing with them? They broke the law! The law!"

"So did you. You just killed a sentry."

"As far as I'm concerned, you killed the sentry. Who do you think they're going to believe after I release the evidence against your son?"

Sandra swung the gun out and struck Parks in the head. He toppled to the floor. She holstered her weapon and dragged Parks's body into the room with the sentry, closing the door when she finished.

"Why are you helping me?"

Sandra turned from the door, wiping her eyes of the tears. "I'll explain later."

Veronica stepped out of one of the rooms, her purse around her arm. "I think it's time we all get out of here."

"What were you doing in there?" Sandra asked.

"I heard the sentry checking the rooms, and I hid. I kept a close eye on what happened between you and Parks to see if I could really trust you."

"Do you?"

"Only time will tell."

40 Illusions

David stepped silently down the stairwell, taking each movement slowly, passing the door leading into the eighth floor. Any sound, such as the tapping of his sneakers against the concrete, echoed off the walls as if he were in a shower. He had already found one sentry unconscious on the stairs around the ninth floor. Turquoise had cleared a path, as she said she would, but he doubted she would be able to get them all.

Although he didn't want to use violent force if he didn't have to, David made an attempt to take a weapon off the fallen sentry, but to no avail. Either their weapons were concealed or they didn't need them because of their tremendous strength and shielding.

He continued toward the seventh floor when he spotted another sentry guarding the door to the sixth floor farther down. David made his way to the seventh floor door and gently pushed down on the handle, cranking the door open with meticulous effort. He slipped inside and slowly, gently shut the door behind him. He had no doubt that the sentry, if he bothered to look up, might have been able to see David through his scanners. David wasn't all that sure of what they were capable of, just that they were designed with some of the world's most advanced technology. At least, that's what the news reported.

The hallway stretched out before him, a barren corridor. Empty, soulless, silent—save for the humming of the heaters. He decided to wait where he was, see if the sentry guarding the sixth floor would leave so he could continue down toward the lobby.

David leaned his back against the stairwell door and closed his eyes. He pushed down the fear struggling to rise up in his spirit. The odds were stacked significantly against him. The woman he loved, the girl he had grown up with, was about to marry a ruthless man with ulterior motives that still weren't all that clear. The hotel was filled with Anaishan Sentries, which in single numbers were hard enough to evade or defeat. And the psycho Agent Parks was in the building somewhere, no doubt looking for David.

But he remembered that the odds had been stacked against him many times before. Maybe not to this extent, but he had made it out of many a hopeless situation both by himself and with Veronica, Carrie and Sean. David nodded. He had to keep pressing on. He couldn't give up, couldn't give in to the odds. He had to rise above them to save Carrie's life, to stop this heinous wedding before things really got out of hand and spiraled into a pool of chaos.

"David."

He opened his eyes. "You?"

The farmer's daughter stood before him, her soft, disturbingly innocent demeanor making him question whether she was human.

"Don't worry," she whispered. "The sentry on the sixth floor is there to stall you, to prevent you from dying on your way to the wedding."

David rubbed his eyes, hoping the girl was a figment of his tired mind. "What are you doing here?"

"I'm here to help you."

"Help me?" He laughed. "Help me? You caused all of this, all of this trouble, just by alerting your dad to Kimberly in the gas station. And then you led us along that route at the facility where your dad shot me in the back. I can't tell you how much I appreciate that."

"What you perceive to be trouble is simply trouble rerouted to put you on the right path." Olivia's eyes changed color, exhibiting a light blue shade.

He threw his hands up in the air. "Whatever." David slowly opened the stairwell door and looked out over the railing. The sentry still guarded the sixth floor.

"David, I need your help. Anaisha needs your help."

He turned back into the hallway, slowly shutting the door behind him. "I'm concerned with one thing right now, and that's getting out of here and saving Carrie's life."

"This world is in danger. You aren't going to like what's to come, but you must understand this is all how it was meant to happen. You're the only strand left to build the resistance."

"I don't even know what that means, but I'm sure it doesn't matter. I'm getting out here before your crazy dad decides to show up and put another bullet in my back."

"Evil is here, David. It is here for your friend, Kimberly.

It is here for you and Veronica. It is even here for Turquoise. You can't see it, though it is all around you. As is the good, at least what little is left of it in this world, in this reality."

"I have a wedding to stop. A girl to save." He suddenly felt warm, as if the heaters were turned up too high in the hallway.

"The wedding is only the beginning. The beginning of a journey that will determine if you are truly Anaisha's greatest hero or not."

"I don't want to be a hero! Don't you get it? Doesn't fate or the gods or whatever you believe controls our lives get it? I'm not a hero, not anymore. I did my time, I saved the world, I brought peace to the land. Now I just want to be with Carrie, go live somewhere where nobody is going to bother us for the rest of our lives. Do you get that?"

"You are the only one who can save us, David. You and your friends, you're the only ones who can stop what's coming."

"I don't care. Just…just get rid of the guard down there and let me be on my way." *Boy, it's getting warm in here.* He unzipped the front of his hoodie, sweat forming in the small of his back, in the nooks behind his ears, the pits of his arms. His face felt flush with warmth, and he wondered if he was getting sick or developing an overly aggressive anxiety attack.

"Fine," Olivia snapped, taking a few steps back. "If you won't take what I say seriously, then I'll show you what I'm talking about. There is too much at stake to allow you to be so careless and arrogant, putting your needs before those of the world. I'll let you see what you're up against. I will give you the sight to see the one formed by darkness."

Her eyes were a deep blue now. He decided he didn't want to wait any longer, didn't want to linger another moment in this hotel, in this hallway, before this mentally unstable young girl. He turned toward the door, but, to his fright, it was gone. The door handle, the door, all of it were gone, and in their place stood a solid wall. When he turned back toward Olivia, she too was gone. The corridor began to stretch out in front of him, doubling, tripling, quadrupling its length through the hotel. The lights flickered and dimmed to a dark red glow. A mist filled the corridor, seeping in from the walls, from the vents, filling the space in front of him.

"What's going on?" he called out. "Joke's over. I want my door back."

"Heh, heh, heh, heh," a deep, raspy voice boomed. The clouds in front of David moved, as if someone or something was making its way through it.

"Who's there?"

A tall man strolled toward David. He wore a crimson-colored suit, had a bald head and a clean-shaven face. David noticed something unpleasant about the man's face, something about its roundness, the very small rolls of fat dripping from under his neck. His jaw line was carved into a shape that reminded David of the gargoyles perched at the very top of some of Lysallis's city buildings, the lower jaw coming out a little farther than the top.

But it was the man's eyes, his bluish-white pupils that triggered the nightmare in David's memory. An apartment, the burning credits, the murder of a girl, those same glowing eyes and Drather.

The lighter, the hotel and now the creature standing before me.

"It seems the young lady has given you the sight to see me. That sort of ruins my element of surprise."

David glanced at his watch, knowing he was running out of time. The face on the watch was blank, just a green circle missing the numbers and hands. He glanced up at the man in the red suit. "Who are you?"

The man grinned, revealing sharp teeth. "It all depends. I used to be something great, a general in the dark army. Now? Well, you can call me Chaos. It's a watered-down version of my real name, a name for which you would not understand the genuine interpretation.

"As I said before, the girl has given you the gift of sight. It's remarkable she was able to do that, but I do have to admit it's quite annoying. My work, my plans, my strategies, all hinge on the element of surprise, and it seems she has taken that from me."

David stared at the man, into his glowing eyes, recounting the nightmare, his mind trying to study every detail of it to piece together what was really going on. He had found the lighter, the same lighter that burned the credits. *But where are the credits? Who is the dead girl? And why does the layout of the apartment seem so familiar?*

"I can see your mind working behind those eyes. You're crafting an appropriate explanation for everything. It's pathetic to see you working so hard to figure the simple things out."

"I want out of here. I want the door back so I can get out of this place."

"If it were only as simple as that. Olivia is the one who took away your door. She has forced confrontation between you and me, for purposes I can only assume. I think she has the presumption that if you were to see what you are up against, it might somehow force you to take up a mantle and wage a war you do not have the power or ability to wage. That's okay. Her ignorance can be blamed on her young age.

"Your ignorance cannot. You have experience, you have lived a life other mortals have only sought after in books and films. You have lived, David. And if you want to continue living, if you want to continue enjoying this planet, however corrupt and deceiving it may be, you will listen to what I have to say."

"I want to leave. That's all I want to do. Let me out of this place. Now!"

"Giving me orders? I thought you didn't want to be a leader. Or was I wrong? I'm on your side, David. I am a friend, for lack of a better word. I agree that you shouldn't be a leader, or a hero. I think it's a grand idea that you settle down somewhere, out of the way. There will always be evil in the world. It's not something you can completely rid yourself of. But the mantle to stop it must be passed to others, the responsibility given to those who haven't received their battle scars yet.

"In other words, it is time for you to rest, to retire."

David sensed something else moving in the mist. The substance of the air was extremely thick, like the smoke after an explosion.

The man, Chaos, stepped closer to David. His arms behind his back, he grinned again, revealing those sharp teeth. "I think I need to show you who I really am, so you will take me seriously when I tell you what I don't want you to do."

David glanced at the wall behind him, hoping the door reappeared. No luck.

"I want you to see what evil is truly capable of. You've fought some very challenging and sinister enemies in the past. Mr. Big, Scarlet Rogue, even yourself at certain points. It is…

impressive…that you have triumphed over these adversaries, although I sense you were being helped by outside forces."

"What are you talking about?"

Chaos shook his head. "Never mind that. Since that clever child has opened your eyes to the real world around you, I will use it to my advantage and show you the powers I have been given." The man stepped back, the toothy grin on his face, and waved his arms in the air like a magician about to perform a trick. "Abra…cadabra!"

Everything around David disappeared, replaced with black space.

Panic kicked in, but David quickly pushed it down. Although he wasn't entirely certain this man was human, he had to stay calm, had to keep his wits about him, or he would fall here and now and never make it to the wedding. He wondered what time it was. The darkness shrouded all of his sight, preventing him from looking at his watch. *It's probably still messed up anyway.*

The darkness began to disperse, and in its place a tunnel of lattice formed, wrapped in ivy and crimson-colored solaris flowers. A stone pathway materialized under his feet, and benches lined the sides of the tunnel.

The air grew cold as a white fog settled in front of him.

"Where am I?"

Nobody replied. He stepped forward, reached out to touch the lattice and recoiled when his hand felt real wood. He peered through the side of the tunnel and saw grassy lawn spreading out toward a large castle in the distance. People loitered on the lawn, dressed in fancy gowns and tailored suits. Examining them, David found that they were all frozen in place, frozen in expressions of laughter, of socializing, giving them the appearance of cardboard cutouts.

Has time somehow stopped here? Where is here? Where am I?

David looked away from the wall of the lattice tunnel and heard laughing in the distance, in the direction of the tunnel's mouth. He started through the lingering fog, making his way toward the jovial sound. He peered through the squares of lattice along the wall at different points, capturing glances of people frozen in a time of what he perceived to be a wedding reception or celebration of some kind. He spotted a large wedding cake through part of the lattice, but ivy blocked a majority of his view, preventing him from seeing what sat at the very top of the dozen-tiered white cake.

The surrealism of the scenes made David shiver, but he pressed on, his curiosity getting the very best of him. Whatever this Chaos man had done—drugged or hypnotized David—David wasn't going to succumb to the fear he felt.

The laughter grew louder as he got closer to the end of the tunnel. He shivered, wanting a jacket or a blanket, anything to warm him. The sound of light rain pitter-pattered across the ivy-covered roof of the tunnel. The environment gave him a sense of peace. In all of his adventures through Anaisha, he couldn't ever remember coming across a tunnel like this. He thought of the castle he spotted in the distance and became aware that he had never seen one that tall or magnificent.

When he stepped across the threshold of the tunnel into a thick cloud of fog, the laughter exploded. When it died down, the fog began to dissipate, giving a clear view to the scene in front of him.

A long table draped in white cloth stretched before him.

Dozens of people sat at the table, all of them with wine glasses in hand, raising them to the sky.

One particular woman, dressed in a dark blue strapless gown, was standing, arm stretched over the table with her glass full of dark red wine. "And that was how I remember these two wonderful people meeting each other."

The crowd erupted in cheers, everyone clinking their wine glasses together, creating a high-pitched ringing that forced David to cover his ears momentarily. The woman took her seat, and it was then that David noticed who sat at the other end of the table.

Jerad Montlier.

The man wore the typical tuxedo that men wear on their wedding day. And then it dawned on David what this scene represented. He turned to head back into the tunnel, but the table scene moved in front of him, no matter what direction he tried to turn.

Everyone's gaze suddenly fell on him, as if he had just been identified as an intruder.

"David, so nice of you to come. I don't remember sending an invitation to you," Jerad said from his seat.

David didn't know how to respond. He focused on the people staring at him, their eyes like wolves who have found someone trampling across their turf. Then, as if on cue, every wine glass on the surface of the table fell over, spilling its contents across the once-white tablecloth. David watched as the red wine seeped into the cloth, the stains gathering with each other until the whole tablecloth was doused in red.

"See what you've done?" Jerad asked.

"What do mean?"

Another figure materialized from the fog encompassing the table and its occupants—a female. As she sauntered through the mist and took a seat in Jerad's lap, David suddenly felt the urge to scream.

Carrie, dressed in a dazzling red gown that flowed across the floor like the wine that marred the table, smiled. "Hello, David. I didn't expect to see you here. In fact, if I remember right, you weren't invited."

"I..."

She wrapped her arms around Jerad's neck and smashed her crimson-painted lips into his. David turned to look away, but once again, the scene followed his vision wherever it went. He closed his eyes, but the vision remained there, in the darkness behind his eyelids. There was no sanctuary from his agony, from the harsh spell placed on him.

When they finished kissing, Carrie stood up and strolled toward David. He felt paralyzed, frozen, like the people he had seen through the lattice walls. When Carrie reached him, he couldn't help but lunge toward her to kiss her. She shoved him back with her arms, disgust splashed across her face.

"What do you think you're doing?"

The guests at the table stood to their feet, angry.

"I love you!"

Carrie's grimace turned into a smile, and she began giggling. "Love me?"

Those behind her laughed hysterically. It sounded like the laughter he heard from the tunnel.

Jerad was up and making his way toward them.

David closed his eyes, rubbing them frantically, in an attempt to wipe away this dreaded illusion or dream, or whatever it was. *How did I get here again?* Something to do with the man in the red suit…Chaos. This was a trick, something to prevent him from reaching the wedding. *But I'm at the wedding now, aren't I? The castle in the distance, the tall, towering castle is Jerad's, isn't it?*

David felt someone grab his hand, and when he opened his eyes, Carrie held his palm in hers.

"Let go of me, David."

He looked down and realized he was holding her hand. He let go and took a step back. "What is this? What is going on?"

Jerad wrapped his arms around Carrie's waist from behind, buried his face into her neck and began to peck her skin with soft kisses.

"Stop that!" David screamed.

The guests at the table moved toward him. Some had picked up their wine glasses and broken the tops of them across the edge of the table, apparently planning to use them as weapons.

Carrie's eyes closed with the kisses Jerad planted on her. "That feels so nice," she whispered. "So much better than anything David ever gave me."

David found himself surrounded. The dozens of wedding guests had suddenly multiplied into hundreds.

Jerad stepped away from Carrie, his face flush. He wiped his lips on his sleeve. "You weren't invited here, David. How did you get here?"

"I…" he looked at Carrie, as if expecting her to approve of his presence there.

She shook her head. "I sure didn't invite you."

How did I get here again? Wasn't it…I came here to save her? "I came here to save you. I…I came through crooked cops and

376

sentries, and I was shot and…and…"

"I don't care what you came through."

"What?"

"I don't care," Carrie reiterated. "Why would I care?" Her arms hung at her sides, her hands balling into fists. "What do I care that you came all this way? To save me from what? This is my wedding, idiot. My wedding!" she screamed.

David noticed the crowd moving in a step or two closer toward him. The sharp, jagged edges of the broken wine glasses glistened with drops of wine.

Carrie jabbed her long-nailed finger into his chest. "You let me go a long time ago. You didn't come after me when I ran. You didn't stop me from meeting Jerad. You should have told me how you felt about me sooner, instead of waiting for the 'right moment.'" Carrie did the quotes with her fingers. "What did you think was going to happen? Did you think I was just going to rot in the absence of your love? No! No!"

David wanted to run. Anywhere. He wanted this nightmare to be over, wanted to wake up in his bed at the apartment. He could call Veronica, and she would comfort him, help him through this. His stomach fell ill and he understood if he didn't do something quickly, if he didn't get away, he might vomit on Carrie or any of the crowd members slowly creeping closer to him.

Carrie's temper seemed to die down, and her face returned from redness to a pale complexion.

"You see, David, I don't want you anymore. I did, at one point, but you blew it. You lost your grand opportunity to take me as your own. Now I'm Jerad's. I'm his property. I'm his to do what he wants with…."

David felt bile shoot up his throat, but he swallowed it quickly before it could leave his mouth. The tart, bitter taste lingered on his tongue.

"It's for the best. For both of us. See, you could never offer me what Jerad offers me. Wealth, power, prestige. I live like a queen, because I am one now. And you," she waved her hand at him as if he was a passing thought, "you're a washed-up hero with no direction. You have no ambition, no goals, no drive to move you forward."

"You're my drive!" he heard himself shout. "You're why I did this, why I came all this way, why I fought and fought and fought." He crumpled to his knees, tears pouring from his eyes. He had to touch her, had to keep a piece of her with him. He reached out and grabbed hold of the hem of her gown, but the cloth melted into wine that passed through his fingers.

Carrie knelt to his level. He looked into her eyes, into those bright green eyes and noticed they had turned a menacing shade of bright blue. "You need to pull yourself together. Move on without me. I am no longer yours to have."

"I can't."

When the words slipped out, David noticed a change in the atmosphere. What he felt coming from the crowd as anger and hostility, though minimal, turned to rage and malice. They were ready to tear him to pieces, ready to cut him into tiny particles with the broken wine glasses, with their bare hands. Carrie had developed this attitude as well.

"You will," she said firmly. "You will move on, you will forget about me. I'm no good to you now. I love Jerad. Jerad loves me. I love my riches and my castle and my new friends. You have Veronica, you have your family. Go back to them and let me be. Let me live in peace."

He couldn't stop the words from slipping out again. "I can't."

Carrie stood up tall. "Then you'll die."

The crowd descended on him, and he was thrust into darkness again.

The hotel hallway began to materialize. David found himself on the floor, his back against one of the hotel room doors. He had been crying, tears staining his cheeks, dotting the T-shirt under his hoodie.

Chaos sat, cross-legged, in front of him. "Welcome back."

"What....where was I?"

"Carrie's wedding. That should have been obvious."

"I—..."

"Just don't talk right now. I want you to keep quiet, to let everything you saw sink in. I need you to understand, David, that the wedding you're on your way to stop needs to be forgotten. Dispose of your heroic notions and go back to Lysallis. Now. I'll even guarantee you and your friends a safe journey home."

Disorientation lingered with David, and he found himself unsure of what was real and what was his overactive imagination. Maybe he had taken a bullet to the head in his attempt to escape the hotel, and now he lay sprawled somewhere in a hallway or stairwell, blood seeping from his skull, mentally trapped in this morbid merry-go-round.

Chaos stood. "I'll leave you to ponder your options. You better hurry, though, because your time is running out. Not just to stop the wedding, but to get out of here."

David buried his face in his knees, yelling at his mind to calm down, to bring reality back into focus. He knew the wedding...experience...was only an illusion. *Right?*

"Lift your head, David. Time is running out."

He looked up and saw Olivia standing there. Chaos was gone. Or at least, invisible again.

David got to his feet, a bit of a dizzy spell flashing over him. "What happened?"

Olivia helped steady him against the wall. "That man, the one who came to visit you, is Chaos. Literally. He is by far the most powerful enemy you have come up against. I have given you the gift of sight. It is necessary to fulfilling your destiny."

"Destiny?" David glanced at his watch. 7:29 p.m.

"What did he tell you?"

"To go home."

"You can't do that. You have to continue on the path you've started."

The wedding vision hung in the front of his mind. It was real for him, at one point. Carrie, Jerad, the riches that he gave her, the friends she surrounded herself with. The hatred she had toward him.

Olivia grabbed David's wrist, staring up at him with bright green eyes. "You mustn't doubt. That's what Chaos wants you to do. To doubt your path, your destiny."

David nodded. "I'm going to save Carrie." He realized if this Chaos man was real, and not a frightening figment of his imagination, then David had an advantage by being able to see him when he was in the vicinity. This would allow David to prepare himself mentally for any other visions the man wanted to bestow upon him. Then again, the vision of the wedding…it had to have been more than a vision. David felt like he was really there in the outskirts of the castle.

Whatever Chaos was able to do, it was far more powerful than any illusion.

"I must warn you, David. Carrie will not be yours tonight."

He glanced toward the stairwell door that had been returned to its rightful place. "She will be. If that Chaos character shows up, I'll make sure to teach him a lesson for messing with me."

Olivia shook her head. "You cannot stop him alone. It is impossible."

David sneered. "I'll save Carrie. I've always been able to protect her, and now won't be any different. I'm not about to let some sadistic magician threaten me."

"Chaos is more than a magician."

"Whatever he is, I'll stop him!" David shouted. "I'll resist his mind games. I've fought enemies worse than him before." He knew it was a lie. The reality Chaos had created, the playground of the mind Chaos had erected and trapped David in was like nothing he had ever experienced before. But he knew he would overcome the man's trickery, would have to, if it meant Carrie's life being saved.

"There are some enemies you cannot defeat, David, not by yourself. You will need help in this matter. You will need help saving the world this time around."

David turned the handle on the stairwell door. "I'm through saving the world. I'm going to save Carrie and then I'm going to live my life. I deserve that much."

On his way into the stairwell, David heard Olivia's last words before the door shut softly on her, "This has nothing to do with what you think you deserve. If your destiny calls you to save the world, you will have no choice but to save it or perish with it."

41

Relentless

Carrie lay in the darkness, in the silence, wondering what time it was, how much closer she was to marrying Jerad. She dozed off once, but nightmares of Jerad prevented her nap from lasting long. Each time she shifted her body across the floor of the garage, the cement chilled her bare legs. She wished herself out of the maid outfit, wished herself out of the plastic restraints. She hated the darkness, the lack of sight, the absence of David. She wanted badly to see his face again. She wanted him to rescue her, just one more time.

The door to the house opened, and the garage lights flickered on. Carrie squinted to adjust her eyes.

Jerad walked in, cane in hand, and stopped over her. "I hope you got enough rest. You're going to need it for what's ahead."

"I told you, I'm not marrying you."

"You don't have a choice." He grabbed her by the hair and pulled her to her feet. She yelped, pain spreading across her skull as he shoved her against the wall and grabbed her jaw, squeezing it. "You will marry me! If you don't, all of your friends will die. All of them. I mean David, I mean Veronica, and I will even kill your maid friend. So I would think twice before you mouth off to me." He slammed her head against the wall, dazing her.

When he let go of her jaw, she stared into his demonic gaze. "I won't be scared that easily. You can't stop my friends, nor will I let you think you can tame me." She tasted blood in her mouth and realized the inside of her cheek was cut.

Jerad grabbed her by the arm and shoved her through the doorway leading into the house. "You and little miss maid are going for a ride." He pushed her through the kitchen area, beyond the guards she had snuck past earlier in the day and into the living area. She struggled to stall by dragging the heels of her shoes into the carpet, but he shoved her as hard as he could, causing her to stumble to the floor. Then he picked her up by the hair again and led her through the front door.

A limo sat on the curb, engine running.

Jerad grabbed Carrie's jaw again, crushing her teeth into the wound in her cheek. "I have many, many connections, my dear. Dangerous connections. If you even think about screwing this up tonight, I will make sure you regret it. Your friends will be tortured, in front of you, especially David. I know how much you love him, but you will be marrying me tonight. Nothing, and I mean nothing, will stop that from happening."

"You underestimate me. You underestimate my friends."

Jerad shoved her toward the car. The limo driver stepped out and ran around to the back passenger door, opening it for them. Jerad gave a good shove as Carrie tripped and fell halfway into the car, banging her knees.

The driver shoved her into the seat and swung the door shut. Carrie sat up, wishing she could rub the sting from her knees. She looked down and saw that they were dark red. Across from her sat Angel, frowning, still dressed in the nightgown, her hands restrained behind her back.

The car started moving, and Carrie feared that her time was running out. If David was going to save her, he would have to be quick about it. Carrie wasn't prepared to marry Jerad, but if he threatened Angel's life, what could she do?

"Stay alert, Carrie, for an opportunity."

"What?"

"Help is on the way."

***

Turquoise dropped the sentry's body on the stairs and opened the door leading into the lobby. The place had been deserted. Turquoise guessed that might have been because of the sentries. Their presence usually sparked fear in civilians.

She found the absence of personnel at the front desk especially strange. She knew the hotel manager, Cedric, would have kept to his post, keeping things going in the hotel as well as keeping her updated on any info he received from Jerad's place.

She heard a groan. She leapt over the counter and landed next to a body on the tile floor. "Cedric!" She knelt and lifted his bloody and beaten face in her arms.

"Turq…"

"Who did this?" She watched his swollen eyes slowly open to orange pupils.

"They…" Blood came leaking from the corner of his lip, trickling across Turquoise's arm.

"Easy, Cedric. Easy."

"Threatened….everyone…told…to   leave…or   they would be…killed."

Why would the sentries threaten anyone who didn't have any connection to the teens? And why would they evacuate the hotel?

Cedric's eyes slowly shut, and his head gained weight in her arms. She gently brushed the matted hair from his forehead and softly stroked his cheek. She wished very badly to have the gift of healing. She could heal herself, but nobody else, which frustrated her to no end in times like this. "Why did they evacuate?"

"The man…" He opened one eye. "Man…in black…said you would…" Cedric coughed, spreading a mist of blood across Turquoise's face. She didn't bother to wipe it off. She knew he spoke of Drather when he mentioned the man in black. *But why would Drather—* "He said you would never reach the girl in time."

Cedric's eye closed, and his head grew heavy like a bowling ball.

"Carrie?"

Cedric nodded. Then the word she feared, the word that confirmed a minute assumption in the back of her mind—an assumption as to why the hotel would be evacuated—slipped from Cedric's lips, which were turning purple. "Bomb."

Her heart skipped a beat. She set him down on the floor and stood to her feet, frantically scanning the computer, filing cabinet, telephones, personal mail boxes along the back wall, waiting for an instinct of some sort to save them, to alert her to where the bomb had been placed. "Where?

Where did he put it?"

"Copier."

She rushed to the large machine, which had been positioned behind the counters, off to the side against a pillar. Lifting the scanning cover, she found nothing out of the ordinary. She checked the paper trays and found nothing there either. Then she opened the casing where the toner cartridge should have been and found Drather's handiwork: a skinny black cylinder with a blue digital readout.

The stairwell door burst open, and David ran out. "Turquoise!"

She pulled the cylinder out of the copier and turned toward him just in time to see Parks jump out from behind a pillar and tackle David to the floor.

Turquoise registered the time on the bomb—six minutes, twelve seconds. David and Parks fought, swinging at each other with thuds and groans. Veronica, Sandra and Kimberly burst out of the stairwell door, and with Sandra's help, pulled David out of Parks's grasp.

"Get out of here!" Turquoise shouted to them, gently setting the canister down on the scanning glass of the copier. She thought it would do well as a flat surface for her to work on.

"What are you two doing with her?" David asked, pointing to Sandra, who had her knees in Parks's abdomen, pinning him to the floor.

"We can trust her," Veronica said.

Turquoise didn't hear any argument from David. She knew he trusted Veronica with his life, so if she said someone could be trusted, she could.

David approached the counter, unaware of the gravity of

the situation. "Let's go."

Turquoise wiped the sweat from her forehead. "I'm not going with you right now."

"What do you mean? We have to stop the wedding."

Two sentries charged into the lobby from the hotel entrance. Veronica set herself in a fighting stance in front of Kimberly, but one swing from a sentry's arm knocked her to the floor, dazed. Some of her purse contents scattered across the lobby: lip balm, hair ties, a card wallet, coins, a canister of mace, a small makeup kit, and a ring of keys.

One of the sentries took Sandra by the arms before she could reach her weapon, while the other grabbed Kimberly and restrained her hands behind her back with cuffs. "Officer Sandra Meldramine and Kimberly Sebastien, you are both under arrest by order of Agent Parks of Tindall Detention Facility Hub 4."

"David!" Kimberly screamed.

"Get out of here!" Sandra said. "Both of you, now!"

David helped Veronica to her feet. "Turquoise?"

The sentries finished restraining Sandra and Kimberly and then started toward David and Veronica.

Turquoise wiped the sweat from her brow, the digital clock on the bomb ticking loudly in her ears. "I can't help you guys right now. I'm sorry. If I don't diffuse this bomb, this whole building and anyone left inside it will blow up."

"We have to save Carrie!" David shouted as Veronica swept the scattered contents back into her purse. They both started moving toward the front doors of the building.

"Get to the wedding!" Turquoise demanded. "Stop it at all costs. You and Veronica. An SUV is waiting outside for you. Keys are in the ignition. I'll diffuse this bomb."

"What about us?" Kimberly asked, struggling to free herself from the sentry's grasp.

"I'll save you, soon. Please, just let me stop this bomb from destroying half the block."

Veronica wiped her bleeding lip and pulled David toward the doors.

"David? David, don't leave us here! Please, please help us!" Kimberly pleaded.

Parks drew his gun and fired a few shots toward David and Veronica. They leapt and rolled toward the pillars, taking cover behind them as the bullets struck the tile and shattered the glass of the front doors.

Turquoise thrust her arm out, and a gust of air picked Parks up and tossed him into the stairwell door, breaking it off its hinges.

"Get out of here, now!" Turquoise barked.

Two more sentries entered the building as David and Veronica rushed past them and exited the hotel.

The sentries who held Sandra and Kimberly captive began moving them toward the doors.

"Turquoise? Turquoise, help! Help us!" Kimberly screamed as they passed the counter. "Help!"

As difficult as it was, Turquoise ignored Kimberly's cries for rescue and let the sentries take her and Sandra away, leaving her alone with the bomb, which she had arranged in pieces across the scanner glass. Carrie was her mission, her priority. But her friend, Cedric, lay on the floor next to her, bleeding, beaten by his enemies, and she couldn't leave him, or the rest of those still in the hotel, to die.

David's outburst at the train station ran through her mind as she started work on diffusing the bomb. He went back to save the people in the station. He risked his life. He found the greater worth more than himself. Now Turquoise found the tables turned. She was risking her life—and, in a sense, Carrie's—to save her friend and those still in the building.

She felt supremely confident that David could take down Jerad, though, especially with Veronica's help. At least buy Turquoise some time so she could diffuse the bomb and get to the wedding in time to get Carrie out of there.

The seconds, the milliseconds, ticked by, each passing too fast, edging her and the hotel closer to destruction.

Five minutes, twenty-eight seconds.

42

As Fate Would Have It

David drove the black SUV down Penny Street toward the Seventh Street Stalus. Veronica dug through the glove compartment, convinced she could find a useful item or two to help them save Carrie. David wasn't so optimistic. The confrontation with Chaos seemed to stay with him, feeding into his fear that he wouldn't reach Carrie in time.

Even if I do reach her in time, what if things play out the way they did in the castle scene? What if she has no desire to be with me and really wants to marry Jerad? David admitted that would be more difficult to take than if they simply missed the wedding.

The streets were abandoned, everyone filling the clubs underneath the asphalt they drove over. David wondered what lively things were happening down there. He also wondered if there would be somewhere to escape to if he did indeed miss the wedding or if Carrie refused his feelings for her. The very thin thread of sanity he had been holding onto most of the journey was beginning to break. When it did, he wasn't sure who or what he would become, and it scared him.

Veronica pulled a very small, black satchel out of the back of the glove compartment. "This is like the one Turquoise carries."

They passed through a green light, and that's when David noticed the accident scene in their lane up ahead. He slowed, going around the police cruisers that had just arrived. An upside-down semi-truck rested atop what might have once been a small car.

David drove past the accident and returned to the right lane, sobered by the thought that it could have been them beneath that semi. *Nobody could have survived an accident like that. Nobody.*

David remembered what Olivia had said, about him being stalled to prevent him from dying.

He turned to talk to Veronica about Olivia and noticed the items from the satchel spread across Veronica's lap: a wad of credits, a small vial of white liquid, a few silver discs David knew to be the same kind Turquoise used to blow up the school bus back in North Ryshard.

David glanced in the rearview mirror, thinking of the accident. The blue lights swirling atop a sentry cruiser suddenly glimmered in the mirror.

"We have company."

Veronica craned her neck to see through the back window and nodded. "We sure do." She picked up one of the silver discs and analyzed it for a moment.

David wondered what to do. The stalus wasn't too far ahead. Even if they outran the sentry, when they reached the stalus, the sentry would only cause problems, possibly bring his friends. If they stopped to fight the sentry, they wouldn't reach the wedding in time.

David slammed his foot down on the gas pedal, and the SUV sped forward, right through a red light. The sentry was in the next lane over, catching up fast. David remembered hearing rumors of how the sentry cruisers were some of the fastest vehicles in Anaisha. He was about to test that rumor.

As both vehicles sped down the street, Veronica set the three discs across her lap, side by side, and put the vial of white liquid and the credits back in the satchel. "We're going to have to take out that sentry, David. We don't have a choice."

He couldn't think of another alternative at the moment. They weren't just trying to prevent themselves from being captured, they were trying to save Carrie's life and— according to Turquoise—possibly all of Anaisha.

He reached over and took one of the discs off Veronica's lap. The cruiser was at his left side now, the lights of the buildings reflecting off the flat surface of the cruiser's window. "How does this work?"

Veronica took it from him. "You turn the bezel to activate the timer and then press the button, here." Handing it back to him, she gripped his hand in hers. "We have to do what we have to do to reach that wedding on time, David. Just remember Carrie's life is at stake."

How could I forget?

He took the disc from her as the window of the sentry cruiser slid down. The sentry in the passenger seat pointed his finger at them, speaking loudly over the rumble of the engines. "Pull your vehicle over! You're under arrest!"

"Not tonight," David groaned as he rolled his window down and jerked the wheel to the left, sideswiping the cruiser. The sentries' vehicle lost control and crawled up on the curb of the median briefly before returning to the road and slamming into the SUV. David held onto the wheel, doing his best not to fly off the road as the front of the vehicle pulled and grabbed.

David swerved into the cruiser again, forcing it into a spinout. It didn't take long for the cruiser to regain its course, but before it could fully enter the view in David's mirror, David barely turned the bezel, pushed the button on the explosive, and dropped the small disc out the window. The night filled with a bright orange eruption that sent the cruiser onto its front end and then flipped the car over on its roof.

The crash would have been simple to survive, seeing how they were well-armored sentries. At least that's what David told himself. He didn't want to think about killing anyone, especially those who were in charge of keeping Anaisha safe.

David wondered again about the accident regarding the semi. He didn't know why it bothered him so much, but the thought wouldn't go away, nagging at him like the spirit of a bitter ghost.

"We're only a couple miles out, David. You can see the clock tower from here." Veronica's gentle voice brought him back from his thoughts, but not out of his fears. If anything, those fears intensified being so close to his goal. The demon hybrid, the crooked agents, the tragedy at the train station—it was all to get him here, to this moment in time, to stop the wedding between Carrie Green and Jerad Montlier. To save a girl's life.

The clock tower loomed a mile ahead of them at the end of the street, the blue neon clock face illuminating the night sky. This was it. David sunk his foot into the gas pedal. This was the point of no return.

"Two guards, no weapons drawn yet."

David looked into the distance and saw that Veronica was

right. A black limo sat parked along the curb, two thugs, probably Jerad's, peering down the street toward the explosion. Behind them stood the stalus, a round building with large double doors and a lawn full of lavender flowers blanketing the pathway to them. Beside the stalus rose the tallest building in South Ryshard: the rebuilt clock tower. The tall, black-paneled monument's neon clock face acted as a pinnacle to the city.

He glanced at the dashboard clock and realized they were minutes past the start of the wedding. Only a quarter of a block left to go. Veronica gripped hold of the grab handle above her door. "There's only one way in there," she said. "Don't worry about me, just do what you have to."

David knew what she was hinting at because he had the same idea. They didn't have time to fight through the men who were drawing their guns now.

Bullets hit the windshield, chipping the thick glass, forcing Veronica down in her seat. David didn't waver in his course, relieved to discover that the vehicle was equipped with bulletproof glass. He heard bullets ricocheting off the front grill and skidding off the roof. David saw one of the men drop the cigarette from his mouth as he leapt out of the way just before the SUV jumped the curb and carved a path through the lavenders toward the front doors of the stalus.

David didn't know for sure what would happen next, just that he had to create a distraction, had to announce his presence to give Carrie a chance to say no, to stop the wedding. The double doors of the stalus approached, but David didn't let up on the gas. He closed his eyes and took a deep breath as the vehicle crashed through the doors, ripping them off their hinges.

Moments later, everything went black.

43 Till Death

Angel made her movements slow and deliberate as she zipped up the back of Carrie's wedding dress. Time was not on their side, although they were doing their best to make use of what little they had. While Jerad's goons kept watch outside the bathroom door, Carrie and Angel took their time getting Carrie ready for the wedding that they were both determined to keep from happening.

As the zipper went, Carrie felt her breasts squeeze tight against her chest. The gown was a half size too small, something Jerad had picked out himself without even consulting Carrie. She would admit, though, that it wasn't completely out of her realm of taste —a red bodice and a two-layer skirt that tapered from the waist to the knees and then fanned out just slightly. Red silk acted as a top layer to the skirt, opening in the front as a sort of curtain to the black silk tier underneath. A black floral pattern was stitched from the waist of her left side up across the front of the dress to her right breast.

"I can barely breathe in this thing."

"Doesn't matter," Angel huffed, straightening the night-gown she still wore. "Your friends should be here soon, if they got my message."

Carrie stared into the bathroom mirror, her thin body filling out the dress, making her look more beautiful than she ever imagined she could. None of the gowns Jerad had ever made her wear came close to looking this elegant. The dress's lush design overshadowed the fact that it was too small, and Carrie found herself wishing David was the one she dressed up for.

Then again, in a way, he was. The thought brought a smile to her face. "Is he really coming?"

Angel rifled through the makeup kit on the sink and began to paint Carrie's eyelids a bright shade of red to match the dress. "I sure hope so."

"If he doesn't…"

"Don't even think that way. If David doesn't show up, we'll have to do what needs to be done to make sure you don't marry Jerad. Simple as that."

What needs to be done? Carrie had no doubt what she would be capable of doing if Jerad decided to try and force marriage upon her. But it was getting close. Any minute, after Jerad finished threatening the stalus official, they would barge in here and demand that she marry Jerad. She couldn't. She wouldn't.

Angel finished with the eye shadow, added a little blush to Carrie's cheeks and then began to tie a solaris flower into Carrie's hair.

"I need you to understand something, Carrie. You can't marry Jerad. No matter what. I'm willing to die to make sure you two don't wed, and I need you to be confident in doing the same." The maid stopped for a second and looked Carrie straight in the eyes. "Are you willing to die to make sure Jerad doesn't move forward in his plans?"

Am I willing to die? Die to prevent a marriage? It seems so...heavy...to think in terms of death.

Angel shook her head. "I see the doubt in there."

"What?"

"The doubt." She returned to fiddling with the flower. "I know you don't completely understand what you're in the middle of. Just trust me—you can't marry Jerad. No matter what."

Carrie stared down toward the floor, the fanned circumference of the dress's bottom blocking her view of the black heels she wore. She imagined the red floral pattern on the sides of the heels. She wanted to cry, wishing for this nightmare to end, but she wasn't sure it would, not the way she wanted it to.

A loud crash shook the frame of the building, raining particles of dust from the ceiling of the bathroom.

"What was that?"

Angel grinned. "Your hero."

***

"You see, David, I've already made my decision."

He opened his eyes, found himself at the wedding reception that Chaos had given him a view of earlier. The hostile guests from earlier were in their seats at the large table outside. Carrie stood in her red gown, her arm around Jerad. The man smirked at David, rubbing the little triangle of hair under his lip as if it was a live animal on his face.

"What? How did I get here?"

"Are you serious?" Carrie asked, irritation in her voice. "You tried to stop my wedding earlier. Jerad's men had to stop you. They knocked you out. It's too late. Jerad and I are married. You failed."

David paused to take everything in. He couldn't remember trying to stop her wedding. He remembered his journey here—he glanced out past the green lawn and spotted the tall castle in the distance. The sky behind the castle seemed fake, painted with white and blue strokes as if the person trying to create the illusion was brushing with watercolor instead of oils. At the very top of one of the castle's spires, David spotted a yellow flag with a picture of a black scythe on it. The scythe had a white smile and a white eye drawn on its side.

Carrie grabbed David's jaw and turned his face toward her. "Do you realize what you've gotten yourself into?"

He pulled his face from her grip. "What are you talking about?"

"You tried to stop my wedding. You failed. More importantly, it wasn't just my wedding you tried to stop. It was Jerad's. And he's not too happy about that."

David suddenly became aware of Jerad standing there, his eyes growing dark. Jerad said nothing, but David could feel tension in the air like suffocating gas.

Carrie threw her arms up in the air. "Now what do I do? Huh? Jerad has strict rules in place. You trespassed, you tried to take me away from him. Now, I'm afraid, he's going to kill you. It's the only way to right things."

David glanced at the castle again. The backdrop of sky had changed to orange and yellow. The scythe flag had disappeared, but since he had seen it once, he knew it was there—had been there at one point minutes ago anyway. *Something is hiding it from me now, but why? What has changed? Where am I?*

Carrie grabbed his jaw again, but this time David grabbed her wrist and yanked her hand away from his face.

Jerad moved in close to him, his face within inches of David's ear. David felt the evil in the man's breath, sensed a sick rage in the atmosphere. The air smelled like rotting flesh, like a dead animal one finds in his attic after the putrid scent has made its way through the house via the air vents.

"Now you did it," Carrie whispered. "Now you made him mad. You touched me. You laid a hand on the Ancient Key. There's only one way out of this, David." She held her finger up. "Only one. You have to run. Run as fast as you can, away from this place. Back through the archways covered in ivy, back the way you came. Go back to the beginning and start over. It's the only way."

David turned behind him, to the ivy tunnel he had come through to the reception area. The path looked clear, crystal clear, unobstructed by enemy or obstacle. "I can't." He looked into Carrie's eyes, those glowing blue orbs that he knew to be green. "I can't leave you. You're a piece of me, Carrie. Even if you've already married Jerad, you still own a piece of my heart that I can't let go."

"It's over, David."

"No. No, it's not." He pointed to the sky. "It's not real. None of this is real."

The other guests at the reception had risen to their feet, surrounding him in a wide circle.

Carrie's eyes flashed bright blue. She grabbed his jaw in

her claws and sunk her nails into his skin. "What do you think this is? You think this is some kind of game?!" She drew blood as he pulled his face out of her grip again.

He wiped his chin on his arm. "This isn't real. I know it isn't real. It's all an illusion, by Chaos. He's doing this."

The guests of the party stepped backward and vanished into a black fog hovering around them. Carrie frowned, wiping drops of David's blood on her dress. "You've done it now. I can't stop what's coming, David. I tried to warn you, I tried to give you a way out, but you've forced my hand. You might have been a hero once, against mortals. But now you fight against gods, and you won't win."

Carrie stepped back into the black fog and vanished.

A spotlight of sunlight shone down on David and Jerad while everything outside the small circle was enveloped in black. David looked for the castle, peering into the dark as if he could see a painting that had been covered in tar.

"You're looking for the wrong things, David," Jerad whispered, his voice echoing. Fright crawled up David's spine like a cat moving up the back of a couch. David felt compelled to turn and look upon Jerad, who stood within an inch of him, but fear paralyzed him, fear of what he might find in Jerad's face. "You wanted love but will find death. You wanted Carrie, but you found me."

Jerad disappeared, leaving David alone. The sunlight gave him warmth, but he felt the cold of the shadows closing in. Red eyes suddenly opened in the darkness.

"I want to show you my true form, David, but I do not believe you are ready to see it."

The beam of sunlight thinned. Soon the shadows would

engulf him. *Then what?* He had the chance to run, but he couldn't. *Why would I have come so far only to turn back and start over?* There was no starting over, there was no other direction but forward. Even if it meant his death.

A soft voice pierced the darkness. It sounded familiar to David, but he found himself more concerned with the thinning sunlight and the red eyes than with trying to recognize who was calling him.

"David, please wake up. We're out of time. We have to go, now!"

Veronica.

David opened his eyes, his chest aching. He was slumped over the steering wheel. Smoke poured into the SUV, slithering in from the wrecked front end, which had collided with the wall that separated the lobby from the sanctuary, creating a large hole. He turned to his right and saw Veronica smile with relief. A few scratches and cuts scattered across her face, and a purple bruise marked her neck.

"I thought you were a goner," she whispered.

He leaned back, grabbing his chest with both hands. "Ahh."

"You okay? We have to get in there. I'm sure Jerad knows we're here by now."

"Jerad?" David rubbed the bridge of his nose and forced his mind to adopt his new reality. The other had been a dream, an illusion he saw through. Chaos's tricks hadn't worked this time. David could still save Carrie. All was not lost.

He unfastened his seatbelt, opened the door and dropped out of the vehicle, hitting the carpeted flooring of the stalus lobby. Pain covered his body, from his wounded shoulder blade to his chest. His legs felt like pudding as he wobbled to

401

his feet, grabbing the door for a crutch. Veronica made her way around the SUV and helped steady him.

"You good?"

He shook his head. "No. Not yet."

"We have to get in there. Now."

David nodded. "I know. Okay…" He lifted his legs toward his chest, stretching them. The feeling came back to his lower extremities, and he felt whole again, at least physically. Mentally, his brain felt like a bowl of scrambled eggs. The visions that Chaos blinded him with were real enough to trick his mind into believing them. And even though he had outwitted Chaos by realizing the illusion was just that, an illusion, he was still having some trouble recuperating.

Veronica grabbed his arm and gently tugged him through the hole in the wall leading into the sanctuary. He struggled to get his sense of reality back, his mind still fighting it ever so slightly. *The castle, the fake sky, the smiling scythe. Carrie's nails digging into my jaw.* David reached up to his face and found only the large gashes from the demonic creature back at his apartment.

The sanctuary was nothing more than wood and carpet, pews lined up to face a very small stage with a lectern, microphone stand and a couple speakers. A cluster of trees lined the back wall of the stage, flanking colorful stained-glass windows. Each displayed a scene from the historical texts of Anaisha, the Tolydremon. The book detailed Anaisha's history, from the wars that spanned the planet to the gods who erected chaos and malevolence upon the land.

The window facing him held within it a scene from the wedding of Arcterus the Beautiful to her demon lover, Seran. She wore a bright white dress, illuminated by the artificial lighting mounted just outside the window. The demon, Seran, looked human and wore a suit made of red cloth that glowed just as brightly as the white dress.

"You notice how happy Arcterus looks in the glass?"

David and Veronica both turned toward a doorway off to the side of the room. Jerad stood there, his left palm cupping the gem atop his cane.

"Where's Carrie?" David asked. He took note of the impatience in his voice, and he fought to keep it at bay. His mind clearing, David realized that he and Veronica had probably just walked right into a trap, especially if Jerad knew they were coming beforehand.

Jerad walked toward the stage, leaning on his cane when he felt the need to be dramatic. David had seen gemstones like the one on the top of the cane before, and he knew it was nothing to mess with. Knowing his luck, this one probably had poison inside.

Jerad waved his hand toward the front pew. "Have a seat."

"I don't think so."

Jerad motioned to Veronica. "Will you have a seat?"

She simply smiled at him.

Jerad huffed. "Very well. I think a lot needs to be explained."

"Where's Carrie?" David asked again.

Jerad took a seat in the pew, leaning his cane down beside him. "Carrie is safe. For now. To ensure her safety, you and I need to talk, David."

The illusions Chaos had inflicted him with vanished into mist. His mind began taking notes now that it was awake, analyzing the stalus sanctuary, searching for weapons, for

403

anything that could be used against Jerad. The next few minutes would be critical, as Jerad didn't have his goons with him yet. It was just David and Veronica against Jerad, who appeared to be alone.

"I'll bring your attention to the stained glass behind you. Arcterus, as the scene suggests, was engaged to a demon, Seran. This was no ordinary demon, though. He was a demon who had given up his life of eternal glory and riches to become mortal, so he could be with the love of his life, Arcterus."

"We don't have time for bedtime stories, Jerad," Veronica sneered. "Tell us where Carrie is, or this is going to get ugly for you."

He smiled and continued, ignoring her altogether. "You see, Arcterus and Seran were in love. So much so that Seran gave up immortality to have one lifetime with Arcterus. He traded eternity for a moment. A moment. Do you know the rest of the story? No? On the day of their wedding, another man, one by the name of Visane, showed up and killed Seran with an ancient, holy sword. Hoping to take Arcterus for himself, Visane murdered the one she truly loved. She fled that day, never to be seen again except in the constellations.

"The point of my story is simple. You, David, have obviously shown up here to stop our wedding. But you see, unlike Seran, I saw this coming." Jerad grabbed his cane and used it to pull himself to his feet. "I'll give both of you this one chance to leave. Walk out the way you came, and I'll let you go peacefully."

David picked up the microphone stand in both hands. "How about we give you one chance to tell us where Carrie is?"

Jerad grinned. "So, you came all this way for a fight? If I

had known that, I would have met you halfway. I've wanted to kill you for some time now. The both of you."

David spotted Veronica heading toward the door through which Jerad entered the room. As much as David wanted to go with her to find Carrie, he knew his place was here, to stop Jerad, to put an end to whatever plan he had set in motion in his sick and twisted mind long ago.

Jerad walked up onto the stage, grinning. "You really do intend on stopping me, don't you?"

"Yeah."

Jerad swung his cane at David. As David blocked with the microphone stand, the metals clashed against one another.

"This stops here!" David groaned between gnashing teeth.

Jerad stepped back, twirling the cane in his hand. "You have no clue what you've gotten yourself into, David. This is a finely laid plan that has been months, years, decades in the making. You really think you can put a stop to it by interrupting a wedding?"

David watched the man carefully, timing the revolutions of his cane, the steps of his feet across the stage. There was no doubt by the way he placed more weight on his right leg that his left had been injured, but David wasn't sure if it was enough of an advantage over him. Jerad could very well be faking his handicap.

"I see that brain working, timing my moves. It may have been six months since you fought with your friends, but I see you still have it in you." He swung the cane out, jabbing toward David's head in a decoy shot and then lowered the cane and struck David in the side of the leg.

Pain resonated up his thigh, but he managed to swing the

mic stand out for a blow of his own, smashing Jerad in the shoulder. Jerad charged at David, ramming him into the plastic lectern as both crashed with it to the floor. David caught a glimpse of the cane careening toward his face and rolled out of the way just in time. Then he kicked his foot up into Jerad's stomach, knocking the wind out of him as he stumbled back, giving David room to scramble to his feet.

***

When Veronica left the sanctuary of the stalus, she worried about David and whether or not he could handle himself against Jerad. In his prime, he could handle himself against almost any opponent. But six months had passed, and Veronica was waging David's safety on the fact that he had gotten some practice in over the last couple days.

She ran down the hallway that stretched through the stalus, no sign of any interference yet. Veronica began to put the pieces of a tentative plan together in her head, knowing it wouldn't come out the way she wanted but hoping it would come close. The idea was to grab Carrie, reunite with David and get out of South Ryshard as quickly as possible. Jerad was a powerful man and probably had the law on his side, meaning they didn't have time to squabble back and forth with idiotic bedtime stories and monologues until one side decided to raise the white flag.

No, she was counting on David to buy her some time so she could find and rescue Carrie. From there, it would be a matter of escaping before things got worse.

Veronica stopped and took cover behind a trash can. Up

ahead, one of Jerad's mercenary thugs stood guarding the door to the women's restroom.

Carrie has to be in there. Veronica remembered Turquoise saying something about having an insider or two in Jerad's house. Maybe one of them was in there keeping an eye on Carrie. If this was a typical shotgun wedding, Carrie was probably getting ready in there—maybe even against her own will.

Veronica peeked around the receptacle and analyzed the thug. Just under six feet tall. Common semi-automatic firearm—probably a standard fifteen-bullet clip with recoil reduction added. Veronica spotted a combat knife sheath on his leg. She didn't want this to get violent, but she would resort to violence if necessary to save her friend.

The man grabbed the microphone branching out from his ear. "Yeah?......Yeah, they're both here......I'm sure." He turned toward the restroom door. Veronica took a deep breath and bolted out from behind the trash can, running as fast as she could toward him. Before he could turn his head to face her, she was already in the air, her foot crashing into his face, slamming his skull against the wall.

Veronica landed on her feet and then dropped to the floor, sweeping her leg into his ankle. He fell like a sack of potatoes, cursing in two foreign languages—both of which Veronica understood. He fired the gun, but the bullet hit the tile inches from Veronica's thigh. She leapt to her feet and slammed one knee into the man's chest, knocking the wind out of him.

He reached up for Veronica's neck as she brought her other knee down into his windpipe, cutting off his air supply. He swung his fists at her, but she blocked his attacks easily, as if his hands were flies disturbing her picnic.

If David saw what she was doing, she knew he would try and stop her before she could kill the man. But David wasn't here. He was fighting his own battle. This battle belonged to her, and she intended to win.

The man stopped struggling after a bit, his arms falling to the tile like guillotines. She lifted herself off him and stood to her feet, catching her breath.

The door to the restroom cracked open, and a woman in a red nightgown peered out.

"Veronica?"

Veronica nodded, panting.

The woman opened the door wide. Carrie stood in the middle of the restroom, clothed in an elegant wedding dress, her hair adorned with a bright red solaris flower.

Veronica rushed in and embraced her in a hug. "I'm so glad you're okay."

"I'm fine," Carrie said. "I wondered if you would actually make it in time. I'm so sorry I ran from you guys. I'm so sorry I got myself into this mess."

Veronica pulled away, shaking her head. "None of that matters. Right now, we need to get out of here before Jerad brings in reinforcements."

"Where's David?"

"Keeping Jerad busy, but I don't know how long he'll last."

They entered the hallway. Carrie glanced at the man on the floor and cupped her hands over her mouth. "Is he…?"

Veronica reached down, grabbed the man's gun and pulled the combat knife out of its sheath. She slid the knife into the back of her jeans and the gun into her pocket, then looked at the woman in the red nightgown. "What's your name?"

"Angel. I work with Turquoise."

"She's still at the hotel for all I know. We need to help David and get out of here."

"Agreed."

***

The cane's bottom end swung up, striking David across the chin, causing him to fall backward and hit the floor. Painful waves pulsed through the muscle in his shoulder, causing a groan to escape his lips.

"You really think I'd let you just walk in here that easily and screw up my plans?" Jerad brought the cane down toward David's face, but he blocked it with the microphone stand.

David realized he was tiring. His shoulder ached, as did most of his back. The muscles in his arms were wearing down, exhausted from the fight with Jerad. He pushed himself, though, mentally and physically, trusting that Veronica was doing her best to rescue Carrie while David kept Carrie's captor busy.

Jerad lunged against the cane, forcing the microphone stand to smash against David's chest. David felt his ribs scream in protest. How long could he keep this up? He closed his eyes, gritted his teeth and pushed against the cane with all of his strength, managing only to get it off his chest for a brief moment before Jerad threw all of his body weight against the cane again and forced the mic stand to crash into David's breastbone.

Jerad leaned against David. "You're finished! My men have killed Veronica. I'll finish you here and now, and then I'll marry Carrie and it will all be over." Spit covered David's face when Jerad spoke. "Just relax. Just let it happen. Death in battle is a great way for you to die, don't you think? An appropriate one at least, for a hero."

Jerad pressed his weight against the mic stand again, crushing David's chest. David struggled to find a way out from under the man, but he couldn't use the hands that were grasping the mic stand, holding on for dear life. He kicked his feet, trying to reach Jerad's groin with a lucky shot, but it was no use. He was pinned with no way out.

Someone suddenly tackled Jerad to the ground. The weight of the stand lifted, and David heaved and rolled to his side.

Veronica grabbed him in her arms and sat him up. "You're alive."

"Yeah." *Barely.*

"David! My David!"

He looked up, his vision consumed by a black and red gown. Carrie hit the floor and hugged him.

"Oh, I missed you so much. David, I'm so sorry for leaving. I can't believe I left you!"

He wrapped his arms around her bodice and buried his face in her neck. She smelled like soap. David felt her tremble and realized she was crying. He continued to hold her, trying not to cry himself. The nightmare hadn't come true. Chaos's illusions had all been fake, not prophetic like he feared.

He pulled his face out of her neck and put his mouth near her ear. "I love you, Carrie," he whispered. Then he looked upon her face, taking the moment in. Tears streamed down her cheeks, and her bottom lip quivered with a smile.

She kissed him on the lips, and the world came crashing in around him. The stalus disappeared, Jerad vanished and David's friends faded. All that lay before him was Carrie, dressed in her black and red wedding gown, her head adorned with the red solaris flower. She was his. He was hers. The time for fighting had come to an end, and he now had what he wanted more than anything.

When they pulled apart, David heard her say she loved him back. Those words replayed in his mind, extinguishing every flame of doubt that had cropped up during his treacherous journey to this place.

Carrie reached her hand up to wipe away some of the blood dripping from his chin. Her green eyes sparkled. "I'd rather die, David, than live another day without you."

"I hate to break up the reunion, but we have company!" Veronica shouted.

David and Carrie looked up to Veronica and followed her gaze toward the front doors of the sanctuary. Through the space around the broken-down SUV, the blue lights of sentry cruisers flashed steadily.

"Ahh!" Angel screamed.

David turned just as Jerad leapt off the stage and bolted toward the door leading into the hallway. As much as he would have loved to take him down, David knew their next course of action was to escape the stalus and leave South Ryshard—or, as a plan B, hide in one of the underground clubs.

As Veronica and Carrie helped Angel up, David noticed the large red and black rash forming on the Angel's left arm. He rushed over to her, casting a sidelong glance at the entrance to make sure nobody had entered the sanctuary yet.

Angel rocked back and forth on her side, clawing at the area around the bruise. "He hit me…hit me with that stone on his cane."

"A poisonous stone," Carrie whispered. "We have to get her to a hospital!"

Veronica took a quick peek behind her. "First we have to get out of here. Let's try and find the back door and see if we can get our hands on a vehicle."

"Good idea," David replied. And it was a good idea. Really, it was their only chance now. Going after Jerad would have to wait—indefinitely for all David cared. He had come for Carrie, and now that he had her, he planned on running away with her somewhere nobody but Veronica would be able to find them.

David peered through the hole in the wall again and saw sentries entering the lobby. He reached down and started to lift Angel into his arms.

"Put her down, David, and put your hands above your head."

David gently laid Angel back on her side. "Parks." He turned around, his arms in the air. Parks stood just below the stage, his gun pointed at David.

Veronica pulled the gun from her jeans and aimed it at Parks. "Put it down, or I'll put a bullet straight through the center of your face."

Parks grinned. But his grin was like one David remembered seeing on a patient at the Tindall Sanitarium a couple years earlier. All of a sudden, David remembered the patient's farfetched stories about the end of the world, demons and stars falling from the sky. The patient even babbled on about other realities and wormholes. The guy was crazy and heavily medicated at the time, but seeing the same smile on Parks's face only reminded him that Parks was no saner.

"I have the upper hand here," Parks said as half a dozen sentries entered the sanctuary through the broken wall. "You're under arrest, Mr. Corbin. Seize him!" The sentries approached the stage, their glistening armor creating a radiant blue glow.

David had fought against a sentry. One. And if it hadn't been for Veronica, he would have been killed. Now he faced a half dozen. Veronica had a gun, but so did Parks. David was sure the sentries had weapons as well, hidden on them somewhere, probably beneath their nearly impenetrable armor.

"Put the gun down," Parks demanded. David noticed a small gap between Parks and the wall that ran toward the door leading to where Veronica found Carrie. If he could get Carrie and maybe Angel in there, they could find safety while David and Veronica battled Parks and the sentries. Their odds of winning were slim, but if worse came to worst, David would run. That was his best option under the circumstances. Even if he was able to take Parks out, how would that look to others in the government? David had no hard proof of Parks's involvement in the crooked dealings, so how would he prove himself innocent?

Run. That was the plan. *Escape. Live to fight another day—or maybe not at all.*

Veronica set her gun down on the edge of the stage, putting her hands in the air. She stepped back toward Carrie and whispered something to her, something David couldn't make out. He analyzed the sentries' positions, the stance that Parks had taken below the small stage. If they had any advantage, it was height. The stage sat only about a foot or two off the ground, but it would give David an edge to do what he was considering.

Parks reached up warily toward the stage, grabbing Veronica's gun. "You kids have been a real pain. Now comes your discipline."

David eyed the microphone stand near his left foot. He wished he knew Veronica's plan, just so he didn't do something stupid to offset it. Then again, Veronica knew him better than anyone. So maybe she was counting on him to do something…drastic.

When Parks stepped forward, David reached down, grabbed the mic stand and leapt off the stage, colliding with Parks. As they hit the floor, David rolled to his feet, the pain in his shoulder reminding him how much his body didn't appreciate his actions.

A blue arm swung out toward him, and he ducked, then slid under the sentry's legs. Once behind the armored soldier, David swung the metal pole as hard as he could into the sentry's back, hoping to crack the armor. Instead, the jolt of hitting the armor sent a nasty shockwave through the mic stand, causing it to wobble out of David's hands.

Veronica jumped off the stage to the sentry's back, pulling the helmet off his head in one motion. David saw a knife in Veronica's hand, and before he could hope to stop her, she had already swung the blade, slicing through the sentry's neck as blood splattered through the air.

Parks rushed David, knocking him back into the stage. His head hit the corner, dazing him for a moment. Parks threw him to the floor and took a quick swing at David's face, hitting him in the jaw. "Little brat, I'm going to tear you apart and find that stupid necklace!" He went to swing again when Veronica grabbed his arm and pulled him off David. She jabbed at him with the knife, cutting his necktie. He went to hit her, but she grabbed his fist in her palm and squeezed, dropping him to his knees.

"You've harassed my friends long enough," she growled.

A sentry swung his armored fist at her, hitting her in the back of the head. She fell to the floor, losing the knife. Parks stood to his feet, rubbing his knuckles as he kicked her in the ribs. "Now what? I have these shelled behemoths at my disposal. What do you have? Huh? David? Your washed-up hero friend?" Parks lifted her up by her hair and then threw her against the stage, slamming his fist into her ribs.

David grabbed the mic stand and lunged at Parks, intending to spill rage on the agent for hurting Veronica. A sentry grabbed the pole and lifted David into the air. Using the stand to his advantage, David swung from it and jammed his feet into the sentry's chest, knocking them both to the floor. David quickly recovered and took the mic stand to the sentry's helmet, cracking the plating and the glass in the front.

Another sentry landed his fist on the back of David's head, sending him to the floor.

44 Vengeance

C arrie made her way through the back hallway, the bottom of the wedding gown floating across the tile floor as she searched for another way out of the stalus. At least that's what she had led Veronica to believe she was doing. Her true intention was to find Jerad and make him pay for what he had done not only to her, but to Belgar and to Angel.

If I don't end this, he'll find me again. Somehow. And he'll try to kill David. Again.

Shadows moved in the moonlight spilling out from the stalus official's office. Carrie peeked inside the dim room. A window behind the desk revealed lightning flashing in the distant darkness outside.

"Where are you, Jerad? Coward, come out and face me!" She stepped into the office, her hand sweeping the wall behind her to find the light switch. When she flipped it on, she found the office chair turned around, its back facing her. A tuft of hair stuck out from behind the top of it. "I know you're there. Come fight me without your goons and see what I'm really capable of."

The chair whirled around, and one of Jerad's thugs pressed his finger to the microphone in his ear and smiled. "We have her."

The door slammed shut behind her, and something hard struck her across the back, knocking her to the floor. She struggled to get to her feet when two arms suddenly wrapped around her from behind, restraining her arms at her sides. Carrie bounced up and down, struggling to break free, but whoever was holding her pushed her forward and banged her face down onto the surface of the desk.

"I'm going to enjoy this." Jerad's voice held a mix of determination and desperation as he pressed his hand against her cheek, smashing her face against the oak. "You're a fool for coming after me alone. Now I'm going to make sure you learn a painful lesson."

Carrie glanced up at Jerad's bloodied face. Angel had given him a good beating, but he still held a remarkable amount of strength. Her vision shifted to a small letter opener that lay a few inches from her face. Jerad held her arms behind her together with one hand, and pressed her face against the desk with the other. If she went after the letter opener, she would have to be quick. No room for error.

In a flash, she pulled her right arm free of his grip, reached up and grabbed the letter opener and swung it back, stabbing him.

He released his grip on her, and she shoved her body backward, knocking them both to the floor. He wrapped his arms around her again, holding her on top of his chest as the thug left the chair and started toward them.

"Pretty little thing's going to have to die now," the thug mumbled. He reached to his side to pull out his firearm when the tip of Carrie's high heel found his crotch. She slammed her head back into Jerad's face and rolled off him, struggling in the dress to get to her feet. The thug dropped to his knees, grabbing himself with both hands.

Carrie pulled the gun out of the thug's holster and pointed it at Jerad.

"You stabbed me!" Jerad shouted, pulling the letter opener from his ribs, his white shirt was now a dark shade of red.

"Don't you move or I'll shoot!"

Jerad laughed. "You won't shoot me." He breathed in deeply and let out a moan. "You're a peacekeeper, not a warmonger." Using the bookcase to anchor him, he slowly lifted himself to his feet, holding the sharp, blood-stained letter opener in his hand.

"I'm tired of being underestimated by you." The thug lay in the fetal position on the floor, a few feet from Jerad's cane, the gemstone glistening with the echo of Angel's assault.

"You kill me now, and you'll have more than half of the world after you…for the rest of your life. I have contacts in the highest places, and I am one of the richest men in the world. There is nowhere you can go that I won't find you. You have no safe havens. You will marry me, or I will *take* from you what I have worked so hard to obtain!"

Carrie felt her hands trembling slightly with the gun. She told herself that Jerad was a monster and needed to be killed. But wouldn't that make her a monster? He was right about his connections. She had lived with him long enough to know that. But David was resourceful—incredibly resourceful—and he could find a place for them to hide until the dust settled.

Jerad grinned, shaking his head. "You can't win."

"I guess I'll have to call it a draw then." She lowered the weapon and fired a bullet into his bad leg. He collapsed to the floor, screaming in agony. "Don't you ever bother me, David or any of my friends again, or next time I'll make sure I kill you."

Carrie opened the door and entered the hallway, slamming the door behind her. She leaned against the wall and let the gun slide from her hand as tears broke free.

***

The enormous pounding in Veronica's head and the soreness in her ribs made it difficult for her to stand on the stage. She finally got to her feet, waited a moment for the dizziness to pass and then took in the scene before her. David was fighting the sentries, swinging the microphone stand like it was an extension of his body. She had seen him fight before, but now she observed a new fire in him, the fire to protect Carrie. Parks slinked toward the back wall, no doubt waiting for his moment to take David out. Carrie had escaped to the back hall like Veronica had told her to do. And Angel…she was breathing hard, lying on the floor of the stage, her bruise turning her whole arm black.

Veronica knew it was time. She had waited long enough, had kept her secret long enough. The lost sleep, the guilt at hiding something so…uncanny…from her best friends for so long. She couldn't hide it anymore. Her friends needed her help.

Another dizzy spell hit, and Veronica dropped to her

knees. A gust of cold wind seeped in through the destroyed wall, carrying with it the refreshing scent of rain. A thunderstorm had arrived. The smell calmed her nerves. She closed her eyes and began to focus on the environment around her. The dark arts she had learned so long ago were the advantage they needed right now.

Veronica slowed her breath, relaxed her shoulders and buried her face in her knees. Suddenly, she could feel the pain in David's shoulder in her own. The sore muscle, the raw skin. His painkillers had completely worn off, yet he continued to fight with everything he had.

She heard Carrie's crying from the back hallway, felt her fear toward Jerad, his hand of power and influence, his ability to hunt her, David and Veronica down to kill them in their sleep.

The bitter taste of approaching death formed on Veronica's lips, and she knew Angel would soon pass from this world to the next. The girl had been strong, sacrificed her own life to save Carrie's, but her time had come. The poison, with its burning power, ignited Angel's arm in fiery pain, causing her to lose consciousness.

Veronica soaked in these emotions, these thoughts into her own mind, her own bones, her own muscles. Her body tingled with the sensations as she felt the rhodenine, the conduit to these things, moving through the atmosphere, fluttering toward her like moths to a flame.

When Simper Creed had taught her to harness rhodenine to use as a powerful weapon, she nearly destroyed herself the first time. Rhodenine was one of the most unstable elements in Anaisha—its solid, gas and liquid properties determined the element's different reactions. In liquid form, rhodenine could cause memory loss and expose one to unhealthy amounts of radiation. In gas form, rhodenine could release enough energy to power a city for months. And in solid form, rhodenine could kill with its poisonous properties.

The most dangerous of all, though, was rhodenine in particle, atmospheric form. Found in Anaisha's air all across the planet. Not gas necessarily, not solid and not liquid. More…spiritual. Some believed, at least from what Simper Creed had told her, that the dark arts called upon rhodenine as the power of the gods. Veronica doubted the gods had anything to do with this. They could care less about Anaisha and everyone's petty squabbling.

Her body felt abuzz with the element, and she was careful not to take too much in. Many died performing the dark arts because they didn't know when to stop. Veronica focused the energy into her hands, where she could control it. When she lifted her head from her knees and opened her eyes, her pupils glowed bright purple. She knew she couldn't hold the rhodenine within her body for very long.

She spotted Parks sneaking up behind David, who was fighting two sentries with that mic stand. Veronica stood to her feet and stretched, feeling the energy trying to sneak out of her hands and travel up to her elbows. She fought it back and pointed her finger at the crooked agent. "Parks!"

David glanced briefly over his shoulder, making sure the man wasn't close enough to harm him, and then returned his focus to the fight. Most of the sentries had fallen, leaving only the two David was struggling with.

Agent Parks rushed toward Veronica. One of the sentries picked David up by the hoodie and pile-drove him into one of the pews. As the bench collapsed, David let out a groan. Veronica knew she would have to make this quick. David most likely didn't have it in him to take out the last two sentries on his own. And who knew if Parks had backup coming? They had to finish this and get out of the building as quickly as possible.

Parks jumped up on the stage and took a swing at Veronica. She ducked and then twisted her arms out in front of her, palms facing Parks.

"I'm hoping this will be the last time you underestimate me and my friends." A bright violet current traveled through her arms, standing her hairs straight up as it moved through her bones and across her skin. The energy converged into her palms, turning them violet.

Parks lunged at her again. The purple light left her palms and struck Parks in the chest, tossing him through the air. He crashed into the broken wall and fell to the floor like a worn ragdoll.

Veronica fell to her knees, exhausted. She watched David fight off the sentries, forcing herself to stay awake, to stay conscious. The buzz from the rhodenine wore off, and in its place she felt fatigue and tiredness. The human body couldn't handle rhodenine—wasn't built to handle it the way she handled it—and now the consequences of using the powerful element took their toll. Taking out Parks would prevent him from calling in any more help, if he hadn't already, and left David to focus his efforts on the last two sentries without having to glance over his shoulder to see if Parks was trying to stab him in the back.

45 Plan B

David struggled to get himself out of the broken pew as the sentry lifted him up by the hoodie. "You will be sentenced to death for the actions you have taken today."

David grabbed the zipper of his hoodie and yanked it down. The sweatshirt opened, and he slipped out of the sentry's grip, leaving his hoodie hanging from the sentry's fist. David rolled under one of the pews and kept rolling, hoping to stay out of the sentry's sight.

The second sentry leapt up and brought his fist down into the bench David was about to roll under, smashing it in pieces. David stopped and started to roll back to his right when another fist came down through that bench. He jolted to his feet and turned to make his way toward the stage when an armored fist struck him in the jaw, knocking him backward to the floor.

Blood seeped into his mouth. David shook the pain and struggled to his feet, his body screaming at him to stop. His head hurt, and his sore back was pleading with him to give up.

He crawled up on the stage and took a spot at Veronica's side, wondering how much longer he could last against these two sentries. Parks lay unconscious on the far end of the room, near the destroyed vehicle. No sign of any other help coming to back the agent up.

The sentries approached the stage, one still holding David's hoodie in his tight grip. Veronica leapt through the air and landed on one of their backs, twisted the helmet off and brought it down as hard as she could across the man's skull. The loud crack signaled to David that they had won this fight. As the sentry collapsed to the floor, the last one came toward Veronica. In a final burst of adrenaline, David lunged out and landed on his back, doing his best to twist the helmet off like Veronica had done.

But the sentry grabbed David by the hair and threw him to the floor. Then he lifted one of the benches over his head. David scrambled across the carpet, hoping to get back onto the stage, but before he could, the sentry dropped the bench. David shielded his head with his arms, surprised when a purple glow slammed into the descending furniture and shattered it in mid-air. He could have sworn it came from Veronica's direction, but he wasn't certain what "it" was.

Veronica grabbed the stray mic stand from the floor and swung it at the sentry's face, cracking his front face shield, knocking him back. She took another swing, but the sentry grabbed the stand and tossed it through the air. Then he brought his fist down toward Veronica, but she rolled out of the way just in time.

David got to his feet and hopped on the sentry's back, trying again to pull the helmet off. He managed to get it up over the sentry's head but was thrown off before he could strike, the helmet tumbling between pews.

Veronica lay on the floor, breathing deeply, her eyes fluttering. David got to his feet again, stars flittering in his vision. The sentry took a swing, but David ducked. Then David crawled up on the stage and grabbed the lectern. He lifted it high above his head, the room swaying a bit in his vision, and brought it down on the sentry's skull, killing him.

David fell to the floor, exhaustion consuming him.

"David!"

He looked up as Carrie rushed to his side and helped him to his feet. He felt the warmth of her body and wished to stay here forever, safe in her arms, safe from the insanity of the world.

She ran her hand through his hair and kissed his forehead. "You did it. You stopped them. Now we can leave."

Veronica got to her feet. She held her head and took a few moments before she spoke. "We need to take Angel with us."

David reached down to the girl, felt for her pulse and then shook his head. "She's gone."

Veronica grabbed David's hoodie out of the dead sentry's grip and tossed it to him. He slipped it on as Carrie grabbed his hand in hers, a warm smile consuming her face. The white of her eyes was red from crying. He didn't ask why she had been crying. He didn't care. They were together now, and they had forever to talk to each other about their adventures.

Veronica slammed her body into David's, bringing them both down to the stage floor. David turned in time to watch a white line of smoke travel through the sanctuary and collide with Carrie's neck. Her surprised expression slowly changed to one of dreariness, her lips curving into a frown, her wide eyes blinking rapidly before they rolled up into her head. Her body wobbled, and she collapsed.

David threw Veronica off him and rushed to Carrie, grabbing her in his arms. "Carrie?!" Her eyes slowly rolled back into place, staring at him in wonder, and then they shut as her stiff body relaxed, melting in his arms. He shook her shoulders. "What happened? What happened?!" He glanced frantically around the stalus, searching for the origin of the white smoke. Parks lay unconscious—or dead—on the other side of the room. Angel was dead on the stage. The sentries were out cold.

Veronica put her fingers to Carrie's neck. "Oh…"

David's eyes grew wider with fright as he saw tears coming out of Veronica's eyes. He looked down at Carrie, his heart skipping beats.

"I thought he was aiming for you, David. Not her. I—"

"Who?!"

"I saw a figure over there, near the SUV. It looked like he had a gun aimed on you. I thought he was trying to kill you."

David glanced up toward the hole in the room. *Nobody. Who did this?! It couldn't have been Parks. Was it Chaos? Is this another illusion?* David rubbed his eyes vigorously, telling himself it was an illusion, a dream. He felt dead, like the life had been stripped from his body. The room, the stage suddenly began to tilt out of focus.

He looked up at Veronica, then back to Carrie. His hand felt something in the side of her neck. He pulled it out, causing her body to jerk briefly and then relax again. David held the small dart up to the soft lights of the high stalus ceiling, watching the tiny drop of rainbow fluid swish around in the capsule.

"Poison," he whispered hoarsely. He set the dart on the floor and looked at Carrie again. She looked so peaceful, like she was sleeping. He brushed his hand across her cheek, which was ice cold and turning blue.

"David, whoever that was is probably going to come back and—"

David stood to his feet. Veronica couldn't grab him quickly enough before he leapt off the stage and charged down the aisle toward the back of the sanctuary.

"David! David, you need my help! Don't go out there alone!"

Ignoring her pleas, he shoved his way through the hole in the wall and entered the lobby. He took a good look around, searching, hoping to find Carrie's assailant. *Nobody in the lobby. Nobody outside.*

"Well."

The voice startled him. He swung around to find Chaos standing with his arms crossed.

"This is a fine mess you've gotten yourself into, isn't it?"

David lunged toward him, dove into a wall of red mist and tumbled to the floor. He got to his feet and swung around only to find the mist—and Chaos—both gone.

Chaos reappeared a few feet from him. "I'm sure you know by now that I am a force you cannot control or stop. I figured the lessons I taught you would have sunk in by now."

"Did you do it? Did you kill her?"

"Did I do it? That's an interesting question. I specifically remember warning you of what would happen if you tried to stop this wedding. Now you've made me, and others, mad. Very mad. If you thought what I did with the garden was a

427

show, you just wait, David. The best is yet to come. My finest performance is still far off, but in the meantime you'll get to see what I'm really capable of. Not just illusions and smoke and mirrors. No, you see, I used to be very, very powerful. I was a leader, like you. Now I'm an outcast. I have no physical form any longer, at least not a human physical form, yet I have powers that rival my human counterparts.

"And there is only one thing I am after, David. The book. I was really telling you to stay away from this wedding because I wanted you to stay away from the book."

"A book? Carrie was killed over a book?"

Chaos laughed. David took another swing at him, his fist sailing through red mist. Chaos reappeared at a different spot in front of him, an amused smirk on his face.

"You know what book. Although with Carrie dead, no-body will get their hands on it. I suppose that's better than you getting your hands on it." Chaos brushed his palms to-gether. "Job well done. Well, satisfactorily done, I guess." He stared at David a few moments and then cleared his throat. "Now that everything is said and done, I suggest you get out of here. Your friend, Agent Parks, has awakened, and I believe he, like everyone else you have come up against, has thought two steps ahead of you."

David stood, perplexed. *I remember seeing the Codex of Ra'f mentioned on Cloud's chip, along with Carrie's name, but—*

"Run. Go hide somewhere with your buddy, Veronica. Carrie is dead. There is nothing left for you here."

"What have you done?"

"Not me. You. I gave you two options. Go back the way you came or go forward and lose Carrie. Your actions brought the consequences you experienced tonight."

Thunder peeled outside. Then thumping, like helicopter blades.

Chaos smiled. "Time to run. Run like the bitter wind." The man vanished in a mist of red smoke.

David rushed back into the sanctuary. Veronica sat on the stage, clutching Carrie's lifeless body, tears streaming down her face.

The thumping grew louder.

"Run! Run, Veronica! Get out of here!" He started toward the stage when something hard slammed into his forehead, knocking him on his back.

Parks stood over him, gun pointed in his face. "You're mine now, David. All mine."

A loud explosion rocked the building as chunks of ceiling fell into the sanctuary. Long black ropes dangled down through the new opening as sentries slid into the stalus from the helicopter. They immediately took positions on stage, surrounding Veronica and Carrie and Angel's bodies.

David glared at Parks, his veins filled with the wild fury of an animal. "You're not taking me!" He kicked Parks in the leg and got to his feet, running toward the sentries coming in through the roof. He climbed up on one of them, ripping off his helmet. *I can fight them! I can fight all of them! I have to get us out of here. I have to save Carrie! She can't be dead. She can't be dead!*

David beat the sentry in the head with the helmet over and over again. With his strength drained, the beating was more like tapping until the sentry grabbed David by the neck and held him out in front of him.

"Mr. Corbin, you are under arrest by the order of Agent

Parks."

David glanced at Veronica, surrounded by four sentries who had her on her feet. She shook her head at him and then turned away. "I'm sorry."

The sentry set David on the ground and then snapped his arms behind him, restraining him with metal cuffs. David couldn't get his eyes off Carrie's body lying there on the stage... torn...breathless...dead.

He felt Parks's breath in his ear. "You're going to pay for what you've done."

"I have to see her. I have to see her!" David rushed toward the stage, ignoring the fact that sentries blocked every way to it. One sentry reached out his hand and grabbed David's head, stopping him in his tracks. David kept moving his feet, pushing against the sentry, trying to force his way through the blockade. Until finally he fell to his knees, tears pouring from his eyes. Hopelessness, failure, heartache flowed through him like a disease, taking over his mind, his body, consuming what was left of him.

Parks grabbed the back of David's hoodie and pulled him off the ground, his body lolling about like a giant rubber band. He pointed to Veronica. "Keep her separate from this one."

"What about the dead girls, sir?" one of the sentries asked.

Parks waved his hand toward the bodies as he pulled David toward the stalus exit. "Leave them." They made their way outside. Tire tracks were carved through the field of lavenders where David had sped the SUV into the building. Parks took him to the cruiser parked on the curb and opened the back door. "Take one long look at the last stalus you're ever going to see. When I'm through with you, you will wish we were back at the detention facility."

David took a seat in the back of the cruiser, wishing he were back at the detention facility. Back in time. He could stop this. Stop Carrie's death. Stop whoever had shot her.

Parks took to the driver's seat and started the car. He craned his neck to look at David. "Better get comfortable. We have a long drive to Galtaia Penitentiary."

No!

"I hear your buddy, Mr. Big, is in there, along with some of his friends, all waiting to get their hands on you. I'll be their hero handing you over to them."

The car drifted down the street as David closed his weary eyes and fell into the darkness trapped behind them. *Carrie…gone. Dead. A corpse.* He had his chance to get her back and blew it, only getting her killed in the process. Now there was nothing he could do to change things. Nothing he could do to stop what was already in motion. Chaos had spoken of a book David knew nothing about, but it didn't matter now that Carrie was dead. Nothing mattered now that she was dead. Nothing.

***

Drather made his way through the alleys that cut through the city away from the stalus, moving swiftly to avoid being spotted by Parks, his sentries or David and his friends. In a nearby dumpster, he tossed the sniper gun, burying it under a pile of garbage bags, the smell reminding him of his time on the streets as a kid.

He leaned back against the brick wall and pulled out his cell phone, dialing.

431

"It is done," he said to the person who picked up on the other end. "I want the rest of the credits deposited into the First Imperial Bank by midnight tonight…No…No, it went exactly as planned…What I do next is none of your business. Deposit the credits. My job in South Ryshard is done."

Drather ended the call and quickly dialed another number. He glanced at the street the alley spilled into, making sure nobody had followed him.

A female's voice picked up. *"Hello?"*

"I have your credits. Do you have the ID?"

Silence.

"Do you have the ID?"

"Yes. Yes, I do."

"I'll meet you back in Lysallis in a couple hours. Wait for my call."

He stuck the phone in his pocket and let out a sigh of relief. Everything was going according to plan. He pulled a tattered photo from his jacket and stared at it under the faint glow of the alley light. He and Rebecca Soft were embracing each other in a photo booth at the Winter Festival. He rubbed his finger along her face, his mind struggling to revisit those moments of his younger life.

"Soon, my love. Soon, there will be retribution for you and for me."

46 Doppelganger

Amber hung up the phone and stared at the plastic ID card lying on top of her computer desk. David's innocent-looking picture stared back at her, as if asking why she did this, why she would betray him like this.

She got up from the chair and walked over to the tall mirror on the wall near her bed. Gazing at her ragged self in her gray sweats and pink T-shirt, she wondered if she could go through with this. She had stolen David's ID and back-stabbed him, when all he had ever done for her was treat her like a princess.

Did she miss him? *Yes. I miss him.*

No you don't!

She saw her dark shadow, her doppelganger, in the mirror and sighed. *You again?*

You don't miss him, her copy said. *You miss his attention. Once you do this for Drather, you'll have the credits to get all the attention you want. Just stick with the plan, and don't be a sissy about this.*

Amber caught a quick glimpse of her clock. It was almost nine. By midnight, her deed would be done, and she'd have her ten thousand credits. All for a simple ID card.

47 Smoke & Mirrors

As soon as the last of the sentries left the stalus, Turquoise appeared from behind a large tree on the backside of the building. She had been resting after watching some of the scene play out here tonight.

Regret seeped in, but she quickly countered it. The hotel and the people inside it had been spared, thanks to her explosive defusal training. Cedric was dead. He had been a great operative, and now he was gone. Turquoise tried to get him medical attention, but there just hadn't been time. Parks escaped the hotel, and she knew he was heading to the stalus to stop David. By the time she arrived here, there were too many sentries for her to deal with on her own.

David had been taken by Parks, Veronica by the sentries. Carrie was dead, and there was no sign of Jerad anywhere.

It couldn't have ended any worse.

She made her way to the front of the building where the SUV had collided into the sanctuary wall. Walking into the sanctuary, she saw the gaping hole that had been blown in the roof, pieces of debris still raining down across the pews. Her gaze landed on a figure up on the stage. *Angel.*

The young girl was dressed in a red nightgown, and her arm and half of her face had turned black. Turquoise felt for a pulse, found none and just sat there, cradling the girl's head in her arms. "Why did you have to die in this horrible place?"

The bruise was one Turquoise had seen once before. Contracted by a very lethal poison that no doubt had to have been inflicted by Jerad. If she had shown up earlier, she could have saved them all. She could have helped them all escape before Parks showed up and made things more complicated.

Turquoise stood to her feet, gently laying Angel down on the floor, careful not to touch her poisoned arm. She had seen someone's arm break off and disintegrate before, just from an attack like the one made to her. She looked around the sanctuary, around the stage, for something, anything, that could help her understand what exactly went on here.

A small object led her eyes to the stage. She picked it up, held it to the light and recognized it to be a dart. The rainbow-colored drop of liquid in the small attached vial was a poison, but not a lethal one. And the dart had been lying in the same spot Carrie's body had been in before an ambulance came to pick her up.

Turquoise dropped the vial in her satchel, her spirit lifting, and then took another look at the destruction. Another object on the far side of the stage caught her attention. She picked up a black cell phone, sticking it in her satchel as well.

So Carrie wasn't dead. *Why would someone want us to think she is? And who? Who is driving that ambulance, and where is it headed?*

Turquoise picked up Angel's body, lifting it in her arms.

436

The girl felt like a sack of wet, dead leaves. As much as Turquoise felt the need to cry, she didn't. There had been too many casualties on this mission, and it wasn't over yet.

I have to save the teens. I'll need their help to rescue Carrie. Wherever she went.

Thunder boomed outside, sending a vibration through the air. Hard rain pattered off the roof of the stalus, falling through the large hole above. The storm had arrived, and Turquoise knew it was time to face it head-on.

The adventure continues in *Lost Birth*…

www.ingramcontent.com/pod-product-compliance
Lightning Source LLC
Chambersburg PA
CBHW072335020726
47506CB00004B/887